"TOTALLY ENGROSSING."   —*Orlando Sentinel*

"UNDENIABLY ENTERTAINING."
                              —*Los Angeles Times*

"TIGHT PLOTTING . . . BEGUILING STORY-TELLING . . . ANOTHER STELLAR PERFOR-MANCE."   —*The San Diego Union-Tribune*

Cases don't get much colder than that of Violet Sullivan, who disappeared from her rural California town in 1953, leaving behind an abusive husband and a seven-year-old named Daisy. But PI Kinsey Millhone has promised Daisy she'll try her best to locate Violet, dead or alive. All signs point to a runaway wife—the clothes that disappeared; the secret stash of money Violet bragged about; the brazen flirtations she indulged in with local men, including some married ones. Kinsey tries to pick up a trail by speaking to those who remember Violet—and perhaps were more involved in her life than they let on. But the trail could lead her somewhere very dangerous. Because the case may have gone cold, but some people's feelings about Violet Sullivan still run as hot as ever. . . .

"The freshest, tautest installment in quite a while . . . *S is for Silence* gets it right." —*Entertainment Weekly*

"Strong character portrayals . . . and a stunning climax."   —*Booklist*

"Score another triumph for Kinsey."—*Kirkus Reviews*
continued . . .

"Millhone's complexity is mirrored by the novels that document her cases: books that nestle comfortably within the mystery genre even as they prod and push its contours."   —*The Wall Street Journal*

"One of the darkest and most complex of her stories."
—*The Miami Herald*

"One of the best of the series."   —*The Calgary Sun*

"In a few strokes, she creates vivid, real people."
—Cleveland *Plain Dealer*

Praise for the Kinsey Millhone novels:

"A refreshing heroine."—*The Washington Post Book World*

"Millhone is all too human, and her humanity increases with each novel, each investigation . . . An incredibly even and satisfying series, one that keeps the reader interested in the plot—and in the continuing development of Kinsey Millhone."   —*Richmond Times-Dispatch*

"Grafton's prose is lean and her observational skills keen."   —*Chicago Tribune*

"A confident, likable sleuth with a good sense of humor."
—*Orlando Sentinel*

"A long-lived and much-loved series." —*Publishers Weekly*

"A stellar series." —*The Baltimore Sun*

"The spunkiest, funniest, and most engaging private investigator in Santa Teresa, California, not to mention the entire detective novel genre." —*Entertainment Weekly*

"Grafton's alphabet thrillers just keep getting better." —*USA Today*

"[Grafton] has mastered the art of blending new and old in novels that are both surprising and familiar." —*The San Diego Union Tribune*

"Grafton deserves an A for maintaining her series's high standard of excellence." —*Library Journal*

"Returning for another visit with the perpetually grumpy, smart-alecky and utterly dedicated Kinsey is a treat." —Cleveland *Plain Dealer*

"Kinsey Millhone is Grafton's best mystery, one that has been unfolding deliciously since the letter 'A.'" —*San Francisco Chronicle*

"[A] first-class series." —*The New York Times Book Review*

"Book for book, this may be the most satisfying mystery series going." —*The Wall Street Journal*

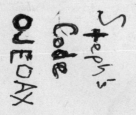

TITLES BY SUE GRAFTON

Kinsey Millhone Mysteries

and

IS FOR
SILENCE

SUE GRAFTON

G. P. Putnam's Sons
New York

S

PUTNAM

G. P. PUTNAM'S SONS
Publishers Since 1838
An imprint of Penguin Random House LLC
375 Hudson Street
New York, New York 10014

Copyright © 2005 by Sue Grafton
Excerpt from *T is for Trespass* copyright © 2007 by Sue Grafton
Penguin supports copyright. Copyright fuels creativity, encourages diverse
voices, promotes free speech, and creates a vibrant culture. Thank you for buying an authorized edition of this book and for complying with copyright laws
by not reproducing, scanning, or distributing any part of it in any form without
permission. You are supporting writers and allowing Penguin to continue to
publish books for every reader.

First Marian Wood/G. P. Putnam's Sons hardcover edition / December 2005
Berkley mass-market edition / December 2006
First G. P. Putnam's Sons premium edition / March 2016
G. P. Putnam's Sons premium edition ISBN: 978-0-399-57520-4

Printed in the United States of America
10 9 8 7 6 5 4 3

For my granddaughter, Addison,
with a heart full of love

ACKNOWLEDGMENTS

The author wishes to acknowledge the invaluable assistance of the following people: Steven Humphrey; Ben Holt, Ben Holt Equipment; Ken Seymour, www.1953chevrolet.com; John Mackall, Counselor-at-Law, Seed Mackall LLP; Greg Boller, Deputy District Attorney, Santa Barbara County District Attorney's Office; John Lindren, D&H Equipment; Bill Turner, Detective Sergeant (retired), Santa Barbara County Sheriff's Department; G. David Dyne, M.D.; T. J. Dwire, Title Officer, Lawyers Title Company; Emily Craig, Forensic Anthropologist, Kentucky State Medical Examiner's Office; John White, KellyCo Metal Detector Superstore; Dale Kreiter, Library Technician, and the Staff of the Santa Maria Public Library; Leslie Twine; Florence Michel; C. L. Burk; and Don Gastiger.

Thank you, Hairl Wilson, for the use of your first name, and Bob Ziegler, for the use of your name in its entirety.

A NOTE FROM THE AUTHOR

This is a work of fiction. All the characters are conjured out of whole cloth, which is to say, the persons inhabiting this novel are figments of my imagination and have no real-life counterparts. Anyone who knows the city of Santa Maria and the surrounding countryside will not only recognize the setting for this book but will also note the many liberties I've taken with geography. There is no abandoned two-story Tudor residence in the center of that flat, agricultural landscape. The towns of Serena Station, Cromwell, Barker, Freeman, Tullis, Arnaud, and Silas are invented. Some of the roads exist, but as I've recently appointed myself Acting Chair and sole member of the Santa Teresa County Regional Transportation Planning Agency, I've relocated, rerouted, and renamed these roads according to the dictates of the story. Please do not write me those notes telling me I got it wrong, because I didn't.

S

IS FOR
SILENCE

1

LIZA

Saturday, July 4, 1953

When Liza Mellincamp thinks about the last time she ever saw Violet Sullivan, what comes most vividly to mind is the color of Violet's Japanese silk kimono, a shade of blue that Liza later learned was called "cerulean," a word that wasn't even in her vocabulary when she was fourteen years old. A dragon was embroidered in satin-stitch across the back, its strange dog-shaped face and arched body picked out in lime green and orange. Flames twisted from the dragon's mouth in curling ribbons of bloodred.

That last night, she'd arrived at the Sullivans' house at 6:00. Violet was going out at 6:15 and, as usual, she wasn't dressed and hadn't done her hair. The front door was open, and as Liza approached, Baby, Violet's three-month-old buff-colored Pomeranian, started yapping in a shrill little doggie voice while she pawed at the screen, punching holes here and there. She had tiny black eyes and a black button nose and a small pink bow affixed to her forehead with stickum of some kind. Someone had given Violet the dog less than a month before, and she'd developed a fierce attachment to it, carrying the dog around in a big straw tote. Liza disliked Baby, and twice when Violet left the dog behind, Liza put her in the coat closet so she wouldn't have to listen to her bark. She'd gotten the idea from Foley, who disliked the dog even more than she did.

Liza knocked on the door frame, a sound barely audible above the dog's *yap-yap-yap*. Violet called out, "Come on in. I'm in the bedroom!"

Liza opened the screen door, pushed the dog aside with her foot, and walked through the living room to the bedroom Violet and Foley shared. Liza knew for a fact that Foley often ended up sleeping on the couch, especially when he'd been drinking, which he did almost every day, and even more especially after he'd busted Violet in the chops and she'd stopped speaking to him for two days or however long it was. Foley hated it when she gave him the silent treatment, but by then he'd be sorry he'd slugged her and he wouldn't have the nerve to protest. He told anyone who would listen that she brought it on herself. Anything bad that happened to Foley was someone else's fault.

Baby pattered into the bedroom behind her, a fluff ball of nervous energy with a party favor of a tail. She was too small to jump up onto the bed, so Liza scooped her up and put her there. Violet's tow-headed daughter, Daisy, was lying on the bed reading the Little Lulu comic Liza had given her the last time she sat, which was the night before last. Daisy was like a cat—always in the room with you but busy pretending to be doing something else. Liza took a seat on the only chair in the room.

Earlier in the day when she'd stopped by, there had been two brown paper bags sitting on the chair. Violet said it was stuff going to Goodwill, but Liza recognized a couple of Violet's favorite things and thought it was odd that she'd give away her best clothes. Now the brown bags were gone and Liza knew better than to mention them. Violet didn't like questions. What she wanted you to know, she'd tell you outright, and the rest was none of your business.

"Isn't she adorable?" Violet said. She was talking about the dog, not her seven-year-old child.

Liza didn't comment. She was wondering how long it would take to suffocate the Pomeranian while Violet was out. Violet was sitting on the bench at her makeup table, wearing the bright blue kimono with the dragon across the back. As Liza watched, Violet loosened the tie and shrugged the wrap aside so she could examine a bruise the size of Foley's fist that sat above one breast. Liza could see three versions of the bruise reflected in the tri-fold mirror that rested on the vanity. Violet was small and her back was perfect, her spine straight, her skin flawless. Her buttocks were dimpled and ever so slightly splayed where they pressed down against the seat.

Violet wasn't at all self-conscious about Liza seeing her undressed. Often when Liza came to sit, Violet would emerge from the bathroom naked, having dropped the towel so she could dab behind her knees with the violet cologne she used. Liza would try to keep her gaze averted while Violet strolled around the bedroom, pausing to light an Old Gold that she'd leave on the lip of the ashtray. Liza's gaze was irresistibly drawn to the sight of Violet's body. No matter where Violet went, eyes were drawn to her. Her waist was small and her breasts were plump, drooping slightly like sacks filled nearly to capacity with sand. Liza's boobs were barely sufficient for her AA brassiere, though Ty would close his eyes and start breathing hard every time he felt her up. After they kissed for a while, even if she resisted, he'd find a way to unbutton her shirt, nudging aside her bra strap so he could cup a budding breast in his palm. Then he'd grab Liza's hand and press it between his legs, making a sound somewhere between a whimper and a moan.

In her church youth group, the pastor's wife often lectured the girls about heavy petting, which was not recommended, as it was the quickest road to sexual intercourse and other forms of loose behavior. Oh, well. Liza's best friend, Kathy, was currently taken up with the Moral Rearmament Movement, which preached Absolute Honesty, Absolute Purity, Absolute Unselfishness, and Absolute Love. The last was the one that appealed to Liza. She and Ty had started dating in April, though their contact was limited. He couldn't let his aunt hear about it because of things that happened at his last school. She'd never been kissed before, had never done any of the things Ty introduced her to in their times together. Of course, she'd drawn the line at going all the way, but she couldn't see the harm in Ty's fooling with her boobs if it made him feel good. This was exactly Violet's point of view. When Liza finally confessed what was going on, Violet said, "Oh please, Sweetie, what's it to you? Let him have his fun. He's a good-looking boy, and if you don't give in to him some other girl will."

Violet's hair was dyed an astonishing shade of red, more orange than red and not even intended to look real. Her eyes were a clear green, and the lipstick she wore was a pinky rose shade. Violet's lips formed two wide bands across her mouth, as flat as the selvage on a remnant of silk. Her pale skin had an undertone of gold, like fine paper in a book printed long ago. Liza's complexion was freckled, and she tended to break out at "that time of the month." While Violet's hair was as silky as an ad for Breck shampoo, Liza's ends were crinkled and split from a miscalculation with the Toni Home Permanent Kathy'd given her the week before. Kathy had read the directions wrong and fried Liza's hair to a fare-thee-well. The strands still smelled like spoiled eggs from the lotions she'd applied.

Violet liked going out, and Liza babysat Daisy three and four times a week. Foley was gone most nights, drinking beer at the Blue Moon, which was the only bar in town. He worked construction, and at the end of the day, he needed to "wet his whistle" was how he put it. He said he wasn't about to stay home babysitting Daisy, and Violet certainly had no intention of sitting around the house with her while Foley was out having fun. During the school year, Liza ended up doing her homework at the Sullivans' after Daisy was in bed. Sometimes Ty came to visit, or Kathy might spend the evening so the two could read movie magazines. *True Confessions* magazine was preferable, but Kathy was worried about impure thoughts.

Violet smiled at Liza, their eyes connecting in the mirror until Liza looked away. (Violet preferred to smile with her lips closed because one of her front teeth was chipped where Foley'd knocked her sideways into a door.) Violet liked her. Liza knew this and it made her feel warm. Being favored by Violet was enough to make Liza trot around behind her like a stray pup.

Breast inspection complete, Violet shrugged herself

back into the kimono and tied it at the waist. She took a deep drag of her cigarette, then rested it in the ashtray so she could finish putting on her face. "How's that boyfriend of yours?"

"Fine."

"You be careful. You know he's not supposed to date."

"I know. He told me and that is so unfair."

"Unfair or not, his aunt would have a fit if she knew he was going steady, especially with someone like you."

"Gee, thanks. What'd I do to her?"

"She thinks you're a bad influence because your mother's divorced."

"She *told* you that?"

"More or less," Violet said. "I ran into her at the market and she tried to pump me for information. Someone saw you with Ty and ran blabbing straight to her. Don't ask who tattled because she was very tight-lipped. I told her she was nuts. I was polite about it, but I made sure she got the point. In the first place, I said, your mother wouldn't let you date at your age. You're barely fourteen . . . how ridiculous, I said. And in the second place, you couldn't be seeing Ty because you spent all your spare time with me. She seemed satisfied with that, though I'm sure she doesn't like me any better than she likes you. Guess we're not good enough for her or her precious nephew. She got all pruney around the mouth and went on to say that at his last school, some girl got herself in trouble, if you get my drift."

"I know. He told me he felt sorry for her."

"So he did her the big favor of screwing her? Wasn't she the lucky one?"

"Well, it's over now anyway."

"I'll say. Take it from me, you can't trust a guy who's hellbent on getting in your pants."

"Even if he loves you?"

"Especially if he loves you, and worse if you love him."

Violet picked up a wand of mascara and began to sweep her lashes, leaning into the mirror so she could see what she was doing. "I've got Cokes for you in the fridge and a carton of vanilla ice cream if you and Daisy want some."

"Thanks."

She recapped the wand and used a hand to fan her face, drying the dramatic fringe of black goo. She opened her jewelry box and selected six bracelets, thin silver circles that she slipped over her right hand one by one. She shook her wrist so they jingled together like tiny bells. On her left wrist she fastened her watch with its narrow black-cord band. Barefoot, she got up and crossed to the closet.

There was very little evidence of Foley in the room. He kept his clothes jammed in a pressed-board armoire shoved in one corner of Daisy's room, and as Violet was fond of saying, "If he knows what's good for him, he better not complain." Liza watched while she hung the kimono on a hook on the inside of the closet door. She was wearing sheer white nylon underpants but hadn't bothered with a bra. She slipped her feet into a pair of sandals and leaned down to fix the straps, her breasts bobbling as she did. Then she pulled on a lavender-and-white polka-dot sundress that zipped up the back. Liza had to help her with that. The dress fit snugly, and if Violet was aware that her nipples showed as flat as coins she made no remark. Liza was self-conscious about her figure, which had begun developing when she was twelve. She wore loose cotton blouses—usually Ship'n Shore—mindful that her bra and slip straps sometimes showed through the fabric. She found this embarrassing around the boys at school. Ty was seventeen and, having transferred from another school, didn't act stupid the way the others did, with their mouth farts and rude gestures, fists pumping at the front of their pants.

Liza said, "What time are the fireworks?"

Violet reapplied her lipstick and then rubbed her lips together to even out the color. She recapped the tube. "Whenever it gets dark. I'm guessing nine," she said. She leaned forward, blotted her lipstick with a tissue, and then used an index finger to clean a line of color from her teeth.

"Are you and Foley coming home right afterward?"

"Nah, we'll probably stop by the Moon."

Liza wasn't sure why she'd bothered to ask. It was always like that. They'd get home at 2:00 A.M. Liza, dazed and groggy, would collect her four dollars and then walk home through the dark.

Violet took the bulk of her hair, twisted it, and held it high on her head, showing the effect. "What do you think? Up or down? It's still hotter than blue blazes."

"Down's better."

Violet smiled. "Vanity over comfort. Glad I taught you something." She dropped her hair, shaking it out so the weight of it went swinging across her back.

That was the sequence Liza remembered—beginning, middle, and end. It was like a short loop of film that ran over and over. Daisy reading her comic book, Violet naked, and then being zipped into the polka-dot sundress. Violet lifting her bright red hair and then shaking it out.

The thought of Ty Eddings was wedged in there some-where because of what happened later. The only other brief moment that stayed with her was a time jump of maybe twenty minutes. Liza was in the cramped, not-quite-clean bathroom with its moldy-smelling towels. Daisy, her fine blond hair caught up in a barrette, was taking her bath. She was sitting in a cloud of bubbles, scooping them up and draping them across her shoulders like a fine fur coat. Once Liza had Daisy bathed and in her baby doll pajamas, she'd give her the pill Violet left for her whenever she went out.

The air in the bathroom was damp and warm, and smelled like the pine-scented bubble bath Liza had squirted into the rush of running water. Liza was sitting on the toilet with the lid down, watching to make sure Daisy didn't do something dumb, like drown or get soap in her eyes. Liza was already bored because babysitting was tedious once Violet left the house. She only did it because Violet asked, and who could turn her down? The Sullivans didn't have a television set. The Cramers were the only family in town who owned one. Liza and Kathy watched TV almost every afternoon, though lately Kathy had been sulky, in part because of Ty and in part because of Violet. If Kathy had her way, she and Liza would spend every waking minute together. Kathy had been fun at first, but now Liza felt like she was suffocating.

As Liza leaned over and swished a hand in the bath-water, Violet opened the door and stuck her head in, holding Baby in her arms. The dog yapped at them, bright-eyed and happy in a braggy sort of way. Violet said, "Hey, Lies, I'm off. See you kids later."

Violet liked to call her "Lies," a shortened form of "Liza" but spelled differently, or at least as Liza pictured it.

Daisy tilted her face up, puckering her lips. "Kiss!"

Violet said, "Kiss, kiss from here, Honeybunch. This lipstick's fresh and Mama doesn't want it messed up. You be good now and do everything Liza says."

Violet blew Daisy a kiss. Daisy pretended to catch it and then blew it back, her eyes shining at the sight of her mother, who was looking radiant. Liza waved, and as the door closed, a waft of violet cologne entered the room on a wisp of chill air.

2

The puzzle of Violet Sullivan was dumped in my lap via a phone call from a woman named Tannie Ottweiler, whom I'd met through my friend Lieutenant Dolan, the homicide detective I'd worked with the previous spring. My name is Kinsey Millhone. I'm a licensed private investigator, typically working twelve to fifteen cases that range in nature from background checks to insurance fraud to erring spouses in the midst of acrimonious divorces. I'd enjoyed working with Dolan because he provided me a reason to leave my usual paper searches behind and get out in the field.

The minute I heard Tannie's voice, an image popped to mind: forties, good face, little or no makeup, dark hair held back by tortoiseshell combs and framed in a halo of cigarette smoke. She was the bartender, manager, and sometime waitress at a little hole-in-the-wall known as Sneaky Pete's. This was where Dolan had first talked me into helping him. He and his crony, Stacey Oliphant, who'd retired from the Santa Teresa County Sheriff's Department, were investigating an unsolved homicide that had been sitting on the books for eighteen years. Neither man was in good health, and they'd asked me to do some of the legwork. In my mind, that job and Tannie Ottweiler were inextricably connected and generated feelings of goodwill. I'd seen her a couple of times since then, but we'd never exchanged more than pleasantries, which was what we did now. I could tell she was smoking, which suggested a minor level of uneasiness.

Finally, she said, "Listen, why I called is I'm wondering if you'd sit down and have a chat with a friend of mine."

"Sure. No problem. About what?"

"Her mother. You remember Violet Sullivan?"

"Don't think so."

"Come on. Sure you do. Serena Station, north county? She disappeared years ago."

"Oh, right. Gotcha. I forgot about her. That was in the '40s, wasn't it?"

"Not that far back. Fourth of July, 1953."

When I was three, I thought. This was September 1987. I'd turned thirty-seven in May and I noticed I was starting to keep track of events in terms of my age. Dimly I dredged up a fragment of information. "Why am I thinking there's a car involved?"

"Because her husband had just bought her a Chevrolet Bel Air and that disappeared, too. Great car—a five-passenger coupe. I saw one just like it at the car show last year." I could hear Tannie take a hit from her cigarette. "Rumor had it she was having an affair with some guy and the two ran off."

"Happens every day."

"Don't I know it. You ought to hear the stories I get

told, people crying in their beers. Tending bar has really warped my point of view. Anyway, lot of people are convinced Violet's husband did her in, but there's never been a shred of proof. No body, no car, no evidence either way, so who knows?"

"What's this have to do with the daughter?"

"Daisy Sullivan's an old friend. She's here on vacation, hanging out with me for a couple of days. I grew up in north county, so we've known each other since we were kids. She was two years behind me from grade school all the way through high school. She's an only child, and I'm telling you this business with her mother has messed her up bad."

"How so?"

"Well, for starters, she drinks too much, and when she drinks she flirts and when she flirts she gloms on to the nearest loser. She has terrible taste in men . . ."

"Hey, half the women I know have bad taste in men."

"Yeah, well, hers is worse. She's always looking for 'true love,' but she doesn't have any idea what that's about. Not that I do, but at least I don't marry the bums. She's been divorced four times and she's sitting on a ton of rage. I'm the only friend she has."

"What's she do for a living?"

"Medical transcription. Sits in a cubicle all day long with a headset, typing up all this crap dictated by the docs for their medical charts. She's not unhappy, but she's beginning to see how she's limited herself. Her world's been getting smaller and smaller until it's coffin-sized by now. She figures she'll never get her head straight until she knows what went on."

"Sounds like this has been going on for years. How old *is* she?"

"Well, I'll be forty-three this month, so Daisy must be forty, forty-one . . . somewhere in there. I can hardly keep track of *my* birthday, let alone hers. I know she was seven when her mother bugged out."

"What about her father? Where's he at this point?"

"He's still around, but his life's been hell. Nobody wants to have anything to do with him. He's been shunned, like that old tribal shit. The guy might as well be a ghost. Listen, I know it's a long shot, but she's serious. If he did it, she's gotta know, and if he didn't, well think about the service you'd be doing. You have no idea how screwed up she is. Him, too, for that matter."

"Isn't it a little late in the game?"

"I thought you liked challenges."

"After thirty-four years? You gotta be kidding."

"I don't think it's *that* bad. Okay, so maybe a few years have gone by, but look at it this way: the killer might be ready to bare his immortal soul."

"Why don't you talk to Dolan? He knows a lot of north county cops. Maybe he can help, at least steer you in the right direction."

"Nah, no deal. I already talked to him. He and Stace are taking off on a three-week fishing trip, so he told me to call you. He says you're a terrier when it comes to stuff like this."

"Well, I appreciate that, but I can't track down a woman who's been gone thirty-four years. I wouldn't know where to start."

"You could read the articles in the newspaper at the time."

"That goes without saying, but Daisy's capable, I'm sure. Send her to the library periodicals room—"

"She already has all that stuff. She said she'd be happy to give you the file."

"Tannie, I don't mean to sound rude, but there are half a dozen other PIs in town. Try one of them."

"I'm not comfortable with that. I mean, it'd take me forever just to fill them in. At least you've *heard* about Violet Sullivan. That's more than most."

"I've heard about Jimmy Hoffa, too, but that doesn't mean I'd go out and start looking for him."

"All I'm asking you to do is *talk* to her—"

"There's no point in talking—"

"Tell you what," she cut in. "Come on over to Sneaky Pete's and I'll make you a sandwich. Gratis, on me, completely free of charge. You don't have to do a thing except listen to her."

I'd already zoned out, distracted by the promise of free food. The sandwich she referred to was the Sneaky Pete house specialty, which Dolan claimed was the only thing worth ordering—spicy salami on a kaiser roll with melted pepper Jack cheese. Tannie's innovation was to put a fried egg on top. I'm ashamed to admit how easily I can be seduced. I glanced my watch: 11:15 and I was famished. "When?"

"How about right now? My apartment's only half a block away. Daisy can walk over from there quicker than you can drive."

I elected to walk the six blocks to Sneaky Pete's in a futile effort to delay the conversation. It was a typical September morning, the day destined to be a carbon copy of the days on either side: abundant sunshine after patchy morning clouds, with highs in the mid-seventies and lows sufficient to encourage sleeping under a down comforter at night. Above me, migrating birds, alerted by changes in the autumn light, were making a V-line to winter grounds. This was the upside of living in Southern California. The downside was living with monotony. Even perfect weather palls when that's all there is.

That week, local law enforcement was preparing for the California Crime Prevention Officers Conference, which was set to run from Wednesday through Friday, and I knew Cheney Phillips, who worked Vice for the Santa Teresa Police Department, would be tied up for the duration. That suited me just fine. Being a woman with a prickly disposition, I was looking forward to the time alone. Cheney and I had been "dating" for the past three months, if that's a word you want to use to describe a relationship between divorced singles in their late thirties. I wasn't clear about his intentions, but I didn't expect to marry again. Who needs the aggravation? All that togetherness can really get on your nerves.

Without even having heard Daisy's long, sad tale, I could calculate the odds. I didn't have a clue how to search for a woman who'd been missing for three decades. If she was alive, she must have had her reasons for running away, electing to keep her distance from her only child. Then, too, Violet's husband was still around, so what was his deal? If he'd wanted her found, you'd think he'd have hired a PI himself instead of leaving it to Daisy all these years later. On the other hand, if he knew she was dead, why go through the motions when he could save himself the bucks?

My problem was that I liked Tannie, and if Daisy was a friend of hers, then she was automatically accorded a certain status in my eyes. Not much of one, I grant you, but enough for me to hear her out. Which is why, once we were introduced and I had my sandwich in front of me, I pretended to pay attention instead of drooling on myself. The kaiser roll had been buttered and laid on the grill until the bread was rich brown and crunchy at the edge. Rings of spicy salami had been soldered together with melted cheese—Monterey Jack infused with red pepper flakes. When I lifted the top, the yolk of the fried egg was still plump, and I knew it would ooze when I bit into it, soaking into the bread. It's a wonder I didn't groan at the very idea.

The two sat across the table. Tannie kept her comments to a minimum so Daisy and I would have the chance to connect. Looking at the woman, I had a hard time believing she was only two years younger than Tannie. At forty-three, Tannie's skin showed the kind of fine lines that suggested too much cigarette smoke and not enough sun protection. Daisy had a pale, fine-boned face. Her eyes were small, a mild anxious blue, and her lank light-brown hair was pulled back and secured in a messy knot held together with a chopstick. Several loose strands were trailing from the knot, and I was hoping she'd remove the chopstick and have another go at it. Her posture was poor, her shoulders hunched, perhaps because she'd never had a mother nagging her to stand up straight. Her nails were bitten down so far it made me want to tuck my own fingertips into my palms for safekeeping.

While I savored my sandwich she picked away at hers, breaking off small portions she mounded on her plate. One out of three bites she'd put in her mouth while the others she set aside. I didn't think I'd known her long enough to beg for one. So far I'd left her in charge of the conversation, but after thirty minutes of chitchat, she still hadn't brought up the subject of her mom. This was my lunch hour. I didn't have all day. I decided to jump in myself and get it over with. I wiped my hands on a paper napkin, crumpled it, and tucked it under the edge of my plate. "Tannie tells me you're interested in locating your mother."

Daisy glanced at her friend as though for encouragement. Having finished her meal, she started gnawing on her thumbnail in much the same way a smoker would light a cigarette.

Tannie gave her a quick smile. "Honestly, it's fine. She's here to listen."

"I don't know what to say. It's a long, complicated story."

"I gathered as much. Why don't you start by telling me what you want?"

Daisy's gaze flicked across the room behind me as though she were looking for a way to bolt. I kept my eyes fixed politely on her face while she struggled to speak. I was trying to be patient, but silences like hers make me want to bite someone.

"You want . . . what?" I said, rolling my hand at her.

"I want to know if she's alive or dead."

"You have any intuitions about that?"

"None that I can trust. I don't know which is worse. Sometimes I think one thing and sometimes the opposite. If she's alive, I want to know where she is and why she's never been in touch. If she's dead, I might feel bad, but at least I'll know the truth."

"An answer either way would be a stretch by now."

"I know, but I can't live like this. I've spent my whole

life wondering what happened to her, why she left, whether she wanted to come back but couldn't for some reason."

"Couldn't?"

"Maybe she's in prison or something like that."

"There's been absolutely no word from her in thirty-four years?"

"No."

"No one's seen her or heard from her."

"Not that I know."

"What about her bank account? No activity?"

Daisy shook her head. "She never had checking or savings accounts."

"You realize the implications. She's probably dead."

"Then why weren't we notified? She took her purse when she left. She had her California driver's license. If she was in an accident, surely someone would have let us know."

"Assuming she was found," I said. "The world's a big place. She might have driven off a cliff or she might be at the bottom of a lake. Now and then someone slips through the cracks. I know it's hard to accept, but it's the truth."

"I just keep thinking she might have been mugged or abducted, or maybe she had some disease. Maybe she ran away because she couldn't face up to it. I know you're wondering what difference it makes, but it matters to me."

"Do you really believe she'll be found after all this time?"

She leaned toward me. "Look, I have a good job at a good salary. I can afford whatever it takes."

"It's not about that. It's about the probabilities. I

could waste a lot of my time and a shitload of your money, and at the end of it, you'd be right back where you are. I can as good as guarantee it."

"I'm not asking for any kind of guarantee."

"Then what?"

"Help me, that's all. Please tell me you'll try."

I sat and stared at her. What was I supposed to say? The woman was earnest. I had to give her that. I looked down at my plate, then used an index finger to pick up a fallen glop of cheese that I put on my tongue. Still tasty. "Let me ask you this. Didn't someone investigate the disappearance at the time?"

"The sheriff's department."

"Great. That's good. Have you asked what they did?"

"That's something I was hoping you'd do. I know my dad filled out a missing-persons report. I've seen a copy so I'm sure he talked to at least one detective, though I don't remember his name. He's retired now I think."

"That's probably easy enough to find out."

"I don't know if Tannie mentioned this, but Dad thinks she was having an affair and the two of them ran off."

"An affair. Based on what?"

"Based on her past behavior. My mother was wild . . . at least that's what everybody says."

"Assuming there's a guy, do you have any idea who?"

"No, but she did have enough money tucked away to support herself. For a while, at any rate."

"How much?"

"That's a subject of debate. She claimed fifty thousand dollars, but that was never verified."

"Where'd she get that kind of money?"

"From an insurance settlement. As I understand it,

there was a problem when I was born. I guess the doctor botched the delivery, and she had to have an emergency hysterectomy. She hired a lawyer and sued. Whatever she collected, she signed a confidentiality clause promising she wouldn't disclose the details."

"Clearly, she did."

"Well, yes, but nobody believed her. She did keep something in a safe-deposit box she rented in a bank down here and she emptied that the week she left. She also took the Chevy my dad bought her the day before."

"Tannie says there's been no sign of that either."

"Exactly. It's like she and the car were both vaporized."

"How old was she when she disappeared?"

"Twenty-four."

"Which would make her what, now, fifty-eight or so?"

"That's right."

"How long were your parents married?"

"Eight years."

I may be lousy at math, but I picked up on that. "So she was sixteen when she married him."

"Fifteen. She was sixteen when I was born."

"How old was he?"

"Nineteen. They had to. She was pregnant with me."

"I could have guessed that." I studied her face. "Tannie tells me people in Serena Station think he killed her."

Daisy flicked a look at Tannie, who said, "Daisy, it's the truth. You have to level with her."

"I know, but it's hard to talk about this stuff, especially when he's not here to tell his side."

"You can trust me or not. It's up to you." I waited a couple of beats and then said, "I'm trying to make a decision here. I can't operate in a vacuum. I need all the information I can get."

She colored slightly. "I'm sorry. They had what you'd call a 'volatile relationship.' I can remember that myself. Big screaming fights. Slaps. Broken dishes. Doors slamming. Accusations, threats." She put an index finger in her mouth and began to worry the nail with her teeth. I was getting so tense watching her, I nearly slapped her hand.

"Either of them ever hit you?"

She shook her head with certainty. "I usually stayed in my room till it was over."

"Did she ever call the cops?"

"Two or three times that I remember, though it was probably more."

"Let me take a guess. She'd threaten to file charges, but in the end, she'd always back down and the two of them would get all lovey-dovey again."

"I think someone from the sheriff's department was working on that. I remember him coming to the house. A deputy in a tan uniform."

"Trying to talk her into taking action."

"That's right. He must have made headway. Somebody told me she'd asked for a restraining order, but there was some kind of screwup and the judge never signed."

"So given their marital history, after she disappeared, the sheriff's department talked to your dad because they thought he might've had a hand in it."

"Well, yes, but I don't believe he'd do that."

"But what if I find out he did? Then you've lost both parents. At least now you've got him. Do you want to take that risk?"

Tears formed a bright line of silver along her lower lids. "I have to know." She put a hand against her mouth to still the trembling. Tears had made her complexion a patchy red, like a sudden case of hives. It took courage to do what she was doing, I had to give her that. Stirring up old dirt. Most people would have been happy to sweep it under the rug.

Tannie pulled a tissue from her jeans pocket and passed it over to her. Daisy took a moment to wipe her eyes and blow her nose, composing herself before she put the tissue away. "Sorry about that."

"You could have done this years ago. Why now?"

"I started thinking. There are still a few people left who knew her back then, but they're scattering and a lot of them are dead. If I put it off much longer, they'll all be gone."

"Does your dad know what you're up to?"

"This isn't about him. It's about me."

"But it could affect him nonetheless."

"That's a chance I'll have to take."

"Because?"

She sat on her hands, putting them under her thighs, either to warm them or to keep them from trembling. "I'm stuck. I can't get past this. My mother took off when I was seven. Poof. She was gone. I want to know why. I'm entitled to the information. What did I do to deserve that? That's all I'm asking. If she's dead, okay. And if it turns out he killed her, then so be it. At least I'll know it wasn't about her rejecting me." Tears welled and she blinked rapidly, willing them away. "Have you ever been abandoned? Do you know how that feels? To think someone just didn't give a shit about you?"

"I've had experience with that," I replied with care.

"It has been the defining fact of my life," she said, enunciating every word.

I started to speak, but she cut me off. "I know what you're going to say. *'What she did had nothing to do with you.'* You know how many times I've heard that? *'It wasn't your fault. People do what they do for reasons of their own.'* Well, bullshit. And you want to know the hell of it? She took the *dog*. A yappy Pomeranian named Baby she hadn't even had a month."

I couldn't think of a response so I kept my mouth shut.

She was silent for a moment. "I can't have a man in my life because I don't trust a soul. I've been burned more than once and I'm petrified it's only going to happen again. Do you know how many shrinks I've been through? Do you know how much money I've spent trying to make my peace? They fire me. Have you ever heard of such a thing? They throw up their hands and claim I won't do the work. What *work*? What kind of work can you do around that? It sticks in my craw. Why'd she leave *me* when she turned around and took the fuckin' dog?"

3

I met Daisy Sullivan at my office at 9:00 the next morning. Having shown me a glimpse at her rage, she'd retreated into calm. She was pleasant, reasonable, and cooperative. We decided to set a cap on the amount of money she'd pay me. She gave me her personal check for twenty-five hundred dollars, essentially five hundred dollars a day for five days. When we reached that point, we'd see if I'd learned enough to warrant further investigation. This was Tuesday, and Daisy was on her way back to Santa Maria, where she worked in the records department at a medical center. The plan was that I'd follow her in my car, drop it off at her place, and then we'd take hers and head out to the little town of Serena Station, fifteen miles away. I wanted to see the house where the Sullivans were living when her mother was last seen.

Driving north on the 101, I kept an eye on the rear end of Daisy's 1980 Honda, dusty white with an enormous dent across the trunk. I couldn't think how she'd done that. It looked like a tree trunk had fallen on her car. She was the kind of driver who stayed close to the berm, her brake lights flashing off and on like winking Christmas bulbs. As I drove, the flaxen hills appeared to approach and recede, the chaparral as dense and scratchy-looking as a new wool blanket. A gray haze of dried grass undulated at the side of the road, whipped by the breeze created by the passing cars. A recent fire had created an artificial autumn, the hillsides as bronze as a sepia photograph. Tree leaves were scorched to a papery beige. Shrubs were reduced to black sticks. Tree stubs, like broken pipes, protruded from the ashen earth. Occasionally, only half a tree would be singed, looking as though brown branches had been grafted onto green.

Ahead of me, Daisy activated her turn signal and eased off the highway, taking the 135, which angled north and west. I followed. Idly I picked up the map I'd folded into thirds and laid on the passenger seat. A quick glance showed a widespread smattering of small towns, no more than dots on the landscape: Barker, Freeman, Tullis, Arnaud, Silas, and Cromwell, the latter being the largest, with a population of 6,200. I'm always curious how such communities come into existence. Time permitting, I'd make the rounds so I could see for myself.

Daisy's house was off Donovan Road to the west of the 135. She pulled into a driveway that ran between two 1970s-era frame-and-stucco houses, mirror images of each other, though hers was painted dark green and the one next door was gray. Against her house, bougainvillea grew from thick vines that climbed as far as the asphalt shingle roof in a tangle of blossoms the shape and color of cooked shrimp. I parked at the curb and got out of my car while she pulled the Honda into the garage and removed her suitcase from the trunk. I stood on the porch and watched her unlock the door.

"Let me get some windows open," she said as she went in.

I stepped in after her. The house had been closed up for days and the interior felt hot and dry. Daisy moved through the living and dining rooms to the kitchen, opening windows along the way. "The bathroom's off that hall to the right."

I said, "Thanks," and went in search of it, primarily because it gave me the opportunity to peek into other rooms. The floor plan was common to houses of this type. There was an L-shaped living-dining room combination. A galley-style kitchen ran the depth of the house on the left, and on the right, a hallway connected two small bedrooms with a bathroom in between. The place was clean but leaned toward shabby.

I closed the bathroom door and availed myself of the facilities—a polite way of saying that I peed. The tile in the bathroom was dark maroon, the counter edged with a two-inch beige bullnose. The toilet was the same deep maroon. Daisy's robe hung on the back of the door, a silky Japanese kimono, dense sky blue, with a green and orange dragon embroidered on the back. I gave her points for that one. I'd imagined something closer to a granny gown, rose-sprigged flannel, ankle-length and prim. There must be a sensual side to her that I hadn't seen.

I joined her in the kitchen. Daisy had put a kettle on the stove, flames turned up high to speed along the process. On the table, she'd set out tea bags and two heavy ceramic mugs. She said, "I'll be right back," and disappeared toward the bathroom, which allowed me the opportunity to peer out the kitchen window. I studied the neatly kept yard. The grass had been trimmed. The rose bushes were thick with blooms—pink, blush, peach, and brassy orange. Tannie had told me Daisy drank to excess, but whatever angst had been generated by her mother's disappearance, her exterior life was in order, perhaps in direct counterpoint to the emotional mess inside. While she was gone . . . as a courtesy . . . I refrained from peeking into the trash to see if she'd tossed any empty vodka bottles. The kettle began to whistle, so I turned off the burner and poured sputtering water into our cups.

When she returned she carried a manila folder that she placed on the table. She settled in her chair and put on a pair of drugstore-rack reading glasses with round metal frames. She removed a sheaf of newspaper articles, clipped together, and a page of notes, neatly printed, the letters round and regular. "These are all the newspaper accounts I could find. You don't have to read them now, but I thought they might help. And these are the names, addresses, and phone numbers of the people you might want to talk to." She pointed to the first name on the list. "Foley Sullivan's my dad."

"He now lives in Cromwell?"

She nodded. "He couldn't stay in Serena Station. I guess a few people reserved judgment, but most thought poorly of him to begin with. He'd been a drinker before she left, but he quit cold and hasn't had a drop since. This next name, Liza Clements? Her maiden name was Mellincamp. She's the babysitter who was watching me the night my mother ran off . . . escaped . . . whatever you want to call it. Liza had just turned fourteen and she lived one block over. This gal, Kathy Cramer, was her best friend—still is for that matter. Her family lived a couple of houses down—big place and nice, relative to everything else. Kathy's mother was a dreadful gossip, and it's possible Kathy picked up a few tidbits from her."

"Is the family still there?"

"The father is. Chet Cramer. Foley bought the car from his dealership. Kathy's married and she and her husband bought a place in Orcutt. Her mother died seven or eight years after Mom disappeared, and Chet married some new gal within six months."

"I bet that was a popular move." I indicated the next name on the list. "Who's this?"

"Calvin Wilcox is Violet's only brother. I think he saw her that week, so he may be able to fill in a few gaps. This guy, BW, was the bartender at the dive where my parents hung out, and these are miscellaneous customers who witnessed some of their famous public shoving matches."

"Have you talked to all these people?"

"Well, no. I mean, I've known them all for years . . . but I haven't asked about her."

"Don't you think you'd have better luck than I would? I'm a stranger. Why would they open up to me?"

"Because people like to talk, but a lot of stuff they might not be willing to say to me. Who wants to tell a woman how often her dad punched her mother's lights out? Or refer to the time when her mom got mad and threw a drink in some guy's face? Now and then I get wind of these things, but mostly people are falling all over themselves keeping the truth under wraps. I know they mean well, but I get weirded out by that. I hate secrets. I hate that there's all this information I'm not allowed to have. Who knows what's being said behind my back even to this day?"

"Well, I'll be giving you regular written reports, so whatever I learn you'll be hearing about."

"Good. I'm glad. About time," she said. "Oh, here. I want you to have this. Just so you'll know who you're dealing with."

She handed me a small black-and-white snapshot with a scalloped white rim and then watched over my shoulder as I studied the image. The print was four inches square and showed a woman in a floral-print sleeveless dress, smiling into the camera. Her hair, which could have been any color, was a medium-dark tone, long and gently wavy. She was small and pretty in a 1950s kind of way, more voluptuous than we'd consider stylish in this day and age. Over one arm she carried a straw tote from which a tiny fluffy pup appeared, staring at the camera with bright black eyes. "When was this taken?"

"Early June, I think."

"And the dog's name is Baby?"

"Baby, yes. A purebred Pomeranian everyone hated except my mom, who really doted on the little turd. Given the chance, Dad would have taken a shovel and pounded her into the ground like a tent peg. His words."

A two-by-four porch post appeared to be growing from the top of Violet's head. Behind her, on the porch rail, I could read the last two house numbers: 08. "Is this the house where you lived?"

Daisy nodded. "I'll take you by when we're over there."

"I'd like that."

We were silent on the drive to Serena Station. The sky was a flat pale blue, looking bleached by the sun. The hills rolled gently toward the horizon, the grass the color of brown sugar. Daisy's was the only car on the road. We passed abandoned oil rigs, rust-frozen and still. To my left I caught a glimpse of an old quarry and rusting rail-road tracks that began and ended nowhere. On the only visibly working ranch I saw, ten head of cattle had settled on the ground like brawny cats in the slatted shade of a corral.

The town of Serena Station appeared beyond a bend in the two-lane road, with a street sign indicating that it was now called Land's End Road. The street ran in a straight line for three blocks and ended abruptly at a locked gate. Beyond the gate, the road wound up a low hill, but it didn't look like anyone had traveled it for quite some time. There were numerous cars parked in town—in driveways, along the streets, behind the general store—but nothing seemed to move except the wind. A few houses were boarded up, their exteriors bereft of color. In front of one, the paint on the white picket fence had been stripped to the wood, and portions of it sagged. In the small patchy lawns, what little grass remained was dry, and the ground looked hard and unforgiving. In one yard, a camper shell sat under an overhang of corrugated green plastic sheets. There were tree stumps and a tumble of firewood. What had once been the automobile-repair shop stood open to the elements. A tall, dark palm tree towered above a length of chain-link fence that extended across the rear. A stack of fifty-five-gallon oil drums had been left behind. Weeds grew in dry-looking puffs that, in time, the wind would blow free, sending them rolling down the middle of the road. A hound trotted along a side street on a doggie mission of some kind.

Behind the town the hills rose sharply, not mountains by any stretch. They were rugged, without trees, hospitable to wildlife but uninviting to hikers. I could see power lines looping from house to house, and a series of telephone poles stretched away from me like hatch marks on a pencil drawing. We parked and got out, ambling down the middle of the cracked blacktop road. There were no sidewalks and no streetlights. There was no traffic and, therefore, no traffic lights. "Not exactly bustling," I remarked. "I take it the auto-repair shop went belly-up."

"That belonged to Tannie's brother, Steve. Actually, he moved his operation into Santa Maria, figuring if someone's car broke down, the owner would never manage to get it out here. He wasn't about to offer to go get them. At the time, he only had one tow truck and that was usually out of commission."

"Not much of an advertisement for auto repair."

"Yeah, well he was bad at it anyway. Once he moved, he hired a couple of mechanics and now he's doing great."

Daisy pointed out the house where Chet Cramer lived with his current wife. "The Cramers were the only family with any sizeable income. They had the first television set anybody'd ever seen. If you played your cards right, you could watch *Howdy Doody* or *Your Show of Shows*. Liza took me over there once, but Kathy didn't like me so I wasn't invited back."

The Cramers' house was the only two-story structure I'd seen, an old-fashioned farmhouse with a wide wooden porch. I'd stuck a pack of index cards in my jacket pocket, and I used one now to make a crude map of the town. I'd be talking to a number of current and former residents, and I thought it would help to have a sense of where they'd lived relative to one another.

Daisy paused in front of a pale green stucco house

with a flat roofline. Up came the hand so she could gnaw on herself. A short walkway led from the street to the walk-out porch. A chain-link fence surrounded the property, with a sign hanging from the open gate that read NO TRESPASS. The yard was dead. Raw plywood sheets had been nailed over the windows. The front door had been lifted from its hinges and left leaning against the outside wall. The house number was 3908.

"That's where you lived. I recognize the porch rail from the photograph."

"Yep. You want to come in?"

"We're not trespassing?"

"Not now. I bought it. Don't ask me why. My parents rented from a guy named Tom Padgett, who sold it to me. You'll see his name on the list. He was in the bar on a couple of occasions when the two of them pitched a fit. Daddy worked construction so sometimes we had money and sometimes not. If he had it, he'd spend it, and if he didn't have it, too bad. Owing people money never bothered him. Bad weather he'd be out of a job or else he'd get fired for showing up drunk. He wasn't exactly a deadbeat, but he operated with a similar mentality. He'd take care of the bills if he was in the mood, but you couldn't count on that. Padgett was forever pounding on him for the rent because Daddy tended to pay late, if he paid at all. We'd be threatened with eviction, and when he finally coughed up the rent, it was always with the attitude that he was being abused."

I followed her through the gate. I knew she must have been back a hundred times, but looking for what? An explanation, a clue, an answer to the questions that were plaguing her?

Inside, the layout was elementary. Living room with a

dining cove, a kitchen with just enough room for a table and chairs, though those were long since gone. The kitchen appliances had been removed, pipes and wires sticking out of the wall. Blocks of relatively clean linoleum indicated where the stove and refrigerator had once sat. The sink was still there, along with the chipped Formica counters with metal rims. Cabinet doors stood open, revealing the empty shelves where paper was curling up from the corners. Without even meaning to, I moved forward and closed one of the cabinet doors. "Sorry. Things like that bug me."

"I'm the same way," Daisy said. "You wait. Leave the room and come back and the door will be open again. Almost enough to make you wonder about ghosts."

"You're not tempted to fix it up?"

"Maybe one day, though I can't imagine ever living here again. I like the house I'm in."

"So which bedroom was yours?"

"In here."

The room was barely nine feet by twelve, painted an unpleasant shade of pink that I supposed was meant to be girlish.

"My bed was in this corner. Chest of drawers there. Armoire. Toy box. Little table and two chairs." She leaned against the wall and surveyed the space. "I felt so lucky to have a room of my own. I didn't know from tacky. Most of the people we knew were as bad off as we were. Or that's what I realize now."

She moved from her room to the second bedroom and paused in the door. This one was painted lavender with a wallpaper border of violets along the low ceiling line. I backtracked three steps and checked the bathroom, where the sink and bathtub were still anchored in place. The toilet had been removed and a rag was stuffed in the hole, which still emitted the spoiled-egg smell of flushes gone by. This was possibly the most depressing house I'd ever been in.

She moved in behind me, perhaps seeing the house as I did. "Believe it or not, my mother did what she could to pretty things up. Lace curtains for the living room, throw rugs, doilies for the furniture—stuff like that. One of the last fights I remember, my dad went berserk and tore down one of her precious lace panels. I don't think he could have done anything worse. That's how they were, always going to extremes, pushing each other over the edge. She tore down the rest, ripped them off the rods and threw them in the trash. I could hear her screaming she was finished. Done. She said he destroyed everything beautiful she tried to do and she hated him for that. Blah, blah, blah. That was a couple of days before she left."

"Did it scare you? The fights?"

"Sometimes. Mostly I thought that's just how parents behaved," she said. "Anyway, the upshot is I'm a chronic insomniac. Shrinks have a field day with that. The only time I remember sleeping well was when I was a little kid and my parents went out. It must have been the only time I felt safe, because Liza was in charge and I knew I could trust her to take care of me."

"You remember anything else from those last few days?"

"A bubble bath. It's the little things that get you. I was sitting in the tub and she was on her way out. She stuck her head in the door . . . that little yappy dog in her arms . . . and she blew me a kiss. If I'd known it was the last one I'd ever get, I'd have made her come back and kiss me for real."

4

Daisy took an alternate route on our return to Santa Maria, swinging north in a wide loop that, according to the map, encompassed the townships of Beatty and Poe. In point of fact, I didn't see either one. I squinted, saying, "Where's Poe? The map says it's right here close to a little town called Beatty."

"I think those are company names. Poe, I don't know about, but there's a Beatty Oil and Natural Gas. If there were ever towns in those spots, they might've left the names on the map so the area wouldn't seem so desolate."

The surrounding countryside was flat, entirely given over to agriculture: fields of lettuce, sugar beets, and beans as far as the eye could see. The air smelled of celery. Bright blue port-o-potties stood like sentinels along the road. Cars were parked along the berm adjacent to some fields. Wooden crates were stacked high on flatbed trucks, and migrant farmworkers bent above the rows, harvesting a crop I didn't recognize on sight, flying by as we were at sixty miles an hour. The road made a wide curve north. Oil rigs dotted the land and in one section, there was a small refinery that threw off an odor reminiscent of burning tires. In sections, I could see a line of stationary boxcars that must have stretched for a quarter of a mile.

I looked past her through the driver's-side window. Tucked in a stand of pines, a grand old stone-and-stucco house sat close to the road, abandoned to all appearances. The architecture had elements of English Tudor with a touch of Swiss chalet thrown in, the whole of it incongruous in the midst of tilled and untilled fields. The second story was half-timbered with three gables punctuating the roofline. "What the heck is that?"

Daisy slowed. "That's why we came this way. Tannie and her brother, Steve, inherited the house and three hundred acres of farmland, some of which they lease out."

Two massive stone chimneys bracketed the house on each end. The narrow third-story windows suggested rooms reserved for household servants. A magnificent oak had been planted at one corner of the house, probably ninety years before, and now overshadowed the entrance. Across the road, there was empty acreage.

The yard was completely overgrown. Weeds had proliferated and once decorative shrubs were close to eight feet high, obscuring the ground-floor windows. Where there had been a gracious approach, defined by boxwoods on both sides of a wide brick path, the passage was now close to impenetrable. Someone was using a small tractor to clear the overgrowth near the road, piling it in a mound. The brush closer to the house would probably have to be hacked away by hand. Daunting, I thought.

"Catch the back side," she said as we passed.

I shifted in my seat and glanced over my shoulder, looking at the house from another angle. A wide dirt-and-gravel lane, probably the original driveway, now doubled as a frontage road with a service road splitting off to the right. I was guessing that the service road intersected one of the old county roads that was rendered obsolete once New Cut Road went in.

On the back side of the house, most of the third-story windows in the rear were missing, the frames and timbers charred black from a fire that had eaten half the roof. There was something painful in the sight and I could feel myself wince. "How'd that happen?"

"Vagrants. This was a year ago. Now there's a raging debate about what to do with the place."

"Why was the house built so close to the road?"

"Actually, it wasn't. The house used to sit dead center on the land, but then the new road was cut through. The grandparents must have needed cash, because they sold off a big chunk, maybe half of what they owned. The ink wasn't dry on the check before negotiations were under way for a housing tract that never went in. Talk about local politics. Now Tannie's in a quandary, trying to decide whether to restore the house or tear it down and build in a better location. Her brother thinks they should sell the property while they have the chance. Right now, the market's good, but Steve's one of those guys who's always predicting doom and gloom, so they've been butting heads. She'll have to buy him out if she decides to hang on. She's hired a couple of guys to help her clear brush on her days off. The county's been testy about the fire hazard, given last year's burn."

"Does she want to farm the land?"

"I doubt it. Maybe she plans to open a B-and-B. You'd have to ask her."

"Amazing." I could feel the shift in my perception of Tannie Ottweiler. I'd pictured her barely making ends meet on a bartender's salary, never guessing she was a land baroness. "I take it she's thinking about moving up here."

"That's her hope. She's been driving up Thursdays and Fridays, so if she's here again this week maybe the three of us could have lunch."

"Sounds great."

There was a silence that lasted fifteen miles. Daisy was communicative in small doses, but she seemed to feel no obligation to chatter full time, which suited me fine.

"So what's your story?" she asked, finally.

"Mine?"

"You've been asking questions about me. Fair is fair."

I didn't like this part, where I was forced to pony up. As usual, I reduced my past to its basic elements. I didn't want sympathy and I didn't want additional questions. In any version I told, the ending was the same and I was bored with the recitation. "My parents were killed in a car wreck when I was five. I was raised by a maiden aunt, who didn't parent all that well."

She waited to see if I'd go on. "Are you married?"

"Not now, but I was. Twice, which seems like plenty."

"I've got four divorces to your two so I guess I'm more optimistic."

"Or maybe slower to learn."

That netted me a smile, but not much of one.

When we got back to Daisy's house, I picked up my car and drove the hour back to Santa Teresa, returning to my office, where I worked for the balance of the afternoon. I took care of the phone messages that had accumulated in my absence and then sat down and read the newspaper accounts about Violet in the weeks following her vanishing act. The initial item about the missing woman didn't appear until the eighth of July, Wednesday of the following week. The article was brief, indicating that the public's help was being sought in the disappearance of Violet Sullivan, last seen on Saturday, July 4, when she'd left to join her husband at a park in Silas, California, nine miles from her home in Serena Station. She was believed to have been driving a violet-gray two-door Chevrolet Bel Air coupe, with the dealer's sticker displayed on the windshield. Anyone with information was encouraged to contact Sergeant Tim Schaefer at the Santa Teresa County Sheriff's Department. The telephone number for the north county substation was listed.

Daisy had clipped two more articles, but there was little additional information. There were references to Violet's having money, but no dollar amount had been confirmed. A bank manager in Santa Teresa had called the sheriff's department to report that Violet Sullivan had arrived at the Santa Teresa Savings and Loan early in the afternoon on Wednesday, July 1. She'd spoken first to him, presenting her key and asking for access to her safe-deposit box. He was already late for lunch so he'd turned her over to one of the tellers, a Mrs. Fitzroy, who'd dealt with Mrs. Sullivan previously and recognized her on sight. After Mrs. Sullivan signed in, Mrs. Fitzroy verified her signature and accompanied her into the vault, where she was given her box and shown into a small cubicle. She returned the box some minutes later. Neither the teller nor the bank manager had any idea

what was in the box or whether Violet Sullivan had removed the contents.

In a third article, which ran on July 15, the county
sheriff's department's public relations officer stated they
were interviewing Foley Sullivan, the missing woman's
husband. He was not considered a suspect, but was a
"person of interest." According to Foley Sullivan's account, he'd stopped off to have a beer after the fireworks
ended at 9:30. He got home a short time later and saw
the family car was gone. He assumed that he and his wife
had missed each other at the park and that she'd arrive
shortly. He admitted to being mildly intoxicated and
claimed he'd gone straight to bed. It wasn't until his
daughter woke him at 8:00 the next morning that he
realized his wife had failed to return. Anyone with information, etc.

Occasionally, in the years since then, feature articles
had been written about the case—puff pieces in the main.
The tone was meant to be hard-hitting but the coverage
was superficial. The same basic facts were spun out and
embellished with little in the way of revelation. As nearly
as I could tell, the subject had never been tackled in any
systematic way. Violet's uncertain fate had elevated her
to the status of a minor celebrity, but only in the small
farming community where she had lived. No one outside
the area seemed to take much interest. There was a
black-and-white photograph of her and a separate photo
of the car—not the identical vehicle, of course, but a similar make and model.

The car caught my attention and I read that part
twice. On Friday, July 3, 1953, Foley Sullivan had filled
out the loan papers on a purchase price of $2,145. Since
the vehicle was never seen again, he'd been compelled to

make payments for the next thirty-six months until the terms were satisfied. Title had never been registered. Violet Sullivan's driver's license had expired in June of 1955, and she'd made no application for renewal.

What struck me as curious was that Daisy had described her father as close to a deadbeat, so I couldn't imagine why he'd continued paying for the car. How perverse to have to go on forking out the dough for a vehicle your wife may or may not have used in running off with another man. Since there was no way the dealer could repossess the car, Foley was stuck. I couldn't understand why he cared, one way or the other, whether the dealer sued him for the balance or turned him over to a collection agency. Big deal. His credit was already shot, so what was one more debt? I put the question in a drawer at the back of my mind, hoping an answer would be sitting there the next time I looked.

At 5:00 P.M. I locked the office and went home. My studio apartment is located on a side street a block from the beach. My landlord, Henry, had converted the space from a single-car garage to a rental unit, attached to his own house by a glass-enclosed breezeway. I've been living there quite happily for the past seven years. Henry's the only man I know whom I'd be willing to marry if (and only if) we weren't separated by a fifty-year age difference. It's tough when the perfect man in your life is an octogenarian . . . though a *young* eighty-seven years old. Henry's trim, handsome, smart, white-haired, blue-eyed, and active. I can go on in this manner, reciting his many virtues, but you probably get the point.

I parked and passed through the squeaky gate that announces my arrival. I went around to the rear and let myself into my apartment, where I wrestled with my conscience briefly, and then changed into my running clothes and did a three-mile jog along the beach. Home again forty minutes later, I found a message from Cheney Phillips waiting on my machine. He proposed a quick bite of supper and said unless he heard otherwise, he'd meet me at Rosie's close to 7:00. I showered and got back into my jeans.

"Well, it's an interesting proposition. I'll give you that," Cheney said when I'd laid it out to him. Rosie had taken our order, asking us what we wanted, and then writing down what she'd already decided to serve—an unpronounceable dish that she pointed to on the menu. This turned out to be a beef-and-pork stew with more sour cream than flavor, so we'd spent a few minutes surreptitiously adding salt and enough pepper to make our eyes sting. Rosie's cooking is usually tasty, so neither of us could figure out what was going on with her. Cheney was drinking beer and I was drinking bad white wine, which is all she serves.

"You know what's hanging me up?" I asked.

"Tell."

"The thought of failing."

"There are worse things."

"Name one."

"Root canal. IRS audit. Terminal disease."

"But at least those things don't impact anyone else. I don't want to take Daisy's money if I can't deliver anything, and what are the odds?"

"She's a grown-up. She says this is what she wants. Do you have any reason to doubt her sincerity?"

"No."

"So why don't you put a cap on the money end?"

"I did that. It doesn't seem to help."

"You'll do fine. All you can do is give it your best shot."

In the office Wednesday morning, I made a series of phone calls, setting up appointments with the principals on my list. I didn't think the order of interviews would make any difference, but I'd arranged the names in order of personal preference. In quick succession, I talked to Sergeant Timothy Schaefer, who'd been the investigating officer when Violet disappeared. I wanted to see how things had looked from his perspective and I thought he'd be good at laying in the background. We agreed to meet that afternoon at 1:00, and he gave me directions to his house in Santa Maria. Foley Sullivan was next on my list. Daisy had told him I'd be calling, but I was still relieved to find him cooperative. I made an appointment to talk to him after my interview with Sergeant Schaefer. My next call was to Calvin Wilcox, Violet's only sibling. I got a busy signal on that number so I moved to the next.

Fourth on my list was the babysitter, Liza Clements, née Mellincamp, one of the last people who'd spent time in Violet's company. I was hoping to create a calendar of events, starting with Liza and working my way backward as I reconstructed Violet's activities and encounters in the days before she vanished. I dialed Liza's number and she picked up after six rings, just at the point where I'd about given up.

When I identified myself, she said, "I'm sorry, but could we talk another time? I've got a dental appointment and I'm just now walking out the door."

"How about later this afternoon? When will you be home?"

"Really, today's a mess. What about tomorrow?"

"Sure, that would work. What time?"

"Four o'clock?"

"Fine."

"Do you have my address?"

"Daisy gave it to me."

"Great. See you then."

I moved on to Kathy Cramer. She and Liza were fourteen at the time, which put them in their late forties now. I knew Kathy was married, but she'd apparently elected to keep her maiden name, because Cramer was the only reference I had. I dialed her number and once I had her on the line, I told her who I was and what I was doing at Daisy's behest.

"You're kidding," she said, her voice flat with disbelief.

"Afraid not," I said. So tedious. I didn't relish having to go through this routine with every other call I made.

"You're looking for Violet Sullivan after all these years?"

"That's what I was hired to do. I'm hoping you can fill in some blanks."

"Have you talked to Liza Mellincamp?"

"I see her tomorrow afternoon. If you could spare me half an hour, I'd be grateful."

"I can probably manage that. Can we say tomorrow morning at eleven?"

"Sure thing."

"What address do you have? We just moved."

I recited the address on my list, which was out of date. She gave me the new one with a set of directions that I scribbled down in haste.

My last call was to Daisy, telling her I was making a run to Santa Maria and back. On Thursday, I expected to have a block of free time, so I was proposing lunch and a quick verbal report. She was agreeable and said we could try a coffee shop close to her work. Since Tannie would be in Santa Maria on Thursday as well, she'd give her a call and see if she could join us. Her lunch hour was flexible, so I agreed to call as soon as I had a break.

After I hung up, I folded the list and gathered my index cards, gassed up the VW, and headed north. I was already getting bored with the hour drive each way and not all that happy about the miles I was putting on my thirteen-year-old car.

5

KATHY
Wednesday, July 1, 1953

Kathy Cramer was working in the office at her father's Chevrolet dealership when Violet pulled up in Foley's rattletrap pickup and started looking at cars. She carried a big straw tote with a little dog tucked inside, its head popping up like a jack-in-the-box. This was Kathy's first real job, and her father was paying her a dollar an hour, twenty-five cents over the minimum wage and twice what her best friend, Liza, made for babysitting. A dollar an hour was pretty good for a fourteen-year-old, even if his hiring her was not entirely voluntary. When his secretary left to get married, he'd wanted to advertise for a permanent full-time replacement, but Kathy's mother put her foot down, insisting he could find somebody in the fall when Kathy went back to school.

Her responsibilities entailed answering the phone, filing, and "lite" typing, which she generally messed up. At the moment business was slow, so she occupied her time reading the movie magazines she kept in her lap. James

Dean was already her favorite of the new Hollywood stars. Also Jean Simmons, with whom she completely identified. She'd seen *Androcles and the Lion* and, most recently, *Young Bess*, in which Jean Simmons had starred with her husband, Stewart Granger, who was second only to James Dean in Kathy's mind.

This was July and the office was small. Glass on all sides let the sunlight slant in, heating the space to unbearable temperatures. There was no air-conditioning, so Kathy kept an electric fan beside her on the floor, the face tilted toward hers for maximum effect. The air was still hot, but at least it was moving. She didn't think it was possible to sweat so much sitting down. In the spring, her gym teacher had suggested it really wouldn't hurt if she lost thirty-five pounds, but Kathy's mother was having none of it. Girls paid entirely too much attention to superficial matters like weight, clothing, and hairstyles when what counted was inner beauty. It was more important to be a good person, setting an example for those around you. Kathy's mother said her complexion would clear up in time if she'd just quit picking at it. Kathy used Noxzema every night, but it didn't seem to help.

Kathy took off her glasses and polished the lenses with the hem of her skirt. These were new glasses with stylishly tilted black cat's-eye frames that Kathy thought looked especially wonderful on her. She found herself following Violet's progress across the lot. She had vulgar dyed-red hair and wore a tight purple sundress with a deeply scooped neckline. Winston Smith, the salesman Kathy's dad had hired the month before, had his eye on the crevice between her boobies. Everybody was always mooning over Violet, which made Kathy sick. Especially her friend, Liza, who thought Violet could do no wrong.

Kathy was struck by a sharp emotional jolt, which later in life she might concede was a feeling of jealousy. At the moment she wondered if it was possible to have hot flashes at so young an age. She'd seen her mother fanning herself, suddenly dripping with sweat, and thought what she experienced might be similar.

Winston worked strictly on commission, which probably explained why he was so interested in talking to Violet as she strolled between the aisles of used cars. Winston was twenty years old. His hair was dark blond with a ridge of curls on top. The sides were swept back and met at the nape in a style known as a DA, which was short for "duck's ass," though that wasn't a term Kathy would dream of saying out loud. Kathy could see him gesturing, pretending to be knowledgeable when, in fact, he'd never made a sale. She found it endearing, how transparent he was to her. His goal was to make enough money to pay for his sophomore year in college, and he'd confided his belief that selling cars was the perfect way to jack up his savings. He admitted he didn't have quite the knack for it that he'd hoped. He didn't even enjoy it much, but he was determined to develop his skills, taking Mr. Cramer as his role model. Temporarily, of course.

He was easily handsome enough to be a movie star himself. She thought he looked wonderful in his front-pleated slacks, open-neck shirt, and white bucks. He actually reminded her of James Dean—same cheekbones and long lashes, and the same slender build. His expression was soulful, suggestive of troubles untold. Kathy could picture him working for her father after graduation, but he had bigger dreams, possibly law school, he said. Kathy often asked him about himself, encouraging him to open up to her.

In her pencil drawer, she kept the box of pretty pink stationery she was using for the volume of poems she was writing. She liked the roses around the edge and the pale blue butterfly in each corner. She did the actual composition on wide-lined tablet paper and then transcribed the finished verse onto good paper when she was finally satisfied. Originally she'd bought the stationery for Liza, whose birthday was coming up on Friday, July 3, but when she realized how perfect it was, she'd decided to keep it for herself. She could always give Liza the lily of the valley dusting powder someone had given her last year.

The poem she was working on was half-finished. This was only the fourth poem she'd written, but she knew it was her best. Maybe not perfect yet, but her English teacher said every good writer did constant revisions, and Kathy'd found that to be the case. She'd been working tirelessly on this poem for the better part of the morning. She took out the lined sheet and read it to herself. She was thinking of calling it "To W . . ." without giving any other hint of whom the poem was written for. She knew many poets, such as William Shakespeare, wrote sonnets and titled them that way.

To W . . .

When I gaze in your beautiful brown eyes
I feel my throbbing heart increase in size
With all the love I hold inside for you
I promise, my darling, I will always be true.

I loved you deeply right from the start
And now no one can ever sunder us apart.
If I could only hold you tightly in my arms . . .

She hesitated. That word "arms" was a stumper. "Charms" would rhyme, but she couldn't figure out how to work it in. She tapped her pencil against her lips and then crossed it out. She'd come up with something better. Her thoughts returned to Winston. As a seventh grader, she'd taken a class in dating etiquette, anticipating the opportunities that would crop up for her in eighth grade. She'd learned what topics were suitable for conversation with a boy and what to say at the door at the end of a date. In her mind, the boy's face was amorphous, his features shifting to resemble whatever movie star she was currently smitten with. She imagined him kind and gentle, appreciative of her many fine qualities. She'd had no idea then how soon Winston would appear in her life, the epitome of all her dreams. She did think he'd exhibited a certain interest in her, at least until Violet showed up.

Violet and Winston were approaching the showroom floor, where the best car on the lot—a two-door Chevrolet Bel Air coupe—was displayed under bright lights to emphasize its sleek lines. Violet had spotted the vehicle from halfway across the lot, and Winston was laying on his spiel as though his life depended on it. Like Violet might actually buy it. Very funny! Ha ha! She'd heard Violet and Foley were so poor they could barely afford the rent.

Winston held open the plateglass door, allowing Violet to pass through. Kathy caught sight of a big blue bruise on her chin. Violet was all the time walking around like that, making no effort whatever to cover the marks. No dark glasses. No makeup. No wide-brimmed hat, which might have helped. She went about her errands—supermarket, post office, walking Daisy to school—with one or both eyes black, cheek swollen, her lips puffy and plump from one of Foley's blows. She made no excuses and she never explained, which left Foley looking like a fool. How could he defend himself when she never accused him of anything? Everyone in town knew he hit her, but no one intervened. That was considered their personal business, though Kathy's mother often said it was a total disgrace. Kathy's mother thought Violet was trash and she said Liza was asking for trouble if she hung out with her. Just the night before, sitting at the top of the stairs while her parents were in the living room, she heard her mother talking about Violet and Jake Ottweiler, who'd been seen slow-dancing at the Blue Moon. Violet was oversexed, a regular nymphomaniac (whatever that was), and her mother was disgusted that Jake would have anything to do with her. She was getting all worked up, her voice rising (which made it easier for Kathy to hear) when her father blew his stack. "Christ, Livia! Is that all you have to do, sit around and pass along ugly gossip? What the hell is wrong with you?!"

They'd argued, and her mother had hushed him because she was worried Kathy might overhear them. Personally, she'd agreed with her mother. Violet was a tramp. Kathy picked up a batch of papers and crossed to the filing cabinet by the door so she could hear what Violet and Winston said. The two were focused on the car and didn't seem to notice her hovering nearby. Winston was saying, "Make no mistake, this is not your basic sedan. This is Chevrolet's five-passenger coupe. A 235 engine, Powerglide, dual carbs, and exhaust. Full hubcaps, even has a beehive oil filter, if you can imagine such a thing."

Violet clearly didn't know a filter from a fish fillet. "It's the color I love," she said, running a hand along the front fender. The hood ornament looked like an eagle or a hawk in full flight, beak foremost, wings back, speeding through the air in a stylized pose.

"The color's custom—only one of its kind. Know what it's called? 'Violet Slate.' I kid you not."

Violet flashed him a smile. She made a point of wearing shades of violet: purple, lavender, lilac, mauve. Winston leaned past her and opened the door on the driver's side, revealing the orchid pink trim on the lower dash panel. "Here, have a seat." He cranked down the window and then stood back so she could get a better view. The seats were plush, trimmed in a robin's egg blue with insets and side panels in a pink-and-blue pattern that looked like flame-stitching, the two colors bleeding into each other to form violet shade. When the car had come in, Mr. Cramer had opened the trunk for Kathy, showing her the interior, which was upholstered in the exact same two shades. Even the spare tire in the wheel mount was covered in blue plush, like a tire cozy.

Violet slid in behind the wheel, hands at ten o'clock and two o'clock, nearly feverish with excitement. "It's beautiful. I love this!" She ran a reverent hand across the seat. "How much?"

Winston laughed, thinking she was making a joke.

"What's so funny?"

He stared at the toe of his shoe, looking up at her from under dark lashes, dimples showing, his brow furrowing. "Well, nothing, Mrs. Sullivan, but I believe it's beyond your means. I know it's beyond mine."

"I've got *money*."

"Not this much," he said, in a jocular tone, keeping

things light. Kathy could see he was trying to cushion her disappointment when he told her the price. She thought Violet was getting a bit above herself, putting on airs. Boy, was she in for a rude surprise.

Violet's smile faded. "You think I can't afford to buy a nice car like this?"

"I didn't say that, Mrs. Sullivan. By no means."

Kathy couldn't believe the woman was still pushing the point, but Violet said, "Then answer my question."

"Sticker price is $2,375. My boss might be willing to dicker some, but not a lot. Car like this is considered top of the line and there's not much wiggle room, as we like to say."

Kathy checked Violet's expression, hoping she'd realize how far out of line she was. Violet kept her eyes on Winston, who seemed somewhat distracted by the gap that appeared at the neck of her dress, which was cut low to begin with. She said, "I'd want to take it for a test drive."

"Well, sure. We can arrange that."

She extended her hand out the window, palm up. "You have the keys?"

"No, not *on* me. They'd be in the office . . . in there," he said, gesturing unnecessarily.

"Well, Winston, you'll have to go and get them. You think you can manage that?" Her tone was silky and flirtatious even though what she said seemed insulting to Kathy's ear.

"Unfortunately, my boss has gone to lunch, and I'm the only one on the lot."

"And?"

"And, you know, I can't just take off, because he left me in charge."

"If I'm not mistaken, there's a mechanic on the premises. Two of them, in fact. What's that one's name? Floyd, isn't it?"

Both Kathy and Winston checked the service bay where Floyd could be seen, servicing a used car that had just come in. Mr. Padgett had been talking about a trade-in but then decided he'd hold off until fall when the new '54 models arrived. In the meantime, he'd said he'd just as soon have the cash in hand, so he'd sold it outright.

Winston seem relieved, as though Violet had given him the perfect out. "Mrs. Sullivan, Floyd can't work the floor. He wouldn't know what to do any more than I could go back in the service bay and do his job for him."

"Why do I need you? All I'm going to do is drive around the block. Don't you trust me?"

Winston's Adam's apple dipped. "I do. It's not that. I just think it'd be better to wait until my boss gets back so you can talk to him. He knows this car inside and out, far better than I do. Besides, if it comes to that, he's the one who handles all the paperwork, so it only makes sense."

"Paperwork?"

"You know, down payment, terms—stuff like that. You'd have to have your husband come in and sign."

Violet was amused. "Why? Foley doesn't have a dime. I intend to pay cash."

"Outright?"

"Do you know how much money I have? I'm not supposed to tell, but I know I can count on your discretion," she said, lowering her voice.

"You shouldn't be telling me anything personal, Mrs. Sullivan. You should talk to Mr. Cramer about your finances."

"Fifty thousand dollars."

Winston laughed, unnerved. "Seriously?"

"Of course. Why would I joke about a thing like that?"

"What'd you do, rob a bank?"

"It was an insurance settlement. I wanted more, but that's what the company offered me right off the bat. My lawyer said take it, so that's what I did. The two were probably in cahoots. I've never even told Foley the full amount. He'd be on me in a flash and squander every dime. See this?" Violet pointed to the bruise on her chin. "One day Foley's going to push me too far and that's it. I'll be gone. The money's my ticket out." She held out her hand. "Now. May I have the keys?"

Kathy watched Winston struggle with the request. She knew he wasn't much for confrontation, especially with a woman like Violet. On the other hand, she knew her dad had given him explicit instructions: No test drive without a salesman. No leaving the floor unattended.

"What's your commission on a sale like this?" Violet asked, as though the sale were a foregone conclusion.

"Somewhere in the neighborhood of four percent."

"Enough to cover your tuition and books for the next two years, or am I wrong about that?"

"That seems about right," he said.

Even Kathy was transfixed by the notion of all that money coming to him.

"So do you want the sale or not?"

Winston glanced at his watch. "I don't know what to tell you, Mrs. Sullivan. Mr. Cramer's due back any minute now . . ."

"Oh for Christ's sake! Give me the keys and let's get on with it. I'm just taking it around the block."

Kathy closed the file drawer, rolling her eyes in disgust. Pushiness was unbecoming in a woman—everyone knew that—but blasphemy was inexcusable. She returned to her desk and took a seat. The woman was insane. There was no way Winston was going to let her drive away in that car. Without so much as a dollar changing hands? Very funny. Ha ha. Kathy picked up a stack of papers and tamped them against the desk, then opened and closed a drawer, pretending to be absorbed in her work.

Winston appeared at her desk. There were big damp circles under his shirt sleeves, and she could smell his sweat. "I got a problem."

"I know. She is so full of herself, it makes me sick."

"Can I have the keys to the Bel Air?"

She stared at him, blinking. "Why ask me?"

"Could you give them to me, please? She's buying the car and she wants to see how it drives."

"I don't have them."

"Yes, you do. I saw him give them to you."

Kathy didn't move because she'd suddenly had a thought. At dinner the night before, her dad told her mom he was top-heavy on inventory and light on cash. What if Violet really had the money and the sale got messed up? If Kathy made a fuss and then the deal fell through, she'd never live it down. She could feel her face burn.

Exasperated, Winston leaned over and opened her pencil drawer. There, big as life, were the keys on a ring with the Chevrolet logo, the make and model of the car inked on a round white tag. He helped himself to the set.

"You'll be sorry," she said, not looking at him.

"No doubt," he said, and then returned to the floor. Violet was still sitting in the car.

Kathy's dad would have a fit the minute he found out, but what was she supposed to do?

Winston held out the keys to Violet. She took them without a word and then started the car. She put the gear in reverse and began backing toward the wide steel door at the rear of the showroom. Kathy watched as Winston crossed to the door and gave the handle a yank. The door ascended on its track with a low rumbling sound. He leaned toward the driver's-side window, probably to offer her advice, but Violet swung the car into the alley and took off without so much as a backward look.

Kathy saw Winston glance at his watch, and she felt a little thrill of fear because she knew exactly what was on his mind. Even if Violet took the long way around, the drive couldn't take more than five minutes. Which meant he could have the car on the floor again before her dad returned from lunch.

6

I found Sergeant Timothy Schaefer in a workshop at the back of his property on Hart Drive in Santa Maria. The house itself was built in the 1950s by the look of it—a three-bedroom frame structure so uniformly white that it had been either freshly painted or recently covered in vinyl siding. His workshop must have been a toolshed at one time, enlarged by degrees until it was now half the size of a single-car garage. The interior walls were all raw wood and exposed studs. He'd used layers of newspaper as insulation, and I could probably read a year's worth of local news items if I peered closely enough.

Schaefer had told me he'd retired from the Santa Teresa County Sheriff's Department in 1968 at the age of sixty-two, which made him eighty-one years old now. He was heavyset, his loose gray pants held up with tan suspenders. The brown and blue in his plaid flannel shirt had been washed to a blend of softly faded hues. His hair was a flyaway white, as fine as spun sugar, and he wore bifocals low on his nose, fixing me with an occasional sharp look over the rims.

In front of him, on a chunky wooden workbench that lined the shop on three sides, he'd set a newly refinished rocking chair, its seat in need of recaning. His tools were neatly lined up: a pair of needle-nose pliers, two ice picks, a knife, a ruler, a container of glycerin, and loops of cane held together with clothespins. On the chair he was currently caning, he'd used golf tees to hold the cane in place until he could tie them off underneath.

"My daughter got me into this," he said idly. "After her mother died, she thought a hobby would keep me out of trouble. Weekends, we make the rounds of flea markets and yard sales, picking up old beat-up chairs like this. Turns out to be a money-making proposition."

"How'd you learn?"

"Reading books and doing what they said. Took a while to get the hang of it. Glycerin helps the cane slide. Don't soak it long enough and it's hard to work with. Soak it too long and it'll start to weaken and break. Hope you don't mind if I keep on with this. I promised a fellow I'd have his rocker ready by the end of the week."

"Be my guest."

For a while, I was content to watch without saying a word. The mechanics of it reminded me of needlepoint or knitting, something close to a meditation. There was a certain hypnotic quality to the process, and I might have stood there observing for the better part of the day if time had permitted.

When I'd called the day before, I'd mentioned Stacey Oliphant by name, thus according myself instant credibility since the two had worked together for a number of years. Schaefer and I had spent a few minutes on the

phone discussing the man. When I told him I was looking for information about Violet Sullivan, I'd asked if he
needed to clear anything with the department before we
spoke. "Nobody cares about that anymore," he'd said.
"Only a few of us remember the case. She's still classified
as a missing person, but I don't think you'll have much
success after all these years."

"It's worth a try," I'd said.

"Did you know her?" I asked now.

"Sure did. Everybody knew Violet. Feisty little thing
with that fiery red hair. She was a beautiful girl with a
defiant streak. If Foley blackened her eye, she made no
attempt to hide it. She'd sport a bruise like a badge of
honor. Damndest thing you ever saw. Black and blue, she
was still prettier than any other woman in town. I wasn't
smart enough to keep my trap shut, and my wife was so
jealous I thought she'd spit nails. Violet was the kind of
woman men fantasize about. A lot of wives ended up
with their noses out of joint."

"How well did you know Foley?"

"Better than I knew her, given his numerous contacts
with law enforcement. That's how I ended up dealing
with him in the first place, because of his smacking her
around. I probably went to the house half a dozen times.
None of us liked going out on domestic calls. Dangerous
for one thing, and for another, it made you wonder what
the hell was wrong with folks. Violet and Foley were
skating close to the edge. Bad situation. Her little girl
was of an age where she'd end up standing in the line of
fire. Abuse spills over. It might start with the spouse, but
the kids aren't far behind."

"What about Violet? Did she have any criminal history?"

"Nope."

"Foley never had her arrested for assault?"

"Nope. If she hit him, he must have been too embarrassed to call us."

"Shoot. No mug shots and no fingerprints. That's too bad," I said.

"She was clean as they come. She didn't have a Social Security number because she never held a job, so that's one more dead end. The only outside dispute she had, she took Jake Ottweiler into small-claims court. His pit bull attacked her toy poodle and killed it outright. I think she collected a couple hundred bucks. Foley probably borrowed every cent of it to pay the bills."

"Daisy remembers the two brawling. She says neither one went after her, but it had an effect."

"I don't doubt that," he said. "We sat Foley down more than once and gave him a talking-to, but like most abusers, he was busy blaming someone else. He maintained Violet was provoking him, which made it her fault, not his."

"This was over what period of time?"

"Two, three years, running right up to the last anybody ever saw of her. After we spoke yesterday, I called one of the deputies and had him pull the old file. He went back through the reports and says the two got into a bad one on June 27, a Saturday, the week before she disappeared. Foley flung a pot of coffee at her and it caught her on the chin. She called us. We went out to the house and arrested his sorry ass and then held him overnight until he had a chance to cool down. Meanwhile, she filed a complaint charging him with misdemeanor battery . . ."

"Why misdemeanor?"

"Injuries weren't that serious. He'd broken her jaw, it'd have been another matter. We advised her right then to get a restraining order out against him, but she said she was fine. Minute he got out, he went straight to the house. He begged her to drop the charges, but before anything could come of it, she was gone and that was that."

"When did he report her missing?"

"July 7. In those days, the law required a seventy-two-hour wait if there was no suggestion of foul play, which there wasn't. So Sunday passed, and then Monday without a word from her. Tuesday morning, Foley came over to the station and asked to file a report. I was the one who took the information, though the story was already out by then, and we knew we had a problem on our hands."

"How did he seem?"

"He was obviously upset, but in my estimation, mostly for himself. Given his history, he had to figure he'd be first in line when it came to close scrutiny. We put out a countywide bulletin, giving a description of Violet and the car she was believed to be driving, and then expanded that to statewide within two days. We contacted the papers up and down the coast. Didn't generate much interest, to tell you the truth. Most ran two column inches in the second section, if they bothered at all. Radio, same thing. The story got some local airplay, but not that much."

"Why no splash? What was that about?"

"The media wasn't prone to jumping on stories the way they do now. Violet was an adult. Some had the feeling she'd run off of her own accord and she'd come back when it suited her. Others leaned toward the notion she'd never left at all, at least not alive."

"You think Foley killed her?"

"That's what I thought at the time."

"Why?"

"Because the violence had escalated and she was serious about pressing charges, which would've been bad news for him. It's like the deputy DA told me, 'You don't have a witness, you don't have a case.' If he'd gone to trial, chances are he'd have ended up in jail. It certainly worked to his advantage that she was gone."

"I'm assuming there was an investigation."

"Oh, yes. We could pretty much trace her activities up until the time she left the house that night. This would have been six fifteen or so, after the babysitter showed. It wasn't dark yet and wouldn't turn dark until closer to nine o'clock. Couple of people saw her drive through town. They said it looked like she was alone except for her little dog, standing in her lap yapping out the window. She stopped and bought gas, filling up her tank at a service station near Tullis, so we know she made it that far."

"What time was that?"

"Six twenty-five, round about then. The fellow at the pump cleaned her windshield and checked her tires, which he needn't have done. The car was brand new and he was interested in hearing how she handled. They spent a few minutes talking about that. I asked him if he noticed anything unusual because I was curious about her mood. If she was leaving her little girl for good, you'd think she'd be down in the mouth, but he said she seemed happy. 'Giddy' was his word. Of course, he'd never laid eyes on her before, so as far as he knew, she was always that way. I was hoping she'd said something about her destination, but no such luck. Her dog was barking up a storm, jumping from the front seat to the back. She finally let it out to do its business in the grass. After she put the dog back in the car, she went in the office, paid the clerk for her gas, and bought a Coca-Cola from the cooler. Then she got in the car and off she went, driving toward Freeman."

I opened my shoulder bag and took out a pen and my map of Santa Maria. "Can you show me the location of the service station? I'd like to take a look."

He adjusted his bifocals and studied the map, opening it to the full and then refolding it. "That'd be here," he said, making a mark on the page. "Place is still there, though the pump jockey and clerk have both left the area. From that point, she could have gone anyplace. Down one of these side roads and out to the 101—south to Los Angeles, north to San Francisco. She could have circled back and gone home. We calculated how far she could get on a tank of gas and checked with every station within that radius—no easy task. No one remembered seeing her, which struck me as odd. That car was a beauty and so was she. You'd think someone would have noticed if she'd stopped for anything—meal, restroom, to walk the dog. I don't know how she could have vanished like that, literally, without a trace."

"The papers said Foley wasn't considered a suspect."

"Of course he was. Still is. We put that out, hoping to coax him into telling what he knew, but he was a wily one. He went straight out and hired an attorney, and after that, he wouldn't say a word. We never did come up with anything to hang him on."

"He gave no explanation at all?"

"We managed to get a little bit out of him before he clammed up. We know he stopped by the Blue Moon and had a couple of beers. He claimed he got home a short time after that, which would have made it somewhere between ten and ten thirty. Trouble is, the babysitter, Liza Mellincamp, said she didn't see him until sometime between midnight and one, which means if he killed her he had time to dispose of the body."

"He must have done a good job of it if she's never been found."

Schaefer shrugged. "I imagine she'll turn up one of these days, assuming there was something left of her once the critters got through."

"Also assuming he killed her, which he might not have."

"True enough."

"Not that I'm arguing for or against," I said.

"I understand. I go back and forth myself, and I've had years to ponder the possibilities."

"Did anybody support Foley's claim that he got home when he said?"

Schaefer shook his head. "Far from it. They know roughly when he left the Moon, but no one seems to know where he went after that. Might or might not have been home. Liza's word against his."

"What about the car? I understand there's never been any sign of that either."

"My guess is it's long gone, probably broken down for parts. If not that, there's always a demand for stolen cars in Europe and the Middle East. In California, L.A. and San Diego take the biggest hits."

"Even back then?"

"Yes ma'am. The numbers might be different, but percentages are the same. Something like eighty-five thousand cars stolen out of those two cities just this past year. They steal 'em, take 'em to local ports, and crate 'em up for shipping. The other option is to drive a car across the border and dispose of it down there. Places in Mexico and Central America, if a vehicle doesn't find a buyer, it's left on the street and ends up sitting in an impound lot. You go down to Tijuana, you can see thousands—cars, trucks, RVs. Some have been there for years and never will be reclaimed."

"Was the car his or hers?"

"He was the one signed the loan papers, but the car was hers. She made sure everyone knew that. In those days, wives couldn't get credit even if they worked. Everything was done in the husband's name."

"But why would he do that? Buy her a car and then kill her the next day. That doesn't make sense."

"He might have killed her on impulse, struck her in a rage. Doesn't have to be something he planned in advance."

"But why buy the car at all? Daisy told me he could barely pay the bills. I've also heard she had enough cash to buy it outright."

"I'll tell you what I think. He did it out of guilt. That was his pattern. He'd get mad, beat the hell out of her, and then do something nice to make up for it. Maybe he realized she was on the verge of taking him to court so he tried to buy her off. She was nuts about that car."

"From what I heard, Foley was stuck making all the payments even though he never had a thing to show for it. That seems strange."

"Depending on his agreement with the dealer," he said. "The fellow you want to talk to on that subject is Chet Cramer of Chet Cramer Chevrolet in Cromwell. I'll give you his address."

"Thanks. Daisy mentioned him. I'm surprised he's still in business after all these years."

"Oh, sure. He'll never retire. He's got his hands on the reins and he'll be happy to drop dead before he ever lets go."

Mentally I went back and skimmed the newspaper accounts I'd read. "One of the papers reported Violet going into a Santa Teresa bank that week and getting into her safe-deposit box. Any idea what was in it?"

"Nope. I'd assume valuables of some kind. Like you, I've heard she had a sizeable sum of cash, but you'd have to take that on faith. We got a court order and had the box drilled when it was clear she was gone. It was empty."

"What about since then? I know how Stacey feels about a case like this. An open-ended situation bugs the hell out of him."

"You're right about that. Once in a while someone goes back to take a look, but there's not much to go on. We never got a break on this one and we haven't had the manpower to devote to a second full-on investigation. Detectives down in S.T. have enough on their plates. Some rookie might noodle around with it from time to time, but that's about it."

"What about the theory she was having an affair?"

"That's what Foley maintains, but I have my doubts. Ask around and you'll find out most people who heard the rumor heard it from him. Violet screwed around— no question about that—but if she ran off with someone, how come no one else was gone?"

7

The service station where Violet was last seen was near Tullis, a dot-sized town you could probably miss if you weren't paying strict attention. Several hamlets, like stars in a constellation, were clustered in a patch with small two-lane roads forming the irregular grid that connected them. Tullis was to the east on a straight line that led to Freeman and from there to the 101.

Service stations in the area were few and far between, so it was easy to see why Violet had chosen this one. At that point, she'd only had the car for one day, but she'd apparently done sufficient driving to empty her tank. Or maybe she was topping it off in preparation for whatever she did next, which is to say died or left town. I noticed myself shifting from one position to the other. She behaved like someone who was on her merry way, but to where? And more important, did she ever arrive?

When I reached the service station, I pulled in to one side and parked near the entrance to the ladies' room, taking advantage of the facilities while I had the chance. The toilet did flush, but the hand dryer was busted and since paper towels had been eliminated in the interest of sanitation, I ended up drying my hands on my jeans while I walked around outside.

The station sat at the junction of two roads, Robinson and Twine. The afternoon was hot and still, the sunlight relentless. This was September, and I was imagining the heat in July was fierce. There were endless flat fields on all sides; some looking ragged from the harvest and some newly planted with sprigs of green. It had been late day when Violet stopped here, and it must have looked then much as it did now. The area was windy and dry, without so much as a stand of trees to provide shade. I pictured Violet's red hair whipping across her face while she stood chatting with the fellow who pumped her gas that day. What did she think was coming next? That's what bothered me—the idea of her intentions and her innocence.

In my car again, I headed west, turning left out of the station onto Twine Road. I passed a sign for New Cut Road and realized Tannie's property had to be less than a mile away. Sure enough, the big farmhouse loomed in the distance, hugging the blacktop as though hoping to thumb a ride. The incongruity of the house in the flat agricultural landscape struck me anew.

Once in Cromwell, I consulted the directions Daisy'd given me. Foley Sullivan worked as a custodian for the Cromwell Presbyterian Church on Second Street. The building was plain in the nicest sense of the word, white frame with a steeple, set on a wide lawn of green. A large brick wing had been added to one end. I parked in the side lot and took the walkway to the front of the church.

Starting with the obvious, I tried one of the big double doors and I was surprised to find them unlocked. I let myself in. The foyer was empty. The doors to the sanctuary stood open, but there was no one in sight. I said yoo-hoo-type things to announce my presence, hoping to avoid any appearance of trespassing in a house of God. The sanctuary was bathed in quiet, and I found myself tiptoeing down the center aisle in response. There were elaborate stained-glass windows on each side of the room and deep wine-colored carpeting underfoot. The massive brass organ pipes made an inverted V behind the chancel. The empty wooden pews were gleaming in the light. The air smelled of carnations and lilies, though there were none in evidence. To the right, behind the pulpit, the choir loft was visible. At the front of the church on the right-hand side, I could see a door that I was guessing led into the minister's study. To the left, double doors with glass uppers probably opened into the corridor that connected the church with its more modern addition.

I pushed through the double doors and found myself in a broad carpeted hallway. Sunday school rooms opened off to the right, most with folding chairs, two with low tables and chairs designed for little kids. Everything was in order. I could smell Windex, Endust, and furniture polish. I pushed through a second set of double doors into a large social hall. Long banquet-style tables had been set up, but the metal folding chairs were still stacked on rolling carts pushed up against the wall. I imagined the room could be furnished or emptied for just about any activity or any size crowd. I wondered if church members still held potluck suppers. I hoped so. Where else could you get beef-and-macaroni pies and green-bean casseroles made with cream of mushroom soup? As a child I'd been expelled from numerous denominations of Sunday schools, but I bore no grudge. As usual, thoughts of food prevailed, softening the experience to recollections as rich and sweet as warm homemade brownies.

I entered the kitchen through a swinging door, again saying "Hello?" and pausing to see if there would be a response. The room was flooded with sunlight. The counters were stainless steel, and huge soup cauldrons hung from racks above the two restaurant-sized stainless-steel stoves. The white enamel sinks were snowy. I was running out of places to look. Any minute now, Foley, I thought to myself. I was so focused on finding him that when he appeared behind me and tapped me on the shoulder, I jumped and clutched my chest, barking with surprise.

"Sorry if I scared you."

"I just wasn't expecting it," I said, wondering how long he'd been trailing me. The notion generated an uneasiness I had to struggle to suppress. "I appreciate your seeing me on such short notice."

"That's quite all right."

He was tall and gaunt, with sleeves slightly too short for the length of his arms. His wrists were narrow and his hands were big. He was clean shaven, his cheekbones prominent and his jawline pronounced. His face reminded me of certain black-and-white photographs taken during the Depression—haunted-looking men in breadlines, whose gazes were fixed on the camera in despair. His eyes were a deep-set blue, the orbital ridge darkly smudged. I'd seen someone else with the same demeanor, though the reference eluded me in the moment. There was no animation when he spoke. He looked out at me from some remove, a curious distance between his inner self and the life of the outside world. I could see nothing of Daisy in his features, except perhaps the marks of unhappiness for which Violet was the source. He was only sixty-one years old, but he might have been a hundred from the wariness in his eyes.

"Come on with me. I'll show you where I live. We can talk down there where it's private."

"Sure, fine," I said, and followed him, wondering at the wisdom. Alone with a guy like him in this big empty church. Daisy was the only one who knew where I was. We descended one flight of stairs to the basement level, which was dry and well maintained. Foley opened the door to what I first mistook for a large storage closet.

"This is my apartment. Help yourself to a chair."

The room he'd shown me into was maybe ten feet by ten, white walls, gleaming beige linoleum tile floor. In the center was a small wooden kitchen table with four matching chairs. He had a hot plate and a small refrigerator tucked into a counter along the wall, a sofa, one upholstered chair, and a small television set. Through a doorway I could see a smaller room with the suggestion of a roll-away bed poking into view. I was guessing at the presence of a bathroom beyond that.

I sat down at the table. In the center was a bowl of unshelled peanuts. He sat in apparent relaxation. The gaze he rested on mine was direct but curiously empty. He indicated the nuts. "Have some if you want."

"Thanks. I'm fine."

He picked up an unshelled peanut, broke open one end, and tilted the kernel into his mouth. He opened the second half of the nut and ate that kernel, too. The sound reminded me of a horse crunching on its bit. He held on to the empty shell. I could see him feeling the waffled surface, the tips of his fingers moving across the edges where the fibers extended from the shell. I've been known to eat peanuts shell and all to eliminate the mess.

He took a fresh one from the bowl and rolled it, pressing slightly, measuring its give. His fingers might have been moving with a will of their own. Rolling, pinching. "You're a private detective. Where from?"

"Santa Teresa. I've been in business ten years. Before that, I was a cop."

Foley shook his head. "Why's Daisy doing this?"

"You'll have to ask her."

"But what'd she say when she hired you on?"

"She's upset. She says she's never made peace with her mother's leaving her."

"None of us made peace with that," he said. He looked away from me and then shrugged, as if in response to some inner debate. "All right. I guess we best get it over with. You can ask anything you like, but I want to say this first: Pastor of this church is the only man in town with any charity in his heart. After Violet left, I got laid off and I couldn't get work. I did construction before, but suddenly no one would hire me to do anything. Based on what? I was never arrested. I was never charged. I never spent a day in jail in regard to her. The woman ran off. I don't know how many times I have to say that."

"You hired an attorney?"

"I had to. I needed to protect myself. Everybody thought I killed her, and what was I supposed to do? I had Daisy to support and I couldn't get a paying job to save my soul. How can you prove you didn't do a thing when the whole town believes you did?"

"How'd you earn a living?"

"I couldn't. I had to go on welfare. I was ashamed of myself, but I had no choice. All the time we were married, Violet wouldn't take a job. She wanted to stay home with Daisy and that was fine with me, though I could have used the help. Some months, I couldn't pull in the money we needed to cover the bills. That was hard. There's people who seem to think I didn't care if I was behind on my bills, but that's just not true. I did what I could, but once she was gone, I didn't know where to turn. If I left Daisy for a single minute, she'd come unglued. She had to have me in her sights. She had to know where I was. She had to hang on my pant leg for fear I'd up and disappear. That's how it was. Violet did what suited her, regardless of us. She was a self-centered woman, and mothering wasn't something she did all that well."

"What was?"

"Come again?"

"What did she do well? I'm asking because I'd like to get a sense of her . . . not just how she behaved, but who she was."

"She was a party girl. She stayed out late and drank. Sometimes she danced."

"What about you? Did you go dancing as well?" I asked, wondering if he was using the word as a metaphor.

"Not often enough to suit her."

He replaced the unshelled peanut in the bowl and put his big hands in his lap under the table. I could hear a popping sound and I knew he was systematically cracking his knuckles.

"Did she have hobbies or interests?"

"Like what, did she do macramé?" he asked with a touch of bitterness. "Not hardly."

"Cooking, for instance. Anything like that?"

"She fixed things out of cans. Tamales wrapped in paper. Sometimes she didn't even bother to dump them in a pan and put them over heat. I know I sound negative and I apologize. She might have had good qualities, just none I could see. She was beautiful, I'll give her that. She had her hooks in me deep."

"Why'd you stay?"

"Dumb, I guess. I don't know, it seems so long ago. Sometimes I can hardly remember what it was like. Not good, I know. Why I stayed was I loved that woman more than life itself."

"I understand," I said, though the statement was preposterous, given what I'd heard.

He went on. "Anyway, I'm not the only one who had complaints. She wasn't happy, but she stayed on, too. At least until she went."

"Daisy tells me you believe she was having an affair."

"I know she was."

"What makes you so sure?"

"Aside from the fact that she told me?"

"Really. What'd she say?"

"She said he was twice the man I was. She said he was a tiger in bed. I don't want to go into that. She cut me to the quick, which is what she intended."

"Maybe she was making it up."

"No, ma'am. Not her. There was someone all right. You can trust me on that."

"Do you have any idea who?"

"No."

"There was no one you suspected even the tiniest bit?"

He shook his head. "At first, I thought it was some-one from Santa Maria or Orcutt, somewhere like that, but there was never a claim from anyone else about a missing spouse, which is why no one gives credence to anything I say."

"Let's talk about you. What's your story?"

"I don't have a story. Like what?"

I shrugged. "Were you ever in the military?"

He shook his head, his expression sour, as though I was adding one more item to his list of grievances. "Army wouldn't take me: 1941 when the war broke out, I was fifteen years old. As soon as I turned eighteen, I tried to enlist, but the physical messed me up. Teeth were bad. You were supposed to have six biting teeth and six chewing teeth lined up right. I didn't get mine fixed until later. By then, I could see how being in the army wasn't such a hot idea. Bunch of boys from around here went off and never did come back."

"Daisy told me Violet was fifteen when you married her."

"Bet she told you why, too."

"I know she was pregnant. Did you ever think about putting the baby up for adoption?"

"Violet would have done that or worse, but I stood in her way. I wanted that child. I wanted to get married and raise a family. She acted like I forced it on her, which maybe I did, but I thought she'd adjust."

"Fifteen is young," I said, stating the obvious to keep the conversation afloat.

"Violet was never young. She told me once she was fooling around by the time she was twelve. I wasn't the first to have her and I certainly wasn't the last."

"Did that bother you?"

"Her past? I didn't care about that. What bothered me was everything she did after. You probably heard I hit her, but there's two sides to every story. She was unfaithful—time and time again—and I defy any man who says he can live with a thing like that. Could you live with it?"

"That's what divorce is for," I said, blandly.

"I know, but I loved her. I didn't want to live without her. I thought I might knock a little sense into her. That's all I was trying to do. I know I was wrong. Sometimes I can't believe I ever thought that way, but I did. She was stubborn . . . willful . . . and she never changed her ways. I was as good to her as I knew how and she left us anyway. About broke my heart."

"And you've never remarried?"

"How could I? I have nothing to offer. I can't say I'm divorced, can't say I'm a widower. Not that any woman's asked. Once Daisy left home, I took this job. Pastor gave me a place to live and I've been here ever since." He was silent for a moment, emotion churning under the surface.

"Tell me about the car."

"I can tell you exactly. Her and me had a fight. I forget now over what. I tore down a panel of her lace curtains and she went berserk, tore down the rest and threw them in the trash. She went over to the Moon and I followed her. We started drinking and she calmed down some. I thought everything was okay, but that's when she up and told me she was leaving me. She said it was over and she'd be gone the next day. I didn't believe a word. Violet said things like that every other week. This time she was crying so hard it tore me up. I was sorry for what I'd done. I knew those lace curtains meant something to her. I wanted to make up for that and everything else.

"She'd seen the car a couple days before and that's all she talked about, so I went down to the dealership and bought it. I drove it home that same day and parked it out in front, then went in and told her to look outside. When she saw the car, she was like a little kid. It's the happiest I'd ever seen her."

"When was that? What date?"

"July third. Day before she left."

"Did she talk about going somewhere, a road trip?"

"Not a word. She was nicer than she'd been in a long, long time, so I thought things were fine. We spent Saturday morning together, the three of us—her, me, and Daisy. I had a job at work to take care of in the early afternoon, but after that I came back and we did some stuff around the house. At five, she fixed Daisy's supper—bacon and scrambled eggs, which was Daisy's favorite. Violet had a babysitter coming at six. She was going to put Daisy in the bath and get her ready for bed. She wanted to change clothes and she said we'd meet at the park in time for the fireworks.

"I stopped by the Blue Moon on the way. I'll admit I had a couple of beers . . . more than a couple, if you want to know the truth. By the time I got to the park, it was almost dark and the fireworks display was about to begin. I looked everywhere for her and finally took a seat and enjoyed the show by myself."

"People saw you there?"

"Yes, indeed. That's one thing people had to give me. Livia Cramer was sitting right there talking to me, big as life. When I got to the house, I could see the car wasn't in the drive. I went in and realized Violet was gone as well."

"But the babysitter was there, yes?"

"That's what she says. My thinking wasn't all that clear."

"Why was that?"

"I had a couple more beers at the park and then stopped off at the Moon on my way home. That's why I wasn't too steady on my feet. I went in the bedroom and laid across the bed. I didn't look in Daisy's room because it didn't occur to me. I thought she was out with Violet, riding in the car. I figured Violet changed her mind and decided Daisy should see the fireworks. Next thing I know it's morning and Daisy's tugging on my hand."

"And then what?"

"Then I went through the roughest two days of my life. Sunday morning, I called the sheriff's department to see if they knew anything. I thought she might have been arrested, or in a car wreck. Deputy said no, but if I hadn't heard from her by Tuesday, I could come in and file a missing-persons report, which is what I did when she hadn't come back. I gave up drinking that day and I haven't touched a drop of alcohol since."

"And she never got in touch?"

"Not a call. Not a postcard. No word of any kind from that day to this."

"Why'd you keep making payments on the car?"

"To show I loved her. To show I was sincere about changing my ways. I believed she'd come back, and on the day she did, if she ever did, I wanted her to know that I'd never lost faith."

"It didn't make you angry to have to pay for the car she went off in?"

"It made me sad, but in a way . . . if she had to go . . . I was happy she had that. Like a parting gift."

"By then, everybody thought you'd done something to her."

"That's been my burden to bear and I hope I've done it like a man. I might sound bitter, but it's not about her. It's about the fact that I've been judged and condemned." He reached for the bowl of peanuts and took one, then changed his mind and put it back. The dark sunken eyes came up to mine. "Do you believe me?"

"I don't have an opinion. I've been on this one day. You're only the second person I've talked to so I'm not in a position to believe or disbelieve. I'm gathering information."

"And I'm telling you what I know."

"What about the fifty thousand dollars she was said to have?"

"That was after Daisy's birth. I don't know the details except the labor went on for hours. Her water broke at nine o'clock on a Friday night, but nothing much went on. She was having contractions now and then, but she wasn't in much pain. She thought it might not be as bad as she'd heard. I don't know why but the minute any woman finds out she's pregnant, other women haul out some terrible tale about how hard it was, how somebody's cousin ended up hemorrhaging to death, about babies born deformed. She was scared to death and she wanted to hold off going to the hospital as long as she could. We stayed up all night playing cards—gin rummy—and she played me for a penny a point. I think she took something like fifteen dollars off me. After a while, the pains started coming harder and she got so she couldn't concentrate. I told her we ought to go and she finally gave in. We got to the hospital and they took her off to the labor room. That was at six A.M. The nurse came out and said she was only four centimeters dilated, so they took me in the back and let me sit with her. She was suffering something awful, but the doctor didn't want to give her anything for pain for fear it'd slow her down. Noon, I went out to get something to eat. I got back to the waiting room as the doctor arrived. The nurse had called him because she didn't think Violet's labor was progressing like it ought. I don't know the particulars about what happened next. I know something went wrong and Dr. Rawlings was at fault. Daisy was okay. She was finally born around seven that night by forceps. There were female complications and the upshot was that he removed Violet's womb. There she was, sixteen years old, and she could never have another child. I don't think she gave a hoot about that, but she saw the opportunity to get some cash. I think she sued him for half a million dollars and got considerably less. She was tight-lipped about that and never would tell me the amount. She said the money was hers and it was none of my affair. Said she earned it the hard way and she wanted to make sure I never got my hands on it. She wouldn't put it in a regular savings account because she was afraid of community property laws. She got a safe-deposit box and kept the cash in there. I told her it was foolish. I said she ought to invest, but she was adamant. I think the money made her feel powerful."

We sat and stared at each other while I digested the information. Finally, I said, "I appreciate your candor. At the moment, I can't think what other ground we need to cover. I may have questions for you later on."

"I understand," he said. "All I ask is you'll keep an open mind."

"I'll do that," I said. "And if further questions come up, I hope I can talk to you again."

"Of course."

8

After I left the church parking lot, I found a quiet side
street and pulled over to the curb. I shut off the engine
and took out a handful of index cards, jotting down what
I remembered about the conversation. During interviews early in my career, I tried using a tape recorder, but
the process was awkward. It made some people self-
conscious, and both of us tended to watch the tape reel
going around and around, assuring each other the device
was working. Sometimes a reel came to an end and
clicked off while the interviewee was in the middle of a
sentence. I'd have to turn the tape over and then back-
track, which was off-putting to say the least. Transcribing
a tape afterward was a pain in the rear because the sound
quality was often poor and the ambient noise made some
of it impossible to hear. Taking notes in longhand was
just as distracting. I finally gave up and started winging
it, quieting the chatter in my brain so I could hear what
was being said. My memory has improved to the point

where I can remember the bulk of an interview, but I still find it helpful to nail down the details while they're fresh in my mind. Over time, a portion of any recollection fades, and while I might remember the gist, it's the minutia that sometimes makes all the difference.

Cynic that I am, I did wonder if Foley had quit drinking because he was afraid alcohol would one day loosen his tongue, tricking him into saying something he shouldn't. For the same reason, I questioned his reasons for the lack of an intimate relationship since Violet had disappeared. Guilt produces a loneliness of its own. The temptation to confide has to be overwhelming at times. His suffering had been intense, but he'd never sought solace, or so he claimed.

I looked at the map again, noting the distance between the service station where Violet had filled her tank, the park in Silas, and the Sullivans' house. Must have been fifteen or twenty miles from point to point. It was possible, I supposed, that Violet had bought gas and then driven home, in which case she might well have been there when Foley returned. If that were the case, surely the babysitter would have said so. I put a rubber band around my fat stack of cards, then fired up the engine, put the car in gear, and headed for home.

As I was unlocking my front door, Henry emerged from his kitchen and locked the door behind him. He was looking very spiffy for a guy who favors shorts and flip-flops. He waved and I waited while he crossed the patio. It was close to cocktail hour and I figured he was on his way to Rosie's. "Actually, I'm driving down to Olvidado to take Charlotte to the movies. We'll catch the five-o'clock show and have dinner afterwards." Charlotte was a real estate agent he'd dated twice. I was happy to see him take an interest after his recently failed romance.

"Sounds like fun. What are you seeing?"

"*No Way Out* with that actor, Kevin Costner. You think this is okay?" He held his arms out, asking me to make a judgment about his slacks and collared T-shirt.

"You look fine."

"Thanks. What are you up to?"

"I'm on a job up in the Santa Maria area. I'll be driving back and forth, but I don't want you to worry if you don't see me for a couple of days. You better get a move on. Traffic's tricky at this hour."

I watched him cross to his two-car garage, pausing long enough to see which car he took. His pride and joy is a 1932 Chevrolet, the five-window coupe, painted bright yellow. His other car is a workaday station wagon, which is serviceable but no great shakes. He backed down the drive in the vintage Chevy, waving at me as he disappeared from sight.

Once in my apartment, I dropped my shoulder bag on a kitchen stool and went through my usual ritual of phone messages and mail. Cheney had called to say hi and he'd catch me later. Mail was boring. When I peered into the refrigerator, the sight that greeted me was no big surprise. The contents consisted of condiments— mustard, pickles, olives, and a jar of jalapeños—a stick of butter, a head of browning lettuce, and a six-pack of Diet Pepsi. I hadn't been to the grocery store for days, which meant I'd either have to make a supermarket run or eat out again. While I debated, I returned Cheney's call. I knew he'd be gone, but I left a lengthy message, telling him what I was up to. I wasn't sure what my schedule would look like after tomorrow, but I said I'd be in touch. Already this was feeling like the same sort of absentee relationship I'd had with Robert Dietz. How do I get myself into these situations with men?

I was halfway to Rosie's, less than thrilled with the prospect, when I thought about Sneaky Pete's. I knew Tannie would be working, and it occurred to me that we could chat about Daisy and Violet while I indulged in another spicy salami concoction on a kaiser roll. I trotted back to my car and drove into town.

Sneaky Pete's is a neighborhood hangout, serving a loyal clientele in much the way Rosie's does. Tannie spotted me when I walked in. I took a stool at the bar, waiting while she finished drawing two beers for a couple near the window. It was not quite six and quiet for a Wednesday night. Even the volume on the jukebox had been turned down to a tolerable level.

She returned to the bar and took out a wineglass and a bottle of Edna Valley, saying, "You drink Chardonnay, right?"

"Good memory."

"That's my job. Daisy says the three of us are having lunch tomorrow."

"That's the plan. I told her I'd call her as soon as I'm free. What time are you driving up?"

"I'm not sure yet, but early. I'll find out where you're going and I'll meet you there." She poured my wine and then picked up her cigarette and took one last drag before she stubbed it out. "One of these days I'll quit. Working here, you have to smoke in self-defense. So how goes the battle? Daisy says you're already hard at work."

"Well, I'm doing what I can. She drove me around the area so I could get the lay of the land. Serena Station's depressing."

"Isn't it," she said. "You meet Foley?"

"I spoke to that retired sheriff's department sergeant first and then to him."

"That must have been intense."

"Very," I said. I took a sip of my wine. "You didn't tell me you had a house up there. Daisy took me by yesterday afternoon so I could see. Too bad about the fire."

"We're lucky they caught it when they did or the house would be gone. We've got a deputy patrolling now to keep the riffraff out. My brother hates the place."

"Daisy says you hope to buy him out."

"If I can get him to agree. He's being his usual bullheaded self, but I think he'll knuckle under in the end. His wife's on my team. She's got no interest in being saddled with a house like that. I love it, but talk about a white elephant."

"The land must be worth a fortune."

"You ought to see our tax bill. The tricky thing is there's a move afoot to rezone. The rumor around town is that the old packing plant has been sold and the buildings will be demolished. That property butts right up against ours, so I've had developers wooing me all year, trying to get the jump on it before word leaks out. I'd love to hang on, but we'd net ourselves a bundle if we sell out to them." She reached under the bar and pulled out a roll of paper, secured with a rubber band. "You want to see what they have in mind?"

I took off the rubber band and opened the large furl of heavyweight paper. What I was looking at was a watercolor mockup, showing the grand entrance to a walled community called the Tanner Estates. There were two big stone pillars leading into the development, with lush lawns on both sides of a winding drive. A few rooftops were visible in the distance, the houses widely spaced and nestled among mature trees. To the left, Tannie's house was beautifully rendered, restored to its original state, thanks to the artist's skill. "Geez, what I saw this afternoon didn't look anything like this. Where are all the big nasty oil tanks and barbed-wire fences?"

"I guess if you have bucks enough, you can make it look any way you please. I can't believe the county will approve the plans, but Steve says that's all the more reason to sell while we can."

"That makes no sense. If the rezoning's approved, the value of the land would go up, which is reason to hang on."

"Try telling that to him. He wants out from under."

I released the edges of the paper and it rolled itself up of its own accord. "Was that where you grew up?"

Tannie shook her head. "It belonged to my grandparents, Hairl and Mary Clare. Mom and Steve and I lived there while Pop was away at war. When he joined the army in 1942, my mother moved back into the house. She didn't have job skills to speak of and Pop couldn't support us on his military pay."

"Did you say your grandfather's name was 'Hairl'?"

She smiled. "His name should have been Harold, but my great-grandmother couldn't spell so that's what she wrote on his birth certificate. My mother was named for both her parents—Hairl and Mary Clare—so she became 'Mary Hairl.' Thank god the linking names stopped there or no telling what I would have been called."

"Where'd 'Tannie' come from?"

"It's actually 'Tanner'—my mother's maiden name."

"I like it. It suits you."

"Thanks. I'm fond of it myself. Anyway, Hairl and Mary Clare lived in the house from 1912, when it was built, until 1948, when she had a stroke and went into a nursing home. Granddaddy bought a duplex in Santa Maria to be close to her."

"You guys stayed in the house?"

"My mother couldn't manage on her own so we moved into the other side of his duplex. That way, she could make sure he was taking care of himself. He ate all his meals with us."

"Big change for you."

"And a tough one, too. I missed living in the country. I didn't have any friends, but I was free to roam. We had dogs and barn cats. It was idyllic from my perspective, but as she pointed out, the new place was closer to town, which meant I could walk or ride my bike to school. I finally got used to the idea. Once Pop came out of the army, he went through a series of jobs, the last of them at Union Sugar. He'd always loved farming—not that he ever made a dime—but after the war his heart wasn't in it and he couldn't handle the work. Mom would have pitched in if we'd had the chance to move back. Even after my grandmother died, I held on to that hope, though I can see now the chances were getting dimmer with every passing year. Granddaddy would have left the house to my mother, but she died before he did."

"How old was she?"

"Thirty-seven. She was diagnosed with uterine cancer in 1951 and died two years later, when Steve was sixteen and I was nine."

"Must have been hard on all of you."

"My dad in particular. He was a mess. We moved from Granddaddy's duplex to a little house in Cromwell. I went to various schools in north county, which is how I knew Daisy. She and I were a couple of sad sacks in those days. We'd both lost our mothers and our lives had been turned upside down."

"You were coping with a lot."

"I was and I could have used some continuity. Steve and I saw Granddaddy every chance we got, but he was a sour old man by then and very bitter about life. There was a time when he'd ruled over his very own magic kingdom. Then suddenly, his wife was gone and his only child was dead. It was like he held Pop responsible for everything that went wrong."

"Your father? How so?"

"Who knows? Maybe by association. Seeing Pop must have been too painful a reminder of the past. Granddaddy was probably happiest those three years when my father was gone and he ruled the roost. He died a month after my mom."

"I'm sorry."

"Hang on." She broke away and picked up a food order from the kitchen window, delivering it to the guy at the end of the bar. I could see him tuck into the kaiser roll, fried egg dripping onto his plate, and I could taste the hot salami and cheese. When Tannie caught sight of my face, she placed an order for me without my even having to ask. I must have looked as mournful as a dog begging for table scraps. "Tell you who you ought to talk to is Winston Smith. Is he on your list? He's the guy who sold Violet the car."

"Name doesn't sound familiar, but I can check. What's the story on him?"

"Nothing in particular. It's just this feeling I have. I always thought he knew more than he let on."

"What's your opinion of Foley? I don't believe you've said. I'm talking about him as a person, not what he may or may not have done."

I saw her attention shift. Another customer had come in and she moved halfway down the bar, as he was claiming a stool. He told her what he wanted, and I watched her make his drink, though it was not one I recognized from the liquors she poured. She obviously knew the guy and chatted with him while pulling bottles from the shelf, doing pours with a carelessness that comes from long experience. Having served him, she took advantage of the interruption to make a round of the tables, where she picked up three drink orders and tended to them before she came back to me. She paused to light a cigarette, answering the question as though she'd never been gone: "He was always a creep. I don't buy into that pious act of his. I've heard he's given up booze, but that doesn't cut any ice with me. A guy like that—scratch the surface, he's the same as he's always been. Only now he hides it better."

"Did you have much contact with him?"

"Enough. Daisy and I were friends, but my dad never let me spend the night at her house. For one thing, the place they moved into was a nasty little dump, and for another, he saw Foley as the kind of guy young girls shouldn't be left alone with. Daisy was welcome to come to our house. When Foley dropped her off, he'd try to chat me up. I'm only ten years old and I can already tell that he's a world-class jerk."

"You thought that at ten?"

"I could see straight through him. Kids operate at gut

level and they're hard to fool. I never told Daisy what I thought of him—she had problems enough—but I avoided him like the plague. Even Pop, who's what they call 'a man's man,' didn't have any use for him."

"Your father's still alive?"

"Oh, sure. Hale and hearty. Daisy says she put his name on the list of people you should talk to. I don't think he knew Violet. I mean, he *knew* her—everybody knew Violet—but mainly because she and Foley hung out at the Blue Moon. Pop's a part owner now."

"Isn't that the Blue Moon where the Sullivans threw some of their big screaming fights?"

"That's it," she said. "You can ask the bartender, BW. He witnessed most of 'em. In fact, he and Pop pooled their resources and bought the Moon not long after Violet disappeared. They've talked me into taking over the management, if I move back to town."

The crowd was picking up, and after Tannie brought my sandwich, I left her alone to tend to business. In my bag I had my index cards, so while I ate, I shuffled through my notes, trying to get a sense of where I was and where I needed to go next. The wall of years between me and Violet Sullivan felt as impenetrable as ever, but I was catching glimpses of her.

9

CHET
Wednesday, July 1, 1953

Chet Cramer was late getting back from lunch, having spent an interminable three hours in discussion with Tom Padgett about a partnership in his heavy-equipment business. In Chet's opinion, Padgett was a fool. He'd married a woman fifteen years older than he was. Tom was forty-one now, which put her somewhere in the neighborhood of fifty-six years old, a shriveled-up old bag. Everyone in town knew it was her money he was after. She'd been widowed after twenty-five years of marriage to Loden Galsworthy, who'd died of a heart attack. Loden owned a string of funeral parlors, and Cora not only inherited those, but the rest of his estate, which was valued at a million dollars and included the house, two cars, stocks, bonds, and life insurance. Tom was a man with big schemes and precious little in the way of common sense. He'd hit her up for one loan in order to set up his business in the first place. He'd borrowed an additional sum from the bank. He admitted he'd been underfunded from the get-go, but now he wanted to expand, capitalizing on the inevitable demand for John Deere equipment as Santa Maria grew. The builders had to lease from someone and why not him? Chet could see his point, but he didn't much like Padgett, and he sure as shit didn't want to go into business with him. His suspicion was that Tom had a big balloon payment coming up, and this was nothing more than a push to find the dough before the note came due. Cora must have put her foot down and refused to bail him out.

At the country club, over grilled trout, Chet had been polite, feigning interest when, in truth, he had an agenda of his own. He and Livia were eager for membership, and he was hoping Tom and Cora would agree to sponsor them. The place had an old-money respectability he'd always admired. The furnishings were refined, though he noticed a touch of shabbiness in the corridor on his way in to the dining room. Only rich people had the confidence to offer leather chairs so old they had cracks along the seat. The point was that members here were movers and shakers in town, and membership would put Chet on a first-name basis with most of them. Even at lunch, men were required to wear jackets and ties. He liked that. He'd looked around the room, picturing the entertaining he could do here. Livia was an avid but lousy cook, and he'd done everything he could to steer her off inviting folks for dinner. She didn't believe in alcohol consumption, which she said was against Scripture. That made meals a dreary proposition. From his perspective, heavy drinking was the only way to survive her enthusiasms, and he employed every manner of ingenuity to keep his glass filled with something more palatable than the sweetened iced tea she served.

Here he could see that members and guests to a man were enjoying midday cocktails—martinis, Manhattans, whiskey sours. Chet wanted to take up golf, and he liked the idea of Livia and Kathy lounging around the pool while colored waiters in white coats served them sandwiches held together with frilly toothpicks. You weren't even expected to pay for the meal. You signed your name to a chit and then paid in full at the end of the month.

Of course, Padgett was sly. He seemed to sense Chet's ambition, and he was probably hoping to use it as leverage for the so-called partnership. Chet had stalled him off, suggesting that Tom put together a business plan so he and his accountant could take a look. Chet said as soon as he knew what kind of money they were talking, he'd have a chat with the bank. Which was all a bunch of crap. He didn't need his accountant to point out the folly of underwriting Padgett's proposal when he, Chet, was struggling to keep his dealership afloat. In some ways, he and Padgett were in the same fix. Chevrolet expected him to expand his salesroom, services, parts and accessories facilities, along with his presence in the used-car market. The company also insisted that he pay for a product sign, a service sign, and "other necessary signs," none of which were cheap. He was in hot competition with nine other car dealerships in town—Studebaker, DeSoto, Packard, Buick, Dodge, Plymouth, Chrysler, Hudson, and Cadillac. At the moment, he was holding his own, but he knew it would require a sizeable investment if he wanted to pull ahead.

Poor dumb Padgett had bombed out twice with his get-rich-quick schemes: the first, an amusement park that would have cost the moon; the second, some harebrained idea about buying a television station. Televisic was fine, but it wasn't going anywhere. An Ardmore table-model TV set—like the one he owned—was retailing for $359.95, and how many people could afford to pay that? Less than ten percent of households in the country owned a TV. Besides which, there were already 326 television stations in the country. Los Angeles had nine. What was the point of one more?

The heavy-equipment business was at least practical, though Padgett would probably find a way to drive it into the ground, figuratively speaking. Chet was banking on the fact that Padgett didn't know the first thing about putting together a business plan. If he managed to come up with the numbers, Chet could always blame his accountant when he finally turned him down. If he was clever about it, he could hold him off long enough for his country club membership to be approved before he delivered the bad news. He'd have to come up with the ten thousand dollars' initial club-membership fee, but he'd figure that out.

Chet pulled into the dealership and parked in his usual spot. Passing through the showroom, he noticed the big gleaming coupe was gone and he felt a flash of hope. The car was prime, high-powered and streamlined, with all the latest gadgets. Of course, the factory had shipped the car with accessories he hadn't ordered, but he was good at persuading buyers to accept pricey options. The car had arrived on the lot only two days before, and a sale this quick would be impressive in his ten-day report. Every month, he had to provide the factory with a sales estimate r the next three months. These figures were used to de- ne factory production, but if he didn't have the sales, accorded the inventory, and if he didn't have a n of cars his business would steadily diminish.

The dealership felt deserted that afternoon because two of his three salesmen were off for a variety of reasons that annoyed him no end. One had called in claiming he had a head cold, for pity's sake. What kind of man was that? In all his years in the business, he'd never taken a sick day. Jerry Zimmerman, his other salesman, had come up with an excuse just as lame, which meant he was left with Winston Smith, the new hire, in whom he had no particular faith. Winston had been through the same extensive training every Chevrolet salesman enjoyed, but he didn't have the fire. Chet wasn't sure what the kid wanted out of life, but it wasn't selling cars. His ambitions were airy-fairy, all talk and no substance. He probably pictured sales as a means to an end instead of a calling, which is how Chet saw it. At first Chet thought the boy had promise, but it hadn't come to much. Winston wasn't hungry and he couldn't for the life of him get the concept of closure. Selling wasn't about having nice long chats with folks. It was about making the deal, getting a signature on the dotted line. He'd have to learn to take control and bend others to his will. In the meantime, the boy was earnest and good-looking, and maybe that would be sufficient to carry him while he developed a spine.

Chet passed through the outer office, ignoring the fact that his potato-faced daughter was busily scribbling on a piece of pink notepaper that she slipped into a drawer as soon as she caught sight of him. It galled him that he was paying a dollar an hour when she had no office skills. Her phone manners were atrocious, and he was forever scrambling around behind her, trying to make amends for her moodiness and her snippy tone of voice.

She was their only child. Livia had lobbied for three, eager to start a family as soon as possible. Chet hadn't married until he was thirty-two, hoping to be properly settled in life. At the time he met Livia, he was selling Fords in Santa Maria and he was tired of working for someone else. He'd been carefully setting money aside, and according to his reckoning he'd be able to buy his own dealership within the year. He'd insisted on postponing children for at least five years until he'd bought the franchise and gotten the business on solid ground. Livia had "slipped up," or so she said, and she was pregnant within six months of the wedding, which meant his life plan had taken another hit. He was fine now, but it grieved him to think how much better off he'd be if she'd done as he asked. He'd made a surreptitious visit to a doctor in Santa Teresa, investing in a quick snip that eliminated any further slipups in that department.

Even so, when Kathy was born—six weeks premature—he'd felt so proud he thought his heart would burst. He'd first seen her in the nursery through the plateglass window, with a hand-printed sign that said BABY GIRL, CRAMER. She was such a tiny little thing—three pounds, fourteen ounces. Livia had been in the hospital for two weeks, and the hospital kept the baby for an additional four weeks until she topped five pounds. That bill had set him back yet again, and he didn't recuperate for years. He hadn't complained. He was happy the baby was healthy with all her fingers and toes. He'd pictured her developing into a beautiful young lady, smart and accomplished, devoted to her dad. Instead, he'd been saddled with this lump of a girl, pudgy and sullen, who had the brains of a sprinkler head.

Chet went into his office and took a seat in

his leather chair, swiveling so he could look out at the side lot with its row after row of gleaming trucks. The Advance Design Series truck had hit the market in June of 1948, and he still marveled at its features—the front-opening hood; the concealed door hinges; the tall, fixed two-piece windshield. Two years later, the company had introduced the NAPCO four-wheel-drive conversion. Since the kit wasn't factory installed, the customer first had to buy a new Chevrolet or GMC truck, but the light truck was coming into its own and profits had soared.

He knew the specs on every vehicle that came onto the lot and he knew the needs of workers in the area—farmers, plumbers, roofers, and carpenters. As a result, he moved more trucks than any other dealer in the county, and he intended to keep it that way.

"Mr. Cramer? Could I speak to you?"

Chet turned to find Winston in the doorway. The afternoon temperatures had climbed into the nineties and Winston was sweating unattractively. He'd have to find a way to instruct him in the use of antiperspirant. Chet got to his feet and moved around his desk, holding out his hand for Winston to shake. "Good, son. Glad you're back. I saw you'd taken the coupe. I hope you've got a live one on the line. Let's see if you remember what I taught you about reeling in a sale."

He intended to go out to the showroom with Winston so he could offer the potential buyer a handshake and his personal greeting. Customers liked to meet the man who owned the place. It made them feel important. He'd answer any questions the fellow had, ask a few of his own, and generally smooth the way. Winston was inexperienced, and Chet thought he'd appreciate his boss stepping in to show him how it was done.

Winston's forehead was beaded with perspiration, and he had to use his pocket handkerchief to mop his upper lip. His Adam's apple dipped. "Well, that's just it. The customer took the car out to get a feel for how she handles . . ."

"With one of the mechanics? Son, that's a very bad idea. This is a sales situation. That's your job. Any question about the nuts and bolts can wait until the deal's in place. I'll find a way to turn the situation to our advantage, but you can't let this happen again."

He could see Winston was uncomfortable at the correction, but there was a right way and a wrong way to go about these things, and he might as well conform to management guidelines straight off the bat. Chet passed Kathy's desk on his way to the floor, with Winston hard on his heels. Kathy was suddenly very busy, fussing around her desk, but she flicked a look at Winston as the two men went by. Chet had seen her mooning around and he knew she had a crush on the young man, but her expression today held a touch of guilt. Surely Winston hadn't made a pass at her. He couldn't be that dumb.

He caught sight of both his mechanics in the service bay, but there was no sign of the car. He stopped in his tracks, and Winston nearly bumped into him like a cartoon character.

"Mr. Cramer? What happened was . . . the customer? She's extremely interested in the car. I talked to her at length and she as good as said she'd be buying it. She even went so far as to mention an all-cash deal. So when she asked for a test drive, I explained for sure that I couldn't leave the lot, and she said that was fine—she didn't need my help, because all she was going to do was drive around the block and she'd be right back."

Chet turned and stared. He felt his heart give a thump, as though someone had punched him, *boom boom*, in the chest—blows that pumped a thick, cold liquid through his veins. He must have misunderstood, because what he heard Winston say simply couldn't be true. Cora Padgett was the only woman in town who had the wherewithal to walk into a dealership, take a car off the floor, and pay cash on the spot. But Tom had told him over lunch that she was out of town. Cora had gone to Napa to tour the wineries with her sister, Margaret, who lived in Walnut Creek. She wouldn't be back until Wednesday of the following week—unless this was meant as a surprise and she'd told Tom a story so she could buy the car without his knowing in advance. "What are you talking about? What customer?"

"Mrs. Sullivan."

"Sullivan?"

"Yes, sir. Violet Sullivan came in. She's in the market for a car—"

"You let Violet Sullivan take that car out by herself? What's the matter with you?"

"I'm sorry. I can see how it might look, what with company policy and everything like that. I told her to come right back, you know, that it wasn't a good idea—"

"How long has she been gone?" His voice sounded shrill and he knew he was losing control. He made a point of never speaking to an underling in anything other than a civil tone. But the enormity of the error, the possible consequences . . .

"I didn't check the time—"

"Approximately, you dolt!"

"I'd say sometime around noon. Well, I don't know, maybe a little bit before then, but close enough."

Assume he minimized and what were we talking about here, four hours? Five? Chet closed his eyes and his voice dropped. "You're fired. Get out."

"But sir. I can explain."

"Get off the lot. Right now. I want you out of my sight or I'm calling the police."

The boy's cheeks flamed with embarrassment, and the look Winston pinned on him was bleak.

Chet waited until he could see the boy was leaving, and then he turned and walked back to his office. He'd have to notify the sheriff's department and the highway patrol. If she'd been involved in a wreck, or if she'd stolen the car outright, she could be anyplace by now. He had liability insurance, blanket coverage for anything on the lot, but his premiums would double the minute he made a claim. Money was already tight. He sat down in his swivel chair and reached for the phone.

"Daddy?" Kathy was in the doorway.

"What!"

"Mrs. Sullivan just pulled in."

Through the glass he spotted the car and relief washed over him. The vehicle didn't appear to be damaged, at least the parts he could see. He went out to the floor, knowing that in no way possible could she afford to buy the coupe. Violet turned as he approached, and he was startled by her vibrancy—the flaming hair, the creamy skin, her eyes a vivid green. He'd never seen her at close range because Livia made a point of crossing the street, tugging him by the arm, if she spotted Violet anywhere in town. She thought Violet was a tramp, wearing those sheer nylon blouses you could see right through. The sundress Violet wore today emphasized the suppleness of her arms, and the flowing skirt showed her legs to advantage. Livia was thick-waisted and narrow-minded, critical of others whose circumstances or beliefs or behaviors were an affront to her own. Chet was irritated by her scathing pronouncements, but he'd kept his mouth shut. From afar, he'd seen Violet's flirtations with married men, and he'd wondered how it would feel to have her attentions lavished on him.

"Hello, Chet. Sorry I was gone so long."

He circled the car until he was satisfied no harm had come to it. On impulse, he leaned in and checked the odometer: 257 miles. For a moment he was speechless. She'd turned this beautiful new Bel Air into a piece-of-shit used car. "Come into the office," he snapped.

Violet caught up with him and tucked a hand through his arm, forcing him to slow his pace. "Are you mad at me, Chet? May I call you 'Chet'?"

"You can call me 'Mr. Cramer' like everyone else. You put two hundred fifty-seven miles on that car? Where the fuck did you go?" He regretted the swear word the minute it was out of his mouth, but Violet didn't seem to care. As he opened his office door, she passed in front of him and he could smell her cologne.

His heart gave another double thump, this time warming his blood. He moved away from her. "Take a seat."

"Yes, sir."

He went around and sat down behind his desk, suddenly conscious of the power he wielded. She had to know she was in the wrong, that he could extract any price he named. Two hundred and fifty-seven miles on a brand-new car? He wondered if she'd set it up that way. Maybe she'd had her eye on him at the same time he'd had his eye on her. She stared at him with interest, appar-

ently undismayed by his rage or the fact that he was ordering her around.

She extracted a pack of cigarettes from her purse. Ever
the gentleman, he took out his lighter and fanned the
striker. She leaned across the desk, allowing him a
glimpse of the swell of her breasts as she accepted his
light. There was a bruise on her chin and he knew what
that was about. She reclaimed her seat and crossed her
legs. He glanced at Kathy, visible in the outer office beyond his glass-enclosed cube. She was watching the back
of Violet's head with her mother's same spiteful stare,
constructing new and better ways to feel superior. When
Kathy caught him looking at her, she got up and walked
to the water cooler. Fourteen, and she was already as
rigid, nasty-minded, and prissy as her mom. She'd taken
out a piece of pink notepaper and it sat squarely in the
middle of her desk. He could see the heavy black writing
on it even at that distance, an angry-looking scrawl that
slanted across the page.

He picked up a pencil and tapped on his desk while
he rearranged his thoughts. He had no idea how he
should play it, but he loved feeling in command. "So
what are we going to do about this, Mrs. Sullivan?"

Her smile was slow, smoke drifting from her lips as
though she was smoldering at the core. "Well, Mr. Cramer, Sweetie, I can make a suggestion, but I'm not sure
you want to talk about it here. Buy me a drink and I'm
certain we can work something out."

Every syllable she spoke was weighted with promise.
Her gaze was fixed on his mouth with a hunger he'd
never seen in a woman and had certainly never experienced in himself. How could this be happening? She was
his for the taking. He knew that as surely as he knew his

name. Though he'd never admit it, he was a man of conventional inclinations. He was forty-seven years old, and in fifteen years of marriage, he'd never been unfaithful to his wife, not for lack of opportunity, but for lack—he saw now—of comprehension. After the first few months with Livia, the sex was workaday—pleasurable, and of course a blessed relief, but in no way compelling. Livia might not be wildly attractive, but whatever his ordinary irritations with her, she'd never denied his needs, and she'd never implied that she found sex onerous. While he wasn't dissatisfied, he'd never understood what all the fuss was about.

In one stroke that had changed.

Here before him, Violet Sullivan, with her insolence and her boldness, had ignited him, sparking a desire so consuming he could barely breathe. He thought maybe this was what it meant to sell your soul to the devil, because he knew in that moment he'd be willing to rot in hell for her.

10

Thursday morning, I went through my usual routine, waking at 6:00 to do my three-mile jog. I prefer to have exercise under my belt before I start my day. In the late afternoon, it's too easy to think of reasons to sit around on my buns. The morning air had a faint chill to it, and the sky was layered with salmon and amber clouds, overlapping like ribbons sewn on the borders of a bright blue tablecloth. I used the brief walk to the beach as a way of warming up before I eased into a trot. Along the bike path, the palm trees were still, no breeze at all ruffling the fronds. A fifteen-foot expanse of ice plant stretched between the bike path and the beach. Beyond that the ocean tumbled and churned. A man had parked his car in the public lot and he was tossing breadcrumbs in the grass. Gulls were wheeling in from all directions, shrieking with delight. I picked up my pace, feeling my body warm and my muscles become loose. It wasn't the best run I ever had, but it felt good nonetheless.

Home again, I showered, threw on my jeans, my boots, and a T-shirt, and then ate a bowl of cereal while I cruised through the local paper. I reached the office at 8:30 and spent an hour on the phone, taking care of business unrelated to Violet Sullivan. At 9:30 I locked up, hauled my portable Smith-Corona typewriter out to the car, and drove to Santa Maria for my meeting with Kathy Cramer. I didn't expect to get much from her. At the time, she'd been too young to qualify as a keen observer of adults, but I figured it was worth a try. You never know when a fragment of information or an off-hand remark might fill a blank spot on the canvas I was painting bit by bit.

The Uplands, the golf course subdivision Kathy Cramer had just moved into, was still a work in progress. The course itself was an irregular series of fairways and bright greens that formed an elongated V the length of a shallow valley. A man-made lake sat in the angle between the front and back nine holes. View homes were perched on the ridge that ran along one side of the course while on the opposite hill, I could see the lots laid out and marked with small flags. Many homes had been completed, with sod lawns and an assortment of shrubs and saplings in place. Other houses were under construction, some framed and some consisting solely of the newly poured slabs. Across the low undulating hills, I could see a hundred houses in various phases of completion. Kathy's house was finished, but the landscaping wasn't in. I'd seen its twin or its mirror image replicated up and down the street—buff-colored stucco with a red tile roof. I parked at the curb, where moving boxes had been piled in anticipation of a garbage pickup. I took the walkway to the front door. The shallow porch had already been furnished with a faux-wicker couch, two faux-wicker chairs, and a welcome mat.

As I was knocking, a car pulled into the driveway and a woman got out, her frizzy mane of blond hair held back with a navy headband. She was dressed in tennis shoes and navy shorts and a matching navy jacket, with a white leotard visible where the jacket was unzipped. Her legs were as lean and muscular as a biker's. She said, "Sorry. I hope you haven't waited long. I thought I'd get here before you did. I'm Kathy."

"Hi, Kathy. I'm Kinsey. Nice meeting you," I said. "Your timing's perfect. I just arrived."

We shook hands and then she turned and unlocked the front door. "I switched to an earlier Jazzercise class, but got caught in traffic coming home. You want ice water? I need to rehydrate."

"I'm fine, thanks. You like Jazzercise?"

"I should. I'm taking six to eight classes a week." She dropped her bag on a console table just inside the front door. "Make yourself at home. I'll be back in a sec."

She disappeared down the hallway, moving toward the kitchen, her rubber soles squeaking on the gray ceramic tile. I turned right and went down two stairs into the sunken living room. The walls were painted a dazzling white, and the only artwork in sight was an oversize painting from a chain of commercial galleries devoted to one man's work. The autumnal scene was of a mare and foal in a gauzy-looking pasture at dawn.

There were no window coverings and the light spilled in through a haze of construction dust. The powder blue wall-to-wall shag carpeting had been installed recently, because I could still see bits and pieces—tufts and scraps—left behind by the flooring guys. The couch and two matching chairs were upholstered in a cream-colored chenille. On the coffee table, she'd arranged a stack of decorator magazines, a centerpiece of pale blue silk flowers, and a cluster of color photographs in silver frames. The three girls portrayed were variations of their mother—same eyes, same smile, and the same thick blond hair. Their ages seemed to fall within a six-year range. The oldest was probably thirteen, braces gleaming on her teeth. The other two girls stair-stepped down from eleven to nine. The middle girl was decked out in a majorette's uniform, a baton held aloft.

Kathy returned to the living room with a tumbler of ice water in hand. She found a coaster and moved toward a conversational grouping of navy blue club chairs with a glass-topped table in the center as though for a conference of some kind. I pictured a meeting of the neighborhood association during which other people's tacky yard ornaments would come under fire. She took one chair and I sat across from her, taking a mental snapshot without having to stare. I pegged her at a youthful forty-eight or forty-nine. She was thin in a way that suggested strict attention to her weight. She seemed high-strung, but having caught her on the back end of a workout, I knew her energy level might have been the result of an hour of strenuous exercise. She looked as though she'd spent the summer working on her tan, and I imagined an aboveground pool in the backyard of the house she'd just left.

"Those are your daughters?" I asked.

"Yes, but the pictures are out of date. Tiffany was twelve when that was taken. She's twenty-five now and getting married June of next year."

"Nice fellow?"

"A doll. He's in law school at UCLA, so they'll be living down there."

"And the other two?"

"Amber's twenty-three; she was a majorette in her junior high school band. She's technically in her senior year of college, but she's taking a year off to travel. Brittany turns twenty next month. She's at Allan Hancock," she said, naming the local community college.

"They look just like you. Must be quite a crew."

"Oh, they're great. We have a good time together. You want to see the rest of the house?"

"I'd love to."

She got up and I followed her.

"When did you move in?"

"A week ago. The place is still a mess," she said, talking over her shoulder as we moved down the hall. "I've got half the boxes unpacked and most things in place, but some of the rooms won't be furnished until god knows when. I need to find a decorator I can get along with. Most are so pushy. Have you ever noticed that?"

"I've never worked with one."

"Well, don't if you can help it."

She walked me through the house, pointing out the obvious: the empty dining room, butler's pantry, eat-in kitchen, mud room, and laundry room. Through the kitchen windows I could see the backyard, which consisted of a poured concrete patio sitting like an island in a sea of raw dirt. Upstairs there were five bedrooms—a master suite, a bedroom for each of the girls, and a guest room, devoid of furniture. She chattered on and on, her prime interest focused on her decorating schemes. I found myself making chirpy, insincere remarks. "Oh, I've always been *crazy* about Louie the Fourteenth. That'll look great in here."

"You think?"

"Absolutely. You couldn't do better than that."

Tiffany's bedroom walls were painted a pale cream. The furniture was in place, but I got the impression that she wasn't moving in. Her sights were set on the future, when she'd be married and coming back for holidays with her husband and kids in tow. Amber's room was stark purple and had the same unoccupied air. Brittany, at nineteen, still clung to her collection of stuffed animals. The color scheme she'd chosen was pink and white—stripes, checks, and florals. Everything had ruffles, including the dressing table, the bed skirt, and the canopy that arched over her four-poster bed. Kathy detailed a number of triumphs each of the girls had chalked up, but I'd tuned her out by then.

Tramping down the stairs, I said, "The house is wonderful."

"Thanks. I like it," she said, flashing me a smile.

"What sort of work does your husband do?"

"He sells cars."

"Like your father."

"He works for Daddy."

"Great. I'll introduce myself. I'll be going by the dealership in the next couple of days to chat with your father about Violet. Didn't he sell her that car?"

"Yes, but I doubt he can tell you any more than I can."

"Every little bit helps. It's like working on a jigsaw puzzle without the picture on the box. Right now, I don't even know what I'm looking at."

Returning to the living room, Kathy sat on the couch

and I took a matching upholstered chair. She picked up her glass and rattled the ice, drinking off the half an inch of water that had accumulated in our absence.

"How well did you know Violet?" I asked.

"Not well. I was fourteen years old and never had much to do with her. My mother hated her guts. The irony is, six months after Mom died, Daddy married a woman who looked just like Violet—same dyed red hair, same white-trash ways. Caroleena's pushing forty-five, three years younger than me, if you can believe that. I'd hoped it was a phase, but they've been married twenty years so I guess she's here to stay. More's the pity."

I said, "Ah," for lack of anything better.

She caught my tone and said, "It's embarrassing, but what're you going to do? I guess I should be glad he has someone to look after him. Saves me the aggravation. Of course, I'd be willing to bet if he ever gets sick, Caroleena's heading out the door."

"What's the age spread between the two?"

"Thirty-six years."

"Wow."

" 'Wow' is right. When they married, he was sixty-one and she was twenty-five. Don't even bother asking me what's in it for her. She lives well and she knows how to get anything she wants," she said, rubbing her thumb against her index finger, indicating money.

I felt my brow lift, wondering if the "new" Mrs. Cramer would be acing Chet's only daughter out of her inheritance. "What about Violet? You must have had some sense of her."

"Oh, please. I had the same opinions my mother did. She made sure of that. Violet was flashy, but that was about it. Men followed her around like a pack of dogs so

I guess she had something. Whatever it was, it went over my head."

"You went to the fireworks that night?"

She straightened the edges of the decorator magazines. "Yes. Liza and I were supposed to go together, but Violet asked her to babysit so that was that. I think Liza went over there at six o'clock to get Daisy bathed and ready for bed."

"Did you happen to see Foley at the park?"

"Sure. For a while, he was talking to my mom. He'd stopped off at the Blue Moon and he was drunk as usual, so he and my mom got into it."

"About what?"

"Who knows?"

"Did you talk to him yourself?"

"Not me. I was scared of him as it was and I didn't want to have anything to do with him."

"Did you ever keep Liza company when she was babysitting?"

"Once in a while. I'm glad Mom never found out, or she'd have had a fit. She was a teetotaler who thought all the evil in the world came out of a bottle."

"What was it about Foley that scared you?"

"What didn't? His violence, his temper, the way he lashed out. With him, you never knew what was coming next. I figured if he was willing to hit Violet, why not Liza or me?"

"Did you ever see him hit Violet?"

"No, but I saw the evidence after the fact. That was good enough for me."

"When did you hear Violet was gone?"

"Sunday morning. I didn't know she was *gone* gone, but I knew she hadn't come home. Mr. Padgett came over for lunch after church and he was the one who told my mom."

"How'd he hear about it?"

"Town the size of Serena Station, everybody knows everything. Maybe someone noticed the car wasn't parked out front. That would've set tongues to wagging."

"Was there any gossip about who Violet was seeing? Someone must have come under suspicion."

"Not necessarily. Violet was a tramp, so it could have been anyone. Some guy she picked up in a bar."

"I gather it didn't surprise you to think she'd run off."

"Oh, heck no. Not her."

"Even though it meant leaving Daisy behind?"

Kathy made a face. "Daisy was a whiny little brat in those days. And look how they lived. The Sullivans were dirt poor, their house was disgusting, and Foley beat Violet up every chance he could. The better question is why she waited as long as she did."

I drove from Kathy Cramer's subdivision into Santa Maria proper, where I found a phone booth in the parking lot of a strip mall. I dialed the work number I'd been given for Violet's brother, and the woman who picked up on the other end said, "Wilcox Construction."

"Hi. My name's Kinsey Millhone. I'm trying to reach Calvin Wilcox."

"May I ask what this is in reference to?"

"His sister."

A pause. "Mr. Wilcox doesn't have a sister."

"Maybe not now, but he did. Would you ask him if he can spare a few minutes? I'd like to talk to him."

"Hang on and I'll see if he's in."

I figured she was saying that so she could comfortably claim he was "away from his desk," but the next thing I knew, the man himself picked up the call. "Wilcox."

I went through my spiel again, trying to be succinct since he sounded like a man who liked to get right to the point.

"If you can make it over here in the next half hour, fine. Otherwise, I can't do it until early next week."

"I'll be right there."

Wilcox Construction was located out on Highway 166, housed in a prefabricated steel building on a narrow lot surrounded by a chain-link fence. Both exterior and interior were utilitarian. At a desk just inside the door, there was a secretary-receptionist whose responsibilities probably included typing, filing, coffee making, and walking the sleeping German shepherd beside her desk. "He's the yard dog," she said, giving him a fond glance. "May look like he's sleeping on the job, but he's called into service once the sun goes down. I'm Babs, by the way. Mr. Wilcox is on a call, but he'll be right out. You want coffee? It's already made."

"I better not, but thanks."

"Well, have a seat in that case."

She filled her mug from a stainless steel urn, and once she sat down again, her phone gave a chirp. "That's him. You can go on in."

Calvin Wilcox was in his early sixties, wearing a short-sleeve denim work shirt and jeans belted under a modest swell of abdomen. I could see the outline of a hard-pack of cigarettes in his shirt pocket. He had thinning red hair and ginger freckles on his arms. His cheeks were wind-burned, which made his green eyes look electrified in the ruddy glow of his face. I knew I was looking at a male variation of Violet's green eyes and her faux red hair.

We leaned toward each other across the desk to shake hands. He was a big guy, not tall, but solid. He waited until I sat down and then settled in his swivel chair. He tipped it back in what was probably a typical move, one work boot propped on the edge of his desk. He lifted his arms and laced his fingers above his head, which gave him an air of relaxation and openness I doubted was there. Behind him, on the wall, was a black-and-white photograph of him at a construction site. His hard hat shaded his eyes, while the businessmen on each side were bareheaded and squinting. One held a shovel and I assumed the occasion was a ground-breaking ceremony.

He smiled, watching me with a certain shrewdness evident in his eyes. "My sister, Violet. Here she comes again."

"Sorry about that. I know the subject comes up every couple of years."

"I should be used to it by now. What's that old saying? 'Nature abhors a vacuum.' People want closure. Otherwise you're always waiting for the other shoe to drop. How long have you worked for Daisy?"

"Not that long."

"I guess she can spend her money any way she wants, but what's she hope to accomplish?"

"She wants to find her mother."

"Yeah, I get that and then what?"

"That depends on where Violet is."

"Hard to believe it's still bugging her after all this time."

"What about you? Does it bother you?"

"Not a bit. Violet did what suited her. Her life was her business. She seldom consulted me, and if I offered her advice, she'd turn around and do just the opposite. I learned to keep my mouth shut."

"Did she ever talk about Foley beating her?"

"She didn't have to talk about it. It was obvious. He broke her nose, broke her tooth, broke two ribs. I don't know why she put up with it. If she'd wanted out, I'd have helped, but she went back time and time again, so I finally gave up."

"Were you older or younger?"

"Older by two years."

"Any other siblings?"

"Don't I wish. Parents get old, it'd be nice to have someone to help shoulder the burden. Violet wasn't about to do it, that's for sure."

"Are your parents still alive?"

"No. My father had a series of heart attacks in 1951. Three in rapid succession, the last one fatal. The doctors blamed it on a defect he'd carried since birth. He was forty-eight years old. So far I've managed to outlive him by thirteen years. Mother died a couple of years ago, at eighty-four."

"You're married or single?"

"Married. How about yourself?"

"Single, but my parents are both gone."

"You're fortunate. My mother was in a nursing home for years. Well, let's call it a 'facility.' I wouldn't label it a home. She used to phone me six and seven times a week, begging me to come get her. Up to me, I'd have done it, but my wife was opposed. She's a stockbroker. No way would she have given that up in order to take care of Mother. I didn't blame her, but it was tough."

"You have children?"

"Four boys, all grown and gone. Two live here in town. I got one in Reno and another one in Phoenix." He took a quick peek at his watch. "You want to ask about Violet, be quick about it. I got a meeting coming up."

"Sorry. I get curious about people and I forget myself."

"All right with me. It's your call."

"I take it you and Violet weren't close?"

"You got that right. Last time I saw her, she came by the office and asked for money that I was dumb enough to give."

"How much?"

"Two grand. That was the first of July, in case you're wondering. After she left here, she went over to my mother's house and hit her up as well. Mother didn't have much, but Violet managed to wheedle five hundred dollars out of her. Month later, we found out she'd stolen Mother's good jewelry: diamond bracelets, earrings, two pearl necklaces—the works. Three thousand dollars' worth we never saw again."

"How do you know it was her?"

"Mother remembered her asking to use the bathroom, which you could only get to by going through her bedroom. Jewelry box was on the dressing table. Mother didn't have occasion to open it until her birthday that year when Rachel and I were taking her to dinner at the club. She wanted to get all gussied up and that's when she realized everything was gone."

"Did you report it to the police?"

"I wanted to, but she refused. She said if Violet needed it that bad, she could have it."

"Had Violet stolen things before?"

"No, but she borrowed money every chance she got, usually small amounts. She'd claim it was for Daisy so we wouldn't turn her down."

"That seems curious. She bragged about having fifty thousand dollars of her own, which Foley says she got from an insurance settlement. He can't confirm the amount, but he knows she collected."

"She told me the same thing, but I thought it was b.s. If she had that much money, why bother to weasel the two grand from me?"

"Suppose she was putting a stash together so she could take off?"

"Always possible."

"Could she have kept in touch with your mother? I keep thinking that even if she managed to make a new life for herself, she might still want *some* tie to the past."

"Certainly not with me. Violet didn't have any sentimental attachments that I know of. There's no way Violet could have made contact with Mother without my knowing. For one thing, her number was unlisted, and any mail she got had to go through me first. For a while, the scam artists had her on their radar screens and they were sending her letters proposing 'lucrative' financial schemes or telling her she'd won the lottery and needed to send in the processing fee. She was so gullible she'd give away the furniture if anybody asked."

"And security at the facility was tight?"

"You're thinking Violet could have sneaked in? Forget it. She had no use for Mother beyond ripping her off. Of course, it's irrelevant now since Mother's passed away, but if Violet had managed to make a new life, she wouldn't risk discovery for a woman she didn't give a shit about."

"Any idea where she might have gone?"

"Wherever the road took her. She was a creature of impulse, not one for long-range plans."

"But what's your take on it? You think she's out there somewhere?"

"I never said that. If she were alive, she'd have come back to beg, borrow, or steal what she could. I don't think she went a month without a handout." He took his foot off the desk and leaned in on his forearms. "You want my take on it?"

"Sure, why not?"

"You want to make Daisy happy? Fine. Earn a few bucks for yourself? It's no skin off my nose. But don't turn it into your holy mission in life. You find Violet, you'll only be making trouble."

"For whom?"

"Everyone—and I'm including Daisy in that."

"What do you know that I don't?"

"Nothing. I know Violet. It's just a wild-ass guess."

11

Chet Cramer Chevrolet was located on Main Street in Cromwell, three acres of shiny cars, fifteen capacious service bays, and a two-story showroom with floor-to-ceiling plateglass windows. Inside, at ground level, there were six small glass-fronted offices, each outfitted with a desk, a computer, a run of file cabinets, two chairs for customers, and prominent displays of family photographs and sales awards. One cubicle was currently occupied by a heavyset salesman in earnest conversation with a couple whose body language suggested they were not as eager to do business as he had hoped.

I didn't see a reception desk, but I spotted a sign with an arrow pointing to the parts department. I walked down a short hallway, passing the restrooms and a lounge with comfortable chairs, where two people sat reading magazines. Doughnuts were available and a vending machine dispensed tea, hot chocolate, coffee, cappuccino, and lattes without charge. I found the cashier and told her I had an appointment with Mr. Cramer. She took my name and rang his office to tell him I was there.

While I waited, I wandered back to the showroom floor, moving from a Corvette convertible to a Caprice station wagon. The best-looking car was an Iroc-Z Camaro convertible, bright red with a tan interior. The top was down and the leather seats were soft. Try tailing someone in a car that slick. I turned to find Mr. Cramer standing with his hands in his pockets, admiring the car as I did. I knew from counting on my fingers that he was in his early eighties. I could see he'd been handsome in his youth, and I sensed, like an aura, the volume of air he must have displaced before he shrank from age. His suit was a size that a young boy might wear. He said, "What kind of car you drive?"

"1974 VW."

"I'd make you a pitch, but you look like a woman knows her own mind."

"I'd like to think so," I said.

"You're here about Mrs. Sullivan."

"I am."

"Let's go on up to my office. People see I'm down here, I never get a moment's peace."

I followed him across the showroom floor and up the stairs. When we reached his office, he opened the door and stepped aside to let me in. The room was plain—a straight-legged wooden desk, a couch, three chairs, and white walls on which he'd mounted numerous black-and-white photographs of himself with various local bigwigs. The Cromwell Chamber of Commerce had given him a citation for community service. The furniture might well have been the set he started business with. "Did you graduate from college?" he asked as he rounded his desk and took a seat.

I sat down across from him, putting my shoulder bag on the floor at my feet. "Hardly. I had two semesters of junior college, but I don't think that counts."

"Better than I did. My father dug ditches for a living and never saved a dime. My senior year in high school, he was killed in an auto accident. It'd been raining for a week, highway was slick as glass, and he went off a bridge. I was the oldest of four boys and I had to go to work. One thing my dad taught me was never do manual labor. He hated his job. He said, 'Son, if you want to make money, find a job where you have to shower before you go to work instead of when you get home.' He maintained there was always someone for hire when it came to the dirty work, and I've followed that to this day."

"How'd you end up selling cars?"

"Desperation. Everything turned out fine in the end, but it didn't look so promising at first. The only fellow who'd hire me was George Blickenstaff, owner of the local Ford dealership. He was an old family friend and I guess he took pity on me. I started selling Fords when I was nineteen years old. That was 1925. I didn't much care for it, but at least I wasn't working with my hands. Turns out I had a knack for sales. Four years later, the stock market crashed."

"That must have put a dent in the business."

"Some areas, yes, but not as much out here. We were always small potatoes and we didn't take the same hit the bigger dealers did. By the time the Depression came along, I was doing pretty well, at least compared to what a lot of other folks endured. By then, I'd turned into

Blickenstaff's star salesman. You'd have thought it was something I was born to do. Of course, I was full of myself and thought I deserved a dealership of my own."

"Is that when you bought this place?"

"Took me years. Problem was, every time I had money in the bank, something came along that took the wind right out of my sails. I put my brothers through college and just about had my mother's house paid off when she got sick. The hospital bill alone was enough to wipe me out. Factor in the funeral expenses and the headstone and I was flat broke. I didn't marry till I was thirty-two years old and that set me back again because suddenly I was saddled with a family."

"But you did persevere," I said.

"Oh, I did better than that. By 1939, I could see what was coming. The minute Germany invaded Poland, I talked old man Blickenstaff into stockpiling tires, car parts, and gasoline. He didn't want to listen, but I knew it was an opportunity we couldn't pass up. U.S. involvement was a given. Any fool could see that—except him, of course. I knew when the time came, rationing would be inevitable, and we couldn't afford to be caught short. He argued the point, but I knew I was right and I never let up. My instincts were dead on. Once the war started, there wasn't another dealer in the area who'd had the same foresight. Guys were coming out of the woodwork, begging for gasoline, begging for tires, which was music to my ears. I told 'em I was happy to be of help as long as sufficient cash changed hands. The point was delivering product and service to the customer, and if Chet Cramer could make a buck in the process, then what's wrong with that? Blickenstaff didn't have the stomach for it. He lost a son in the war and he thought it was morally repre-

hensible—that was the phrase he used, 'morally repre-
hensible'—to profit when all those boys had sacrificed
their lives. In truth, he was tired and it was time he
stepped aside."

"You bought the dealership from him?"

"No ma'am. I bought the Chevrolet franchise and
drove that old geezer into the ground: 1945 he closed
his doors and I picked up his dealership for pennies on
the dollar. May sound cold, but it's a simple fact of life:
You can't accomplish anything unless you're willing to
act. Make a plan. Take a risk. That's how you get what
you want."

"What about your brothers? Did any of them come
into the business with you?"

"This is mine. I don't share. I did enough for them
and now they're on their own." He shifted in his chair,
leaning forward on his desk. "Anyway, you didn't come
here to talk about me. You want to know about Violet
Sullivan."

"I do, but I'm also curious about the car. Can we start
with that?"

He made a dismissive gesture. "Foley had no business
buying that car. He ought to've been ashamed of himself. The Sullivans didn't have a pot to piss in—I hope
you'll forgive the language."

"Doesn't bother me," I said.

"Violet got it in her head she had to have that car, and
Foley knew better than to stand in her way. I wasn't
about to turn away a sale, so I cut him a deal."

"Which was what?"

"I took his truck in trade, for whatever that was
worth. Purely a courtesy on my part, but I made one
thing clear: The first time he missed a payment, I'd re-

possess. No excuses, no slow pays, and not one penny short. I didn't care what the law said, that car was coming back."

"Given his history, you were taking quite a chance."

"Oh, I never thought he'd do it. I fully expected to have the car on the lot again within three months and then I'd take it for myself."

"I thought Winston Smith made the sale."

"He's the one Violet dealt with up front. He was a pipsqueak, all of twenty years old. Woman like Violet, she's always going to find a way to get what she wants. She comes waltzing in here when I'm off the lot and she starts working on him. I'd've put a stop to it if I'd seen what was going on. First thing you know she talks him into letting her take that Bel Air on a test drive—alone. I'm serious. Without him in the car. He never should have agreed, but he's so busy trying to impress her, he doesn't know what hit him. When she finally shows up again, she's put two hundred and fifty-seven miles on a brand-new car. I fired him on the spot and then called Foley and told him to get his butt in. He finally came around Friday morning and I completed the deal— approved the loan and handled all the paperwork."

"I still don't understand why you sold it to him. From what I've heard, his finances were a mess."

"I have no use for Foley; man doesn't have a brain in his head. I felt sorry for Violet. I thought she deserved something nice for putting up with him, fool that she was."

"What was in it for you?"

His smile was sheepish. "Hey, even an old dog like me can do a good turn now and then. Everybody thinks I'm a hard-ass, but I can be generous when it suits. Of course that might've been the last time I ever did a good deed. When that car went missing, I was sick to death. Foley did pay it off. I have to give him that."

"So you weren't out anything?"

"Not one red cent."

"Violet didn't tell you how she managed to put two hundred and fifty-seven miles on the odometer?"

"No, but I can make a pretty good guess. That's the day she showed up at a Santa Teresa bank and emptied her safe-deposit box. I figured it out afterward, because the distance was about right—hundred and twenty-five miles each way. She said the day was gorgeous and she couldn't resist. At the time, I was under the impression she drove north along the coast, but she never said as much."

"If she wanted to drive to Santa Teresa, why not take Foley's truck?"

"That thing was on its last legs. No surprise she'd prefer to tool around in a fancy car like mine. Maybe she was planning to sweet-talk the bank manager into making her a loan."

"Did she give any indication she intended to leave town?"

"Never said a word. Not that she had any reason to confide in me. I barely knew the woman. So what was in her safe-deposit box? I never heard."

"Foley thinks it was cash from an insurance settlement. Fifty thousand is the number I've heard. In addition to that, her brother says he lent her two thousand dollars on Wednesday of that week."

"Calvin Wilcox. Now there's a piece of work."

"As in what?"

"Those two were always at each other's throats. He

assumed the full care of their parents and Violet wouldn't lift a hand. He didn't give a damn if she disappeared or not. I'm sure it cheered him no end that when his mother died, all the money came to him. If his sister had been around, he'd have had to split it with her."

I felt my attention narrow like a cat's at the sound of a little mousie scratching in the wall. "Money?"

"Oh, yes. It was a sizeable estate. Roscoe Wilcox made a fortune perfecting phosphorescent paint. Got a patent on some new, improved formula, or so I've heard. Every time you see a paint job that glows, it's money in the bank—or Calvin's pocket in this case."

"How well do you know him?"

"We're both members of the same country club and the same association of local businessmen. He built that company from scratch, which I've always admired, but the fellow himself? I got my doubts about him. Maybe it's just that he and that wife of his have never cared for me."

"What happened to Winston Smith? I'd like to talk to him if you know where he is."

"That's easy. The week after I fired him, I took him back and he's worked for me ever since. It's like I told him: You don't want to act in haste. What seems tragic in the moment can sometimes turn out to be the best thing in the world."

"Meaning what?"

"He ended up married to my daughter and now they have those three gorgeous girls. He's a very lucky man."

12

JAKE
Wednesday, July 1, 1953

Jake Ottweiler pulled up a chair beside his wife's hospital bed and sat with her as he had every evening since June 17 when she'd been admitted. Mary Hairl was on heavy medication. She slept deeply and often, her face in repose as sculpted as stone. Her hand lay in his, her palm against his, her cold fingers threaded through his warmer ones. She was as pale as a piece of paper, lavender veins showing through the skin on her arms. She was thin, brittle-looking, and she smelled like death. He was ashamed for noticing, ashamed of himself for wanting to recoil.

Mary Hairl was thirty-seven years old and she'd given Jake two wonderful children. Tannie, at nine, was a sturdy, fearless girl, boisterous and outgoing, all bony elbows, skinned knees, and joy. She had a talent for playing the piano, and she read books way above her grade level. She'd never be pretty, he knew that about her without even waiting to see what puberty would bring. The growth spurt—the breasts, the loss of baby fat—none of this would alter the basic plainness of her face. But she was a bright, funny child, and he treasured that in her.

At sixteen, his son, Steve, was not only handsome, he was smart as well—not at the top of his class, but not far from it. Played varsity football and won his letter jacket as a sophomore, the first season he played. Eagle Scout. Sang tenor in the church youth choir. He'd signed a pledge that he'd abstain from alcohol for life, and Jake knew he'd do it, no matter the peer pressure brought to bear. Steve was baby-faced and had a boyish demeanor Jake was hoping he'd outgrow. Hard enough to be a man in this world without looking half his age. Mary Hairl had been a good mother to those kids, and he wasn't sure how he'd manage when she went. He'd do what she did—be firm, listen carefully, and let them make their own mistakes as long as it wasn't anything too serious. It would never be the same, but they'd muddle through somehow. What choice did they have?

He put his head down and rested his face against the edge of the hospital bed. The sheet was crisp and cool against his sunburned cheek. He was incredibly weary. After he'd come back from overseas just after the war, he hadn't had the will or the strength to return to farming. He'd taken a series of jobs, most recently with Union Sugar. He'd missed so many days of work because of Mary Hairl's illness, he'd been fired. Now money was impossibly tight, and if it weren't for her father's financial help, they'd be out on the street. He hadn't understood how much work his wife did. Now that he was essentially sole parent, he was in charge of the meal planning, grocery shopping, laundry, and most of the major household chores. Mid-April, just before she was hospitalized for surgery, she'd put in the truck garden, which was flourishing. She'd always been an uncomplaining soul, and by the time she'd seen the doctor for abdominal tenderness and bloating, the tumor was advanced. Surgery confirmed the cancer, which had spread to so many organs there was nothing to be done. The surgeon closed her up again and now they were waiting for the end. The weeding, mulching, and plucking of suckers from the numerous tomato plants was another set of tasks Jake'd added to his list. After school, Steve pitched in with mowing the lawn and washing the truck, while Tannie was in charge of keeping the house tidy and making their brown-bag lunches. Hairl Tanner, Mary Hairl's father, was still joining them for the evening meal, so the four of them ate supper together nightly, a ritual that seemed cheerless without Mary Hairl. Once the meal was finished, Hairl would disappear, leaving Tannie to clear the table. Steve washed the dishes while Tannie dried them and put them away. At that point, Jake would pick up his jacket and head over to the hospital, arriving about 7:00 P.M.

Jake was scarcely aware that he'd fallen asleep. He'd been thinking about the night in early May when Mary Hairl was admitted for the second time in as many months. She'd made sure her father and the kids were fed before she finally, reluctantly, agreed to call the doctor, who'd met them within the hour in the emergency room. Steve had stayed at home to look after Tannie, and when Jake and Mary Hairl left the house, both the kids were doing their homework. She'd been in excruciating pain for much of the day, and he'd handed her over to the charge nurse that night with the blessed sense that at least now she'd get relief. Her suffering only reminded Jake how ineffectual he was in the face of her illness. He'd stayed with her until 9:00, watching the drip in her IV line, waiting for the medication to take effect. He'd kept an eye on the clock, willing the hands to move, and when she'd finally fallen asleep, he'd fled the premises.

He retrieved his truck from the hospital parking lot in Santa Maria and headed straight for the Blue Moon, the only place in Serena Station where a fella could buy a beer. It had been raining intermittently. The May evening was chilly, and he cranked up the heat until the cab felt like an incubator. The roads were dark, and the lighted houses in Serena Station seemed as isolated as campfires. He needed to drink. He needed to unwind in an atmosphere that carried no suggestion of blood, suffering, or impending loss.

The Moon was close to empty. Tom Padgett sat at the bar, nursing a Pabst Blue Ribbon beer, chatting with Violet Sullivan and the bartender, BW McPhee. BW was a stocky fellow, barrel-chested and tough, who doubled as a bouncer when the occasion arose. Jake took a stool at the bar, glancing idly at the two sitting four stools down. Violet's eyes were puffy with tears and her hair was disheveled. Clearly something had gone on. Tom was trying to talk her out of whatever funk she was in. Jake was inclined to ignore Violet, minding his own business, but while BW uncapped his bottle of Blatz, he told him she and Foley had gotten into a shoving match that ended with her slapping him square across the face. Foley had gone berserk, overturning a table and breaking a chair. BW'd given him one minute to clear out or he was calling the police.

By the time Jake arrived, Foley was gone. While Padgett's comments were too low to hear, Violet's responses were audible. She was talking about her money in a tone that was half braggadocio and half aggrieved. He'd heard the claim before, usually when Foley'd just popped her one and she was threatening to leave. He didn't know if it was true or not, the bit about her personal funds. She never mentioned an amount, and it struck him as odd that she didn't simply take the cash and get on with it.

For a while, Padgett dropped a steady stream of coins into the jukebox, and he and Violet danced. The dress she wore was an emerald green, cut low in the back. Behind the bar, BW was watching them as they moved around the floor. Now and then Jake would turn, looking over his shoulder, following their progress with a shake of his head. He and BW exchanged glances.

"That's what got Foley raging in the first place, her dancing with him," BW remarked.

"Just about anything sets him off. Piece of shit," Jake said.

BW studied him. "I don't suppose you want to talk about Mary Hairl."

"Not especially. No offense."

"None taken. You tell her we're thinkin' about her, Emily and me."

"I'll do that."

"How's that beer coming?"

"I'm fine for the moment."

Violet and Padgett settled at the bar again, but he'd no more than sat down than he glanced at his watch, startled at the time. Jake watched as he threw some bills on the bar and said his good-nights. Once the door shut behind him, Violet turned her head, looking down the bar in Jake's direction. He made a point of looking the other way to avoid her gaze. She was the type who went to bars intent on conversation, while he was the type who went in hopes of being left alone. Dimly he was conscious of her crossing the room behind him, heading for the ladies' room. He ordered another beer and was in the process of lighting a cigarette when she appeared at his side. Her hair was now combed and her green eyes assessed him with curiosity. She was holding a cigarette and, well-mannered fella that he was, he extended his match. By then the flame was burning so close to his fingers, he was forced to drop it and strike another one for her. She eased onto the stool next to his. "You want company?"

"No."

"That's funny. You look like a man who could use a friend."

He had no reply to that. Jake probably hadn't exchanged more than a dozen words with Violet in the six years he'd known her. There'd been that business about the dog, but that was about as far as it went. He'd heard the rumors about her. The whole town of Serena Station buzzed with stories about the Sullivans—Foley's drinking, the fisticuffs, her screwing around. Quite the happy little pair. Jake despised Foley. Any man who raised a hand to woman or child was the lowest of the low. Violet, he wasn't sure about. Mary Hairl seemed to like her, but his wife was a good-hearted soul, who'd put out a bowl of scraps for any stray cat that wandered up on the porch. He put Violet in that camp—hungry, wary, and needy. "You still mad about the dog?"

"I got my money. Not that it was mine for long," she said. "How's Mary Hairl?"

"He just asked me that," Jake said, indicating BW with a wave of his cigarette.

"What'd you tell him?"

"Said I didn't want to talk about it, thanks all the same."

"Because it's painful."

"Because it's nobody's business." He was quiet for a moment and then surprised himself by going on. "They've got her on a drip. Morphine, most likely. The doctor won't tell me anything and what he says to her, she keeps to herself. She doesn't want me to worry."

Violet said, "Well, I'm sorry."

"Don't be. It has nothing to do with you." He glanced off across the room. He could feel tears sting his eyes. He'd made a point of not discussing his wife's illness. Acquaintances would ask, but he tended to cut them short. He didn't like the idea of exposing the intimate details of Mary Hairl's condition. He couldn't talk particulars with her father, even if he'd known. Hairl had been a surly son of a bitch ever since his wife died. He was burdened enough as it was, knowing he was on the verge of losing his only child. Which left who? Jake certainly couldn't talk about her sickness with the kids. Both he and Mary Hairl had agreed early on to spare them. Steve, at sixteen, was aware of what was happening, but he kept himself detached. Tannie was mercifully oblivious, which left Jake on his own.

Violet studied him. "How're you holding up? You don't look so hot yourself."

He lifted his beer bottle. "This helps."

"Ain't that the truth," she said, and clinked her wineglass against his bottle. "Why is it men are always trying to prove how tough they are? Situation like yours, what harm would it do to talk about it?"

"What for? I live with it from day to day. Last thing I need is talk on top of that."

"You sound just like me. Too proud to admit when you're hurting. I can sit here in tears and everybody thinks it's just something I do. You're the first guy ever offered to have a decent conversation."

"I don't call this a conversation."

"But there's hope of one," she said.

"What about Padgett? He was talking to you."

"He's about as popular as me. People think I'm a whore and he's a fool. Gives us something in common."

"Is that true?"

"What, about him or me?"

"I couldn't care less about him. What's the deal on you?"

She smiled. "It's like that song about the Whiffen-poofs. . . . What the hell's a Whiffenpoof? You ever ask yourself that?"

"What song?"

"The duet Bing Crosby and Bob Hope sang in *Road to Bali*." She started to sing a fragment in a voice that was surprisingly sweet. " 'Damned from here to eternity. Lord have mercy on such as we.' " Her smile was weary. "That's the deal on me. Damned."

"Because of Foley?"

"Everything wrong in my life is because of him."

"I thought you liked tussling with him. You do it often enough."

"Tussling? Well, I guess that's one way to put it. Foley pounds the shit out of me on a regular basis and I got the black eyes to prove it, but does anybody ask how I'm doing? He could knock me to the floor and nobody'd offer me a hand. I don't want pity, but once in a while I'd like to think someone gives a shit." She stopped and then smirked. "Listen to me. I sound like a victim. Nobody likes a victim, least of all me."

"Why do you put up with it? That's what I don't get."

"What choice do I have? I can't leave him. He's threatened to kill me and I know he'd do it for sure. Foley's a psychopath. Besides, if I left what would become of Daisy?"

"You could take her with you."

"And do what? I got married at fifteen and never held a job in my life. I wouldn't even know where to begin."

"What about that money you're always talking about."

"I'm biding my time. I figure I've got one shot and I'm not about to blow it. Anyway, Daisy's crazy about her daddy."

"Most girls are crazy about their daddies. I'm sure she's crazy about you, too. What's that got to do with it?"

"Daisy's crazier than most. She thinks Foley hung the moon, so why should I get in the way? Sometimes I think they'd be better off without me. I mean, it's one thing if I leave, but take away his little girl? He'd rip my heart out, if he hadn't already done it."

Jake shook his head. "He doesn't deserve either one of you."

"No fooling."

"So what'd you see in him?"

"He was a sweet guy when the two of us hooked up. It's the alcohol does him in. Sober, he's not all that bad. Well, some bad, but not as horrible as you'd think. Of course, he says he's forced to drink to put up with the likes of me."

"What's he have to put up with? You're a beautiful woman. I can't picture any big hardship living with you."

"I'm a pain."

"How's that?"

"I got a reputation as a party girl for one thing. According to him, I don't do anything right and that sets him off. No matter what I do, he's never satisfied. After work, he walks in the door and starts in on me. Either the house is a mess or his dinner's not hot enough or I forgot to take the dirty clothes to the Laundromat again. He wants to know where I've been, wants to know who I talked to, and where I was every time he tried to call me during the day. I'm thinking, what am I, his slave? I'm entitled to a life. I try to keep my mouth shut, but he lays into me and I have to fight back. How else can I hang on to my self-respect?"

"There's bound to be a way out."

"Well, if there is I'd sure like to hear it." She put out her cigarette. "You have any change?"

"What for?" he asked, but he was already digging in his pants pocket, coming up with a handful of coins.

She took a nickel and slid off the stool. He watched her cross to the jukebox, where she inserted the coin and punched in a number. After a moment, he heard the opening strains of Nat King Cole singing "Pretend."

She came back to him, holding out a hand. "Come on. Let's dance. I love this song."

"I don't dance."

"Yes, you do." She looked over at the bartender. "BW, tell the man he has to dance with me. It's time to lighten up the mood."

Jake felt himself smiling as she tugged on his hand, pulling him toward the tiny bare spot between tables that served as a dance floor. She slid into his arms, ignoring the awkward back-and-forth rocking motion that was the only kind of dancing he knew. She sang against his neck, her smoky wine breath tickling his ear. He could smell violets and soap and the same kind of shampoo Mary Hairl had used before she got so sick. Over Violet's shoulder, he could see BW busy himself behind the bar, studiously ignoring what was going on. Jake had never much cared for music, but he could see now how it might have the power to make you forget. If there was one thing Jake needed, it was the blessedness of forgetting, even for a little while.

At midnight, BW started turning off lights. "Sorry about that, folks," he said, as though the bar were filled with people. His tone was bored, but Jake could hear the underlying irritation. BW didn't want to be a party to what was going on. Jake went up to the bar and paid the tab, peeling off bills and adding a generous tip, in part to remind the man of his place.

BW said, "You driving her home?"

"I might, if it's any of your business."

"I know you mean well, but you don't know what you're getting into when it comes to her. Ask Padgett. He'll tell you the same thing."

"Thanks, BW, but I don't believe I asked for your advice."

"I'm saying this as a friend."

"I don't need that kind of friend. Your job is to tend bar. I can look after myself, but thanks all the same."

"Don't ever say I didn't warn you."

Jake helped Violet into her raincoat and held the door for her. As they emerged from the bar, the air seemed as fresh as a florist's shop. The May rain had passed, leaving a mist in the air. The blacktop was damp, looking shiny in places where shallow puddles had formed. He opened the truck door on the passenger side and handed her in. There were no lights in the parking lot, except for the reflected blue from the sign for the Blue Moon, the neon pulsing and blinking. Jake got in on his side and sat, watching the light, fascinated, not really sure what came next. It wasn't as though he hadn't strayed occasionally in the course of his marriage, but he was never sure what he was getting into and that lent a sick thrill to the proceedings.

Violet said, "This is like a time-out. It doesn't count for anything. I like Mary Hairl."

"Me, too," he said. He kept his hands on the steering wheel as though he might actually start the car and drive away.

BW turned the neon sign off and moments later, he came out of the rear door, locked it, and walked to his car.

Jake knew both their faces must have flashed with white as BW passed, his headlights raking across the front of Jake's truck.

And then he was gone.

Violet was drunk and Jake'd had too much to drink himself, but he needed a friend, someone to feel close to for just this one night. Blindly he held a hand out and she took it. They made love. The leather seat was surprisingly commodious. The night was growing cold, and through the open window he could smell the orange blossoms from the orchard nearby. The scent was so dense he could scarcely breathe. He could hear crickets and frogs, and then the night became dead quiet except for the rustling of clothes and his harsh, rasping breath. He felt as though he'd had to run for miles just to get to her.

13

Downstairs, Chet Cramer introduced me to his son-in-law and then excused himself. Winston Smith was the same heavyset salesman I'd seen earlier, and I wondered if his sales pitch had been successful. Probably not, given his energy level, which seemed low if not depressed. We sat in his cubicle, my back to the glass partition that looked out onto the floor. Winston's desk was arranged so he could keep an eye out for customers without appearing inattentive.

At close range, the word "corpulent" was more appropriate than "heavyset" in capturing his girth. He looked as though a simple walk to his car would leave him wheezing and short of breath. There was no ashtray in sight, but I smelled the cigarette smoke that clung to his clothes and breath. Under his chin, a second chin bulged, leaving his shirt collar so taut it might choke him to death if he bent to tie his shoes. He still had most of his hair, which he wore long and curly on top, brushed back in a style I hadn't seen since the days when Elvis Presley got his start.

I'd scarcely sat down when his telephone rang. "Excuse me," he said, and picked up. "This is Winston Smith." And then, with caution, "What's up?"

I had no way of knowing who was on the other end of the line, but he flicked a quick look in my direction and angled his body for privacy. "Hang on a sec." He put the caller on hold. "Let me take care of this and I'll be right back."

"Sure thing."

He left the cubicle. I watched line one blink red until he picked up the call from a nearby phone. On the wall across from me, his sales manuals were lined up on a built-in credenza. In a prominent position, there was a color photograph of a bride and groom on what I assumed was their wedding day. I crossed and picked up the framed photo for closer scrutiny. Winston must have been in his midtwenties, slim, handsome, curly-haired, and boyish, his tuxedo contributing an air of casual elegance. At his side, a hefty Kathy Cramer was squeezed into a wedding dress so tight it must have hurt to breathe. Above the sweetheart neckline, her breasts were plumped like two homemade yeast rolls that had risen and were ready to pop in the oven. In the years since that day, the two had reversed roles. Now she was trim, an exercise addict, while he'd apparently surrendered all hope of getting into shape. What was up with that? I kept thinking about Tannie's offhand remark, that Winston knew more about Violet than he'd admitted.

I replaced the photo and took my seat again mere moments before he returned, murmuring, "Sorry about that." He sat down again, but something in his manner had shifted. "My wife," he said, by way of explanation. "She called while I was with a customer and I had to put her off. Don't want to do that twice."

"No problem. I had a chat with her earlier and she showed me the house. Nice place."

"Should be for the price we paid," he said with a quick forced smile.

"You play golf?"

He shook his head. "She's the golfer. I keep my nose to the grindstone. If you notice me limp, it's from dragging my ball and chain." He laughed when he said it and I smiled in response, thinking, *Ding, ding, ding, ding.*

I said, "I could never see the point of golf myself. Chasing a ball and then hitting it with a stick? Though now that I think about it, that describes a lot of sports. What about your daughters? Are they golfers?"

"Amber was taking lessons before she left for Spain, but we'll see where that goes. She's easily bored so she'll doubtless move on to something else. Brittany's not athletic by any stretch. I'm sure Kathy'd tell you that she takes after me."

"I understand Tiffany's getting married in June."

"Ka-ching, ka-ching," he said, pretending to punch up sales on a cash register. "You know how much weddings cost these days?"

"Not a clue."

"Me, neither. Kathy keeps me in the dark so I can't object. I'm sure it's something close to the national debt."

We both laughed at that, though the observation didn't seem at all funny to me. Clearly Winston and his wife weren't operating off the same page.

He pulled out a handkerchief and blotted his upper lip where a subtle sheen of moisture had appeared. He returned the handkerchief to his back pocket. "Anyway, she tells me you have questions about Violet Sullivan."

"If you don't mind," I said, expecting the standard assurance that the subject was really no big deal.

"Doesn't matter if I do or not, I'm under orders," he said, again with that quick, easy laugh to show what a wag he was.

Mentally I squinted, listening to the second set of comments embedded in the first. I'm not a fan of doublespeak. His asides were the sort offered by married couples who banter in public, airing their grievances with an eye to soliciting outside support. If Kathy had been with us, she'd have countered with a few ha-has of her own, thus guaranteeing a laugh at his expense. He would have joined in the merriment, which is what seemed pitiful to me. The man was in pain.

"What orders?"

"What?"

"What orders did she give?"

"Skip it. Long story."

"I love long stories."

"You don't have other people you have to talk to?"

"I'm supposed to meet Daisy, but if you let me borrow your phone, I can change that. You want to go somewhere and grab a cigarette?"

I called Daisy at work and had a quick conversation with her, telling her something had come up and I wasn't going to make it for lunch. I suggested that if Tannie was driving up I could hang out in Santa Maria and the three of us could have dinner at the Blue Moon instead. She seemed to like that idea, so I said I'd call her again later in the afternoon and we could finalize our plans.

I'd expected Winston to step out into the vestibule to grab a smoke, but he took out his car keys and walked me to the side lot where he'd parked his car. He handed me into the passenger side of a metallic blue 1987 Chevrolet Caravan station wagon. When he got in on his side, he said, "This is only mine until the '88s come in. Then they swap it out."

"Slick."

"You think so until you look at the underlying attitude. No matter how fond you are of what you have, there's always something hotter coming down the pike. It's a recipe for discontent."

"If you buy into it," I said.

"That's my job—promoting the concept. Coaxing the gullible into taking the bait."

"So why don't you quit and do something else? No one has a gun to your head."

"I'm fifty-four years old, a little long in the tooth for any big career change. Can I buy you lunch?"

"In matters of food, you can always count me in."

I pictured McDonald's, but then I was always picturing McDonald's. I'd take a Quarter Pounder with Cheese over just about any other foodstuff on earth.

He drove us across town and pulled into a supermarket parking lot where a fellow and his wife had set up a portable barbeque that was attached to a camper shell. The rolling metal rig was black, about the size of a double-wide utility sink, with a pulley and chain that allowed for the raising and lowering of a rack. Chunks of meat had been laid on the grill over hot coals, and the smoky smell of charred beef filled the air. To one side, buttered rolls had been cut in half and placed on the grill.

A steady stream of cars was turning into the lot, taking advantage of the numerous empty parking spaces. On a card table, I could see piles of paper napkins, paper plates, plastic cutlery, and numerous plastic tubs of salsa and beans. Nearby three portable picnic tables were set up with aluminum lawn chairs. An ice chest contained cold cans of soda for a quarter apiece.

We parked as close as we could and eased into a line that was easily twenty-five people long. The wait was worth it, and I made no attempt to tidy up my manners as we ate.

"Geez, how do they do this? It's great!" I said with my mouth half-full.

"Santa Maria barbecue. That's tri-tip," he said. "You rub it with salt, pepper, and garlic salt, and cook it over red oak."

"Fabulous."

Both of us licked our fingers before opening the moist towelette packets provided with the meal. When my hands were clean, I said, "Thanks. What a treat."

"You're welcome."

We walked back to his car, freeing up our lawn chairs for the people waiting to sit down. We lingered outside his car while he lit his aftermeal cigarette. His thin candy-coating of mirth had dropped away and something darker had emerged. This was not a happy man. There was a heaviness about him that seemed to taint the very air. Apropos of nothing, he held up his cigarette. "Know why I'm doing this?"

"She won't let you smoke inside."

He flicked a look at me. "How'd you know?"

"I was in the house. No ashtrays."

"She runs a tight ship."

"A lot of people feel that way about smoking," I said mildly, not mentioning that I was one.

"Hey, don't I know it. Anyway, I don't want to talk about that."

I didn't ask what "that" he was referring to. Instead I said, "Fine. We can talk about Violet, then."

He was quiet for a long moment. "She was a tramp."

Kathy had used the same term. I said, "Come on. Everybody says she was a tramp. Tell me something I haven't heard."

I watched his face, wondering what was going on behind his eyes.

He studied the bright ember of his cigarette. "Kathy's jealous of her."

"Is or was?"

"Is."

"That takes some doing. Violet's been gone for thirty-four years."

"Try telling her that."

"I thought they barely knew each other."

"Not quite true. Liza Mellincamp was Kathy's best friend. Then Violet came along and Liza got caught up in the Sullivan family drama. Liza's parents were divorced, which in those days was a much bigger deal than it is today. Now it's the norm. Back then it wasn't scandalous, but it was looked on as low-class. And there was Violet, already outside the pale. She took Liza under her wing. Kathy couldn't stand it."

"Is that why she hated Daisy?"

"Sure, she hated her. Daisy was another link to Violet. Liza spent a lot of time at the Sullivans'. She also had a boyfriend that summer, though he broke off the relationship the same weekend Violet disappeared."

"I don't get it. So many events seem connected to Violet. Maybe not directly, but peripherally. You got fired. Tannie's mother died."

"Sometimes I think there are people who generate that stuff. They don't mean to do it, but whatever happens to them ends up affecting everyone else. Day I got fired was the worst day of my life. Twenty years old and there went any hope of a college education."

"What were you planning to do?"

"I don't even remember. Something better than what I got. I'm not a salesman. I don't like manipulating people. Cramer sees it as a game and it's one that he wins. The whole deal makes me sick."

"But it looks like you're doing okay."

"You ought to see my credit card bills. We can barely make ends meet. Kathy's out there spending money faster than I can earn it. Country club membership. The new house. The clothes. Vacations. She doesn't like to cook, so most nights we eat out . . ." He stopped and shook his head. "You know the irony?"

"Oh, do tell. I love irony," I said.

"Now she tells me she needs her 'space.' She broke the news to me last night. She says with the girls as good as gone, she thinks it time for her to reevaluate her goals."

"Divorce?"

"She's not using the word, but that's what it amounts to. Tiffany's wedding will keep her entertained, but after that, it's every man for himself. Meanwhile, she thinks I should find a place of my own. When she called earlier today? I was hoping she'd changed her mind, but all she wanted was to make sure I didn't mention it to you."

"Oops."

"Yeah, oops. I've spent years doing what I'm told, giving her everything she wants, for all the good it did. Now it's freedom she wants and I'm supposed to foot the bill for that, too. She probably has a stud in the wings. Not that I've asked. She'd lie to me anyway so what's the point? The only good part is I don't have to take any more crap off of her."

"Counseling's not an option?"

"Counseling for what? She won't admit we've got a problem, just that she needs 'distance' so she can get 'clarity.' I should get a little clarity myself—hire some hotshot attorney and file before she does. That would shake her to her shoes."

"I'm sorry. I wish I had advice for you."

"Who needs advice? I could use some comic relief."

"Maybe she means what she says; she needs breathing room."

"Not a chance. She must have been planning this for months, waiting until we moved before she lowered the boom." He smoked in silence, leaning against the door on the driver's side while I leaned against the fender near him, both of us watching the crowd thin around the barbecue. Like a trained therapist, I let the silence extend, wondering what he'd offer by way of filling it in. I was just about to get antsy and jump into the breech myself, when he spoke up. "Here's something I never told anyone about Violet. This is minor, but it's weighed on my mind. The night she disappeared? I saw the car."

I didn't look at him for fear of breaking the spell. "Where?"

"Off New Cut Road. This was long after dark. There was road construction going on so everything was torn up. I'd been driving around for hours, more depressed than I've ever been in my life. Except maybe now," he added, drily.

I could feel the hairs go up along the back of my neck, but I didn't want to push. "What was she doing?"

"I didn't see her, Just the Bel Air. I figured she was having car trouble . . . like maybe she'd run out of gas . . . but I didn't give a shit. I thought, she's so smart, let her figure it out herself. Later, when I heard she was gone, I should have mentioned it to the cops. At first, I didn't think it was relevant, and later, I worried it would look like I'd had something to do with it."

" 'It'?"

"Whatever happened to her."

"Why you?"

"For obvious reasons. I'd lost my job because of her and I was pissed off."

"Weird. If she'd run out of gas, you'd think the pump jockey would have seen her at the station again."

"Well, yeah. I thought maybe somebody else had seen the car, but nobody ever said. It was way out in the boonies, but I still can't believe I was the only one who spotted it. When the sheriff's department didn't come up with anything, I decided to leave it alone."

"And you've never told anyone?"

"Kathy," he said. "This was after we were married. I don't believe in couples keeping secrets and it bothered me a lot. So one night I'd had too much to drink and I blurted it out. She didn't think it was a big deal. She told me to forget about it and that's what I did. The detective had already talked to me a couple of times, same way he was talking to everyone else, but he never asked when I'd seen her last and I didn't volunteer."

"And the car was just sitting there?"

"Right. Maybe fifteen, twenty yards off the side of the road. I could see it in my headlights, plain as day."

"You're sure it was hers?"

"Positive. There was only one like it in the county. She'd been driving it around since the minute Foley gave it to her. Absolutely, it was hers."

"Had she had a flat tire?"

"That's possible. I didn't see a flat, but it could have been that. Could have been anything."

"Was the engine idling or off?"

"Off and the headlights were off. The road was really rough, and I'd slowed to a stop, intending to turn around. That's when I saw the car. I rolled down the window and looked out, but everything was still as stone. I actually sat there a couple of minutes, but nothing happened, so I said to hell with it and went back the way I'd come."

"Could she have stopped to let the dog out?"

"I didn't see the dog. At the time, it didn't occur to me there was anything creepy going on. Now, I don't know."

14

Winston drove us to the location on New Cut Road where he'd seen Violet's car. I wanted to take a look at the spot but didn't intend to press the point since he was due back at work.

He laughed when I expressed my concern. "Don't sweat it. Chet won't fire me. I'm the schmuck who pays his daughter's bills."

He took Highway 166 east out of Cromwell and after three miles, turned right onto New Cut Road, which was laid out on a diagonal that intersected Highway 1 to the south. Before September of 1953, when New Cut was finished, drivers were forced to go miles out of their way when heading from Santa Maria to Silas, Arnaud, or Serena Station. The old Tanner homestead appeared, its Tudor façade jarring now that I saw it again. The acreage across the road had been planted and harvested, leaving a pale haze of wispy stalks interspersed with lush weeds.

Winston pulled into the Tanner driveway and we got

out. I left my shoulder bag in the car but carried the map with me.

"Somewhere along in here," he said, gesturing vaguely. "I remember the heavy equipment and big mounds of dirt. The road was being graded, and there was this line of big orange cones and a temporary barricade across the unpaved portion to discourage through traffic, not that there was much. Now that I'm looking at it though, it's hard to pinpoint the spot."

He crossed the road and I followed, watching as he pivoted. He walked backward for a few steps, trying to get his bearings. "I didn't realize the road ran so close to the Tanner property. I'm almost sure the barrier was off in that direction, like a big detour, but I might be wrong."

I said, "Maybe it's like a house under construction. When all you have is the slab, the rooms seem so small. Then the walls go up and everything suddenly looks much bigger."

He smiled. "Right. I never have figured out how that works. You'd think it'd be the other way around."

"Any chance you passed her on the road? If she had car trouble she might have tried walking to the nearest phone."

"Oh no. There's no way I'd have missed her if she'd been out there. I did keep an eye out, but you can see for yourself, she'd have had to hike for miles. Funny thing is, until now I put the incident out of my mind because I felt guilty and I didn't want to deal with it. I should have stopped to see what was going on."

"Don't do that to yourself. It's probably not important in the overall scheme of things."

"I suppose not. She was going to do whatever she did

regardless of me. I just wish I'd been a gentleman and done the right thing."

"On the other hand, she didn't do you any favors."

I opened the map and then folded it in thirds so I could check the relative distances between points. "Here's what puzzles me. The service station near Tullis couldn't be more than three miles away. She filled her tank at roughly six thirty so it's hard to believe she'd run out of gas so soon."

Winston shrugged. "She could have been waiting for someone. This is a hell of an isolated spot. I was only out here by happenstance. I'd been driving around randomly. I got this far and realized there wasn't any place else to go. This was literally the end of the road."

"Did you see any other cars?"

"No. I just remember the pitch-black dark. It was a clear night, and I could hear the muffled sound of the fireworks in Silas, off in that direction."

"Which means it had to be before nine thirty when the fireworks display ended."

"True. I hadn't thought about that."

"Foley swears he was at the park and I gather there were people willing to vouch for him. Meanwhile, what was she doing out here? By nine thirty she should have been two hundred miles away."

We chatted idly of other things on our way back into town. When we pulled into the dealership, Winston dropped me at my car. I got out and then leaned in the window. "Thanks for lunch," I said. "I can't tell you how much I appreciate your telling me about the car. I'm not sure it's significant, but it's fresh information and that's encouraging."

"I'm glad."

"One more quick question and then I'll let you get back to work. This business about you and Kathy. Is that classified?"

"You mean, is it a secret? By no means."

"I'm asking because I'll be talking to Daisy later, bringing her up to speed. I can certainly keep the information to myself if you'd prefer."

"I don't care who knows. Kathy's always airing our problems, blabbing to her girlfriends and then sharing their opinions, as long as they coincide with hers. You can tell anyone you want. The more the merrier. Let her see how it feels."

Once I left him, I pulled off on a side street and made notes. I'd been the happy beneficiary of Winston's anger at his wife. His report about the car had created more questions than it answered, but at least he'd placed her on New Cut Road when the sheriff's department assumed that she'd already left town. Or died. But if Foley killed her and buried her, how had he pulled it off? The Sullivans had only one car, and if it was parked out on New Cut Road, how did he get there and back? The park in the little town of Silas was six miles away. Granted, there was a three-hour gap between the end of the fireworks and his arriving home, but it would have taken him that long just to walk as far as New Cut Road and back. And what could he have done with the car? Winston had speculated that Violet might have been out there waiting for someone, in which case they might have hightailed it out of town as soon as he showed up. That possibility was at least compatible with the facts. What seemed worrisome was the dog. From all reports, Baby yapped incessantly, so why hadn't Winston heard her bark?

At 4:00 I presented myself at Liza Clements's front door. The house itself was plain, a long wood-frame box with a nondescript porch built across the front. The Santa Maria neighborhood was nicely maintained, but it had seen better days. Trees and shrubs had grown too large for the lots, but no one had had the nerve to cut them down. Consequently, the yards were dark and the windows were obscured by evergreens that towered above the rooflines. The shade created a chilliness that seemed to shroud all the houses on the block.

The woman who answered the door looked much younger than her years. She wore tennis shoes, baggy pants, and a double-breasted white chef's jacket that buttoned across the front. Her fair hair was shoulder-length, parted down the middle, and pulled back behind her ears. She had blue eyes, wide straight brows, and a wide mouth. Her complexion was pale and creamy, with a smattering of freckles across her nose. She wore a silver heart-shaped locket that glinted in the V of her shirt. She stood and looked at me blankly. "Yes?"

"You're Liza?"

"Yes."

"I'm Kinsey Millhone."

It took another half a beat before she remembered who I was and then she put a hand to her mouth. "I'd forgotten you were coming. I'm so sorry. Please come in."

"Is this an okay time?"

"Fine. I didn't mean to cut you short yesterday, but I was halfway down the walk when I heard the phone ring."

I stepped into a living room that was ten feet by twelve, furnished out of Pier 1 Imports with very little money but a good eye for design: wicker, plump Indonesian tan-and-black block-print pillows, a reed rug on the floor, and lots of houseplants that, on a second glance, turned out to be fakes.

"No problem. Thanks for seeing me today. Are you a chef?"

"Not with any formal training. I bake as a hobby, but I've been doing it for years. I make wedding cakes in the main, but just about anything else you'd want. Why don't you have a seat?"

I took one of the white wicker chairs with sturdy canvas cushions forming both the seat and the back. "My landlord was a commercial baker in his working days. He's retired now, but he still bakes every chance he gets. Your house smells like his—vanilla and hot sugar."

"I've lived with it so long I don't even notice it. I guess it's like working in a brewery. Your nose eventually goes dead. My husband always thought that was just how our house smelled."

"You're married?"

"Not now. I've been divorced for six years. He owns a party rental business in town. We're still good friends."

"You have kids?"

"One boy," she replied. "Kevin and his wife, Marcy, are expecting their first baby, a little girl, sometime in the next ten days unless the little bugger's late. They're naming her Elizabeth, after me, though they plan to call her Libby." Her fingers moved to the silver locket, touching it as though for luck.

"You look too young to be a grandmother."

"Thanks. I can hardly wait," she said. "What can I help you with?"

"Daisy Sullivan's hired me in hopes of finding her mother."

"That's what I heard. You talked to Kathy Cramer earlier."

"Nice woman," I lied, hoping God wouldn't rip my tongue out.

She smiled, tucking a strand of hair behind one ear. "I wish you luck. I'd love to know where Violet ended up. She changed the course of my life."

"Really. For better or for worse?"

"Oh, for better. No question. She was the first adult who ever took an interest in me. What a revelation. I'd grown up in Serena Station, which has to be one of the crappiest little places on earth. Have you seen it?"

"Daisy showed me around. It's like a ghost town."

"Now it is. Back then, a lot more people lived there, but everyone was so boring and conventional. Violet was like a breath of fresh air, if you'll pardon the cliché. She didn't give a hoot about obeying the rules and she didn't care what other people thought about her. She was such a free spirit. She made everybody else seem stodgy and dull by comparison."

"You're the first person I've talked to who's had anything nice to say."

"I was her lone defender even back then. I can see now she had a self-destructive streak. She was impulsive, or maybe 'reckless' is the better word. People were attracted to her and repelled at the same time."

"How so?"

"I think she reminded them of all the things they wanted but didn't have the courage to pursue."

"Was she happy?"

"Oh, no. Not at all. She was desperate to get away. She was sick of being poor and sick of Foley's knocking her around."

"So you believe she left town?"

She blinked at me. "Of course."

"How'd she manage it?"

"The way she managed everything else. She knew what she wanted and she outfoxed anyone who got in her way."

"Sounds ruthless."

"Again, that's a matter of semantics. I'd say 'determined,' but it sometimes amounts to the same thing. It about broke my heart that she left without saying good-bye. Then again, I had to say 'Go and God bless.' I wasn't that articulate at fourteen, but that's how I felt. I couldn't bear it for my sake, but I was glad for her. Do you know what I mean? She saw a chance and she took it. A door flew open and she zipped right through. I admired her for that."

"You must have missed her."

"It was awful at first. We always talked about everything and suddenly she was gone. I was crushed."

"What'd you do?"

"What could I do? I learned to get by on my own."

"She never got in touch?"

"No, but I was so sure she would. Even if it was a postcard with one line, or no message at all. A postmark would have been sufficient. Anything to let me know she'd made it to wherever. I used to imagine her in Hawaii, or Vermont—someplace completely different than this. I haunted the mailbox for months, but I guess she couldn't take the chance."

"I don't see how a postcard could have put her in jeopardy."

"You're wrong about that. Sonia, the woman at the post office, would've spotted it when she was sorting the mail. I wouldn't have told a soul, but word would've gotten out. Sonia was a blabbermouth, which Violet well knew."

"You were the last person who had any substantial contact with her."

"I know and I've thought about that night. It runs like a loop in my head. You ever get a song on your brain and no matter what you do, it keeps playing and playing? That's how it is with her. Even now. Well, maybe not so much now. The images do fade, but you know what? I smell violet cologne and bang, she's there again. It brings tears to my eyes."

"Did it ever cross your mind something might have happened to her?"

"You mean, foul play? People talked about that, but I didn't believe it for a minute."

"Why not? You'd seen what Foley did to her. Didn't it occur to you she might have come to grief?"

She shook her head. "I thought it was something else. I was there earlier that day and saw these brown paper bags sitting on the chair. I recognized some of her favorite things on top and I asked her what she was doing. She said she'd cleaned out her closet and the stuff was going to Goodwill. Well, that seemed looney even at the time. Later—this was after she was gone—it occurred to me that she'd been packing."

"To go where?"

"I don't know. A friend's house? There must have been some place."

I blinked. "Did she say anything to that effect?"

"Not a word. Foley was gone—I don't know where—and I'd gone over to the house to hang out. She went on talking about something else so I let it drop."

"How come this is the first I've heard of it? I've read all the articles about Violet, but I didn't see a reference to any bags of clothes."

"I don't know what to say. I told the sheriff's deputies, but they acted like they didn't want to hear. By then they were busy quizzing Foley about where he was on Saturday night. I didn't want to make a big deal of it. I figured since she hadn't mentioned it, she didn't want anyone to know."

"But you had to think someone would have been in touch with the authorities once word got out that she was considered a missing person. Surely someone could have contacted the police without compromising her safety."

"Exactly, but the papers ran the story twice and no one came forward, so then I figured I must have made a mistake. She might have left town instead."

"And that's what you told them?"

"Well, no. I got worried that if they thought she'd run off, they'd put up road blocks or something."

"What for? She was an adult. If she left of her own accord, they'd have no right to interfere. Cops aren't in the business of chasing runaway spouses, assuming that's what she did." I was trying not to sound accusatory. She'd been fourteen years old and the account she was giving me was her adolescent reasoning, untempered by later maturity or insight.

"Oh. I guess what you're saying makes sense, but I didn't understand it at the time. Foley was a basket case by then, and I didn't want him hearing about it either, for fear he'd go after her."

"But this was what, five or six days later? She could have been in Canada by then."

"Exactly. I thought the bigger head start she had, the safer she'd be."

Inwardly I was rolling my eyes. "It didn't bother you that your silence left Foley on the hot seat?"

"He put himself there. I didn't do anything to him."

"He's always maintained she ran off. You could have backed him up."

"Why would I help him? He beat her up for years and no one ever said a word. She finally got away from him and good for her. He could stew in his own juices as far as I was concerned. I wasn't going to lift a hand."

"I'm curious why you'd tell me when you never mentioned it before. Reporters must have asked."

"I wasn't under any obligation to them. For one thing, I don't like journalists. What do they call themselves . . . 'investigative reporters.' Oh, please. Like they think they'll get a Pulitzer out of the deal. They're rude, and half the time they treated me like I was on the witness stand. All they cared about was selling papers and promoting themselves."

"What about the sheriff's department? You didn't think to go back and set the record straight?"

"No way. By then they'd made such a federal case of it I was scared to say a word. I'm willing to admit it now because I'm fond of Daisy and I'm glad she's doing this."

I thought about it briefly, wondering how this fit in with what I knew. "Something else came up today. Winston Smith told me he saw her car out on New Cut Road that night. This was sometime before the fireworks ended because he could hear 'em in the distance. He didn't see Violet or the dog, but he knew the Bel Air. I can't understand why she wasn't gone by then if she'd left the house at six fifteen."

Liza shook her head. "I can't help you there. How does that fit in?"

"I have no idea."

"So why didn't *he* bring it up before? You talk about me keeping quiet. He could have said something years ago."

"He did. He mentioned it to Kathy and she shrugged it off. It was one of those occasions where the longer he kept quiet, the harder it was for him to speak up. If she'd given him any encouragement, he might have passed the information on."

Liza's expression held a tinge of distaste. "I'm not sure how much credence you can give him. He and Kathy are having a hard time. He'd probably say anything to make her look bad."

"Maybe so, but the point is it shores up Foley's claim."

"I never said Foley killed her. Just the opposite."

"But a lot of people thought he did. His life has been ruined. The point is, with the car all the way out there and him at the park, how's he going to kill her and get away with it?"

"Dumb luck, I guess."

"I'm serious."

"Sorry. I didn't mean to be flippant."

"Am I overlooking something here?"

Her gaze shifted to the floor and I could see her running the possibilities through her mind. "Not that I believe this, but just for the sake of argument, what if she was already dead by then?"

"That's not out of the question," I said. "But if Foley was the one who killed her, how'd he pull it off? He was at the park until the fireworks ended, then he went to the Moon. How's he going to get out there, get rid of her body, and then dispose of the Bel Air. He doesn't have transportation because he's traded in his truck and she's driving the only car they own."

"He could have borrowed a car or even stolen one. He drives out and buries her. What's so hard about that?"

"But then he's stuck with two cars, the Bel Air and the one he borrowed or stole. You said he came in after midnight, but the timing's still too tight. What'd he do with her car? If he drove it off a cliff or pushed it down a ravine, he still has to walk back to the stolen-slash-borrowed car, pick that up, and drive home. It's too elaborate and it's way too labor intensive. It would have taken him all night."

I saw a tint of pink rise in her cheeks. She said, "You really don't even know if she was there. You're just arguing for the sake of it. She could have abandoned her car and gone off with someone else."

"Ah. You're right about that. I like that. But then what? A car thief conveniently arrives and makes off with her Bel Air?"

Liza was getting impatient. "Oh, who knows? I don't even care by now. I care what happened to her, but not the car."

"All right. Skip that. Let's go back to your point and say she ran off with some guy. Any idea who?"

"I never saw her with anyone. Besides, I'm not sure I'd tell you even if I had."

"You still feel protective?"

"Yes, I guess I do. If there was a guy and they figured out who, it might tip them off to where she went."

"I thought you said you wanted to help Daisy. If you have any ideas, it'd be nice to hear."

"I didn't say that. I said I was glad she was doing this for her sake. It's not like I'm withholding information. I mean, what if Violet doesn't want to be found? Shouldn't she be left in peace?"

"Unfortunately, Daisy's interests and her mother's may not coincide."

"Look, all I know is I don't like being put in the middle like this. I've told you as much as I know. The rest of it is your problem. I hope Daisy gets what she wants, but not at Violet's expense."

"Fair enough," I said. "I guess in the long run, it's theirs to deal with. I'll find her if I can. What the two of them do with it is up to them. Daisy's struggling with the notion of rejection. She doesn't want to think her mother walked off and left her without a backward glance."

"Violet wasn't necessarily rejecting her. Maybe she was saying yes to something else."

"Bottom line in that case? She put her interests above Daisy's."

"Wouldn't be the first time a woman did that. Sometimes the choices are hard. If she had a guy and he was really good for her, it might have been worth the price. I don't mean to keep defending her, but the poor woman isn't here to defend herself."

"That's fine. I understand. She meant a lot to you."

"Correction. Not 'a lot.' She meant everything to me."

"Which puts you and Daisy in the same boat."

"Not quite. I didn't think I'd recover, but here I am and life goes on. Daisy should learn to do the same."

"Maybe she'll get to that one day, but for now she feels stuck." There was a momentary pause while I roamed over the stories I'd heard, looking for something else. I'm sure she was wishing I'd leave her alone. "What happened to your boyfriend?"

"What?"

"Your boyfriend. Weren't you going steady with a guy back then?"

"That was Ty Eddings. How'd you hear about that?"

"Somebody mentioned him. I forget now who. We were talking about all the stuff that went on in the same time frame. The two of you broke up, right?"

"More or less. He left the day after Violet."

"Because?"

"I have no idea. I mean, it's not like we had a falling out. Sunday morning, we were going to meet and spend the day together. Instead, his mother drove in from Bakersfield and hauled him off. I never heard from him again."

"That's a tough one."

"Yes, it was. He was the love of my life. He was a bad boy, but so adorable. I was crazy about him. He was seventeen—three years older than me. He'd been in trouble—truancy and poor grades—things like that. His parents sent him to Serena Station so he could start fresh. I thought he was doing fine."

"There was no relationship between him and Violet?"

"You mean like he's the one she ran off with?"

"Bad boys can be appealing if you have a reckless streak."

"Ah, I see what you mean, but there's no chance. We spent every waking minute together, and if I wasn't with him I was with her."

"Just a thought."

"It wasn't him. I can guarantee you that."

"You really suffered a double whammy, losing Ty and Violet virtually the same day."

Her smile was fleeting. "Luck of the draw. You play the hand you're dealt. There's no point in dwelling on it afterwards."

15

TOM
Wednesday, July 1, 1953

Tom Padgett sat in the Blue Moon, working on his second beer while he brooded about life. Thinking about it later, he could visualize that sequence of events—narrow slivers of reality lined up like the pickets in a fence. Or maybe not the pickets so much as the spaces between. Over the course of three months, his perception had shifted, and suddenly he realized the world was not as he'd imagined it—fair, equitable, or just. People were grasping and self-centered. People were busy looking out for themselves. That had actually shocked him, discovering that truth, though it was apparently obvious to everyone else. In a remarkably short period of time, he'd gone from hope and optimism to a much bleaker view of human nature until, finally, reluctantly, he'd realized he was among the disenfranchised, which was perhaps where he'd been all along.

The first glimpse he'd had of what was coming his way occurred in a counseling session back in the spring. April

Fool's Day in point of fact, which should have been a clue. He and Cora had been married for three years, knocking heads for the better part of two. They were like two dogs tugging on opposing ends of a towel, going round and round, yanking and jerking, but neither one giving ground. Basically the struggle was about power, and the measure of power was related to control of the funds, of which she had the bulk. He couldn't remember who'd suggested the meeting with the minister at the church where he and Cora attended services. He wasn't a religious man himself, but Cora felt church was important and that was good enough for him. She was, of course, fifty-six years old, closer to her demise than he was at the age of forty-one, so that might have had its effect. Where he'd sworn up and down the age difference between them didn't mean a thing to him, he could see that it was going to be tougher as the years went by. Cora looked every bit of her fifty-six years. Her face, not beautiful to begin with, had suffered a collapse in the course of one year, right after she turned fifty-five. He had no idea why, but it was as if somebody yanked a chain and a curtain of wrinkles descended with a thud. Her neck looked like something that had sat unattended in the dryer for days. Her hair had thinned. She started going to the beauty parlor twice a week to have it fluffed and back-combed into an appearance of volume. The problem was he could see right through the ratting to the scalp beneath. She needed constant reassurances, anything to soothe her insecurities. The one thing that gave her confidence was all the money she had. Tom was coming into his prime, but he hadn't made quite the success of himself that he'd hoped. Part of that was Cora's fault because she had the wherewithal to help, but she refused to lift a finger. Which is what had brought them to the pastor's study. Tom had made a cursory study of the Old and New Testaments, and he was pleased with the many admonitions about a wife's duty to her spouse. She was meant to be his helpmeet, submissive in everything. It said so right there in 1st Peter 3, verses 1 through 12.

That's what he was hoping to get down to.

Here's how it went instead.

The pastor, in a mild and caring tone, had asked him what he saw as the problem.

Tom had his answer all set. "In a nutshell, I see marriage as a partnership of equals, like a team, but that's not what I'm dealing with here. She has no faith in me, and that undercuts any faith I might have in myself. I'm no expert on the Bible, but Scripturewise, that doesn't seem right."

Cora had jumped in, giving the minister her side. "But we're not equals. I brought a fortune into this marriage and he didn't have a dime. I don't understand why I have to sacrifice half of what I have so he'll feel like a whole man."

The minister said, "I understand what you're saying, Cora, but there has to be a little give here."

Cora blinked at the man. "Give?"

The minister turned to him. "Tom?"

"I'm not asking for a nickel of her money. All I want is a little help getting on my feet."

"Why don't you direct your comments to her?"

"Sure. Of course. I'd be happy to. What I can't understand is your attitude. It's not like you earned the money. Loden Galsworthy did that. When you met him, you were clerking in a dry goods store. He was a shrewd businessman. His funeral parlors are a big success, and I admire that about him. Who else would be ghoulish enough to make money off the dead? I'm asking for the chance to show you that I'm just as good or better."

"Why do you insist on seeing yourself in competition with him?"

"I don't. I'm not. How can I compete when the man is dead? Cora, I'm not a taker. That's not my nature. Given half a chance, I can prove it to you. All I need is a stake."

"Loden didn't have money handed to him. He earned it all himself."

"But he was born a man of privilege as you well know. I admit I come from humbler stock. You come from humble stock yourself and that's nothing to be ashamed of. What I don't see is why you'd begrudge me the opportunity."

"What do you call the twenty thousand dollars I loaned you last fall?"

"That wasn't enough to do me any good. I tried telling you at the time. You might as well have made it twenty dollars instead of twenty thousand. You can't start a business without capital outlay, especially one like mine. But look at what I've accomplished. I got myself up and running and I did it on my own. What I'm talking about now is a little boost."

"If your business were up and running, you wouldn't be sitting here trying to browbeat me into giving you more."

Tom looked at the minister. "Browbeating? Is this browbeating when I'm practically down on my hands and knees?"

The minister said, "I think Cora can appreciate your position in this."

Tom said to Cora, "No, wait a minute. Whose idea

was this? Mine. I'm here trying to work things out, try-ing to resolve our differences with precious little help from you."

"You're here because you thought you could use him to pressure me into it. I'm sorry, but I won't give you a cent. It's out of the question."

"I'm not asking you to *give* me the money. We're talking about a loan. We can draw up any kind of papers you like and I'll sign on the dotted line. I don't want charity. I want your trust and respect. Is that too much to ask?"

Cora stared at her hands.

Tom thought she was formulating a reply, but then he realized this *was* her reply. He could feel the heat rise in his face. Her silence said everything. She had no respect for him and she had no trust. What it all boiled down to was she'd married him knowing full well that his financial situation was limited. She'd said it didn't matter, but he could see now that what she wanted was the upper hand. Money was control and she had no intention of surren-dering her advantage. When she'd been married to Loden he'd held the whip and she'd been dependent, jumping through hoops. Now she was doing the same thing to him.

He couldn't remember how the session ended. Cer-tainly not with Cora making a concession of any kind.

They'd been silent walking to the car, silent on the way home. He'd dropped her at the house and headed straight for the Moon. Violet was there that night. She'd perched on the stool next to his and he'd bought her a glass of red wine. She was half in the bag, but then again, so was he by this time. "What has you so down in the dumps?" she'd asked.

"It's Cora. We had a counseling session with the minister and somewhere in the middle, the light finally dawned. The woman doesn't trust me and she has no respect. I don't understand it. She married me for better or for worse. This is worse, where I am, but she won't lend a hand to pull me out of a hole."

"What kind of hole?"

"Money, what else? My business needs a boost. That's all I'm talking about."

Violet had laughed. "She's supposed to give you money? Why should she do that?"

"I'd do it for her. What's marriage about if not sharing fifty-fifty? Doesn't that sound fair?"

"Sure, but in this case, both halves belong to her. What do you have to offer?"

"Business savvy. I'm a businessman."

"You're a horse's ass. You sound just like Foley. He'd love to get his big mitts on my money. It's like the Chinese water torture. Drip, drip, drip."

"You don't see yourselves as a team?"

"Sure. We're made for each other. He's the boxer and I'm the punching bag."

"You wouldn't give him anything? Even if it might make a difference in his life?"

"Of course not. Why should I? He'd piss it away."

"You women are hard. I've never seen anything like it. The Bible says wives should be submissive to their husbands. Didn't you ever hear about that?"

"No."

"Well, neither did my wife. It's not even her money. She got it from that old fart she was married to. Hell, I'd have married the man myself if he'd asked me nice."

Violet's eyebrows went up. "Why? Are you one of them?"

"No, I'm not one of them. I'm just making a point."

"You don't know what women go through to get money."

Tom said, "Well, I can make it easy for you. That money you got? You give it to me and I'll promise you a forty percent return in three months. Guaranteed."

"Bullshit." She took out a cigarette and Tom leaned forward with a light. She blew out a stream of smoke and gave him a speculative look. "I got a question for you. How come you never come on to me? Don't you find me attractive?"

"I do. Of course I do. What kind of question is that?"

"You're a stud. I can tell by looking at you."

Tom laughed, embarrassed. "Well, I appreciate your confidence. I'm not sure Cora would agree."

"I'm serious. How long have we been talking like this? How many times we been in here dancing and clowning around? But you never make a move. What's that all about?"

"I can't believe you'd criticize me when I'm the only guy in town who's not trying to get in your pants. You know why that is? I'll tell you why. I'm more interested in this," he said, tapping his head. "Sure, we could take a tumble in the hay. And then what? You'd move on to someone else. I'd rather be your friend."

"Oh, please."

"You know what grieves me? To see a mind like yours go to waste. You're so busy fending off that psychopath you're married to you don't have the time or energy to do anything else. Why don't you use your brain for a change and get away from the guy."

"I don't know. Foley's kind of sweet in his way."

"That's poppycock and you know it. You can't let

emotion rule you in these things. You gotta be hard-nosed."

"But I'm not."

"Call it practical if you like. Look at me and Cora. There's nothing wrong with her. I admire the woman, but what good is that? The marriage is dead. She knows it as well as I do, but you want to know what happens if I ask for a divorce? I'll be out on my ass. Same thing with you. You can walk away, but all you'll take with you are the clothes on your back."

"That doesn't mean anything. If I could get free, I'd be willing to leave it all behind. Who cares about possessions? Anything I have can be replaced. I got money of my own."

"You just can't get off that, can you?"

"You're the one brought up money."

"Now you sound just like Cora."

"Anyway, what the hell do you have to complain about? You got that big house and those cars. You know what I'd give to have a car like yours?"

"That's what I'm trying to tell you, Violet. Four thousand for a car? That's chump change. You're out there with your head down, hunting for pennies on the ground. You gotta look at the bigger picture."

"You paid four thousand dollars for a car? You can't be serious."

"See, that's what's wrong with you. You think small. You think if you keep a real-tight hold on your money you can keep the dollar bills from flying away. Doesn't work like that. You gotta loosen up. Put your money to work. Okay, so you got what in the bank, twenty?"

Violet jerked her thumb up, indicating more.

"Thirty-five?"

"Fifty," she said.

"That's good. Great, but every day it sits, you're losing money on your money—"

She cut him off. "Nun-hun. I know what you're getting at and it's no deal."

"You have no idea what I'm getting at so would you listen for a change? I'm saying we pool our funds."

"Oh, sure, pool our funds. I bet you'd like that. You know why? Because I got more than you."

"I got money."

"How much?"

He tilted his head, calculating. "I'll be honest with you. I got a lot, but not as much as you. That's what I'm working on right now."

"Super. I'm thrilled on your behalf. I'm still not giving you a dime."

"That's what I like about you. You're stubborn as hell. Tell you what, though, you change your mind, all you have to do is say the word."

"Don't hold your breath."

16

I arrived at the Blue Moon that night in advance of Tannie and Daisy. It was 6:45 and the whole of Serena Station was bathed in golden light. The air smelled of bay laurel, the scent underscored by the faint suggestion of wood smoke. In the absence of a visible autumn, Californians are forced to fabricate, stockpiling wood for the fireplace, hauling heavy sweaters out of the bottom drawer. Many residents live in exile; eastern-seaboard and midwestern transplants who end up on the West Coast in search of good weather. No more ice storms, no 108-degree days, no tornadoes, and no hurricanes. First comes relief at being delivered from bugs, humidity, and climatic extremes. Then the boredom sets in. Soon they're making nostalgic trips home at considerable expense to revisit the very elements they'd sought to escape.

The patron parking lot was full and cars were lined up along the road. I made one circuit of the lot, found a small, probably illegal spot and managed to squeeze in.

As I made my way to the entrance, I glanced back, amused at how conspicuous my VW looked in the midst of all the pickups, camper shells, vans, and RVs.

The exterior of the restaurant was rough-hewn, its weathered board-and-batten façade as squared up and staunch as a saloon on a western movie set. The interior was a continuation of the theme: wagon wheels, oil lamps, and wooden tables covered in red-and-white-checked cloths. Happy hour was under way. Where I'd anticipated the odor of cigarettes and beer, the air was rich with the scent of prime beef being grilled over oak.

Tannie had reserved us a table on the left side of the bar area, which was jammed with people. On the right, through an arch, I could see two or three dining rooms, but my guess was the regulars preferred to eat here, where they could keep an eye out for pals. I was probably one of the few unfamiliar faces they'd seen in a while, judging by the curious looks being turned on me.

The hostess showed me to the table and moments later a waitress approached. She handed me a menu printed on plain white paper. "You want something to drink while you wait for your friends? Wine list is on the back."

I glanced at the list of wines by the glass, bypassing hard liquor in favor of something more familiar. I ordered a glass of Chardonnay and then caught sight of a man, sitting at the bar, whose gaze seemed to be fixed on me. I turned to see if he was staring at someone else, but I seemed to be it. Once the waitress went off to fetch my wine, he eased off the bar stool and headed in my direction. He was tall, with a lean, rangy body, and long arms. His face was narrow, as lined and weathered as a contour map. Broken capillaries in his cheeks made him appear flushed, and exposure to the outdoors had mottled his skin to a nutty brown. His hair, once dark, was now a salt-and-pepper mix.

When he reached the table, he held out his hand. "Jake Ottweiler, Tannie's father. You must be her friend."

"Nice to meet you. I'm Kinsey. How are you?"

"Welcome to the Blue Moon, which most of us refer to as 'The Moon.' I saw you when you came in."

"So did everyone else. You must not get a lot of walk-in trade."

"More than you'd think. Folks from Santa Teresa drive up on a regular basis." His eyes were a piercing blue against the sunburned darkness of his face. Tannie had told me he'd farmed the land for years, but his part-ownership in the Blue Moon had apparently introduced an element of gentility. He'd traded in his work boots and overalls for slacks and a nicely cut navy sport coat over a soft white shirt.

When the waitress reappeared and set down my glass of white wine, he murmured, "I'll take care of that" with scarcely a glance at her. It was clear they'd dealt with each other for so long the need for conversation was reduced to a minimum.

I said, "Will you join me?"

"Briefly. At least until Tannie gets here. I'm sure you girls have lots to talk about." He pulled out a chair and ordered a drink with the lift of one hand. When the waitress had moved off again, he leaned back in his chair and studied me. "You don't look like my idea of a private eye."

"These days, we come in all shapes and sizes."

"How's it going?"

"An investigation like this requires the patience of a saint."

"Seems like a fool's errand, if you want to know the truth."

"No doubt," I said. "Can I ask you a few questions as long as I have you here?"

"Be my guest. I don't know that I can help, but I'll tell you what I can."

"How well did you know Violet?"

"Well enough, I guess. I used to see her in here two and three times a week. She was a troubled soul, but not a bad person by any means."

"I heard she took you to small-claims court because of an incident in which your dog killed hers."

"That was bad. I felt sorry for her, but I had my dog under control. Hers was running loose, so she was as much at fault as I was. In the end, I had to put my dog down, but it had nothing to do with her. Anyway, we settled it. I could have argued the point, but to what end? Her toy poodle was dead and she was brokenhearted until she got Baby."

"Were you at the park for the fireworks the night she disappeared?"

"I was. Tannie was supposed to go with her brother, but he took off with his friends so the two of us went."

"Did you see Foley?"

"No, but I know he and Livia Cramer got into it. She didn't approve of the Sullivans. She thought they were heathens, which was none of her concern, but the woman never could leave well enough alone. She got on him about Daisy. The little girl had never been baptized and Livia thought it was disgraceful. Foley was drunk by then and told her exactly what she could go and do with herself. Livia made sure everyone in town heard what he'd said. In her mind, it was one more example of what a lowlife he was."

"You didn't see Violet?"

He shook his head. "Last time I saw Violet was the day before. She was driving around town in that new car of hers and she stopped to have a chat."

"You remember the subject?"

"Mostly she was showing off. She'd come back from taking Daisy and Liza Mellincamp to lunch and a movie in Santa Maria. She had errands to run, so she'd dropped the girls at the house while she was out and about."

"You've got a good memory."

He smiled. "I'd like to take credit, but the subject comes up every other year—some journalist in town. I've told the story so often, I could do it in my sleep."

"I'll bet. When you talked to Violet, she seemed okay to you?"

"As much as she ever did. She had her ups and downs, what I believe they call bipolar these days."

"Really. That's new. No one's mentioned mood swings."

"That was my observation. I'm not up on these things so it's only a guess on my part. She did a lot of crying in her beer, so to speak."

"Daisy remembers her parents getting into a big fight the night before. This would have been Thursday night. She says Foley tore down a panel of her mother's curtains. Violet blew her stack, tore down the rest of them and threw 'em in the trash. Did you hear about that?"

He shook his head slightly. "Sounds like something she'd do. Why bring that up?"

"I've heard that's why Foley ended up buying her the car, to make amends."

"Must not have done much good if she left anyway," he said. "Fellow you want to talk to is my partner, BW, who tended bar back then. Unfortunately, he's not in tonight or I'd introduce you."

"Daisy suggested his name, too. Could you let him know I'm trying to get in touch?"

"How about I tell you where he'll be at seven in the morning and you can talk to him yourself? Maxi's Coffee Shop. It's right on the road between Silas and Serena Station. He's there every morning for an hour or so."

I could feel my eyes cross at the notion of an early morning drive. I'd have to leave S.T. at dawn. "I'd hate to pop in unannounced. He might not like being quizzed while he's enjoying his morning coffee and eating his eggs."

"BW won't care. He's an easygoing guy and he loves to hold court."

"How would I recognize him?"

"Easy. He weighs three hundred pounds and his head is shaved."

He glanced at the entrance behind me, and I turned to see Daisy and Tannie coming in the door. They spotted us and crossed to the table with Tannie leading the way. She was sunburned from a day spent outside battling the brush, but she'd managed in the interim to shower and change clothes. Her jeans were freshly pressed and her white blouse was crisp, her hair still damp and tucked under a baseball cap. Daisy wore a red cotton cardigan over a red-and-white-print dress. She'd pulled her blond hair back, clamping it in place with a red plastic clip.

Jake rose as they approached. Tannie gave her dad a buss on the cheek. "Hey, Pop. I see you've met Kinsey," she said, and then slipped into the chair beside mine.

He pulled out a chair for Daisy. "How're you doing, Daisy? You're looking good."

"Thanks. I'm fine. Place smells divine."

"I got an eight-ounce filet with your name on it."

Tannie lowered her gaze, but the comment she made was directed to me. "Don't look now, but Chet Cramer just walked in with Caroleena, the Violet Sullivan clone."

Of course, I looked straight up, catching Chet Cramer's eye. His smile was friendly, but I noticed he promptly steered his wife toward another part of the bar. From the glimpse I had, she looked too old to be dying her hair such a harsh shade of red. Her pale complexion was more the result of makeup than the delicate Irish coloring she hoped to simulate. Tight dress, big boobs, getting thick in the waist.

"Does she really look like Violet?"

"Oh, hardly," Daisy scoffed. "That woman's a cow. My mother was a natural beauty. Poor Kathy Cramer. I'd be mortified if my father connected up with someone like that."

The dinner crowd was picking up, so Jake excused himself to tend to business while the three of us settled in with our drinks and a serious contemplation of the menu. We all ordered the filet mignon, medium rare, with a salad up front and a side of baked potato. We were finishing the meal when the subject of Kathy Cramer surfaced again. Having been granted immunity from any accusation of gossiping, I naturally passed along the news about the collapse of the Cramer-Smith marriage.

"Well, good for him. She is *such* a bitch. I'm happy to hear he's finally busting out," Tannie said.

Daisy said, "I'm with you. About time he got a back-bone."

"I'm not sure you can call it 'busting out' when she's giving him the boot," I said.

Tannie made a pained face. "But he used to be so *cute*. And really, the name Winston. Could you just die?" she said. "I do think someone should tell him to drop the weight. Even twenty pounds would make a difference. He goes back on the market, I know half a dozen women who'd snap him up."

"Including me," Daisy said, offended that Tannie would offer him up without consulting her.

"Oh, right. Just what you need, another guy with an ax to grind. Wait till Kathy hits him up for alimony and child support. He'll never get out from under."

"I don't know about that."

"What choice does he have?" Tannie asked. "They've been married close to thirty years. She had a crush on him since eighth grade. Remember that? No, you wouldn't. You were still in elementary school. But I'm telling you, even when I was ten, I'd see her moping around town. So pathetic. She'd find ways to bump into him and she'd be going, 'Oh gee, Winston, I had no idea you'd be here.' She'd sit behind him in church and stare at him like she could eat him alive. The guy never had a chance."

I said, "I saw the wedding photo he keeps in his office. He was very trim."

Tannie said, "True. And she was big as a tank."

"How'd she lose the weight?"

"How do you think? She's popping pills like after-dinner mints."

"You're kidding."

"No, I'm not. Black-market speed. She's got a source, from what I heard."

"Now that I think about it, she did seem amped," I said.

The busboy removed our plates and the waitress showed up again to offer us dessert, which all three of us declined.

I watched as a man leaving the bar did a detour toward our table. From across the room, I placed him in his midforties, but by the time he'd reached us, I'd added thirty years. His wavy hair was dark, but the color was a shade I imagined Grecian Formula would produce. His eyes were blue behind heavy black-frame glasses that had hearing aids built into the stems. He was roughly my height, five-six, but the heels on his boots gave him another couple of inches. He wore jeans, a red plaid shirt with a string tie, over which he'd buttoned a powder blue western-cut sport coat, nipped in at the waist.

He greeted Daisy and Tannie with familiarity, taking each by the hand. When all the air-kissing was over, Tannie introduced us. "This is Kinsey Millhone. Tom Padgett. He owns Padgett Construction and the A-Okay Heavy Equipment yard in Santa Maria. Daisy bought her old house from him."

"Nice meeting you," I said.

We made polite noises at each other and then he and Tannie chatted while Daisy excused herself.

Tannie gestured toward the empty chair. "Join us for a drink."

"I don't want to barge in."

"Don't be silly. I've been meaning to call you anyway to pick your brain."

"What's left of it," he said.

He treated us to a round of after-dinner drinks, and the conversation moved from the general to the specific, that being the Tanner house and the debate about rehabilitation. Padgett's expression was pained. "House

hasn't been lived in since 1948. You forget I did a lot of
work for Hairl Tanner, and he showed me around.
Plumbing and wiring were both a mess even back then.
Recent fire aside, the house looks good from the outside,
but once you go in, you got a real disaster on your hands.
Hell, I don't have to tell you. You know what I'm talking
about."

"Yeah, I know."

"Let a house like that sit empty and first the raccoons
move in. Then the termites, then the bums. It was grand
once upon a time, but try bringing it back and you'll go
broke. You're looking at well over a million bucks."

"So I take it you're opposed," she said, and then
laughed. "I know it's bad, but that's a piece of my child-
hood. I can't see knocking it down. Besides, we do make
some money from the property, between the oil and gas
leases."

"Well, you asked and I'm giving you my opinion. You
know the rumors about rezoning. You want to save the
house, you're better off selling to developers and letting
them do the work. They could turn it into offices or a
party center in the middle of a housing tract."

"Steve's point exactly. Don't tell me you're in league
with him."

"I got no stake in the matter one way or the other.
You ought to get a contractor out there and have him
take a look."

"Why not you?"

"You already know what I think. You need to hear it
from someone else. You'll be happier that way. I'd be
willing to meet with anyone you want and throw in my
two cents."

"You'd poison the well."

"I wouldn't open my mouth until you heard what he had to say."

"Who do you recommend?"

"Billy Boynton or Dade Ray. Both are good men."

"I guess I better do that. I know I'm only postponing the inevitable. I keep thinking, one step at a time, but who am I trying to kid? It's like having to put a dog down. You know the mutt's too sick to go on, but it's just that you don't want to do it *today*."

"I understand. You have to do it in your own time."

"Enough said. I got it and I appreciate your input."

"Anytime," he said. His attention shifted to me. "Pardon my bad manners. Jake was just telling me about you. You've got quite a job on your hands."

"Well, it's a challenge at any rate. At first the idea seemed absurd, but now I'm enjoying myself. Me against Violet. It's like playing hide-and-seek."

"So what's your theory?"

"I don't have a theory. Right now I'm talking to anyone and everyone, filling in the blanks. The questions don't change, but sometimes I get an answer I don't expect. One of these days, I'm going to pick up a thread and then I'll see where it goes. From what I've heard about Violet, she might have been devious, but she wasn't good at keeping secrets. Somebody knows where she is."

"You really think so?"

"I do. Either the guy she ran off with or the guy who did her in. It's really just a matter of tracking him down."

He shook his head, his tone skeptical. "I have to hand it to you, you're an optimist."

"That's what keeps me on my toes. What about you? Where do you weigh in on the debate?"

"What, whether she's dead or alive? Personally, I think she ran off and I said it from the get-go. I spent more than one night listening to Violet bitch. I promise, it was only a matter of time before she found a way out."

"But where would she have gone; have you ever asked yourself?"

"Sure, I've thought about that. She was young and in her own way she was innocent. A small-town kind of girl. She had experience with men, but she didn't know anything about the world at large. I can't picture her in a big town like San Francisco or L.A. I can't even picture her in the state. California's as expensive now as it was back then, relative to income. Given the cash she had—which probably didn't amount to much—I'm guessing she'd go someplace she could afford. Midwest, the South— someplace like that."

"You heard about her money?"

"Half a dozen times. She'd get on a tear and threaten to pull out if Foley didn't straighten up and fly right."

"Like that was ever going to happen," Tannie put in.

The subject shifted. There were only so many ideas you could bounce around with so little information. At 10:30, Padgett made his excuses and headed for the door.

Daisy, meanwhile, was feeling no pain. She'd had enough to drink that some merrier, more loquacious personality had taken over her ordinary self. She was flirting with some guy, laughing too loudly. From a distance, she appeared to be having fun. Up close, I was betting, she was out of control. It was the first indication I'd seen of the trouble she was capable of getting into. Tannie followed my gaze, and the two of us locked eyes briefly. "Once she reaches this point, it's all over," Tannie said. "He'll cnd up in her bed and things will go down-hill from there."

"We can't intervene?"

"This time, sure, but she'll be in here again tomorrow night and the night after that. You want to take on that kind of responsibility? Because I sure don't. After this round, at any rate. Tannie to the rescue. What an idiot. Wish me luck."

She left the table and joined Daisy, who was dancing with her cowboy. She took some persuading, but she did return to the table without her new best friend. By the time we were ready to part company, it was 11:00 and I'd had one too many glasses of wine. I was fine for the short haul, but I didn't like the idea of driving all the way home. "You know what, guys? It's not such a hot idea my being on the road. Is there a motel around here, or maybe a B-and-B?"

17

The Sun Bonnet Motel was stuck out in the middle of nowhere, a one-story stucco building that was plain, shabby at the seams, but allegedly clean. My room was the kind you'd be wise to avoid examining with a black light after dark because the stains illuminated—bedding, carpeting, furniture, and walls—would suggest activities you wouldn't want to know about. It was a family business, Mr. and Mrs. Bonnet having owned the place for the past forty years. Its single virtue was that Mrs. Bonnet—Maxi—owned and ran Maxi's Coffee Shop, which was attached to one end. Oh happy day. In the morning, I could intercept BW within a hundred yards of my bed.

Daisy had been apologetic that she couldn't put me up at her house, but that's where Tannie was staying, and she had only the one spare room.

"Sorry 'bout that, but I got dibs," Tannie injected, clearly pleased with herself.

"You could sleep on my couch," Daisy said.

"Oh no, not me. I'm too old for that stuff. Maybe some other time."

After I checked in, I left the registration desk and returned to my car. Mrs. Bonnet had put me in 109, which was down at the end of the line, the second to last of ten rooms. All the other rooms were dark, but there was a car parked on each side of the slot for 109. I left my car in front of my door, only slightly worried by the sight of the drapery sagging off the hooks. I unlocked the door, went in, and flipped on the light. The room was small, the color scheme leaning toward cantaloupe and peach. A double bed was centered on the wall to my right. The pillows looked flat, and there was a trough down the middle of the mattress where my body would just fit, thus saving me needless tossing and turning. The bed tables and the chest of drawers were paint-grade wood with a wood-laminate veneer. The easy chair didn't look that easy, but I didn't plan to sit.

I went into the bathroom, floor squeaking as I walked, and pulled my toothbrush, toothpaste, and a change of underpants from my shoulder bag, where I keep them for such occasions. My only serious lament was that I hadn't brought a book, but I'd expected to drive up and back without any opportunity to read. I checked all the drawers, but there wasn't so much as a Gideon's Bible or a stray paperback. I stripped off my jeans and brassiere, and slept in the very T-shirt I'd worn all day. During the night, I could hear—like the sound of a train passing—thunder in the walls as the guests in rooms on both sides of mine flushed their toilets at random intervals. My bedspread smelled musty, and I was happy I didn't see the article about dust mites until the following week.

At 6:00 A.M. my eyes popped open. For a moment I couldn't think where I was, and when it finally occurred to me, I was annoyed with myself for waking up so early. I had neither sweats nor running shoes, which meant a morning run was out of the question. I closed my eyes to no avail. At 6:15 I threw the covers back, went into the bathroom, brushed my teeth, and showered, as those were the only options open to me. I put on my clothes again and sat on the edge of the unmade bed. I didn't want to walk over to Maxi's Coffee Shop until 7:00, when I was hoping to meet BW.

I got out my index cards and reviewed my notes, which were beginning to bore me senseless. None of the items were monumental. I'd been asking the same six to eight questions for two days, and while nothing revolutionary had come to light, I had to admit I was better informed. I started working on the timeline for the days leading up to Violet's disappearance. The story I kept coming back to was Winston's account of spotting the Bel Air on New Cut Road at the point where construction ended. What had she been doing out there? I thought his guess had merit, that the site was the rendezvous point of Violet and someone else—male, female, lover, friend, family member, or passing acquaintance, I knew not which. The landscape out there was flat, and Winston's headlights would have been visible for at least a mile. She'd had time enough to move the car, but there was no place to hide it unless she'd driven it to the far side of the Tanner house or across the open fields. A better bet was to conceal herself (alone or with her theoretical companion) in hopes that the approaching driver would turn around and go back without stopping to investigate. If she'd had car trouble and needed help, why not step out of the shadows and flag him down? And what of Baby, the yapping Pomeranian pup? This was not a Sherlockian situation where silence suggested familiarity between the dog and someone else. The dog barked at everyone, at least according to reports. It was still a puzzlement why Violet had chosen the place, but that was an issue I'd have to table for the time being.

At 6:58 I packed my toiletries in my shoulder bag and emerged from my room. The motel parking lot was now packed with cars. I left mine where it was and walked to the coffee shop, which was located in front. The moment I stepped inside, I was assaulted by the noise: conversations, music from the jukebox, laughter, the clattering of china. It was like a party in progress, and the air of comradery suggested the gathering was a daily occurrence. Farmhands, construction workers, oil workers, gang bosses, husbands, wives, infants, and school-age kids— anybody who was out and about apparently made the trek from neighboring towns to have breakfast here. I could smell bacon, sausage, fried ham, and maple syrup.

I was fortunate to capture the one remaining stool at the counter. Specials were posted on a blackboard above the pass-through that opened into the kitchen. The menu was standard: eggs, breakfast meats, toast, muffins, biscuits and gravy, waffles, pancakes, and the usual assortment of teas, coffees, and juices. Two waitresses were working the counter, with another four busy serving the booths and tables that filled the room. I told Darva, the waitress who took my order, that I was looking for BW. I'd scanned the place myself and hadn't seen anyone remotely fitting his description, but it was always possible

I'd missed him in the crush. She did a visual survey, as I had, and shook her head. "Wonder what's keeping him. He's usually here by now. I'll point him out to you the minute he comes in."

"Thanks."

She filled my coffee cup, set the cream pitcher within range, and moved down the line, offering refills and warm-ups before she put in my order. My breakfast arrived and I focused my attention on my orange juice, rye toast, crisp bacon, and scrambled eggs. This was my favorite meal, and I wasted no time putting it away. Darva slipped my check under my plate, and when she topped off my coffee cup she said, "That's him."

I looked over my shoulder at the fellow standing in the door. He was as Jake Ottweiler had described him, though I'd have put him at a good twenty-five pounds over the three hundred Jake had mentioned. His head was shaved, but a nap of white stubble had grown in again. His brows were dark and his features appeared diminished by all the weight he carried. His neck was thick, and I could see a roll of fat along his collar line in back. He wore jeans and a golf shirt. I watched him make his way across the room, pausing to chat with half the people he passed. Two men vacated a booth and he slid into it, undismayed by the dirty dishes they'd left behind. I waited until the busboy had cleared the table, giving him additional time to order before I paid my check and crossed the room.

"Hi. Are you BW?"

"I am." He half-rose from his seat and held out his hand, which I shook. "You're Kinsey. Jake called me last night and told me you'd be in. Have you had breakfast yet?"

"I just finished."

He sat down again. "In that case, you can join me for a cup of coffee. Slide in."

I eased into the booth across from him. "Congratulations on the Moon. It's a great restaurant, and what a crowd."

"Weekends are even busier. Of course, we're the only game in town so that doesn't hurt. First thing we did when we took possession was we bought a liquor license. We remodeled and expanded in the late fifties and then again about five years back. Before that the Moon was just a hole in the wall—beer and wine with a few prepackaged snacks, pretzels, potato chips, things like that. The clientele was mostly locals. We might get someone in from Orcutt or Cromwell, sometimes a few from Santa Maria, but that was about it. You enjoy your dinner?"

"I did. The steak was fabulous."

The waitress appeared with a coffeepot and mugs. She and BW got into a minor conversation while she poured coffee. "Your order's coming right up," she said, and moved away.

He smiled. "I'm a creature of habit. Eat the same thing every day. Same time, same place." He added cream to his coffee and then picked up three packets of sweetener and flapped them briefly before he tore off the tops. I watched five seconds' worth of chemicals disappear into his cup. "So you're making the rounds, asking about Violet. Must be frustrating."

"Monotonous is more like it. People are trying to be helpful, but information is scarce and the story tends to be the same. Violet had a trashy reputation and Foley beat her. Try to make something out of that."

"I don't have much to add. I saw the two of them

three and four nights a week, sometimes together, sometimes one or the other alone, but usually half in the bag."

"So if Violet picked up a stranger, you'd have known about it?"

"You bet, and so would everyone else. People frequented the Moon because they knew the place. We were too small and too far out of the way to attract tourists or traveling salesmen."

"Did you work every night?"

"I'd take a day off now and then, but I was pretty much the man in charge. The guy who spelled me, if I was sick or out of town, died a long time ago. Who else have you talked to?"

I rattled off the list of names and watched him nod in agreement.

"Sounds right. None of them could help?"

"That remains to be seen. I'm collecting bits and pieces, but I have no idea if anything I've picked up is relevant. Do you remember your reaction when you heard she was gone?"

"I wasn't surprised. I can tell you that."

"Were you suspicious of anyone?"

"Besides Foley? No."

"You don't know of anyone she might have run off with?"

He shook his head.

"Sergeant Schaefer tells me the locals were all present and accounted for. He says the rumors about Violet having a lover were all traceable to Foley, so if he did something to her, he'd provided himself a smoke screen."

The waitress reappeared with his breakfast: waffles, fried eggs, link sausage, a side of hash browns, and a second side, of grits with a pat of melting butter.

"Makes a certain amount of sense, assuming Foley's smart enough, which I tend to doubt."

"At the time, did you think he might have killed her?"

"It crossed my mind. I know he decked her on more than one occasion, but it was usually behind closed doors. None of us would tolerate his abusing her in public."

"People tell me the two of them got into wrangles all the time at the Moon."

"Only for as long as it took me to get out from behind the bar with my baseball bat. I'd have been happy to clobber Foley if he put up resistance. He was usually cooperative if I made matters plain."

"Was she abusive as well?"

"She went after him sometimes, but she was such a tiny thing she couldn't do much harm. They'd get into it like two dogs, snarling and snapping. I'd go out there and separate them, put her on one side of the room and him on the other."

"Did you ever hear her talk about leaving him?"

"Now and then," he replied. "You know, she'd be crying and complaining, feeling sorry for herself. But it's like I told her, I'm a bartender, not a damn marriage counselor. I did what I could, but it didn't amount to much. Problem was, they were so used to brawling that as soon as it was over, they went about their business like nothing had gone on. Next thing you know they'd be at it again. I'd have thrown 'em both out for good, but I felt as long as they were in the Moon, at least I could keep an eye on them and intervene if necessary."

"Did they fight about the same thing or was it different every time?"

"Usually the same. She'd be flirting with some guy and Foley would take offense."

"Who, though?"

"Who'd she flirt with? Any guy in range."

"What about Jake Ottweiler?"

"I'll correct myself. Not him. The man was married and his wife was on her deathbed."

"Sorry. I didn't think Violet made many subtle moral distinctions."

"She didn't. I saw her throw herself at Tom Padgett and he was married. There was also a fellow who ran a little plumbing concern. Violet was all over him one night. Must have scared the hell out of him because he never came back."

"Did she ever flirt with you?"

"Sure, if I was the last guy left in the bar."

"I guess there's no point in asking if you succumbed to her charms."

"I wasn't tempted. Maybe I saw too much and the idea lost its appeal. I liked her, but not that way. She was too messed up, but it wasn't anything I could change. She was what she was, her and Foley both. Tell you one thing about him: he hasn't stepped a foot in the Moon since the day she disappeared."

"At what point did you buy the place?"

"Fall of 1953. Before that it was owned by a couple of guys from Santa Maria. I was the one who managed everything—kept the books, did the ordering, saw the bathrooms were clean."

"How'd you end up buying it?"

"After Mary Hairl died that August, Jake was at loose ends. He'd had a series of jobs, but none he'd been happy with. He figured it was time for a change, so when he heard the Moon was for sale, he asked if I'd go into part-nership with him in buying the place. I had a couple thousand dollars in the bank so I tossed that in the pot. I had years of experience, and he knew he could trust me not to skim the till."

"It's been a good deal for both of you?"

"The best."

"Sorry to keep harping on this point, but do you have any idea who Violet might have been involved with? I'm really at a loss."

"I probably already said more than I should. Business I'm in, I don't look, I don't ask, and I don't want to know. Anything I do know, I don't repeat."

"Even thirty-four years later?"

"Especially thirty-four years later. What purpose would it serve?"

"None, I suppose."

"Mind if I offer you a word of advice?"

"Why not? I may not take it, but I'm always willing to listen."

"Something to keep in mind: This is a small community. We look after each other. Somebody like you comes scratching around, nosing in our business, that doesn't sit well."

"No one's objected so far."

"Not to your face. We're too polite for that, but I've heard grumbles."

"Of what sort?"

"Understand, this is not coming from me. I'm repeating what I heard."

"I won't hold you accountable. What's the rest of it?"

"If Violet hasn't been found so far, what makes you think you're going to get anywhere? Seems nervy to some."

"It takes a certain amount of nerve to do anything in

life," I said. "This is a fishing expedition. I may not get a bite and in that case, I'm gone."

"You think if one of us knew where she was, we'd tell you after all these years?"

"I guess that would depend on why she left and how protective you felt. Liza Mellincamp believes she's out there somewhere. She claims she doesn't know where, but she sure doesn't want to be responsible for Violet being exposed."

"Suppose it's true," he said. "Suppose she left town like a lot of people think. Suppose she's made herself a whole new life? Why track her down? Believe me, she's suffered enough. If she managed to escape, then more power to her."

"Daisy hired me to do this. If people have a problem, tell 'em they should take it up with her. My personal opinion? She's entitled to any information I can find."

"Assuming you come up with anything."

"Right, but you know what? The years work on all of us. Secrets are a burden. If someone's teetering on the brink, all it takes is a nudge, which is one of my jobs."

He pushed his plate back and took out a pack of cigarettes. I watched him light up, extinguishing the match with a puff of smoke. He kept his cigarette in one corner of his mouth, squinting against the smoke as he leaned to his left and extracted a money clip from his pants pocket. He peeled off a ten and put it by his plate. "Well, I wish you luck. Meantime, I got business to take care of."

"One more quick question: You think she's dead or alive?"

"I really wouldn't care to say. Happy travels."

"Thanks."

As soon as he was out the door, I took out my index

cards and scribbled down as much of the conversation as I could capture off the top of my head. I glanced at my watch. 7:45. With luck, I could get a call through to Daisy and catch her before she went to work. I grabbed my shoulder bag and moved through the dwindling crowd.

I walked back to my room, intending to do a final quick walk-through before I checked out. I slowed as I approached. My door was ajar. I stopped in my tracks. Maybe the motel maid was in there cleaning the room. I moved forward with caution and used the tip of my finger to push the door open to the full. I did a slow visual survey and then stepped inside. Everything was just as I'd left it, at least to all appearances. I had no luggage, so if someone had broken in, there was nothing to search. The bed was still rumpled, covers thrown aside. In the bathroom, my damp towel was where I'd placed it earlier, over the rim of the tub.

I paused in the doorway between the two rooms and let my eyes do the traveling. Object to object, surface to surface. Nothing seemed to be disturbed. Still, I knew I'd locked the door securely because I'd tested the knob right after I'd pulled it shut. I walked to the front office, my room key in hand. The parking lot was now only half as full, but I didn't spy anyone who seemed to take an interest in me.

Mrs. Bonnet was at the desk. I told her I was checking out, and while I waited for my credit card receipt, I said, "Did anyone come in this morning asking for me?"

"No ma'am. We don't give out information about the paying guests. Were you expecting someone?"

"No. When I got back from breakfast, my door was standing open and I was curious."

She shook her head, shrugging, unable to enlighten me.

I signed the slip. She handed me the carbon and I put it in my bag. I walked back to my car, which was parked in the slot outside my room. I unlocked the door and slid under the wheel, tossing my shoulder bag on the passenger seat. I turned the key in the ignition, wondering for one fleeting paranoid moment if I was about to be blown sky-high. Happily, I was not. I backed out and then shifted from reverse into first. The car seemed to waddle when I accelerated. Even with my limited knowledge of mechanical problems, this was not a good sign. I drove forward another couple of yards, thinking I'd run over an object and I was inadvertently dragging it behind. The waddle was still there. Puzzled, I put my foot on the brake and opened the door, leaning to my left. I shut the engine down and got out.

All four of my tires had been slashed.

18

CHET
Friday, July 3, 1953

Chet Cramer sat in his four-door Bel Air sedan, smoking a cigarette, a pleasure he relegated to the end of his day. The windows were cranked open, including the two wing windows, which he'd angled in hopes of capturing fresh air. He loved this car. The Bel Air series was top of the line, with four models: the two-door sport coupe, the two-door convertible, and the two-door and four-door sedans. All had automatic transmission, radio, and heater as standard equipment. His was two-toned; the top Woodland Green, the lower portion Sun Gold, a combination he'd personally selected for himself. The colors reminded him of the green and gold of the old Lucky Strike cigarette pack. When World War II came along, the government had needed the titanium used in the green ink and the bronze used in its gold, so Lucky Strike had abandoned the color scheme in favor of a white pack with a red bull's-eye. When he first started smoking, he'd been attracted to Lucky Strike because of the slogan—Be Happy, Go Lucky—which seemed ironic in retrospect. He hadn't been happy-go-lucky since the death of his father in 1925. Recently he'd switched brands, thinking to disassociate himself altogether from the notions of happiness and luck. The new Kent cigarette, with its Micronite filter, was billed as "the greatest health protection in cigarette history." He wasn't sure why he was concerned about protecting his health, but he didn't think it hurt to cut down on tar and nicotine.

He popped open the glove compartment and took out the sterling silver flask he'd inherited from his dad. He kept it filled with vodka from his office supply, and he used it to fortify himself before he went home each day. He preferred rye whiskey but couldn't afford to greet Livia smelling like a loaf of delicatessen bread. He unscrewed the lid and took a slug. He felt the heat of the liquor going down, but it didn't dissolve the ache in his chest. He checked the clock on the dashboard. 5:22. By 6:15 he'd be having dinner with his wife and daughter, after which he thought he might as well go back to work. He'd taken advantage of the July 4th weekend to advertise a "Firecracker of a Sale." During special promotions of this sort he devoted long hours to the dealership as a matter of course, and now that he'd fired Winston, he'd have to shoulder the kid's load, such as it was. He saw work as a blessing, a way of immersing himself in the here and now. At the moment, he was only going through the motions, knowing it was easier to stick to his routines than to try to make sense out of what had happened to him.

He'd parked facing south on New Cut Road, halfway between Highway 166 and the point at which the road construction ended. The Tanner house was dead-center in his line of vision. To his immediate left was a gravel road leading back to the old Aldrich packing plant. The swing-arm gate across the entrance was padlocked and had been for years, so the spot was the perfect place to unwind. The midsummer air was humid. In his rearview mirror, he could see a breeze undulating across the fields, ruffling the dark green leaves of the sugar beets. A tractor trundled by hauling a bulldozer on a low-boy flatbed, the only traffic he'd seen for the past hour. While he watched, the driver did a clumsy K-turn and positioned his rig in preparation for unloading. Chet took another slug of vodka, dwelling on the trivial while he tried to assimilate the grand.

Wednesday seemed like a lifetime ago, though it was only two days. He hadn't known how depressed he was until Violet cracked through his life like a lightning bolt. She'd been dazzling, and for the first time in his life he'd been engulfed by desire. He felt like she'd doused him with gasoline and set him afire. The minute she'd proposed a drink, he'd seen where she was headed. Dazed, he'd followed her out to his car, tossing an explanation to Kathy as he left. He couldn't remember now what he'd said to her, some lame excuse she'd accepted with a shrug. For once, he'd been grateful his daughter was such a dunce. Despite her moony crushes on movie stars, she was sexually backward, too naive to recognize the chemistry that had flashed so suddenly between Violet and him.

After leaving the dealership, Violet abandoned all talk of his buying her a drink. They got in his car and she directed him to the Sandman Motel, which was two blocks away. He hadn't noticed it before, but Violet was clearly well acquainted with the place. She'd instructed him to check in as a single, under an assumed name. She waited outside while he registered as William Durant, which was actually the name of the man who founded General Motors back in 1908. He was afraid the desk clerk would catch the joke, but she didn't bat an eye. Having deceived her to that extent, he invented a fictitious home address and a detailed explanation of why he needed a room. He was more imaginative than he'd thought. He went on lying through his teeth, flirting with the girl until she blushed a becoming pink. He paid for the room, took the key, and returned to his car.

Violet was gone, but he spotted her at the far end of the parking lot, leaning against the wire fence that surrounded the swimming pool. She waited until he'd parked outside the room, and then she stepped on her cigarette and ambled in his direction, taking her sweet time. She must have known what a picture she made—sunlight shining on her red hair, her figure fully defined by the tight purple sundress. He was trembling at the prospect of having her.

When she reached him, she held out her hand. He dropped the key in her palm and watched as she unlocked the door. He followed her in, marveling at his calm. He had no idea what she expected of him. She set the key on the bed table and turned to him. "I bought you a bottle of vodka, but then forgot the damn thing and left it at home. Sorry 'bout that. I thought you might need a couple of belts to soothe your nerves."

"You planned this?"

"Sweetie, do I look like an idiot? I've seen you watching me. You think I don't know what's been going through your head?"

"Our paths hardly cross."

"No fault of mine. If you weren't so straightlaced, I'd have done this ages ago. I got tired of waiting for you to make a move. So here we are—surprise, surprise."

"But why?"

She laughed. "Don't underestimate yourself. You're a good-looking guy and you're sexy as hell. I'll tell you something else. You've been working too hard. I can see it in your face. When's the last time you cut loose and had *fun*, for god's sake?"

"I'm . . . I don't know what to say."

"Who asked you to talk? Did I say anything about chatting, Chet?" She was making a little joke of his name, but he found he didn't mind. She sat down on the bed, patting the place beside her. "Look at you. All tense. Come over here and I'll help you relax."

He crossed to the bed, moving as though drugged. When he reached her, she rubbed the palm of one hand against the front of his pants. "My, oh my. This is going to be good."

She'd been gentle and sweet, guiding him through a process so highly charged and novel he felt his heart would stop. Nothing with Livia had ever prepared him for such heat. Violet thought his shyness was a riot after all the bullshit he'd laid on her earlier. She'd said, "Big tough guy" in a way that made him laugh. How could she mock him and make him feel good at the same time?

Later, under her patient tutelage, she'd murmured. "Right there, Sweetie. Oh, that's nice. Keep doing that."

She seemed to enjoy bossing him around, inflicting occasional tiny jolts of pain that sent his pleasure soaring into the stratosphere. She liked being in charge, liked making him groan at certain little tricks she had. They made love for an hour, and at the end of it she pulled away from him, laughing and out of breath. "That's it for you, Stud."

"What's wrong?"

"Nothing's wrong. I gotta scoot, that's all. Daisy's parked with a neighbor and I can't be late picking her up. Foley's a psycho when it comes to how I spend my days. Plus, my neighbor's a bitch and I wouldn't put it past her to mention it to him. How're you doing?"

He laughed. "Fine. I can't move."

"Good. I'm glad. Shows I treated you right."

He remained stretched out naked on the bed as she pulled on her underwear and slipped her dress over her head. She crossed to him and sat down on the edge, holding her hair off her neck so he could run the zipper up the back of her dress. Once her dress was zipped, she continued to sit with her back turned to him. "I know people think I'm cheap, but this is not about that. What happened this afternoon is just between us, something both of us want. I know I could have gone about it some other way, but you wouldn't have agreed. You'd have been worried about Livia, worried about Foley, worried we'd get caught. I don't want you to think badly of me. I knew if I didn't push, we'd never get here."

She turned to look at him and he could have sworn she was on the verge of tears. He reached up and touched her face. She laughed self-consciously, dashing moisture from her cheeks. She pulled the sheet over him. "Gotta cover you up or next thing you know you'll get me going again."

He started to rise, but she put a hand on his chest. "No, no. You stay there. I like your hair all tussled and standing up on end. It looks cute. You ought to wear it like that all the time."

"Don't leave."

"I have to."

"Give me ten minutes more. An hour. Better yet, let's just stay here together for the rest of our lives."

She thought about it briefly. "Thirty seconds, but that's it." She sat down again. She took out a cigarette and lit it, passing it to him. "You're full of surprises, you know that?"

He touched her bare arm, marveling at the silky feel of her skin. "You're beautiful."

"I feel beautiful with you."

"When can I see you again?"

"That's not such a hot idea. You know it's dangerous."

"I like risk. I never knew that about myself until you came along."

"That's enough out of you, Stud. I'm out of here."

She kissed her index finger and pressed it to his lips. She put on her sandals and got up, tucking her purse under her arm. "How about tomorrow at noon? I'll have less than an hour, but that's the best I can do."

"Don't you want me to drive you to your truck?"

"I can walk. It's not far and it's better this way."

She left, closing the door behind her. He could hear her footsteps fading on the pavement. He wasn't sure how he'd survive the hours until he saw her again.

When he arrived home late in the day—after his usual meditation out on New Cut Road—he thought he'd be weighted with guilt, but just the opposite was true. He was happy. Something akin to affection resurfaced, and he sat at the dinner table glowing with goodwill. Livia had made jellied salmon for supper, possibly the most disgusting thing he'd ever eaten except for her chicken livers. Nonetheless, he found himself watching her with a kindness rare for him of late. Where had that gone? He thought of himself as a good man, but he realized that as far back as he could remember, he'd been angry and cheerless. Now that had been erased. Even Kathy didn't seem as tedious. He was secretly amused, knowing she'd never dream what her old dad had been up to. He could hardly believe it himself—the transformation from dead to half-dead to reborn. If she happened to mention his leaving with Violet, he'd invent something on the spot and he knew he'd get away with it. His was a whole new world. That it included lying, adultery, and certain acts that were biblically forbidden only made it all the more titillating. He asked for a second helping of canned lima beans, hoping he wouldn't laugh out loud at the images still floating through his head.

He endured Thursday morning with his eye on the clock. At 11:50 he left the dealership, saying he was going out to lunch. When Kathy asked where, he said he hadn't decided yet, but he'd be back in a bit. Feeling worldly, he checked into the same room at the Sandman. It was all so easy now. Violet arrived and moments later, in a flurry of discarded clothes, feverish kisses, agonizing groans, and grabbing at each other, they were both naked and lying on the bed. Her breath smelled of red wine and cigarettes, but he knew better than to ask what she'd been doing at the Moon so early in the day. What difference did it make?

The sex was even better this time, which he hadn't believed possible. Already he felt comfortable in his skin, sure of himself. This wasn't the lovemaking of strangers, but the intimacy of two adults. Violet could be rough, and she brought out the bawdiness in him. She was also outrageous, using language that sometimes shocked his staid sensibilities. She could be tender as well, in ways that made him want to weep.

Afterward, they shared a cigarette like lovers in a movie. He couldn't get over this new sense he had of himself. Violet was tucked up under his arm, her head on his shoulder, face tilted back slightly so she could look at him. He looked down at her, saying, "What?"

She laughed. "How did you know I had something on my mind?"

"You're not the only one with telepathic powers."

"That's good. I like that." She was quiet, smile fading.

He gave her shoulder a shake. "Come on. Out with it."

"I was thinking about what you said yesterday. You know, spending the rest of our lives in this room. That was sweet. That made me feel I was special to you, not just a cheap piece of ass."

"Hey! Enough. Don't say shit like that about yourself."

"Well, it's the truth. You know my reputation. I'm a wild child. I live fast and loose, but you know what it's about? Under all the trashy talk and screwing around, I'm completely numb, like I'm already dead inside. So at least when I'm crazy drunk and out of control, I feel like I'm alive. Does that make any sense?"

"Jesus, you've just described my life. I don't show it the way you do, but it's exactly the same with me. You think I'm happy because I make a lot of money and live in a nice house? Doesn't work that way. All my life I've been busy taking care of other people. This is the first thing I've done for myself. When I said that about spending the rest of my life with you, I meant it."

"Thanks. That makes me feel good." She seemed hesitant. "What happened yesterday, with the car? I'm really sorry. I shouldn't have taken it. I know I was wrong putting all those miles on it, but something came over me. It was like I'd just gotten out of prison and the world could be anything. The sunshine and the ocean. It was just so beautiful, flying down the road. I had all the windows cranked down and my hair was whipping across my face. I took it all the way up to forty miles an hour—"

"Shit, Violet. Don't tell me that. You'll give me a heart attack."

"Well, it was an amazing experience and I have you to thank."

"And for this."

"Yes, for this."

He was quiet for a moment. "You know I can make it happen."

"Make what happen?"

"The car. I can set it up so it's yours."

She laughed. "Oh come on. Bullshit. You can't do that. Are you nuts?"

"I'm serious. Tell Foley to come talk to me. If he shows up tomorrow morning, I can make him a deal."

"Foley doesn't have a dime."

"I know, but we'll work something out."

"You'd do that for me?"

"Yes."

"You're not just pulling my leg?"

"I'd do anything for you. I mean it. I'm crazy about you."

"You don't have to say that just because we ended up in bed."

"You don't know what you've done for me. Everything's different now. I've changed."

"Not changed at all. You're finally yourself."

"Tell me you'll see me tomorrow," he said. "Otherwise, I'll never make it to next week."

She was quiet again, making a study of his face before she formulated her reply. "All right. Tomorrow at four. I've got something to take care of first so you gotta promise you won't get your undies in a wad if I'm late."

Friday at 3:45, he checked into the Sandman. On Wednesday afternoon when he'd registered the first time, he'd told the desk clerk a pipe had broken in his house, badly flooding the downstairs. He spun the story off the top of his head, never realizing he'd be checking in again the very next day. Thursday, he told her he expected the repairs to be under way, but the contractor stood him up. She'd been sympathetic on the first day and skeptical the second. Today, she was snippy, saying if he was going to check in again, why not just keep the room instead of using it for an hour, checking out, and coming back the next day? He hadn't realized she was keeping track. He felt compelled to elaborate, talking about the smell of mildew, having to put all his furniture in storage. The phone rang in the midst of his recital. She picked up and turned her back to him. She went on chattering with some friend until he realized she didn't intend to listen to another word. He took his key and left. What a bitch. He was a respectable businessman. It was no concern of hers what he did or didn't do, or with whom. He wasn't sure why he'd even bothered to explain himself. There were other motels. Next time around he and Violet could find someplace else.

He returned to his car and drove the length of the parking lot and parked outside the room. On the way over, he'd stopped at the florist's and bought Violet an armload of flowers that he wanted her to see the minute she entered the room. He took the bouquet with him and let himself in. They'd twice been in room 14. This was room 12, and he noticed it was quite a bit shabbier. Not that she'd care. He knew the car was already in her possession, because Foley had driven it off the lot at 10:30 that morning. He'd come into the dealership at 8:45, and Chet had made him a better deal than he had any reason to expect. He'd been jovial through the process, knowing he'd be bedding the guy's wife by 4:15. He'd despised Foley previously, but now he pitied him as well. He was too doltish and too much the brute to appreciate what a rare and precious woman he had. She was clearly more than he could handle—young, sensual, beautiful, spirited. Foley'd tried controlling her with his fists, and all he'd done was drive her away. Chet knew how to treat a lady and he had the wherewithal to do it right. He'd already formulated half a dozen plans for getting her out of Foley's house and stashing her somewhere close. At first he thought he'd have to leave Livia, which he was perfectly willing to do. A divorce would be messy and painful, but he was forty-seven years old and entitled to happiness. Of course, his daughter would be upset, but kids were resilient—everybody said so. Kids sensed when their parents were unhappy, and you didn't do them any favors papering it all over and pretending everything was okay. Better to have it out in the open.

On further reflection, he wondered if his initial impulse was wrong. The more he thought about it, the more he realized how cruel it would be to put Livia through that—the public humiliation, the vituperative shouting matches, not to mention the reduced circumstances divorce would entail. After fifteen years of marriage, she'd be devastated. Better to take the high road and spare her the stigma of divorce and abandonment. His relationship with Violet was his to bear and he'd shoulder it like a man.

He'd checked the classified ads for apartments in Santa Teresa and spotted a rental he thought would serve. Clean and attractive, with an ocean view, it said. He could drive down to see Violet every chance he got. He'd fill her life with riches—clothes, travel, anything she wanted. She might resist at first, not wanting to be beholden, but now that the Bel Air was hers, she'd realize how far he was willing to go.

He filled the ice bucket with water and arranged the flowers, already fantasizing what was coming next. Compared to Violet, he was inexperienced and that was humbling. At the dealership, he was always on top—figuratively speaking—but here he yielded, allowing her to do with him as she would. Violet was the boss and he found himself giving up all power to her. The change was restful, a possibility that had never occurred to him. With Livia, he sometimes had to talk himself into making love. He had his physical needs, but it was just as easy to take care of them himself. With Violet, he was charged, half out of his mind in anticipation of her.

Oddly enough, he'd caught sight of her earlier in the day. Shortly after noon, he'd driven into Santa Maria to do his end-of-the-week banking, forgetting that the bank would be closed for the Fourth of July. He'd parked near the Savoy Hotel, and as he was passing the tea shop window, he chanced to look in. There sat Violet with her little daughter, Daisy, and Liza Mellincamp, having a gay old time of it. He smiled at how happy she looked, probably because the car was now hers. He was tempted to tap on the glass and wave to her, but he thought better of it. From now on, in public, he'd act like he didn't have a clue who she was.

4:20. She was late, which she'd warned him about. At 4:26 he checked his watch again, wondering if something had gone dreadfully wrong. If she'd been unavoidably delayed, there was no way she could call because she couldn't be sure what name he'd used when he was checking in. On the off chance Foley had arrived home unexpectedly, she could hardly excuse herself and go use the phone. Foley was paranoid as it was. Between bouts of lovemaking the day before, she'd let slip some of the things he'd done to her, the threats, promises of retribution if he ever found out she'd betrayed him again. Chet was appalled, but she'd shrugged it off as though it was no big deal. "But I'll tell you one thing," she'd said. "Next time he comes after me, that's it for him. I'm out."

4:29. Chet could feel anxiety roiling in his gut. What if Foley had gotten wind of their rendezvous? Chet didn't dare leave. If she finally showed up and he was gone, she'd be furious.

At 4:36, he heard a tap on the door. He pulled the curtain aside, half-expecting to see Foley with a gun in his hand. It was Violet, thank god. He opened the door and in she strolled without a word of explanation. He waited, thinking surely she'd offer an excuse—errands, Daisy, heavy traffic on the road.

"Jesus, what happened? You said four." He knew his tone was accusatory, but he was so relieved to see her he couldn't help himself.

"That's all you've got to say to me? I risk life and limb getting here and you're pissed that I'm late? I told you not to get your shorts up your crack."

"Of course I'm not pissed. I was just worried, that's all. I'm sorry if I came off sounding like a jerk."

"Where'd the flowers come from? You buy those for me?"

"You like them?"

"Sure, but it's a lot of money for thirty minutes max." She tossed her purse on the chair and slipped off her heels, which she kicked to one side.

"That's all the time you have? I thought you said an hour?"

"That's right. I got an hour and now half of it's gone, so don't hassle me, okay? We've got better things to do." She began peeling off her clothes. Dress. Panties. She unhooked her bra, letting her breasts swing free. He couldn't pinpoint her mood. Under the casual manner, there was an edginess he didn't like. He waited for mention of the car, but she didn't say a word. She might be uncomfortable expressing gratitude. She was staring at him. "Are you going to strip or just stand there and look at me all day?"

He undressed quickly while Violet pulled the covers down and got into bed. They made love, but with not quite the ardor he'd experienced the day before. His performance wasn't all he'd hoped for either, though Violet was nice about it, saying, "Oh, quit fretting. Everybody has an off day. You're fine."

Afterward she swung her feet out of bed and sat up.

Despite her reassurances, he was wary, wanting to make it up to her. He put his arms around her from behind, nuzzling her hair, kissing the smooth skin in the middle of her back. He could feel himself coming to life again where it counted. "Check this," he said.

"Quit slobbering. You're getting on my nerves."

Teasingly he tugged on a strand of her hair. "So how does it feel to have your very own Bel Air?"

That brought a smile. She said, "Good. It's great. When Foley came home this morning he parked it out in front and had me look through the window. I could hardly believe my eyes."

She made it sound like Foley deserved the credit. Chet would have kidded her about it, but he sensed that under it all, she was depressed. "Hey, Henny Penny. What's wrong? Has the sky fallen in on you?"

"I'm fine."

"I know you better than that. What is it?"

"I just don't see how I can keep doing this. Foley and I got into this huge fight last night and the fucker tore up the house. It's like he can sense something's off. He hasn't figured it out, but it won't take him long. Once he picks up the scent, he's a regular bloodhound."

"Has he said anything?"

"No, but there's this look in his eye and it's scaring me to death. I'm skating on thin ice. One wrong move and . . ."

"What?"

"I don't know, but something bad."

"Oh, come on. It can't be as serious as all that."

"Easy for you to say."

He felt a whisper of fear. "So let's take a little break until he calms down again. Tomorrow's a holiday. I have work to do anyway so there's no way to meet. This weekend, you can pal around with him. Go to the fireworks, take a picnic supper, do whatever you have to do. You'll have him eating out of your hand."

"Oh, sure. Make light of it. Good old Violet. Just hang out and jolly him along, kiss his ass, suck his dick, anything to pacify the guy, who's been a maniac from birth."

"I wasn't making light."

"Well, you don't live with him. You don't know what he's like. You're not the one he's busting in the chops every other day. Lookit this, I still got a bruise from where he threw a friggin' coffeepot at me."

"So why not leave?"

"And go where? How far do you think I'd get?"

"As far as you like. If it's a matter of money, I can help you out."

"It's not money, Chet. Is that all you think about?"

"What then?"

"Shit. How can I make myself clear? It's just this feeling I get . . . like I'm in this alone. Who cares about me, right? In this town, I'm dirt, lower than the low."

"I care."

"Uh-hun."

"I'm serious. I care deeply about you."

"I know what you care about. Getting laid."

"Now wait a minute—"

"I'm just kidding you, okay? I'm trying to lighten up. What good's it ever done me to feel sorry for myself?"

"Violet, I'm on your side. That's the point I'm trying to make. I've been thinking about it and it's not a good idea for you to stay under his roof. So what occurred to me was finding you another place to live—"

"Yeah . . . well, not to worry. I'll figure it out."

"But why won't you let me help when I'm seriously concerned?"

"Come on, Chet. 'Seriously concerned?' You think I don't see what's going on? This isn't about me. This is about you and what you want. These past two days, you haven't asked me one thing about myself except do I use birth control. Now how's that for concern? Like you're such a stallion I might get knocked up and ruin the rest of your life."

He could feel his face go blank.

She caught his look and relented. "Sorry. I didn't mean that. I don't even know what I'm talking about. Why don't we just chalk it up to that time of the month."

"Is that it? Why didn't you say so? Come here—"

"Would you quit with the phony tone of voice. That's not going to solve my *problem*. Don't you *get* that?" She got up and paced once across the room before she sat down again. She leaned forward, with her elbows on her knees, and put her face in her hands. She made a low exasperated moan. "You're not hearing me, but it's my fault. I'll take all the blame. I should have made myself clear. What's going to keep me safe, Chet, is to stay the hell away from you. You're a nice guy and a good egg, but when it comes to screwing around, you're an amateur. If I'm in jeopardy—which I am—it's because of you."

"But that's what I'm trying to say. I can get you out of here."

"No, you can't. Look at you, goofy about me and all goofy for love. You think I'm the answer to your prayers, but I'm the quickest road to hell. I know you don't want to hear it, but I'm telling you the truth. You can't live this way, with all the sneaking around. It's not in your nature. Basically you're a decent man, which means you'll miscalculate. You'll make some stupid mistake and there goes my ass. I'm better off calling a halt to it right here."

"You don't mean that."

"You see? That's what I'm talking about. You're not listening to me. You're not only putting me in the path of a train, you're tying me to the tracks. If you care—if you *love* me so much—why don't you give me a fighting chance and keep the hell away. I can manage Foley, but not with you bumbling around. Because here's how it's going to go. One night you'll walk into the Moon with a bullshit grin on your face. Foley will take one look at you and he'll know everything. Then guess who's dead meat? First me, then you, then him."

"That won't happen. He's never going to know. Violet, I talked to him this morning. He sat at my desk not even this far away. I swear he doesn't have a clue."

"You wanna know why that is? Because it was about money and him trying to get something out of you. Also, because right now, we've been together three days and you haven't had a chance to screw it up yet, but you will."

"Wait, wait, wait. Let's just think. No need to do anything rash. Look, how about this? I can rent you an apartment in Santa Teresa . . . under a fake name. You don't like that idea, we'll take off together and settle someplace else. I'd do that for you, I swear."

She smiled and shook her head. "That's your solution? You got a great imagination. I gotta hand it to you." She found her brassiere and hooked herself into it. She bent over and maneuvered her breasts, arranging each in its cup. She retrieved her underpants and stepped into them. She settled her dress over her head and zipped herself up. This was a strip show in reverse. She came back as far as the bed table where she took a cigarette from his pack and tamped it on her thumbnail. "Look at this joint. They don't even provide a friggin' pack of matches. Can you give me a light?"

Numb, he flicked his lighter and watched her lean toward the flame, holding her hair out of the way. She took a drag, inhaled, and blew a stream of smoke at the ceiling. "Thanks." She took the ashtray and her purse and went into the bathroom. Through the open doorway, he could see her putting on her face.

He followed as far as the door and caught her reflection in the mirror. "You're telling me it's over."

"That's right. No offense, but let's bail while we can."

He was silent for almost a full minute, while he thought about the last three days. "You did it for the car, didn't you?"

Her mouth came open and she turned. "You said, what?"

"This was all so you could get the car and now that you have it, you're finished with me."

"Are you saying that I fucked you to get a car?! Thanks so much. What kind of whore does that make me? You're the one telling me not to talk shit about myself, and listen to the shit that comes out of your mouth."

"I'm sorry. I'm sorry—"

"If you're so sorry then why don't you quit pushing me around?" Abruptly she went back to her lipstick, following the outline of her mouth. "You want to be a bully, take a number and get in line. When it comes to abuse, Foley's got it all over you."

"Are you crazy? You're crazy. Don't stand there bragging about how bad the guy treats you. I came here prepared to offer you a life."

"Listen, Buster, I have a life. Might not look like much to you, but I'm doing the best I can so don't you condescend to me."

"Violet . . . don't." He tried to speak, but his throat closed and his voice cracked.

"Jesus, Chet. Be a big boy about this. It's been great, but let's face facts. It's sex. Right now, it might be firecracker hot, but how long does that last? In two months it's gone, so don't make more of it than it is. You're not going to run off with me. You're full of shit."

Chet took the last drag of his cigarette and flipped it out the window. He took one more pull from his flask and put that away. The tractor and flatbed, deck empty now, passed him again, heading back toward the 166. On the Tanner property, the bright yellow bulldozer sat with two others, looking as big as a tank. He hadn't been on a bulldozer since he was eighteen years old, that ball-busting summer before his father had been killed. He'd worked construction, thinking he could set aside some cash for his freshman year of college. Nowadays the union trained guys to operate heavy equipment, but in those days, you got on a 'dozer, fired it up, and hoped you wouldn't drive yourself into a ditch.

He turned the key in the ignition and released the T of the emergency brake. He made a U-turn across the two lanes of deserted road. What he'd been through with Violet was the equivalent of a three-year affair compressed into three days. Beginning, middle, and end. Over and out. He couldn't help thinking she'd made a bigger fool of him than he knew. He'd been set up, duped. She wanted the car. It was obvious now, but she'd played him well and he half-admired her finesse. She'd crooked her little finger and he'd scampered after her, as frisky as a pup. He didn't feel it yet, the shame, but he would very soon, once the liquor wore off. He knew his humiliation was commensurate with his joy, but the joy had been fleeting while the rage would burn at his core like the fire in the bowels of a coal mine, year after year. What wounded him was knowing she felt none of his pain. Now every time he saw the car, every time Foley made a payment, he'd cringe, feeling powerless and small. He'd go home to Livia and that would be that. His life had been barely tolerable before, but what would it be like now that he knew the difference?

At the house, he pulled into the driveway and put his car in the garage. Mentally he shook himself off, struggling for control. He had a part to play. He couldn't let Violet ruin his home life as she'd ruined his work. He let himself in the house. The hall smelled of cabbage that had cooked half a day. He wanted to weep. He couldn't even look forward to a good meal at home. Livia, with her heavy hand and glum notions about food, served nearly inedible fare—mackerel loaf, creamed chicken on waffles, tapioca pudding that looked like a clot of egg-infested mucilage spawned by a fish. He'd eaten it all, every variation on a theme, sometimes too frightened to inquire what it was.

"Daddy, is that you?"

"Yes."

He peered into the living room. Kathy was sprawled on the couch, her heavy legs flung over one end. She wore white shorts and a T-shirt, both inappropriate for someone her size. She had a strand of hair in her mouth and she was sucking on the end while she watched television. *The Howdy Doody Show.* Talk about a waste of time. A cowboy marionette with freckles and a flapping mouth. You could even see the strings that generated his movements, his wobbly boots dangling on tippy-toe as he pranced across the screen.

Chet took off his sport coat and hung it on a peg in the hall. What did he care if the shoulder got pulled out of shape? He undid his collar button and loosened his tie. He had to get a grip. But fifteen minutes later, as he was sitting down for supper, Livia made a half-assed remark, saying how ridiculous it was that the South Korean president, Syngman Rhee, called on Christians and non-Christians to pray for peace.

He stared at her, instantly incensed. "You think it's ridiculous the war might come to an end? After we've lost thirty-three thousand U.S. troops? Where the hell is your head? Rhee's the guy who released twenty-seven thousand North Korean POWs less than two weeks ago, sabotaging armistice talks. Now he's softened his position and you want to sit there *sneering* at him?"

Livia's lips tightened to such an extent he was surprised she could speak. "All I'm saying is there's no point in non-Christians praying for peace when they don't believe in God."

"Non-Christians don't believe in God? Is that what you think? Anyone who doesn't go to your personal church and worship your personal deity is some kind of heathen? Livia, you can't be that idiotic."

He could tell she was offended, but he really didn't care. Cheeks stained with indignation, she snapped his dinner plate on the table in front of him with a force that nearly cracked it in two. He looked down at the meal, which consisted of a main dish and a side of cabbage that had boiled so long all the color had cooked out. He pointed to the entrée. "What's this?"

Livia sat down and arranged her napkin in her lap. "We're having International Night. The first Friday of every month. Kathy prepared the dish and I think it's lovely."

"It's Welch Rabbit," Kathy said, happily, already lifting a fully loaded fork to her lips.

"Welch? There's no such place as *Welch*. Are you out of your minds? This isn't rabbit. It's cheese goo on toast."

"Would you sample a bite before you judge, or is that too much to ask after Kathy's worked so hard?"

"This is shit! I can't work a full day and sit down to a meal like this. There's no meat."

"Please watch your language. There's a young lady present."

He pushed his plate back. "Excuse me." He left the table and went into the downstairs powder room, where he pulled out his flask and downed the remaining vodka in six swallows. It wasn't nearly enough, but maybe he'd managed to survive the next fifteen minutes without going berserk.

He returned to the table and began to eat, trying to imagine how normal men behaved. Husbands all over America must be sitting down to dinners just like this, with wives and daughters like the two he faced. How did they do it? Making small talk? He could do that. Clearly there was no point discussing world peace. He glanced at Kathy, not looking too closely as she tended to chew with her mouth open. He said, "I saw your friend today."

"Who?"

"Liza."

"Oh." She was so intent on stuffing her face, he wondered if she'd heard.

"Whatever happened to her?"

Kathy flicked him a look. "Nothing. Why'd you say that?"

"Six months ago the two of you were like Siamese twins, joined at the hip. She dump you or what?"

"No, Dad. She didn't *dump* me."

"Then how come you don't see each other anymore?"

"We do. All the time. She was busy today. Is that against the law?"

"She didn't look that busy to me. Unless a fancy lunch downtown counts."

"Liza didn't have *lunch* downtown."

"I thought today was her birthday. Didn't you say something to that effect here at dinner last night?"

"So?"

"So nothing. I thought she'd be spending the whole day with you."

"We talked on the phone. She said her mother's been sick and might even be contagious or she'd have come right over to celebrate."

"Ohhh," he said, drawing the word out. "Well, maybe that explains it."

"Explains what?"

"What she was doing all dressed up with Violet Sullivan. The two had their heads bent together over shrimp cocktails."

Kathy put her fork down and stared. "They did *not*."

"Yes, they did. Uh-hum. Yes, indeedy."

"Where?"

"The Savoy Hotel. The tea room's on the ground floor. I saw 'em through the window."

Livia said, "Chet."

"Very funny. Ha ha. And where's Daisy all this time? Did you forget about her?"

"She was sitting right there with a big bowl of buttered noodles she was slurping through her lips."

"You're just saying that to bug me because you're in a bad mood. Liza might have gone out, but it had nothing to do with Mrs. Sullivan."

"Why don't you ask her and see what she says?"

"Chet, that's enough."

"I can't call her *again*. I just talked to her. She's taking care of her mother, who's extremely ill."

"Okay. Fine. If that's the way you want to play it. I'd feel bad if things went sour between the two of you. That's my only concern."

Kathy retreated into silence. Meanwhile, Livia sent him dark, meaningful looks that suggested a serious dressing-down to come. Chet didn't intend to stick around for that. He wiped his mouth on his napkin and tossed it on his plate. He got up, working to control the urge to run. He could feel the spite rising in his chest. What the hell was wrong with him? He was never going to get back at Violet by making trouble somewhere else. Why put his daughter at odds with her best friend? The pettiness of what he'd done only fueled his rage. He thought he was close to madness, irrational, erratic, out of control.

He took his sport coat from the hook and shrugged himself into it. Livia had followed him into the hall. "Are you going *out*?"

"Yes."

"But I'm expecting company. This is my canasta night. The girls are going to be here at eight. You said you'd take Kathy and go somewhere."

He walked out the front door and slammed it behind him, so choked with fury he couldn't utter a word.

19

I went back to the motel office and borrowed Mrs. Bonnet's phone. I contacted the sheriff's office to report the incident and was told they'd send someone out. I then called Southern California Automobile Club and requested assistance. While I waited, I called Daisy's house and Tannie answered the phone. She said Daisy had already left for work. When I told her about my tires being slashed, she was properly outraged. "You poor thing! I can't believe someone would do that to you."

"Personally, I'm thrilled. I mean, on one hand, I'm peeved. I hate to be without transportation and buying four new tires is the last thing I need. On the other hand, it's like hitting all three cherries on a slot machine. Three days into the job and someone's already nervous as a cat."

"You don't think it was vandalism?"

"Absolutely not. Are you kidding? I grant you my car's conspicuous in a parking lot full of trucks, but the choice wasn't random. This was supposed to be a warning, or possibly punishment, but I take it as a good sign."

"Well, your attitude beats mine. I'd be raising six kinds of hell if somebody slashed my tires."

"Shows I'm on the right track."

"Which is what?"

"I have no idea, but my nemesis must think I'm close to figuring it out."

"Whatever 'it' is."

"Right. Meantime, I need the name of a garage, if you know someone good."

"You forget my brother's in the business. Ottweiler Auto Repair in Santa Maria. At least he won't gouge you on the price."

"Great. I'll call him. What about you? What's your day looking like?"

"I'll be out on the property with a couple of guys. If I were so minded, I could be clearing brush for the rest of my life. I'm meeting with a contractor at eleven thirty, but you're welcome to come by."

"Let's see how long it takes me to get my tires swapped out. If everything goes smoothly, I'll stop and pick up some sandwiches and we can have lunch."

"Tell Steve I sent you. That'll surprise him for sure. Better yet, I'll call him myself and tell him you'll be in."

"Thanks."

A sheriff's deputy arrived at the Sun Bonnet within thirty minutes, and he spent an additional fifteen minutes, taking photographs and filling out information for his report. He said I could pick up a copy to forward to my insurance company. I couldn't remember the amount of my deductible, but I'd doubtless end up paying for them myself. Shortly after he left, the tow truck arrived, and the driver loaded my car onto a flatbed truck. I hopped in the cab with him and we covered the fifteen miles to Santa Maria without saying much.

While the car was being unloaded, Steve Ottweiler appeared and introduced himself. He was seven years Tannie's senior, an age spread that seemed to favor him. According to social standards other than my own, a man, at fifty, is just starting to look good, while a fifty-year-old woman is someone the eye tends to slide right past. In California cosmetic surgery is the means by which women stop the clock before the sliding begins. Lately the push is to get the work done earlier and earlier—age thirty if you're an actress—before the slippage sets in. I could see the strong family resemblance between Tannie's brother and their father, Jake, whom I'd met the night before. Steve had the same height and body type, lean and muscular. His face was broader than his dad's, but his complexion was the same sun-stained brown.

I purchased four new tires, taking his advice about which brand I should buy, that being the one he had in stock. We sat in his office while the mechanic put my car up on a rack and started loosening lug nuts. Currently Steve Ottweiler was the only person in the area I didn't suspect of slashing my tires, primarily because this was the first opportunity I'd had to piss him off. Somewhere in the last two days, I'd stepped on some toes, but I hadn't stepped on his—as far as I knew.

I said, "You were, what, sixteen in Violet Sullivan's day?"

"I was a junior in high school."

"Did you know Liza Mellincamp's boyfriend?"

"Ty Eddings? Sure, though more by reputation than anything else. I knew his cousin, Kyle. They were both a year ahead of me so we didn't have much occasion to interact. Actually, I'm not sure anyone knew Ty that well. He transferred in from East Bakersfield High School in March of that year. By the time July rolled around, he was gone again."

"Somebody told me he left the same weekend Violet did."

"No connection that I know of. They were both troublemakers, but that's about it. He'd been kicked out of EBHS and sent to live with his aunt in hopes he'd mend his wicked ways. Guess that idea flopped."

"Meaning what?"

"Word had it that he'd taken up with Liza Mellincamp, who was all of thirteen. The year before, he'd knocked up a fifteen-year-old girl and she ended up dead from a botched abortion. Ty was accorded outlaw status. Very cool in those days."

"He wasn't disliked or avoided?"

"Not a bit. We were all big on drama back then. Ty was regarded as a tragic hero because everyone thought he and the dead girl were deeply in love and her parents had forced them apart. He was Romeo to her Juliet, only he came out of the deal a lot better than she did."

"But is it out of the question that he and Violet might have gotten together? Two black sheep?"

"Well, it's always possible, though it doesn't seem likely. Violet was in her twenties and married to boot, so she hardly registered with us. We lived in a world of our own. You know how it is; the big event for us was two classmates who got killed in a car accident. Violet was a grownup. Nobody cared about her. Liza was the one I felt sorry for."

"I don't wonder," I said. "I talked to her yesterday

and she said she was crushed when Ty left town. What was that about?"

"The story I heard was Ty's aunt got a phone call from someone who told her he was fooling around with another underage girl, namely Liza. That was Friday night. The aunt turned around and called his mother, who'd flown to Chicago for a wedding. She got back to Bakersfield late Saturday night and picked him up first thing Sunday morning."

"You'd think he could have gotten word to Liza. She was dumped without so much as a by-your-leave."

"I guess good manners weren't his thing."

"What happened after that? I asked, but she wasn't happy about the question so I left it alone."

"Things went from bad to worse. Her parents had divorced when she was eight. She'd been living with her mom—essentially without supervision, since her mother drank. When her dad got wind of her relationship with Ty, he flew out from Colorado, packed her up, and took her back to live with him. Of course that went nowhere. The two didn't get along; she hated his new family and she was back the next year. No big surprise. You take a kid like her, used to freedom, and she's not going to react kindly to parental control."

"How'd he hear about Ty if he was in Colorado?"

"He still had contacts in town."

"So she ended up living with her mom again?"

"Not for long. Sally Mellincamp died in a house fire the next year and a local family took Liza in. Charlie Clements was a good guy and didn't want to see her sucked into the foster care system. He owned the auto-repair shop in Serena Station that I bought when he retired in 1962. Liza married his son."

"So everything connects."

"One way or another; it sure looks that way."

Steve was called out to the service bay, but he urged me to stay where I was until my car was ready. His office was small and utilitarian—metal desk, metal chair, metal files, and the smell of oil. Parts manuals and work orders were stacked up everywhere. I took advantage of the moment to review my index cards, playing with the information every way I could. A moment would come when everything would lock into place (she said bravely to herself). Right now, the bits and pieces were a jumble, and I couldn't quite see where any of them fit.

It was Winston's confession I kept coming back to. For years he'd kept quiet about seeing Violet's car. Now I realized how lucky I was his wife was booting him out. Because he was pissed with her, all bets were off, and he felt no compunction about spilling the beans. If I'd talked to him a day earlier, he might not have said a word. It was a lesson I needed to keep in mind: People change, circumstances change, and what seems imperative one day becomes insignificant the next. The reverse is true as well.

My VW was returned within the hour, my tires looking as crisp and clean as brand-new shoes. In addition, I saw that someone had treated me to a complimentary car wash. The interior now smelled new, thanks to a deodorant tag hanging from the rearview mirror. I caught sight of Steve Ottweiler as I was pulling out and gave him a wave.

Heading west on Main, I realized I wasn't that far from the neighborhood where Sergeant Schaefer lived. I took the next right-hand turn and circled back, parking out in front of his house as I had on my earlier visit. When he didn't answer my knock, I followed the walkway around the side of the house to the rear, at the same time calling his name. He was in his workshop and when he heard my voice, he peered out the open doorway and motioned me in.

I found him perched on a stool with a miter box and clamps on his workbench. He'd cut lengths of framing and he was gluing them together. Today he wore denim overalls, and his white hair pushed out like foam from under a black baseball cap.

"I expected to find you working on a chair."

"I finished that project and haven't yet started on the next. These days, I'm so tied up with hobbies, it's lucky I don't work or I'd never fit it all in. What brings you this way?"

"I thought I'd give you an update." I told him about my tires, my call to the sheriff's department, and my subsequent visit to Steve Ottweiler's shop.

"Sounds like you're making someone sweat."

"That's my take on it. The problem is, I have no idea who or how."

"Tell me what you've done and maybe we can figure it out."

I filled him in on my interviews, starting with Foley Sullivan, saying, "I hate to admit it, but I thought Foley made a pretty good case for himself."

"Sounding sincere is a specialty of his. What about the others?"

"Well, the people I've talked to fall into two categories: those who think Violet's dead—you, me, and her brother, Calvin—and those who think she's alive, namely

Foley, Liza, and possibly Daisy. I'm not sure where Chet Cramer stands on the question. I forgot to ask."

"Too bad we can't just put it to a vote," he said. "I can see how Liza and Daisy ended up in the same boat. Neither wants to entertain the idea that Violet's gone for good."

"Maybe we're the cynics, assuming she's dead when she might be alive and well and living in New York."

"Can't rule that out."

I went on down the list, telling him what Winston had confessed about seeing Violet's car.

Schaefer said, "I've been thinking about that car. Couple of us old retirees get together for dinner once a month and talk about the old days. I was telling them about you and what you're up to. The one fellow worked Auto Theft, and he said if the Bel Air landed in a junk yard, the VIN might have been stripped off and switched to another vehicle. You want to make a stolen car disappear, that's how you go about it. The beauty of it is it then allows you to register a stolen car as salvage. You claim you bought some old clunker and fixed it up and who's going to be the wiser? They call 'em ghost cars. Any rate, next day I phoned the SO and had one of the deputies read off the vehicle identification number from Violet's Bel Air."

"You had that?"

"Oh, sure. Chet Cramer gave it to us in one of the early interviews. I called up the Sacramento DMV and had them do a computer search. They show no record of the VIN. Dang. For a minute, I was hoping for a hit, but the car's never surfaced, which sets me back to the notion it was shipped overseas."

"You're assuming the number Cramer gave you was

correct," I said. "All he had to do was alter one digit and the computer would spit it back as a no match."

"That's a troubling possibility. You'll be careful?"

"I will."

"And keep me in the loop."

I assured him I'd be doing that as well.

I stopped at a delicatessen and picked up some sandwiches and Cokes, then took Highway 166 out of Santa Maria until it intersected New Cut Road. By now the route was familiar and I drove with only half my attention focused on the road. With the balance of my mental energy, I was sifting through the miscellany I'd collected over the past two days. I wasn't much wiser but at least I was getting all the players sorted out.

I reached the Ottweiler property at 11:15. Tannie's contractor had arrived early, and he pulled into the driveway the same time I did. She introduced him as Bill Boynton, one of the two Padgett had suggested the night before. I told her about the sandwiches I'd brought and then left her alone to chat with him while I took the opportunity to tour the interior of the house. From the porch, I could see two guys working at the edge of the property, cutting heavy brush as she had. A swath had now been cleared from the foundation to the depth of the yard. The ground looked naked and apologetic without all the high weeds, brambles, and old shrubs.

Even at first glance, I found myself agreeing with Padgett, who considered the place beyond redemption. No wonder her brother was urging her to sell. The first floor had all the charm of an inner-city tenement. I could see touches of former splendor—ten-inch crown molding, beautifully plastered ceilings with ornate medallions and cornices as delicate as cake icing—but in most rooms, decades of leakage and neglect had taken their tolls.

When I reached the stairs, I began to pick up the acrid scent of charred wood, and I knew that the floors above would be damaged not only by the fire, but by the water from the firemen's hoses. I went up, following a once beautiful oak banister that was now dingy with soot and age. A fine layer of broken glass crunched underfoot, making my progress audible. Fixtures had been stripped. In the largest of the bedrooms at the front of the house, I was momentarily startled by what appeared to be a vagrant curled up in one corner. When I moved closer, I could see that the "body" was an old sleeping bag, probably left by a drifter taking shelter uninvited. In the large walk-in linen closet, I could still see labels written in pencil on the edges of the shelves—SINGLE SHEETS, DOUBLE SHEETS, PILLOW CASES—where the maids had been directed to place the freshly laundered linens.

The third floor was inaccessible. Yellow CAUTION tape had been stretched across what was left of the stairs. Gaping holes in the stairwell traced the course of the fire as it ate its way through the rooms above. There was something unbearably creepy about the ruin everywhere. I returned to the second floor and made a circuit, pausing at many of the windows to take in the view. Aside from the field across the road, there wasn't much to see. One field over, a new crop of some kind was sprouting through layers of plastic sheeting that served to keep the weeds down. The illusion was of ice. Closer to the house, Tannie's battle with the brush had uncovered meandering brick paths and a truck garden now choked with weeds. During the summer, a volunteer tomato plant had resurrected itself, and it sprawled over a wooden bench, cherry tomatoes in evidence like little red ornaments on a Christmas tree. I could see the outlines of former flower beds and trees stunted by lack of sun for all the overgrowth.

To the left, at an angle, I gazed down at an ill-defined depression that might have been a sunken pool, or the remnant of an old septic system. There wouldn't have been sewer lines in place in the early 1900s when the house was built. A mound of newly cleared snowball bushes was visible along one edge. The uprooted plants boasted once bright blue blossoms as big as heads of cabbage. I felt bad at the sacrifice of bushes that had grown so impossibly grand.

In the side yard of the lot where our trailer had sat, my aunt had planted hydrangeas much the same color, though not quite so lush as these had been. The neighbor's hydrangeas were a washed-out pink, and Aunt Gin took delight in her superior blooms. The secret, said she, was burying nails in the soil, which somehow encouraged the shift from pink to the rich blue shade.

Afterward I felt I'd been incredibly dense, taking as long as I had to add that particular two plus two. I stared down at the cracked and slightly sunken oblong of soil and felt a flash, the sudden gelling of facts that hadn't seemed connected before. This was where Winston had last seen the car. Amid dirt mounds, heavy equipment, and orange plastic cones, he'd said. A temporary road barrier had been erected, denying access to through traffic. No sign of Violet, no sound from the dog, but from that night forward, the Bel Air was never seen again.

Perhaps because it was buried here. Maybe all these years, the rich blue hydrangeas had been feeding on the rust.

20

I drove to the service station near Tullis and used the pay phone to call Schaefer. I told him what had occurred to me and asked how we might confirm or refute my hunch about the oblong depression in the earth. Schaefer was dubious but said he had a friend who owned a metal detector. He agreed to call the guy. If the guy could help, they'd meet us at the property as soon as possible. Failing that, he'd drive out on his own and assess the situation. I hadn't told Tannie what I was up to, but now that I'd set the wheels in motion, I worried I was making a colossal ass of myself. On the other hand, oh well. There are worse things in life and I've been guilty of most.

By the time I pulled up at the house again, she'd finished her business with Bill Boynton and he was gone. "Where'd you disappear to? I thought we were having lunch."

"Yeah, well, something's come up. I want you to take a look."

"Can't we eat first and then look?"

"This won't take long."

She followed me to the side yard and I pointed to the irregular rectangle that had attracted my attention. At ground level, the depression wasn't as defined as it appeared from above, especially with half-dead hydrangea bushes piled to one side. At close range, it looked more like a mole had been tunneling across the yard. The soil was uneven, but it took a bit of squinting to see that it was sunken in relation to the surrounding lawn. This was about the same as staring at the night sky, trying to identify Taurus the Bull by visualizing lines between stars. I never saw anything remotely resembling livestock, a failing I attributed to my paltry imagination. Yet here I was pointing like a bird dog, saying, "Know what that is?"

"Dirt?"

"Better than dirt. I think it's Violet Sullivan's grave."

Tannie stared down at her feet. "You're shitting me."

"Don't think so, but we'll find out."

We sat on the porch steps waiting for Tim Schaefer. Tannie had lost her appetite and neither of us was in the mood to talk. "But I got dibs on the braunschweiger once we get around to the sandwiches," she said.

At 1:10 Schaefer drove up in his 1982 Toyota and pulled into Tannie's drive with his metal-detecting pal. The two got out, car doors slamming in unison, and crossed to the porch. Schaefer carried a shovel and a long steel implement, like a walking stick with a point on one end. He introduced his friend, whose name was Ken Rice, adding a two-line bio so we'd know whom we were dealing with. Like Schaefer, he was a man in his early eighties, retired after thirty-eight years with the Santa

Maria Police Department, working first as a motorcycle officer, then foot patrol, Narcotics, and later as the department's first K-9 officer. For the past twenty years, his passion had been the location and recovery of buried relics, caches of coins, and other forms of treasure. We shook hands all around and then Rice turned on his detector, which looked like the two halves of a toolbox, connected by a metal rod. "Let's see what we got."

The four of us trooped across the property to the side yard, me tagging behind Rice like a little kid. "How does that work?"

"System has a directional transmitter and directional receiver built into these interlocking cases. Powered up, it emits an electromagnetic field that penetrates the soil. This is the same equipment used by public-utility employees looking for pipes underground. When the search pattern encounters metal, the signal is interrupted and that generates an audio response."

"How far down?"

"The Fisher's capable of revealing a target as far down as twenty feet. Depending on soil mineralization and ground conditions, it's possible to detect an object even deeper."

When we reached the spot, the three of us watched as Rice swept the detector across the ground. He'd put on a headset, and I gathered the device made a continuous sound that grew louder when he made a find. On his first pass, I saw the needle on the gauge leap hard to the right and stay there as though glued. He pressed a hand to his ear, frowning to himself as he continued sweeping across the area. Having finished, he said, "You've got something the size of a boxcar down there."

I laughed. "We do?"

"Schaefer tells me you're looking for a car, but this might be something else."

"Such as what?"

"A Dumpster, underground storage tank, a chunk of sheet metal roof."

"So now what?" I asked.

"That's what I'm trying to figure out."

He and Schaefer conferred and then Schaefer returned to his car, where he opened the trunk. He came back bearing a ball of twine and a plastic bag full of the golf tees he used in recaning chairs. While Rice made a series of passes with his box, Schaefer followed in his wake and stuck golf tees in the ground, roughly conforming to the signal Rice was picking up. Tannie and I each took a turn listening, passing the headset from one to the other. If Rice moved the device too far left or right, the tone diminished. Schaefer ran a line of twine from tee to tee. When they finished mapping, the string was laid out in a rectangle eighteen feet long by approximately eight feet wide. I could feel the skin pucker on my arms at the notion of an underground object of that size. It must be equivalent to sailing on the ocean and realizing a whale was on the verge of surfacing under your boat. The very proximity seemed ominous. Unseen and unidentified, it radiated an energy that had me edging away.

Schaefer picked up the metal bar he was using as a probe. He chose a spot and pushed down, leaning his weight into the rod. It sank eight inches, but not easily. The soil in this part of the state has a high clay content, larded with numerous rocks and sizeable sandstone boulders. This makes digging tedious under the best of circumstances. Strike a boulder with a shovel blade and the impact will reverberate all the way up your arms.

Rice added his weight to the job. The probe sank another foot and a half and stopped. He said, "What do you think?"

"Let's see if it's rock or we're hitting something else."

Schaefer took his shovel and set to work, cutting into the hard-packed topsoil. I'd thought the ground would yield, but it proved to be slow going. Twenty minutes of steady effort produced a trench eighteen inches wide and about three feet long. Frail roots were exposed and hung from the perpendicular sides of the cut like a living fringe. The dirt pile beside the hole mounted.

At a depth of twenty-six inches, he made contact with an object, or a portion of an object. The four of us paused to stare.

"I've got a trowel if you want to dig by hand," Tannie said.

"Might be smart," Rice replied.

When she returned, she said, "May I?"

Schaefer said, "Have at it. It's your land."

Tannie got down on her hands and knees and began to scrape away the dirt. The object might have once been chrome though it was so badly rusted it was difficult to tell. I found myself tilting my head, saying, "What *is* that?"

By the time she'd dug down and cut an additional five inches, she'd uncovered something with a metal lip that extended over a shallow curve of glass. She looked up. "It's a headlight. Isn't it?"

Schaefer rested his hands on his knees and leaned closer. "I believe you're right."

Tannie scraped away another narrow trough of dirt, revealing what looked to be the rusted metal curve of a front right fender.

Rice said, "One of us better call the station and get some help out here."

By 3:00 there were eight officers at the site: an ID detective and a young deputy from the Santa Maria Sheriff's Department; a sergeant, two homicide detectives, and two nonsworn officers from Santa Teresa. In addition, an investigator had driven up from the State Crime Lab, which is located in Colgate, near the Santa Teresa Airport. A temporary parking area had been set up for official vehicles, including the crime scene van.

The first officer on the scene, the young Santa Maria deputy, had secured the area, relegating Schaefer, Ken Rice, Tannie, and me to a spot twenty-five yards away. Anyone in a secured crime scene is considered the same as a primary witness and might be asked to testify in court, which was why we were kept at such a distance. In addition, if this turned into a homicide investigation, there was always the risk that unauthorized persons might contaminate the site.

The lead investigator, Detective Nichols, came over and introduced himself, then briefed us on strategy for the excavation. He was a good-looking man in his forties, wearing a dress shirt and tie with a windbreaker, but no sport coat. He was slim, his light brown hair trimmed short. He glanced in my direction. "You're Miss Millhone?"

"That's right."

"Could I speak to you?"

"Of course."

We moved some distance away so we could talk in private.

"I understand Daisy Sullivan hired you to find her mother. You want to tell me how you came up with this?" he asked, indicating the site.

I backtracked, filling him in on my conversation with Winston and the tidbit he'd given me about spotting the car. I told him I'd been bothered by the fact that after that last sighting, the car was never seen again. "I was touring the house and when I looked down from one of the second-floor windows, I spotted the depression in the ground. At first I thought I was looking at an old planting bed, but then the car popped into my head. I called Sergeant Schaefer and he drove out with Ken Rice."

"You had no information in advance?"

"None. In fact, I had only the dimmest recollection of Violet Sullivan's disappearance. I'd read the occasional newspaper account, but I hadn't paid much attention until Daisy contacted me this past Monday. Tannie was the one who introduced us, which is how I ended up here."

He settled a look on me that was friendly enough, but had a no-nonsense undertone. "Anything else you find, you make sure I hear about it first."

"Absolutely."

We returned to the others. The five of us watched while one of the ID techs photographed the area and the other tech took measurements and drew a rough sketch, depicting what was believed to be the angle and orientation of the car. Given what they could see in the early phases of the work, the speculation was that whoever engineered the burial had used a bulldozer with an eight-foot blade, probably creating a ramp at a twenty- to thirty-degree angle. The car had been backed into the hole and then covered with fill. According to calculations, it would have taken approximately fifty feet of ramp to a maximum depth of fifteen feet in order to get the whole of the car underground with the front end sunk deep enough to prevent discovery. Now I could see what that pesky high school geometry class was about. There was no point in going to all the trouble of burying a car if the hood ornament was going to wash clear in the first big rain storm. If the job were poorly done, the car would emerge, little by little, over a period of time until it looked like an island in the middle of the lawn. Assuming the whole of the vehicle was there. Maybe we were looking at the bisected front end with nothing else attached. Detective Nichols excused himself and went back to the dig.

If speculation about the depth and angle was correct, the car was tilted beneath the surface like a sunken submarine, hung up on an underwater shelf. That being the case, the roof of the car and the top edge of the windshield would be approximately two paces back and some two and a half feet deep. To test the theory, Nichols whistled the young deputy over, handed him the shovel, and directed him to dig. He set to work, keeping his cuts shallow. Fifteen minutes later, the blade of his shovel scraped the surface of the roof.

There was a long debate about the use of an excavator, a motion that was quickly ratified. The idea of freeing the vehicle by hand was out of the question. The ID detective radioed and a deputy was dispatched to A-Okay Heavy Equipment to ask Padgett if he had one available. This generated an additional delay while the excavator was located, loaded on a low-boy flatbed truck, and driven out from town.

Tannie and I retired to her car, now parked a hundred yards down the road. We sat with the windows rolled down and ate our deli sandwiches, calling it lunch though it was already 4:00 P.M. I had no idea how word got out, but a trickle of people appeared, and before long the road was lined with vehicles. Two deputies controlled public access to the scene, which had been sealed off with tape. Steve Ottweiler arrived and he joined us, talking to his sister through the open window of her car. She said, "Does Pop know?"

"I called him and he's on his way out. Let me go see what Tim Schaefer has to say. He'll know more than we do."

Steve crossed the road. Schaefer was standing in a small knot of men. During the course of their conversation, the flatbed truck arrived. Tom Padgett had followed in his car, and he supervised the off-loading of the compact John Deere excavator, after which the equipment operator was the only one allowed in the magic circle. Padgett was relegated to the sidelines in the same way we were, which seemed to annoy him no end. For the next hour, we watched in amazement as the operator maneuvered his equipment with the delicacy of a surgeon. He was directed by whistles and hand signals, his skill such that he could scrape as little as an inch or as much as a foot of dirt from the hole on command.

Ken Rice found a ride home while Schaefer remained. He stood sipping coffee from a foam cup someone managed to provide. Even retired, he was drawn to the drama unfolding before our eyes. Jake Ottweiler pulled up and parked his car down the road. His son walked out to meet him and the two returned to Tim Schaefer's side. Having worked for the sheriff's department for thirty-some-odd years, he was the reigning civilian expert. I noticed BW McPhee was on hand, having appeared at some point. I also caught a glimpse of Winston, but didn't have a chance to make eye contact before he disappeared again. A local TV station sent a crew, and Detective Nichols gave a brief, uninformative statement, essentially referring the reporter to the sheriff for further comment.

At 5:45 Daisy arrived. Tannie and I got out of the car and waved her over. She joined us, looking pale and subdued. She was still in her work clothes, navy slacks, a cotton sweater, and sensible low-heeled shoes. She was chewing on her thumbnail again but lowered her hand self-consciously when she caught sight of me. She tucked her fingers out of sight and shifted from foot to foot as though to warm herself. She hadn't heard about my tires being slashed, so we talked about that just to get her mind off what was going on. "I don't like the sound of it."

"It's a bit melodramatic, but I took it as a good sign," I said.

"What are your plans for tonight?"

"I was expecting to head home, but now I think I'll hang out until we know what we've got down there."

"You can't go back to the Sun Bonnet."

"No, but there are other motels."

"Spend the night at my place. Tannie leaves first thing tomorrow morning. You'll survive one night on the couch. I've done it before myself. Meanwhile, we can lock your car in my garage and get it off the street in case the son of a bitch comes looking for it."

"If I stay, I'll either need to do laundry or borrow some underwear."

"We'll do both."

"This is such guy stuff. I love it," Tannie remarked, taking in the various gatherings of men.

Detective Nichols joined Tim Schaefer on the far side of the road, introducing himself to Jake and Steve Ottweiler. After a few more minutes of conversation, Nichols returned to us. He knew by then that the Ottweilers owned the property and that Daisy was the only child of the missing Violet Sullivan. He introduced himself to Daisy, and I could see her taking him in—glasses, clean-shaven, nice smile. There was a shift in her posture. Clearly she found him attractive.

He glanced at the clusters of onlookers out by the road. Even with their limited line of sight, there was something compelling about the work. "I'm about to have the deputies clear these people out of here. This is not a spectator sport. If we need to bring in additional equipment or manpower, I don't want to have to work around all the looky-loos and parked cars. I'm going to have you give the deputy contact numbers in case I need to get in touch. I'd appreciate your keeping quiet about anything you've seen or heard. We don't want details getting out. The less information we have in circulation, the better."

"It's all right if we stay?" Daisy asked.

"As long as you do what you're told and keep out of the way."

"How long will it take? I know you can't say exactly . . ."

"I'm guessing two days. No point being hasty and damaging the car beyond what nature's already done."

"But you haven't found anything?"

"Not so far. I understand your concern about your mother and I'll keep you informed. As soon as we free the car, we'll take it to the impound lot. We've got a storage facility, where we can warehouse the vehicle while we go over it. Right now we have no idea what evidence we'll find, if any, after all this time. What about your father; have you talked to him?"

Daisy shook her head. "I came right from work. I assume somebody's called him by now, but maybe not. I'm sure he'd be here if he knew."

"One thing I'll need to ask him—or maybe this is something you can tell me yourself—do you recall what your mother was wearing the day she disappeared?"

"A sundress. Lavender cotton with white polka dots. Leather sandals and thin silver bracelets, six of them. I don't actually remember any of it. It was in the report my father filed at the time." She seemed so tense, I expected her teeth to chatter. "Are you going to tell me if she's down there?"

"I'd do that, of course. You have a right to know."

"Thank you. I'd appreciate that."

As he walked away, she tracked his departure with a calculating eye. "Well, he's cute. Married, no doubt."

Tannie laughed. "Just your kind of guy. Too bad he works. He'd be perfect for you."

Within minutes, we could see two deputies encouraging bystanders to move on. People began to drift away. Car doors slammed, engines coughed to life, and one by one the crowd dispersed. In truth, at that remove, there wasn't much to see. The excavation was being treated like an archaeological dig—sketched, diagrammed, measured, photographed, and documented with a video camera as well. Two-man teams were set up, and as each scoop of dirt was freed, it was loaded into one of two sieves, shaken, and sifted for physical evidence.

At dusk, portable generators were brought in and high-intensity lights were set up. By then Daisy was shivering.

I linked my arm through hers. "Let's get out of here. They're not going to find anything tonight. You're freezing and I'm starving. Plus, I gotta pee so bad I'm about to wet my pants."

"Oh, me too," Tannie said.

21

JAKE
Thursday, July 2, 1953

Jake Ottweiler drove into Santa Maria for his bimonthly haircut, pausing outside the barbershop to put a nickel in the vending machine and extract a copy of the *Chronicle*. In his truck he'd discovered Mary Hairl's soiled nightgowns in a bundle on the front seat, where he'd inadvertently left them the night before. Once he got home, he'd do a load of wash and take her fresh clothes on his visit the next day. He usually went afternoons or evenings without fail, but she'd urged him to take a day off. He'd argued the point, more as a way of disguising his relief than with any desire to prevail.

As for the laundry, she'd insisted the hospital gowns were fine, not wanting to make more work for him when he was already strapped for time, but he'd seen how much happier she was in her own cotton nightie and robe. Now and then she even managed to put on her slippers and venture down the hall to visit the pastor's mother, who was laid up with a broken hip.

Rudy greeted him when he entered the shop. He was finishing up a shave on the fella ahead of him, so Jake waited his turn. He took a seat in the barber chair. Rudy wrapped a paper band around his neck and then secured a cape over his shoulders. The two scarcely exchanged a word. Rudy had been cutting his hair for the past twenty-seven years and didn't need advice. Jake flapped open the paper, skimming for information about the coming three-day weekend. He wasn't much interested in the Fourth of July folderol, but Mary Hairl wanted the kids to enjoy themselves. Steve was old enough to entertain himself—which in fact he preferred to do—but Tannie was another matter. Jake thought he might take her to the annual Fourth of July Rodeo Parade in Lompoc, where the Santa Maria Valley Roping and Riding Club would be performing. His choices for the fireworks show were the Elks Field at 8:30 Saturday night or the little park in Silas, which was closer to home. He planned to take a picnic supper. He didn't know how to cook, but his thought was to buy some hot dog buns and weenies that he could roast on one of the charcoal barbecue grills that dotted the park. He could buy potato salad and baked beans at the market and maybe candy bars for dessert.

As he flipped past the society news, Livia Cramer's name caught his eye. Mrs. Livia Cramer had been the hostess of a home-demonstration party, at which prizes had been given to Miss Juanita Chalmers, Miss Miriam Berkeley, Mrs. R. H. Hudson, and Mrs. P. T. York. Refreshments of pizza pie and cake were served. Now why that was newsworthy was beyond him, but he knew she'd be full of herself at the attention. Livia was pretentious enough as it was. He was tempted to carry the article up to the hospital to Mary Hairl, but if he tried poking fun at the woman, Mary Hairl would only come to her defense. Livia was panting for the day when she could palm off that hulking child of hers on some poor unsuspecting chump. With all the prattling about the engagement party, bridal showers, the wedding, the reception, talk of the gown, the flowers, and the honeymoon details, Livia would have her name and likeness splashed across the society pages for a year and a half. Assuming anyone would have the girl.

He read the comics—*Nancy*, *Freckles*, *Gordo*, and *Alley Oop*—which he never thought were funny but couldn't bear to miss. Then he checked the baseball scores and farm news while Rudy ran the clippers up the back of his neck. He drove home smelling like talcum powder. Despite Rudy's best efforts, his back and neck were already feeling itchy from the newly trimmed hairs that had slipped down his collar.

Once home, he stripped off his work boots, Sears shirt, and overalls, and ran water in the shower. While he waited for the hot water to come through, he put his clothes in the hamper, and as he passed the bathroom mirror, he glimpsed the scabbed-over claw marks Violet Sullivan had left on his back not four days before. He stepped into the shower, feeling both appalled and aroused. If anyone else saw the marks his goose would be cooked. He was always surprised by the damage she managed to inflict. She was small, no bigger than a girl, all energy and sass, red hair hanging halfway down her back, with a waviness that made a pattern when he lifted it from her neck. He liked to thread his fingers through its thickness, grab a fistful of hair, and pull her head back so hard her mouth would come open with surprise. He'd run a rough palm across her breasts and down the length of her spine while she shuddered with desire. He'd never known a woman like her, so savage and so insatiable. She wore a delicate violet perfume, her trademark she said. She dressed in purple and lavender, sometimes a dark vivid green that set her green eyes afire. The fabrics were soft and clung to the front of her legs, making a crackling sound when he pulled the skirt away from her thighs.

He'd never cared for violets himself. Weeds, to his way of thinking, taking over the lawn. Mary Hairl loved them, the white ones in particular, and she fussed at Jake every time he threatened to spray. He couldn't see the point in letting something wild and uncontrollable encroach on the grass. That spring, which he knew now would be Mary Hairl's last, he'd lain facedown among the violets, letting the light, sweet scent saturate his skin. He'd run his hand across the dark green leaves, snatching up the blossoms in the much same way he'd torn into Violet the last time they met. The motel carpeting had a strange metallic smell that he associated with their sex.

At the hospital the night before, he found himself ruminating on the differences between the two women. Of late, Mary Hairl's eyes had begun to look sunken, hollow, smudged dark, and Jake felt as guilty as if he'd struck her. He'd been patient and tender, dogged in his attentions, but his brain had disconnected, returning to Violet in spite of his best intentions. While he'd dabbed Mary Hairl's face with a damp cloth, he'd be thinking about Violet, the last time they'd been to bed, the ferocity with which she bit and sucked at him, clinging like a woman drowning among the bedsheets. She could tease, withhold, letting her red hair sweep over his thighs while he struggled for control, thrusting himself toward her. Violet would pull away, smiling, her eyes glittering. She'd lick the length of him, and he knew he'd never learn to stifle his groan when she finally took him in her mouth.

He looked down. Mary Hairl had asked for ice water, which Jake went to fetch for her, replenishing her glass. She was thirsty, as trusting as a child, sucking at the clear bent glass straw that he held to her lips. She murmured a thank you and lay back against the pillows. He knew he couldn't go on with Violet. Every other day he'd decide he had to break it off, but each time the opportunity presented itself, he'd think *Once more . . . just once more*, and then he'd hope to find the strength necessary to sever the relationship.

There was a weight in his chest, a heaviness reminding him of all he'd betrayed. Sometimes the anxiety was so intense he felt sick. He was grateful to Violet. He'd always be grateful for what he'd learned. She'd brought him to life after years of ministering to Mary Hairl's pain. If Mary Hairl would go—if she'd only get on with it—he knew the suffocating sense of desperation would pass. At the same time, though he could barely admit it to himself, he harbored the fantasy that with his wife gone, Violet might become a permanent part of his life, filling the void that Mary Hairl had left.

He turned off the shower knobs with a screech, stepped out, and then dried himself off. He dressed, pulling on the jeans he'd hung on a peg behind his closet door. He picked up the bundle of Mary Hairl's soiled nightclothes and moved into the mud room, where he'd hooked up the washer and dryer. He opened the washer lid and found himself staring down at the tight coil of wet clothes he'd neglected to remove. He couldn't remember running a load, but when he pulled out the first article, he realized it was Mary Hairl's laundry from the week before. The clothes were still damp and now smelled of mildew because the garments had sat so long. How could he have done such a thing? Bringing Mary Hairl clean clothes was something he'd taken on to demonstrate his care and concern. She'd never mentioned the fact that he'd failed to return her nighties and her step-ins. What had she worn all week?

Face burning, he started the load again, adding this week's clothing to the one before, hoping that a strong dose of soap powder would eliminate the rank odor of wet cotton gone sour. He went into the bedroom and opened Mary Hairl's dresser drawer, relieved to see she had plenty of other nighties. Everything was neatly folded, a plain virginal white. He pulled out four nightgowns and piled six pairs of step-ins on top. He hesitated and then laid the pile on top of the dresser.

He went through the remaining drawers, searching her belongings, something he'd never dreamed of doing before this moment. He wasn't sure what compelled him to forage among her things. Perhaps some morbid curiosity about the personal effects it would soon be his job to pack up and give away. What did he hope to find? A dildo, evidence of some hidden vice—drink, kleptomania, pornography? He knew, without having to look, that the dresses hanging in her closet were washed colorless, starched and fastidiously ironed. Why did this generate such anger in him? Why was his life filled with degradation while hers was so barren and apologetic?

In the second drawer from the bottom, hidden under her cotton slips, he saw the corner of a bright yellow box. He moved the slips aside. The drawer was lined with unopened gift sets of Jean Naté After Bath Splash and Cologne. He couldn't remember the last time he'd thought of giving her anything else. Why would he? Birthdays, she always asked for Jean Naté. He thought she loved it. Opening his gift, which he inevitably prevailed on the clerk to wrap, she'd seemed pleased and surprised, her appreciation sounding so heartfelt that he hadn't thought to question her sincerity. Christmas meant nothing to him. They gave gifts to the children, but the exchanging of gifts between the two of them felt awkward so now they skipped the practice on mutual agreement. Or so he'd assumed.

Seeing the Jean Naté, he was deeply ashamed. He'd been complacent about her, so oblivious that it hadn't occurred to him to give her anything more personal, lavish, or spontaneous. He was embarrassed that she hadn't felt comfortable telling him the truth, that she'd thought so little of herself she hadn't been able to ask for what she wanted. She probably didn't even know what that was. By her birthday, which would fall on September 12, she'd be gone, and in a flash it occurred to him that if he'd betrayed the marriage, so had she. The difference was that she'd die being thought of as saintly and good, and he'd be forced to live on without her, burdened by rage, corruption, and guilt. He might be a man without character, but she was a woman without courage. Of the two, which was worse?

Once the laundry was done, he left the house and drove to Serena Station. It was only 10:35 in the morning, but BW opened the Blue Moon at 9:00. There was no explanation for the absurdity of the hour. The place sat empty most of the day, half dark, door open, as cool and welcoming as a church. He parked and went in. At a table to one side, Winston Smith sat by himself, his back to the bar, his expression withdrawn. He had a Miller beer in front of him, though Jake knew for a fact he wasn't legally of age. Given his dark mood, maybe BW had taken pity on the boy, figuring he'd take his chances with the ABC agent, who'd been in the week before.

Jake took a seat at the bar and BW set a Blatz in front of him. Jake knew Violet stopped by two and three times a week after Foley left for work. He hadn't seen her since Sunday, but he needed to talk to her before he lost his resolve. Sure enough, she walked in twenty minutes later. Winston, in the process of ordering another beer, turned and stared at her sullenly. "I need to talk to you."

Violet paused by his table. "So talk."

"Please join me," he said. He was speaking with care, but Jake noticed that his consonants had turned soft around the edges. Violet sat down. Whatever Winston had to say to her, he kept his voice low, and Violet's expression never registered more than bemusement. Finally, she leaned forward. Her reply was inaudible, but whatever she'd said, Winston seemed taken aback. She got up and moved to the far end of the bar.

Winston said, "Bitch," to himself.

Jake looked from the boy to BW. "What's his deal?"

BW glanced at Winston. "Kid lost his job."

BW moved to Violet's end of the bar. She ordered and Jake watched while BW poured her a glass of red wine. Jake picked up his beer, walked the length of the bar, and took the stool next to hers. He waited until BW put the wineglass in front of her.

"I'll take care of it," Jake said. BW went to the cash register and punched in the charge, adding it to his tab, then disappeared into the back room to leave the two of them alone. Jake had thought he'd feel anxious about what he had to do, but he found himself regarding her with fondness. "I thought I'd see you yesterday afternoon."

"Something came up. I had business to take care of."

"I wasn't complaining."

"It sure sounded like that to me. If you're here to whine, don't bother. I already had a big dose of self-pity from Winston."

"Why's he so mad?"

"Because he's a jerk. Know what he said? He wanted me to lend him the money for his college tuition. Can you picture it? The nerve! I said, 'Why would I do that? What do I look like, a damn bank manager? I wouldn't lend you a dime if my life depended on it, you little creep.'"

"You're always talking about your money. Maybe he thought you'd be willing to help."

"Yeah, well, any money I have is mine and I'm not giving it away. So what are you doing here?"

"We need to talk."

"That's what he said. About what?"

Jake lowered his voice. "I know you've been pulling away. It's been going on for weeks and it's okay. I don't want you to feel bad. That's all I want to say. It's probably for the best and so be it."

Violet's tone was flat. "I don't have a clue what you're talking about."

"Feels to me like you've gone and found someone else."

"What if I have? I can't count on you, that's for damn sure. You've got Mary Hairl and I'm out here in the cold trying to look after myself. I need to get the hell out of Dodge and what do you have to offer? Nothing. A big fat zero."

"I'm not blaming you, I swear. I know I don't have anything to offer and I'm sorry about that because I'd help if I could. I guess the best we can say is we never made each other any promises."

She turned and squinted at him. "Wait a minute, what is this? Are you breaking it off?"

He motioned a palm flat against the air, trying to get her to lower her voice. "I'd just like to be a good husband to Mary Hairl in whatever time she has left. You think I want to do this? You're all I've thought about for months. For a while, I didn't see how I could live without you. Even now, I'm not sure how I'll make it. As much as you've meant . . ."

"As much as I've *meant*? I couldn't have meant much if you're chucking me aside like a piece of garbage. What's the problem, wasn't I good enough? You sure took advantage while it suited you, you dumb fuck, and now that you're tired of me—"

"Don't say things like that. You know how it was. Both of us were hurting so we helped each other out. I'm grateful for that, but you need something better and it seems like you found it. I just want you to know that I'm happy for you and wishing you the best."

"Well, that's damn generous. You're wishing me the best. Wonder what you'll wish for when Foley finds out."

He could feel his heart skip and all the warm feelings drained away. "Let's hope that never happens for your sake as well as mine."

"Oh, it'll happen all right. You know how I know?" She glanced at her watch. "Because about six o'clock tonight, minute he gets home, I'll have an attack of conscience and 'fess right up. I'll tell him how shocked and appalled I was when you forced your unwanted sexual attentions on me and how poor Mary Hairl has no idea you're strutting around with a big old hard-on, rubbing up against every woman who walks by."

"Oh, don't do that." His tone sounded plaintive, even to his own ears.

"Why not? I gotta protect myself."

"He's not going to believe you. Why would he take your word for anything? God only knows how many guys you've screwed—"

Violet picked up her wine and flung it in his face, then tossed the glass aside. It hit the floor, bounced once, and smashed. She took up her purse and walked out without looking back. Winston turned his head, watching her departure, and then his gaze traveled back to the bar, where Jake sat as though shot, his heart pounding at the shock. The jolt of lukewarm red wine had drenched his face and soaked into the front of his shirt. BW appeared from the back room. He took one look at Jake, reached for a towel, and passed it across the bar. Jake pressed the towel against his face, wishing he could disappear. Thank god only BW and Winston were there to bear witness.

Outside he could hear the engine turn over in Foley's rattletrap truck. Violet took off with a squeal, throwing up gravel against the underside with a rapid *rata-tat-tat*. He could feel the panic mount his frame. Surely she wouldn't do anything so dangerous as to tell Foley about him. He knew she was furious, but she'd taken it the wrong way. He wasn't rejecting her, he was setting her free.

He looked up as Tom Padgett appeared in the door. Tom was staring back over his shoulder, the light glinting off his glasses. He brought his gaze around to the scene in front of him: Jake's shirt soaked, Winston drunk, BW behind the bar, looking rooted in place. "What the hell is going on?"

Jake tried calling Violet twice on Thursday afternoon, but the phone rang and rang, apparently to an empty house. The third time he called, Foley Sullivan picked up and Jake returned the handset to the cradle without saying a word. He spent Thursday evening at the hospital with Mary Hairl, which he hadn't meant to do, but she seemed so pleased and grateful to see him, he nearly convinced himself that he'd done it for her. In truth, he was too anxious to stay home. A whisper of fear had settled in his gut. Violet was reckless, and he wouldn't put it past her to bring the roof down around her head if she thought she was getting even with him. He felt safe in Mary Hairl's company, as though in looking after her, he could look after himself. Or maybe it was more accurate to say that by staying at her side, he hoped to ward off the disaster that was heading his way.

He called Friday at lunchtime, but again there was no answer. He drove through Serena Station, looking for any sign of her. He ran an errand in Silas and then swung back through town and parked across the street from the post office so he could pick up his mail. Miraculously he spotted her, driving the brand-new Chevrolet he'd seen in Chet Cramer's showroom. He was just crossing the street when she slowed to a stop. She leaned over and waited until he was even with the open window. "So what do you think?"

She looked radiant. Gone was the dark rage and in its place was a Violet Sullivan as tickled as a kid with a shiny new bike. He found himself smiling. "Where'd you get that? It's pretty slick."

"It's mine. Foley bought it for me."

"Bought it? I thought Foley was broke."

"Oh, he has his little ways. He must have pulled a fast one on Chet because he went off this morning before nine, came home an hour later, and parked this little beauty at the curb."

"What's the occasion?"

"Who needs an occasion? He's nuts about me. Of course it doesn't hurt that he went berserk last night and tore the house apart. My brand-new lace curtains ended up in the trash. Where're you off to? You want a ride around the block?"

"Nah, I got things to take care of. Maybe another time," he said. He noticed a pair of white cardboard glasses sitting on the front seat. "Those your sunglasses?"

She glanced down. "No, what, these?" She picked them up and put them on. "I took Daisy and Liza Mellincamp to that 3-D movie this afternoon. *Bwana Devil.* Daisy's going to have nightmares for a month."

"Kids will do that," he said mildly.

"Anyway, I gotta be some place so I better let you go. Tah-tah," she said. She put her foot on the gas and took off.

He'd never seen her so cheerful or so full of goodwill. He returned to his car with an overwhelming sense of relief. Maybe everything was okay and he could breathe again.

He went back to the hospital late that afternoon, feeling lighter than he had in months. It was not quite 5:00, but the dinner carts were already in the hall. He'd sit with her through dinner and spend the evening with her until she was settled in for the night. He'd bought Mary Hairl a little houseplant to keep beside her bed. The gal at the florist's shop had wrapped it in a high cone of green tissue paper with a bright purple bow. Jake thought she'd be pleased to have something colorful to look at. He got on the elevator and went up to the second floor. As the doors opened, he stopped in his tracks. Mary Hairl's father was standing in the hall, his face stony. Something had happened to Mary Hairl. Maybe she'd taken a turn for the worse; maybe she was dead. Cold seeped up from the floor and climbed his frame.

Hairl held a Bible in one hand, and in the other he clutched a piece of pink notepaper, covered with a slanting scrawl of black ink. "You son of a bitch. Tell me on this Bible you never lusted in your heart. Tell me you never lain with Violet Sullivan and don't you lie. My poor girl, my only girl, she's in there dying as we speak. She probably doesn't have but a week to live. So you tell me you didn't put that pecker of yours in that vile whore's mouth! Swear on this book! This isn't the first time you've done this, Son. You think I don't know that? Word gets around and I heard about every single one of your affairs. You thought you were being sly, but you never fooled me. I could barely stand to look you in the eye, but I kept hush for Mary Hairl's sake. I should have said something years ago, but she worshiped you. Worshiped the ground you walked on. You're a failure. You're worthless. You can't even manage to earn a decent wage. Weren't for me, you'd be on welfare. And now there you are, off in some bar making a public display of yourself."

Hairl lost his momentum. His voice broke and the

pink notepaper shook in his trembling hand. He sobbed once and then gathered himself again. "If I had the strength, I would choke the life out of you. My beautiful girl. She's the soul of goodness and what of you, sir? You are low-down, stinking trash. You've made her an object of pity in this town, and she'll go to her grave looking like a fool, but there's worse in store for you. I can promise you that."

Jake's mind went blank. He was speechless with horror. What had she done? What in god's name had Violet Sullivan gone and done?

22

The three of us drove to Daisy's in separate cars, like a very short motorcade. Having warned them, I peeled off at Broadway and made a stop at JC Penney, where I bought a cotton nightie, two T-shirts, and cheap underwear. I made a second stop at a nearby drugstore and bought three paperback novels, shampoo, conditioner, and deodorant, figuring if I was in town for any length of time I might as well smell good. Even if the Bel Air was magically unearthed and I went home the next day, the purchases would be useful. It's not like the underpants were stamped with a sell-by date.

I reached Daisy's house at 8:00, when the autumn dark had fully settled and the streetlights had come on. She'd left the garage door open, so I pulled my car in, locked it, and triggered the automatic-door device as I emerged. Once in the house, I found Tannie stretched out on the living room floor, trying to get the kinks out of her back after a morning of hacking brush and an af-

ternoon watching cops dig a car out of her lawn. Daisy
was in the kitchen brewing a fresh pot of tea. She'd
changed out of her work clothes and into her sweats, but
she looked just as stressed as she had at the site. Her face
had the pinched look of someone in the throes of a mi-
graine, though she claimed she was fine. The discovery
of the car had generated tension in each of us, but our
remedies were different. Daisy longed for a bath and
Tannie wanted a drink. For my part, I'd have given anything to be by myself, an impossible desire as things currently stood. I couldn't even take to my bed because
Daisy'd brought her cup of tea into the living room and
now sat on the couch, where I would ultimately sleep.
From the floor, Tannie said, "Hey, gang. I don't remember eating dinner, unless I missed an episode. Is anybody
else hungry? I'm about to eat my own arm."

After a brief negotiation, Daisy picked up the phone
and ordered a large pizza, which was delivered thirty
minutes later. We ate with enthusiasm, though Tannie
declined any portion of the pizza that butted up against
the anchovies Daisy and I had voted for. Just when I assumed we were done for the day, free to read or watch
mindless TV, the telephone rang. Daisy picked up. "Oh,
hi, BW. What's up?"

As she listened I watched her expression change. The
color rose in her cheeks as though controlled by a dimmer switch. "How did that happen?" She closed her
eyes, shaking her head at the nature of his response. "I
see. No, no. It's not your fault. I understand. I'll be right
there."

She hung up.

"What is it?" I asked.

"My father's over at the Blue Moon and he's drunk on

his ass. BW wants me to get him out of there before a fight breaks out."

"Foley's drunk?"

"That's what he says. I'll take care of it. Why don't you two stay here?"

"Don't be silly. I'll go. You can't manage by yourself if he's that far gone."

Daisy turned to Tannie. "What about you? It's entirely optional."

"Count me out. I'll go if you need me, but I'm beat. I gotta get up early and hit the road. We get over to the Moon, I'll end up having a drink and that'll be it. I'm tempted, but trying to behave myself."

"Don't worry about it. We'll be back as soon as we figure out what to do with him."

Daisy found her purse and car keys. She said she'd be warm enough in her sweats, but she found a spare jacket for me. The evening was already chilly, and neither of us was sure how long we'd be out. On the fifteen-mile drive from Santa Maria to Serena Station, she kept shaking her head. "I can't believe it. He's been sober for thirty-four years and here we go again."

"He must have heard about the car."

"That's what BW said."

"But why would that set him off?"

"Beats the hell out of me. I don't even want to speculate."

The Blue Moon that Friday night was jammed. Happy hour had ended at 7:00, but the drinking sailed right on. The energy level seemed manic, bespeaking much joy that the work week was done. This time the place did smell of beer and cigarette smoke. Between the loud talk, the jukebox, and alcohol-amped laughter, the noise was overwhelming.

Foley Sullivan sat at the bar, oblivious to everything, like a man submerged in a deprivation tank. He and his whiskey had been separated for three decades. Now, like old lovers, they'd been reunited, and he was busy reestablishing their relationship, leaving no room for anyone or anything else. He sat ramrod straight. His face was still gaunt, but his deep-set eyes were now bright with relief. His was the kind of drunkenness that had him two sips away from a blind, flailing rage.

Daisy approached, making sure he saw who she was before she laid a hand on his back. She leaned in close in order to make herself heard. "Hey, Dad. How're you doing? I heard you were here."

He didn't bother to look at her, but he did raise his voice. "I see you whipped right over to look after me. Well, I'm fine, girl. No need. I can handle myself. Appreciate your concern, but I believe it's misplaced."

"What prompted this?"

"I guess I was born with a taste for brimstone. You ought to have one yourself. Whiskey will melt the sorrow right out of your soul."

The man on the stool next to Foley's had caught their exchange. I wasn't sure whether he knew Daisy and her father or simply understood that this wasn't a conversation he wanted to hear. He vacated his place and Daisy slid onto the stool.

Foley had gone back to his contemplation, staring into his glass as though into the dark heart of mankind. When Daisy touched his arm, he seemed surprised that

she was still there. The smile he gave her was sweet.
"Hello, Sweet Pea."

"Hello, Dad. Could we go outside and talk? I need
some fresh air, don't you?"

"Nothing to talk about. That car was the final tie." He
made a slicing motion with his hand. "Severed. Just like
that. She knew it'd cut me to the core if it ever came to
light."

"If what came to light?"

"The car. She buried it before she left. I paid and I
paid because I loved her and thought she'd be back. Dear
god, I wanted her to know she didn't owe me anything."

"What are you talking about?"

He focused on her face. "They found her Bel Air. I
thought you knew."

"Of course, I knew. The sheriff's office called me this
afternoon."

"Well then, fair enough. We have to accept the fact.
Your mother laid it in the ground and then she went off.
We have to make our peace with her abandonment."

"She didn't bury it. You can't believe that. How could
she manage?"

"Obviously, she had help. Fella she ran off with must
have helped dig the hole."

"That doesn't make sense. If she was running off, why
wouldn't she take the car with her? If she had no use for
it, she could have sold it."

"It was her way of taunting me. The car was my final
gift to her and she rejected it."

"Dad, please stop. You know what's going on. There's
a good possibility she's buried down there. That's why
they're taking their time, so they won't destroy evidence."

He shook his head, his mouth pulled down as though he regretted having to deliver the news. He wasn't slurring his words, but his brain was operating at half speed and his concentration was, of necessity, intense. He thumped his chest. "She's not dead. I'd feel it here if she were."

"I'm not going to argue with you. Can we just get out of here?"

"Sweet Pea, you're not responsible for the state I'm in. I'm doing this in deference to your mother with whom I drank for many years. This is my farewell. I'm giving up all claim. Violet Sullivan is free." He gestured with his whiskey, toasting his wife before he drank it down.

I wasn't sure where his grandiosity was coming from and I couldn't judge his mood. He seemed dangerous—testy and unpredictable despite the formality of his speech. Daisy shot me a look. Our unspoken pact was to sweet-talk him out of there before he blew. I put a hand on his shoulder and leaned close.

When he realized who I was, he rared back slightly. "So she's got you here, too."

"We're both concerned. It's late and we thought you might like to finish your drinking at home."

His gaze was out of focus, giving him a cross-eyed look. "I don't have whiskey at home. Pastor would disapprove. I live in a church cell that's fit for a monk."

"Why don't we go to Daisy's? We can take you out for breakfast and then we'll stop by her place or we'll drop you at home."

"You've never attended an Al-Anon meeting, have you?"

"I haven't. That's correct."

"This is not your job. It has nothing to do with you. I don't need to be rescued. I don't need to be saved. I want to sit and enjoy myself so leave me be. I absolve you of any responsibility." He waved a hand, airily, absolving me.

Out of the corner of my eye, I saw BW approaching, and I remember thinking, thank god. He'd had years of experience dealing with Foley drunk. Though both hands were empty, he was clearly in bouncer mode. Jake Ottweiler was two paces behind him.

BW said, "Foley, I want you out of here right now."

Foley's eyes jerked from BW to Jake and that's all it took. Foley's demons spilled out, though he smiled as he spewed. "There's the man who fucked my wife."

"Dad. Please lower your voice."

Jake had stopped in his tracks. Foley eased off his stool and steadied himself. BW moved swiftly and locked his arms around Foley's so he couldn't move. Foley raised his voice to a shrieking pitch. "You son of a bitch. Admit it! You used my wife and then you cast her aside like she was common as dirt. You never even had the decency to own up to it."

"That's it," BW said. He lifted Foley and force-marched him through the bar. "You ever set a foot in here again and it's the last thing you'll ever do. I'm warning you."

In BW's grip, Foley's feet scarcely touched the floor. He looked like a ballerina, up on his toes, taking light, dainty steps with remarkable speed and grace. "Warn me? Why not warn him? Why not warn every man in town has a wife as beautiful as mine. I'm telling you the truth, which he damn well knows—"

Daisy grabbed BW's arm and she was being dragged

along at the same quick clip. "Stop it! Let go of him. He can't help himself."

"Maybe I can help. Here, try this." BW bumped the door open with his foot and flung Foley out. Foley landed on one hip, his momentum toppling him over onto his hands and knees. Before anyone could intervene, BW swung one boot back and his fast-moving kick caught Foley squarely in the face. The cartilage in his nose went flat with a sound like a watermelon hitting concrete. Blood spurted out of his nose and his mouth welled with red. A row of white teeth, false, had popped out intact, but others were damaged and his tongue seemed swollen as though he'd bitten himself. His eyes rolled back in his head until all we could see were two white slits. Then he went still. Daisy screamed.

My heart was knocking against my chest so hard I thought I'd see bruises the next day. Daisy dropped down beside her father, who groaned and rolled over on his back. She looked up at BW with horror, both of us expecting a second kick to land. BW turned away. He grabbed the door and his tone was filled with disgust. "Fuck. I'll call an ambulance and send out some ice for his face."

23

The ambulance arrived and three paramedics alighted, like firemen on a run. By then Foley had staggered to his feet and was ready to fight the son of a bitch who'd knocked him on his buns. He was belligerent, lashing out, fending off the paramedic who was offering first aid. With the blood oozing out of his nose and welling across his upper lip, he looked like a vampire interrupted in the course of a gory feast. The waitress brought him a plastic bag packed with ice and wrapped in a kitchen towel. Grimacing, she passed it to him and returned to the restaurant as quickly as possible. While his upper bridge had gone flying, his lower teeth had been forced through his lip. He held the ice pack to his mouth, the towel turning a saturated red. He declined medical attention, so the paramedics had no choice but to climb back in the ambulance and drive away.

Foley slumped onto the wooden steps and leaned his head against the rail, talking to himself.

Daisy bent over him. "Dad, listen to me. Would you listen? You need to see a doctor."

"I don't need a doctor. Leave me be." He scanned the area around him, his eyes out of focus. "Where'd my bridge go? I can't hardly talk without my teeth."

"Don't worry about that. I've got it. I need your keys."

He leaned sideways, nearly losing his balance as he dug in his pants pocket and came up with the keys.

Daisy snatched them and passed them to me before she turned back to him. "I want you to get in the car. I'm taking you to the emergency room. Kinsey's going to follow us in your truck. And don't argue."

"I wasn't arguing," he said in a cranky, argumentative tone.

We helped him to his feet. He was woozy from the whiskey and woozy from the blow to his face. The two of us guided him, staggering, to Daisy's car, which was parked on the street and mercifully close. She unlocked the passenger's-side door and opened it. Foley shrugged off any further help, claiming he could manage. He held on to the door frame, eased himself half the distance to the seat, and then fell the rest, groaning at the jolt.

"It's your own fault," she snapped. "Move your hand."

He managed to remove his hand from the frame half a second before she slammed the door. She opened the trunk and snatched a terry-cloth towel from her gym bag. Disgusted, she opened the door again and tossed it to him. "Don't bleed on the upholstery."

She pointed out his truck in the parking lot and then slammed the trunk lid shut as she rounded the back of the car. I walked over to the truck and let myself in while she started her car. She waited until I was nosing out of the parking lot before she put her car in gear and pulled onto the street ahead of me.

She drove him to the ER at the hospital where she worked. By that time Foley had settled down, perhaps recognizing the enormity of his sins. Even having his nose broken wasn't going to be sufficient penance to redeem him in Daisy's eyes. She put his name on the register, and when he was called she accompanied him into the examining room. I sat in the waiting room, leafing through a magazine while Foley was being worked on. After forty minutes, she came out and sank into the chair next to mine.

I said, "How's it going?"

"He'll be fine. They've called in an ear, nose, and throat specialist to reset his nose. The doctor's also ordered a CAT scan since he suffered a brief loss of consciousness. They said they'd bring me in again when he's back from radiology."

"Will they keep him overnight?"

"Doesn't look that way," she said as she got up. "Let me see if I can find a pay phone and call the pastor. There's no way I'm taking him home with me." She took her purse and headed off down the hall. Less than five minutes later she was back. "Blessings on the man. He asked a few questions and then said he'd be waiting whenever Dad was released. The parish house is right next door to the church, and he says he's welcome as a guest as long as he needs help. I don't know where he'd be if it weren't for that man."

Friday night was apparently the equivalent of date night in the ER world, a popular occasion for accidents and mishaps, pain, suffering, and near-death experiences.

A kid was brought in with a bean stuck up his nose. There was a woman hacking and feverish from a case of the flu, and a man with a sprained ankle swollen to elephantine proportions. A teen arrived holding his badly broken thumb, smashed by a car door and looking so mangled I nearly passed out.

Unfazed, Daisy pulled the clip out of her hair and gathered it in a tidy sheaf before she secured it again. Foley's accusation about Jake's affair with Violet seemed to hang in the air between us. "All I can say is thank god Tannie wasn't there."

"She's bound to hear about it," I said.

"You bet. My phone would be ringing off the hook if anybody knew she was there."

I set the magazine aside. "You have to wonder what went on. Was there really an affair, or did your dad imagine the whole thing?"

"He's not famous for his imagination. Tannie's mother was sick for a good two years. It was 'female trouble,' too, so there's every possibility their sex life sucked." She shook her head and let out a deep breath. She extended her legs and slouched down on her spine so that her head was resting on the back of the seat. "Was there anyone she didn't screw? My mother must have been crazy as a loon."

"Well, it's like the fella said. You're not responsible for what she did."

"But I'm responsible for stirring this up. I should have left well enough alone."

The big digital wall clock read 10:16. I got up, too restless to sit another minute in the midst of all the medical chaos. "I'm going to see if I can find a cup of coffee. You want one?"

"Not me. My nerves are jangled enough."

The fluorescent lights in the public hallways shone brightly on the gleaming vinyl-tile floors. Most departments I passed were dark; hospital administration, the cardiovascular, EKG, and EEG departments. I turned a corner and followed the corridor until I reached the main lobby. A sign indicated that the cafeteria was one floor down, but when I got off the elevator in the basement, the place was dark and the door was locked. According to the sign, the coffee shop was open from 7:00 A.M. until 7:15 P.M. on weekdays. I'd missed by hours. A maintenance man appeared with a mop and an industrial-sized bucket. Together we waited for the elevator, which had stopped on the first floor.

"Is there a vending machine around here?"

He shook his head. "Wish there were. I could use a candy bar about now."

The elevator doors opened and we got on. When we emerged on the first floor, I glanced to my left and spotted Liza Clements sitting in the lobby. Her complexion looked washed out and her jeans and T-shirt were wrinkled. I called out to her and moved in her direction. "What are you doing here?" I asked.

"My granddaughter was born a few minutes ago. I'm keeping out of everybody's hair until she's cleaned up. Kevin's upstairs with Marcy, and both of her parents are here. Six pounds, six ounces. She's absolutely beautiful."

"That's great. Congratulations."

"Thanks. It's been pretty intense. What about you? I didn't expect to see a familiar face."

I gave her a quick rendition of Foley's nose-busting adventure, neatly omitting the remarks that had gotten him tossed out of the Moon.

"Is there any way to get a cup of coffee at this hour?" she asked.

"Nope. I tried. I guess we could find a water fountain but that's about it."

We ended up sitting together in the main lobby for lack of any place better. It was a small cheerless area clearly not intended as a waiting room. At least the ER had offered a television set and a few live green plants. I said, "You heard about the car?"

"That's all anybody's talking about. I guess there's no doubt it's hers."

"Not in my mind. I mean, what are the chances another car would be buried out where hers was last seen?"

She shifted in her chair. "I'm going to 'fess up to something, but I don't want to hear you scream. You promise?"

"Scout's honor."

"As it so happens, I saw Foley at the Tanner property that Friday night."

"Doing what?"

"Tinkering with a bulldozer that was parked near the road. I heard him start it up."

"You're positive it was Foley?"

"I couldn't *swear* it was him, but who else could it be?"

"Just about anyone," I said. "In the as-it-so-happens department, what were you doing there?"

"Ty and I had gone out to the house. We weren't supposed to be dating, and it was the only place we could think of where we wouldn't be seen. We were in that second-floor bedroom in front when we heard him drive up."

"And you were . . . what—smoking dope? Making out?"

She rolled her eyes, tucking a strand of blond hair behind one ear. "Oh, please. None of us smoked dope in those days. We're talking about the '50s. We were square as they come."

"So you were doing what?"

"Okay, we were necking if you must know the truth. When the car pulled up, we thought it was a security guard coming to check on the house, so we hightailed it out the back and waited until we heard the 'dozer start up. Ty figured that would cover the sound of the truck."

"So you didn't actually see Foley face on?"

"I just told you that. The point is, if it *was* him, he had plenty of time to dig a hole."

"What kind of car? I'm assuming you'd have recognized the Bel Air."

"Of course. Most of the time I can't tell one kind of car from another, but I know it wasn't Violet's. Her car was pale and it would have stood out. There was enough of a moon that it would have been obvious."

"What do you remember about the car? Two-door? Four-door? Light? Dark?"

She made a face, shaking her head in the negative. "I *saw* it, but I didn't really look. I was scared we'd get caught and that's all I cared about. And before you even ask, no, I didn't tell the guys from the sheriff's department."

"Because you didn't want to admit you were trespassing?"

"Because at the time, it didn't mean anything. Violet wasn't even missing. When we saw the guy—Foley, or whoever—it wouldn't have occurred to me he'd be doing anything like that. Digging a grave. God, it gives me goose bumps. I'm only telling you now because we know the car is buried there."

"You remember anything else?"

"No. Well, yes. The guy was smoking. I remember that because we could smell it through the open window all the way upstairs."

"Height? Weight? Anything like that?"

"Nope. It was dark and I only caught a glimpse. You think I should talk to the detective?"

"Absolutely," I said.

"Even if it gets Foley in more trouble?"

"You can't even claim it was him. All you can say is there was a guy out there working on a bulldozer. The detective's name is Nichols. He needs to know."

By the time I got back to the emergency room, Foley had been released. He emerged from the examining area, clutching a head trauma precaution sheet and the pain pills he'd been given to take home with him. His eyes were already looking bruised, and I imagined that by the next day, the purple would be intense. He had a splint taped over the bridge of his nose, and it made his eyes seem as close together as a collie's. Both nostrils had been packed with half-inch-wide strips of white cloth, and I could see sutures across his chin. I had to guess there were others on the inside of his mouth. Luckily for him, the pain medication was wiping out the ill effects of his drinking binge. He looked subdued. His eyes were fixed on Daisy's with the mute, pleading look a puppy lays on you when there are table scraps at stake.

Daisy drove him into Cromwell, me trailing along behind in his truck as I had before. When she pulled into the driveway of the parish house, the porch light came on. The pastor pushed a curtain aside and peered out, then opened the front door in his slippers, pajamas, and a soft flannel robe. I parked in front, locked the truck, and crossed to Daisy's car, where I handed Foley his keys. He wouldn't meet my eyes and I could feel the embarrassment rolling off him like sweat. The pastor held open the screen door and Foley disappeared inside. Daisy had a few words with the man and then returned to her car.

We got in. For a moment, she sat staring through the windshield, her hands on the steering wheel.

"You okay?"

"I'll tell you what's weird. You know when you see a movie they have those previews of coming attractions? This feels like a preview of past attractions. I don't remember seeing my father drunk, but this has to be what he was like when he was married to my mom. Not nice."

"Yeah, and I'll bet he looks about like she did when he beat the hell out of her."

She turned the key in the ignition. "At least now you know why I'm so screwed up."

"You know something, Daisy? You're not that screwed up. I've seen a lot worse."

"Oh, thanks. I feel much better now that you've said that."

We drove to Santa Maria in silence. The two-lane road was deserted at that hour, dark agricultural land stretching out on both sides as far as the eye could see. We passed a corrugated metal building sitting in a sea of asphalt and surrounded by chain-link fencing. The area was awash in a cold, silver light, but there was no sign of life. To the west, concealing the sight of the ocean beyond, a swell of low-lying hills formed a scalloped silhouette against the night sky. Daisy checked her rearview mirror as a set of headlights popped into view. I glanced over my shoulder, expecting the car to speed up and pass. Daisy was cruising at a sedate sixty miles an hour, but drivers on country roads get impatient.

The car behind us maintained the same distance for a mile and then began closing the gap. Daisy flicked another look in the mirror. "Shit. I recognize the Mercedes. That's Jake."

"How'd he know where we were? You think he was waiting in the ER parking lot?"

"I didn't see him if he was."

We reached Santa Maria and turned down Daisy's street with Jake right behind us. He wasn't doing anything threatening and he made no attempt to conceal himself, but in the wake of the violence, I wasn't crazy about seeing him again. BW might have delivered the kick, but Jake had been the catalyst. Daisy pulled into her driveway and doused her headlights. I checked the house. An overhead fixture burned in the kitchen, but the living room and guest room at the front of the house were both dark. Jake eased in behind us and doused his headlights. He killed the engine, as Daisy had, and then he got out and approached us along the drive.

"You think we ought to get out?" she asked.

I put a hand on the door handle. "Let's. I don't like the idea of his towering over us."

She got out on her side and I got out on mine, moving around the front of the car so we were side by side. It was dark and the night was chilly as anticipated, which made me happy I'd accepted the offer of a jacket. I crossed my arms, not feeling the cold so much as residual tension. The neighboring houses were locked and barred for the night. I wasn't uneasy about Jake, but it did occur to me that if either of us screamed, no one would hear us and respond.

Daisy said, "Hey, Jake. What can I do for you?"

"Sorry to bother you. I stopped by to ask about your dad. Is he all right?"

"I wouldn't go *that* far, but the doctor treated him and sent him home so I guess that tells you something. You know you could have called instead of following us home like this."

"There's something else I wanted to talk about and I didn't think it should wait. I promise I won't take up too much of your time . . ."

"Good because we spent the last two hours at the emergency room and I'm beat. Tannie's gone to bed if you were hoping to see her."

"It's you I'd like to talk to. You, too," he said, with a quick nod at me.

"Why don't you come on in the kitchen and we'll close the door. I don't imagine you want Tannie hearing this."

"Out here is fine. I intend to talk to her myself as soon as I have the chance. My son, Steve, too."

"Smart move," she said.

Jake ignored her testiness. "I came to apologize for what happened to Foley tonight. We're fully prepared to pay his medical expenses. You can send the bills straight to me and I'll take care of them. BW had no right to do what he did."

"Shit, really? Kick a guy in the face and bust his nose?"

"Daisy, I said I was sorry and I mean that. BW was way out of line and I told him so. I'm not saying he was wrong to hustle your dad out of there. Foley had that coming, but not the violence. BW's a hothead. He tends to act first and think about it later. It wouldn't surprise me if Foley pressed charges."

"Forget it. He's not going to do that. So what else? I'm sure you didn't tail us to inquire about his health."

"I feel I owe you an explanation."

Daisy nearly offered him a smart remark, but apparently decided against it. Better to let him fumble through the conversation on his own.

Jake kept his gaze pinned on the middle distance, but his manner was otherwise straightforward. "It isn't true, what he accused me of, but I believe I know how he came by that impression, even if he's mistaken. I hope you'll bear with me."

"Have at it. I'm all ears."

"There was an incident at the Moon . . . this must have been a month and a half before your mother disappeared. I'd been up at the hospital, visiting Mary Hairl, and I stopped off for a nightcap. Both your parents were at the bar and had been for some time. I think it's safe to say neither one of them was feeling any pain. By the time I arrived, your dad was in a sulk. Violet started flirting with me—I think to aggravate him as much as anything else. My wife was sick. I was lonely and maybe I gave your mother the wrong impression. We started dancing, which seemed harmless to me, but after a while she was behaving in a way that was an embarrassment. Community's small. You know how it is. Everybody knows everybody's business. I couldn't have her rubbing up against me, or putting her hands on my butt. Anyway, I'll skip the details out of respect for her. I didn't want to hurt her feelings, but I knew I had to set her straight.

"Problem was, Violet was accustomed to getting her way and she wasn't about to take no for an answer. She got mad and said I'd insulted her. About then she walked off the floor and I followed her. I hadn't meant anything of the sort. I tried telling her it wasn't my intent. I liked your mother . . . don't get me wrong . . . but I was taken aback. Long and short of it, she ended up throwing a glass of wine in my face."

"That was you? I'd heard the story, but I had no idea. Your name was never mentioned."

"That was me all right. Unfortunately, that wasn't the end of it. She started screaming and cussing. She was hot-tempered to begin with and sensitive to slights. She threatened to tell Foley we'd had sex, that I'd come on to her, and when she turned me down, I'd forced myself on her. Nothing could have been farther from the truth, but what could I do? BW could see something was going on and he got Foley out of there on some pretext.

"Once he was gone, I tried to reason with her. I hadn't meant to offend her and I apologized for any mis-understanding. She seemed to calm down. I hoped that would be the end of it, but I couldn't be sure. I was in a sticky position. I couldn't go to Foley and tell him what she'd said. If she never mentioned it herself, I'd only be opening up a can of worms. He'd either take issue with me for rejecting her, or else he'd accuse her of screwing around and she'd deny everything, claiming I'd raped her. In that case, I'd end up looking like my only interest was in covering my tracks. At any rate, I thought it best to keep quiet and that's the last I heard of it until to-night. Clearly, she did what she'd threatened. She must have told him I'd pushed her into something against her will and that's what he believed."

Daisy was quiet. I could see her testing his story in the same way I was. "I don't know what to say. Dad and I haven't talked about any of this. He's a mess right now and I'm sure he's ashamed of himself for getting drunk. I do understand your wanting to set the record straight. If you like, I'll tell him what you said."

"I leave that to your judgment. At least now you know my side of it. You can believe it or not. And your dad, when he sobers up, can do with it what he wants. I don't mean any disrespect to Violet, but he knows how capable she was of turning things around. If he'd stop and think about it, he might be willing to concede the point. As for me, I'm sorry for any part I played. I never meant to cause him any grief."

"I appreciate that, Jake. Is there anything else?"

"No, that's it. I've had my say. I know it's late and I won't keep you."

The two of them went through a bit of conversational back-and-forth before Jake finally said his good-nights and returned to his car.

Once he'd left, I waited half a minute and said, "What do you think?"

"I've got no proof, but offhand I'd say the man is a lying sack of shit."

24

TOM
Thursday, July 2, 1953

The morning after Cora left for Walnut Creek, Tom slept in, sprawled across the bed in a luxury of sheets. Among the many things they disagreed about was the temperature in the bedroom at night; he liked it cold, windows open to the wide, while Cora liked the windows shut and the heat cranked up. They also disagreed about blankets, the firmness of the mattress, and the nature of bed pillows. Alone, he could do it all exactly as he liked. With Cora out of the way, he was an entirely different man. It was like having a separate personality, one he called forth and wore like a smoking jacket while she was gone. He had two such personalities, as a matter of fact. When he drank, especially at the Blue Moon, he relaxed into the blue-collar type from which he sprang. He was a good old boy at heart. He liked his boots and jeans, adding a western-cut sport coat when he felt like dressing up. Here in Cora's fancy house, sober and unobserved, he activated another side of his nature, playing Lord of the

Manor. He was jaunty and dapper. He used a cigarette holder when he smoked and affected a snooty accent when he talked to himself.

He got up at 10:00, showered, dressed, and popped over to Maxi's Coffee Shop for breakfast. He checked on a couple of pieces of equipment that he had out, and when he reached the house again, he saw the mail truck just pulling away. He angled the car in close to the mailbox and retrieved the stack of envelopes and two of Cora's magazines. He left the car in the driveway and entered the house, calling, "Yoo hoo, I'm home!" purely for the pleasure of knowing he was on his own.

He carried the mail into Cora's office and laid it on the corner of her desk, intending to peruse later at his leisure. He sat down in her office chair and began a systematic search. She was secretive about her personal papers, keeping everything locked up—desk drawers, file cabinets, even the closet where she kept her jewelry and furs. The good news was he'd long ago figured out where she hid the keys. It amused him to let her go on believing herself secure while he kept an eye on her every move. He knew better than to try to siphon money from her bank accounts—she could be such a bitch about those things—but he did occasionally fudge an endorsement on a dividend check. One had arrived the day before, and he'd culled it out of the batch before he gave the mail to her. In his bathroom, with the door locked, he opened the envelope to see what his deception had netted him. Ah. $356.45 from some shares of stock she owned. He liked walking-around money, just the odd few bucks. She never seemed to notice. Dividend checks came periodically and the face amount varied, so it wasn't something she counted on as a regular event. He wasn't proud of himself, but he did enjoy his little forays into her private affairs. Really, she brought it on herself.

He opened her desk drawer and found the folder in which she kept her canceled checks. He extracted one, pleased with the sample of her signature. *Cora A. Padgett* with a little loop on the last *t*. He had a nice supply of tracing paper and he could whip out a decent approximation in no time at all. He endorsed the check—well, "Cora A. Padgett" endorsed the check—and then he put his tools away and picked up the stack of mail. He sorted through rapidly, disregarding bills except for the ones he didn't want her to see. The last envelope in the pile was a letter addressed to Loden Galsworthy from an out-of-state bank. He reached for the letter opener, slit the envelope, and read the correspondence signed by a "Lawrence Freiberg," one of two vice presidents. Mr. Freiberg, or "Larry," as Tom was already fond of calling him, was writing to inquire about the above-referenced account on which there'd been no activity for the better part of five years. Interest had been accruing and was, of course, properly credited, but the bank was wondering if perhaps there was something more they might do for him. They'd recently established an investment arm for valued customers. Since Loden Galsworthy was numbered among their very best, Mr. Freiberg suggested that perhaps the bank might put him in touch with one of their financial experts for an analysis of his portfolio. Tom read the letter twice. This had to be an account of Loden's that Cora had either overlooked or knew nothing about. Mr. Freiberg had probably never met his valued customer and clearly had no idea he was writing to the deceased—the *late* Loden Galsworthy. When he turned to the next page and his eye settled on the account balance, he barked out a laugh. $65,490.66.

He couldn't believe his good fortune. For weeks he'd walked around with his head in a noose and suddenly he was free. He knew exactly what to do. He got up from the desk and crossed to the closet where Cora maintained what amounted to a shrine to her dead husband's memory. Being the sentimental fool she was, she'd held on to a number of items that had belonged to him, among them his personalized stationery and his Montblanc fountain pen. Tom extracted an envelope, several sheets of letterhead, and a few pieces of blank paper. He then sat down at Cora's typewriter (Loden's before his death) and flexed his fingers, preparing himself as though for a piano recital. Using the blank paper and a bit of ingenuity, he composed a letter thanking the vice president for his concern. He confessed he'd been out of the country and had just returned to the States after four years away. Having the account brought to his attention was fortunate, as he was currently entertaining an investment opportunity for which the above-referenced funds would be swiftly set to work. He requested that the account be closed and the money forwarded to him at the post office box he'd maintained during his absence. This was, in fact, a post office box that Tom had set up some time ago so that any private business of his wouldn't come under Cora's nose. He rolled a sheet of Loden's stationery into the typewriter and went to work. His typing was clumsy, but he managed to get a clean copy after three tries. If the bank had kept any previous correspondence from Loden Galsworthy, it might be noted that the typeface, the writing paper, and the fountain pen nib were all a match. Now all he needed was Loden's signature.

On Cora's office wall, there was a certificate of appreciation for work she'd done as a Red Cross volunteer in 1918, when she was twenty-one years old. It was a boilerplate document, hundreds of which must have been doled out to the women who'd donated thousands of hours of free labor, but she'd framed it and hung it as though she were the sole recipient. Loden Galsworthy had been one of the three signatories. She'd told Tom that she and Loden often spoke of the amazing coincidence of this link between them before they'd even met.

He took down the framed certificate and spent twenty minutes or so perfecting Loden's signature. Then he signed the letter, folded it, placed it in the envelope, and added a stamp. All in a day's work. He'd drop it in the mail on his way to the bank. This was truly a gift from the gods, an answer to his prayers. He felt incredibly light and free. He hadn't realized how anxious he'd been until the crisis had passed. Now he didn't have to worry about Cora's penury. No more wheedling, no more maneuvering. In one stroke, all his problems had been solved. As icing on the cake, his lunch with Chet Cramer the day before had gone very well. He knew Chet had agreed to listen to his pitch only because he and Livia coveted membership in the country club to which the Padgetts belonged, but he thought his presentation had been effective. Chet had not only seemed interested, but he'd asked Tom to work up a business plan to pass on to his accountant. Tom intended to work on that shortly after lunch.

He drove to the bank and made a deposit, tucking the forged dividend check in with some miscellaneous checks of his own. With the $65,490.66 that would soon be his, he no longer needed the measly $356.45, but he'd already forged Cora's signature so why not proceed? He'd learned never to waste his efforts. Once he made a plan, he carried it out—a principle that had always paid off handsomely for him.

He chatted with the teller, completed his business, and was just on his way out when he ran into the loan officer, Herbert Greer, who'd clearly made a point of intercepting him. Tom had been avoiding him because he knew the guy was going to press him for the money he owed. Now, with his newfound funds waiting in the wings, he greeted Greer like an old friend, shaking his hand with real warmth. "Herb, how are you? I'm glad I ran into you."

Herb was clearly not prepared for Tom's friendliness after weeks of evasions and excuses. Herb said, "I thought you were out of town. I left a couple of messages with Cora earlier this week, and when you didn't respond I assumed you were off gallivanting around."

"Not me. Cora's the one who's gone. She took off this morning to visit her sister up in Walnut Creek. Naughty girl. She didn't mention you'd called. I had no idea."

"It must have slipped her mind."

"No doubt. She's usually good about these things, but she was in a rush to get packed and on the road. Anyway, I was going to stop by your desk earlier, but I saw you were on the phone."

Herb was cautiously pleased at the suggestion, probably imagining he'd have to tackle Tom and bring him down before any such appointment would be made or kept. "Why don't you have a seat at my desk and we can do that right now?"

Tom looked at his watch, his expression tinged with regret. "Can't. Daggone it. I'm having lunch at the country club with Chet Cramer and I'm late as it is."

"I thought I saw you at the club with him yesterday."

"True. I didn't realize you were there. You should have stopped by the table to say hello. I think I might have mentioned we're in discussions about a partnership. He knows the heavy-equipment business, which he says isn't that different from a dealership."

"I had no idea you had a deal in the works. Good for you."

"Well, we've yet to hammer out the details, but you know him. There's a guy who takes his time. No point in pushing him. He likes to have all his ducks in a row before he takes the plunge."

"We've worked with Chet for years. He's solid as they come."

"Tell you what, if we can reach an agreement, I'll bring him along and maybe we can talk about ways to make this thing work."

"Always amenable. I hope you'll give him my regards."

"Happy to."

"Shall we say Monday? Ten o'clock?"

"Perfect. I'll see you then."

And for the first time in his life, Tom left the bank feeling optimistic. As soon as Loden Galsworthy's money came in, he'd be able to expand. Now all he needed was another big whack of cash so he could pay off his bank loan on Monday.

25

By the time Daisy came out of her bedroom at 8:00 Saturday morning, Tannie had left for home. From my makeshift pallet on the couch, I'd heard her come out of the guest room and creep into the bathroom, quietly closing the door. I must have dozed because the next thing I knew, she was slipping through the living room with an overnight case in hand. Out on the street, I heard her car start and then all was quiet again until Daisy got up.

Tannie had stripped her sheets and left them on the guest-room floor with her damp towel on top. Daisy shoved everything in the washing machine and then loaned me a pair of sweatpants so I could add my jeans to the mix. We took turns in the bathroom. I grabbed a quick shower while she started the coffee and then I ate a bowl of cereal while she took my place. By 8:35 we were dressed, fed, and on our way to the Tanner property to check the progress on the excavation. We took her car, leaving mine in her garage. The day was clear and sunny, the air rapidly warming as we made the drive.

The road was still blocked to through traffic, but the deputy waved us past the barrier when Daisy identified herself. I'd apparently been given dispensation to accompany her. We parked the requisite twenty-five yards from the dig and got out of the car. The sagging yellow crime-scene tape trembled in the breeze with a light snapping sound. I recognized the faces from the day before: both crime-scene techs, Detective Nichols, the young deputy, and Tim Schaefer, who'd made himself a permanent fixture, although confined to the periphery like the rest of us. Despite the restrictions, we hovered on the sidelines as though magnetized. Conversations were restrained, and I noticed no laughter at all, unusual in a situation that generated an eerie tension of its own.

Judging by the mountain of dirt, I could tell that the hole had been considerably deepened, and the operation had shifted from machinery back to shoveling by hand. From our vantage point, there was nothing visible of the vehicle, but I gathered a narrow channel had been created on each side as additional sections of the car were exposed. Tom Padgett stood as close to the excavation as he could manage without risking arrest. His bulldozer was on call, as was a flatbed truck that had been brought over from the yard, and he was behaving as though this gave him proprietary rights, which perhaps it did. When he wasn't focused on the excavation, he was chatting with Detective Nichols like an old pal of his.

Calvin Wilcox was parked behind Daisy, about twenty feet down the road. He'd arrived shortly after we had and he was sitting in a black pickup truck with his company name emblazoned on the sides. He smoked a cigarette, his left arm resting on the open windowsill. I could hear his radio blasting country music. Like Daisy, he was permitted at the site by reason of his relation to Violet. There was no interaction between the two of them, which struck me as odd. As far as I knew, Calvin was Daisy's only uncle, and it seemed natural to assume they'd established a relationship over the years. Not so, judging by their manifest uninterest. Neither acknowledged the presence of the other by so much as a nod or a wave.

"What's the deal with you and your uncle Calvin?"

"Nothing. We get along fine. Just no warm, fuzzy feelings between the two of us. When I was growing up, he and my aunt made very little effort to maintain contact. It's been so long since I've seen my cousins, I doubt I'd recognize them."

"Mind if I talk to him?"

"About what?"

"Just some questions I have."

"Be my guest."

Calvin Wilcox watched without expression as I approached. I saw him flip aside his cigarette butt and then he leaned forward and turned off the radio. Up close, I could see he hadn't shaved that morning, and the stubble along his jaw was a mixture of gray and faded red. With his ruddy complexion, his green cotton shirt made his eyes look luminous. As before, I felt I was looking at a version of Violet—same coloring, opposite sex, but electric nonetheless. "Looks like you pulled a rabbit out of a hat," he said when I reached the open driver's-side window. "How'd you come up with this?"

The question seemed ever so faintly hostile, but I smiled to show what a good sport I was. "I'd say 'dumb luck' but I don't want to be accused of false modesty."

"I'm serious."

"Me, too." I went through my standard explanation, trying a variation just to keep the story interesting. "Someone saw Violet's car parked out here the night she disappeared. After that, it was never seen again so it dawned on me maybe it hadn't gone anywhere. In retrospect, it seems dumb I didn't twig to it before."

"Who saw the car?"

I went through a lightning-quick debate with myself and decided naming Winston was a very bad idea. It was as Detective Nichols had said: the less information in circulation, the better. I waved the question aside. "I don't remember offhand. It's one of those things I heard in passing. What about you; how'd you hear about this?" I asked, indicating the excavation.

"I was listening to the radio on the way home from work when it came on the news. I called the sheriff's office as soon as I got home."

"Were you out here last night?"

"For a while. I wanted to see for myself, but the deputy wouldn't let me get anywhere near. They knocked off at ten and said they'd be starting again this morning at six."

"You have a guess about how long it would take to dig a hole that size? I'm talking way back when."

"I don't know the details. You'll have to fill me in."

"From the scuttlebutt yesterday, the guy made a long shallow ramp, eight feet wide and maybe fifteen feet at its deepest point. The back end of the car is buried at the bottom with the front on an incline about like this." I held my arm out at roughly a thirty-degree angle.

He sat, blinking, while he ran the numbers through his head. "I'd have to do the math to give you any kind of accurate answer. In 1953, the guy would've used a bulldozer. If you're telling me he backed the car in, then he must have dug the hole with a long sloping ramp on either end and scooped out dirt until the hole was deep enough at its deepest point to sink the car completely. I'd say two days, maybe a day and a half. It wouldn't take long to fill it in again. Someone must have seen what he was up to, but he might have had a cover story."

"The Fourth fell on a Saturday that year so most people were given Friday off, too. If the road crew was idle for the three-day weekend, then the excavation could have been done without anyone on hand."

"I can see that," he said. "With the road unfinished, there wouldn't have been any traffic to speak of."

"What about the excess dirt? Wouldn't there have been quite a bit left over when the hole was filled in?"

He fixed his green eyes on mine. "Oh, yes. The car would have displaced somewhere in the neighborhood of twenty cubic yards of dirt. Rough guess."

"So what'd he do, haul it all away?"

"Not likely. The biggest dump truck in operation back then had a capacity of five cubic yards, so it would have taken too long, especially if he ferried the load any appreciable distance. The easiest solution would have been to push it across the road and spread it out on that field."

"But wouldn't someone have noticed the sudden appearance of all the fresh dirt?"

"Not necessarily. If I remember correctly, the field you're looking at belonged to a co-op at the time, and it was only being cultivated intermittently. With road construction under way, things were already torn up, so no one would have paid attention to a little more dirt."

"We have to be talking about someone who's worked in construction, don't you think? The average joe doesn't jump on a bulldozer and dig a hole that size. Seems like you'd have to know what you were doing."

"True, but that's not going to help you narrow the field. After World War Two a lot of guys around here worked construction, Foley being one. Building trade was booming, so it was that, farmwork, the oil fields, or the packing plant."

"Well. I guess we don't have to worry about it. I'm sure Detective Nichols will figure it out."

At noon I took Daisy's car and made a run to the delicatessen I'd patronized the day before. Since Tannie had commandeered yesterday's braunschweiger on rye, I ordered one for myself. Daisy said she'd be happy with whatever I picked up, so I had the counterman put together a sliced-turkey sandwich on sourdough bread. I ordered a second one and then added potato chips, sodas, and a bag of cookies. As long as we were stuck there we might as well enjoy ourselves.

We ate in her car, watching the excavation as though we were at a drive-in movie. A tow truck appeared, the most exciting occurrence in the past three hours. Tom Padgett must have gotten bored because I saw him back away and start heading in our direction. He had his fat-stemmed glasses in hand, polishing one lens with a white handkerchief. His jeans, cowboy boots, and western-cut shirt gave him the air of a rodeo rider, complete with slightly bowed legs.

I said, "Hang on." I opened the car door and got out. "Hi, Tom. Are you off to lunch?"

"Come again?" He put on his glasses and cupped a hand to one ear.

"I wondered if you were on your way to lunch."

"Yes, ma'am. I thought I'd grab a bite somewhere."

"I can save you the trip. We have an extra turkey sandwich, if you're interested."

"That'd be nice if you're sure it's okay."

"If you don't eat it, we'll have to toss it out."

He used the front fender of Daisy's car as a makeshift picnic table. I popped open the remaining soda and passed it to him. He shook his head to the offer of potato chips but later accepted a cookie that he downed with enthusiasm.

I said, "How's it going? You've managed to get a lot closer to the hole than we have."

He cleared his mouth and ran a paper napkin across his lips, nodding as he did. "They're making good progress. Looks like they're about to try pulling the car out of the hole."

"Really, that close?"

He wadded up his sandwich wrappings. "That's why they got the tow truck. Might not work, but it'd sure be a lot easier than what they've done."

"How long did you hang around last night?"

"As long as I could. I had paperwork to catch up on, so I left before they called it a wrap. I was surprised how much they'd accomplished. Lot of dirt."

"Was it your equipment they were using when the road was built?"

"Sure was. Those days, there were only two of us. Me and a fellow named Bob Zeigler. Road construction, the county hired private companies like us, so we took advantage of the need. We were competitors, but neither of us had enough equipment to cover the whole job. Most of what I carried was tractors, and he was already spread thin because there were so many housing tracts under construction."

"How'd you get into the business in the first place?"

"I could see the niche and decided to step in. I borrowed from the local-yokel bank and hit up family members for as much as I could. First thing I did was pick up a couple of used farm machines. I didn't have an office or a yard. I worked out of a truck I kept parked beside a public pay phone, and did the mechanical repairs myself. Heavy equipment's low margin, high volume, so every cent I got went right back to the John Deere factory to buy more equipment. Gradually things picked up. Around here, what with the old-boy network, you could slip a few bucks to a private contractor and you were set. At least for a while."

"You have a guess about what the guy used to dig the hole? Calvin Wilcox says a bulldozer."

"Had to be: 1953 the bulldozer or a track loader would've been the only mobile equipment available. The track loader was new technology in those days. I believe Caterpillar brought one out in 1950, but it was too expensive for me, and if Zeigler owned one, I'd have known about it. So a bulldozer for sure."

"One of yours?"

"Had to be mine or his. We were the only game in town."

"You wouldn't by any chance have records going back that far?"

"Can't help you there. You're hoping I can tell you who rented that machine, but no dice. I keep records for as long as the IRS requires and after that, files get tossed. Seven years back is the extent of it."

"Too bad."

"I'm surprised Detective Nichols lets you nose around like this. He strikes me as the type to run a pretty tight ship."

"Right now we don't even know what we're dealing with."

"I guess that's right. Far as I know, there's no law against burying a car. Same token, sheriff's office can get pretty testy about people messing in their business."

"Happily, I'm not 'messing in their business.' Detective Nichols knows anything I learn will go straight back to him. I made a promise."

We heard the steady *peep-peep-peep* of a vehicle backing up. The tow truck driver had the door open, and he was leaning out so he could see where he was going. Most of the law-enforcement personnel had assembled near the hole—detectives, deputies, and crime-scene techs. Daisy seemed rooted to the earth, but both Padgett and I crossed the road to get as close as we could. There was some dickering around while the cable was secured to the front axle of the car. I could hear the high whine of the hydraulic lift and the cable pulled taut. With a groan, the car was wrested from the earth and hauled, rattling and banging, up the long incline. When the vehicle finally rolled into view, the tow truck driver pulled on his emergency brake and got out to take a look.

The sad remains of the Bel Air hunkered in the light like some hibernating beast whose rest had been disturbed. Moisture had chewed into the rubber on all four tires, leaving them flat. The rust was so extensive that the exterior paint might have been any color. The backseat window on the passenger side was gone. On the same side of the roof, the weight of the soil had caused a portion to collapse, leaving it looking as soft as a rotting melon. Dirt must have filtered into the interior, creating the depression that I'd seen from the second floor of the house. Though we couldn't see anything from where we stood, we were later told that condensation had caused the upholstered seats to decay down to the springs. The windshield and hood were intact, but the gas tank had rusted through and all the gas had leaked out, visible as a darkened patch at the bottom of the hole. Even from that distance, I picked up scents, as subtle but unmistakable as a whiff of skunk—rust, rotting upholstery, and decomposing flesh.

One of the techs blew on the windshield, managing to clear a small patch of glass. He directed the beam from a heavy-duty flashlight across the interior. He moved to the missing rear window so he could peer into the backseat. Daisy turned away, gnawing on her thumbnail. The tech motioned the detective over and he peered in. While the second tech took a set of photographs, Nichols approached Daisy and eased her away from the rest of us. He talked to her for some time, his manner serious. I knew the news wasn't good. I could see her nod, but she made very few comments in response, her expression impossible to read. He waited until he'd assured himself that she was okay before he crossed back to the tow truck. At a signal the car was loaded on the deck and secured with heavy chain.

Daisy returned. Her face was drawn and her eyes held the blank look of someone who hasn't yet made sense of the world. "What's left of the dog is on the floor. They can see skeletal remains in the backseat. The body's wrapped in a shroud of some kind, though most of the fabric's rotted away. Nichols says they won't know cause of death until the medical examiner takes a look at her."

"I'm sorry."

"It gets worse. He says the shroud looks like badly disintegrating lace, probably a curtain, judging by the row of broken plastic rings they can see along one edge."

26

We drove back to Daisy's house. My impulse was to have
her drop me off so I could pick up my VW and head for
home, but she asked me to go with her to tell her father
about the discovery of Violet's body. I wasn't sure she'd
fully absorbed the impact of her mother's death. Under
the surface calm, she had to be in a fragile emotional
state. She'd longed for closure, but surely not this kind.
Though she hadn't said as much, she'd probably had her
hopes pinned on the notion that Violet was still alive,
which would have afforded them the option of reconcili-
ation. The certainty about Violet's fate created more
questions than answers, and none of the options seemed
good.

In the meantime, ever practical, I made a quick dash
inside and moved the clothes from the washer to the
dryer so I could have my jeans back before I hit the road.
We drove to Cromwell in Daisy's car, and when we
pulled up in front of the rectory, we could see Foley sit-

ting on the porch in a wooden rocker, his hands in his lap. In the aftermath of the assault, his face looked painfully swollen. His cheeks and eye sockets had ballooned up as though tight with air, and his bruises were a deeper shade of dark blue and more widespread. He'd showered and his clothes were fresh, but the packing in his nostrils and the splint on his nose had precluded washing his hair. A residue of dried blood matted the strands. Watching us approach, Foley had to know the news was bad, in the same way you know you're in for a jolt when a somber-looking state trooper comes knocking at your door.

Daisy stopped a few feet short of the porch. "Has anyone told you?"

"No. Pastor said there was a call, but I refused to take the phone until I heard from you."

"They found her buried in the car. ID hasn't been confirmed, but the dog was buried with her and there's no doubt as far as I'm concerned."

"How was she killed?"

"They won't know until the autopsy tomorrow or possibly the day after."

"At least she didn't leave us. I take comfort in that."

"Not in the way we thought."

"Do you think it was me that harmed her?"

"I don't know what to think."

"I did love her. I know you don't believe me, but I loved her with all my heart." A tear trickled down each side of his face, but the effect was odd, like he'd suddenly sprung pinhole leaks. Personally, I thought it was the wrong time to try defending himself. Daisy didn't seem receptive and she sure wasn't interested in seeing him play victim. We all knew who the real victim was in the overall scheme of things.

"That's no way to love, Daddy. With a fist? My god. If that's what love is about, I'd just as soon do without."

"It wasn't like that."

"So you say. All I remember is your punching her out."

"I can't argue the point. Sometimes I hit her. I don't deny the fact. What I'm saying is you can't fix on one part and think you understand the whole. Marriage is more complicated than that."

"You better hire yourself another lawyer, Daddy, because I'll tell you what's complicated. She was wrapped in a lace curtain and the dog's skull was crushed."

In the car driving back to her place, I kept my mouth shut, sensing she was in a dangerous mood. Finally she said, "I swear to god, if he killed her I want you to nail his ass."

"I wish it were that simple, but it's not up to me. This is a homicide investigation and believe me, the sheriff's department doesn't need my help or interference. I may be a licensed PI, but that cuts no ice with local law enforcement. The quickest way to alienate the cops is to tromp on their turf."

Daisy's face seemed set. "You owe me a day. I gave you a twenty-five-hundred-dollar retainer. Five hundred a day for five days and you've worked four."

"Well, that's true."

"One day. That's all I'm asking for."

"Doing what?"

"I'm sure you'll think of something. I understand what you're saying about the sheriff's department, but at this point you know more about the case than they do."

"True again," I said. I had my own curiosity to satisfy, and I was already thinking of ways to do it that wouldn't entail stepping on their toes. In times past, I may have been a teeny tiny bit guilty of crossing the line, but I was feeling virtuous this round. So far, at any rate.

When we reached her house, I slipped my jeans on hot out of the dryer, gathered my toiletries and the few remaining articles of clothing, and shoved it all in a plastic bag. I grabbed my shoulder bag, tossed both bags in the backseat of my car, and backed out of the garage. It was Saturday afternoon. Government offices were closed, but the Santa Maria public library was open and might be worth a look-see. I drove into town, heading north on Broadway as far as the 400 block, where I pulled into the parking lot.

The library is housed in a two-story Spanish-style structure with the ubiquitous red-tile roof. Santa Teresa architecture shares certain similarities with Santa Maria, though much of the latter looks less than twenty-five years old. I hadn't seen an "old town" or anything resembling the mix of Spanish, Victorian, post-Victorian, Craftsman, and contemporary houses that Santa Teresa boasts. Many neighborhoods, like Tim Schaefer's, date to the '50s, '60s, and '70s, decades in which single-family residences were miraculously charm free.

Once inside, I asked for the reference department and was directed to an elevator that took me to the second floor. My first job was to pull the roll of microfilm for the *Santa Maria Chronicle* covering June 1, 1953, to August 31, 1953. I threaded the film through the machine and scrolled day by day, looking for anything of significance.

On a national level, June 19, Julius and Ethel Rosenberg were executed at Sing Sing. There was apparently new hope for a truce in Korea. On the local scene, according to the advertisements, gas was selling for twenty-two cents a gallon, a loaf of bread cost sixteen cents, and a sixteen-ounce jar of Kraft Cheez Whiz cost fifty-seven cents. Livia Cramer had given a home-demonstration party, whatever that was, and the ladies who'd been awarded prizes were listed. Cecil B. DeMille's *Cleopatra*, starring Claudette Colbert and Warren William, was playing at the local theater, along with a 3-D movie called *Bwana Devil*. Approaching the Fourth of July weekend, I saw that the Santa Maria Indians had a game scheduled with the San Luis Obispo Blues at 8:30 in the Elks Field, and the 144th Field Artillery Battalion was having a Fourth of July Reunion BBQ. As I'd surmised, while many businesses were open on Friday, banks and government offices were closed. Eventually I came across the article about Violet's disappearance, a copy of which Daisy had tucked in her file. I started printing out pages, beginning with June 30 and continuing into the following week.

I went into a room devoted to genealogy and local history. I checked the volumes on the left-hand wall and located the county directory for 1952. The 1953 edition was missing, but I thought the 1952 data would be more useful in any event. I set my shoulder bag on the floor and took a chair at one of the tables.

In going over my notes, I'd come across the map I'd sketched on my first trip to Serena Station. I'd met many people who'd been intimately connected to Violet, but I hadn't talked to those on the periphery. In a murder investigation, anyone with something to hide could lie, obfuscate, or point a finger at someone else. A disinterested observer was a better source of information.

Serena Station was accorded two pages in the city-county directory: roughly sixty families listed by address, name, and occupation. I counted forty-seven homemakers, eleven oil workers, a nurse, a bartender (BW McPhee), a ranch hand, four railroad workers, eight laborers, a postmaster, and a teacher. Foley was calling himself a construction worker in those days, and Violet was listed as a housewife, not a homemaker, I noted. The Blue Moon, a Laundromat, and the auto-repair shop were the only three businesses in town. The Sullivans' neighbors to the left were Jon and Bernadette Ericksen, and on the street behind them, backing up to their rental house, was a couple named Arnold and Sarah Treadwell. One house down from the Ericksens, there was a family named Hernandez. I made notes, not knowing at this point what information would be worth pursuing. I spotted Livia and Chet Cramer's names, but no family named Wilcox or Ottweiler. I checked the five pages devoted to the small town of Cromwell, spotting both sets of names. Businesses there were more numerous but still covered only eight additional columns. I photocopied all the pages on the off chance I'd need to look at them again. No point in being forced to make a return trip.

I put that volume back and pulled the 1956 city directory, checking for the same three names—Ericksen, Treadwell, and Hernandez. Two of the three families were gone, which indicated death, divorce, or a simple move to another town. I noticed that after 1956, the county directory had been converted to a city directory that covered only Santa Maria and Lompoc, with no mention of Serena Station at all. I pulled the 1986 telephone book and searched again, hoping to find a trace. The Hernandez family was a wash, there being so many listed I knew I'd never track down the one I wanted. I had slightly better luck with Ericksen. I didn't find a "J" or a "B," but there was an "A. Ericksen" in Santa Maria, possibly Jon and Bernadette's offspring. A family named Treadwell was living in Orcutt, and though the husband's first name wasn't a match, I thought there might be a connection. I wrote down both sets of phone numbers and street addresses.

At the desk, while I paid for my photocopies, I spoke to one of the librarians and explained what I needed. "Where else can I get information about Serena Station in 1953? I've gone through the old directories."

He said, "You might want to look at the *Index to Precinct Registers* for Santa Teresa County. I believe we have '51 and 1954."

"Great."

Or not great, as it happened. We returned to the shelves and he found me the requisite volume from 1951. Again I sat down and looked up the community of Serena Station. The listings included names, addresses, occupations, and party affiliation (more Republicans than Democrats, for what that's worth), but all the addresses listed were post office boxes, which didn't do me any good. I flipped back to the pages devoted to Santa Maria, running a finger down page after page of residents. I gave up after ten minutes because the numbers were overwhelming, and I was hoping I'd already snagged what I needed. I gathered my notes and took the elevator to the ground floor in search of a pay phone.

I tried the Treadwells' number first and bombed out big time. The Mrs. Treadwell who answered had never lived in Serena Station, had never known the Sullivans, and couldn't be any help at all when it came to tracking down the former Serena Station Treadwells. She suspected I was trying to sell her something and declined any further questions.

I tried A. Ericksen and got a machine, on which I left the following message: "Hi, my name is Kinsey Millhone. I'm a private investigator from Santa Teresa and I'm wondering if you're the same Ericksen who lived in Serena Station in 1953. I'd appreciate a call back when you get this message." I recited my Santa Teresa phone number and repeated my name. Then I went out to my car and headed for the 101.

I unlocked my apartment door at 5:15. I'd been away since Thursday morning, and the living room was stuffy, smelling of old cleaning products and hot dust motes. I put my portable typewriter on the desk. I had two messages from Cheney, asking me to call him when I got home. I tried his number and got a busy signal. I didn't have a duffel, but my newly purchased clothing was folded and packed in a handsome plastic bag. I trotted up the spiral stairs and unloaded the bag.

I fired up the kettle and made myself a cup of tea, which I sipped while I sat at the kitchen counter and sorted through my notes. I thought it was entirely possible that I'd already spoken to Violet's killer. The motive might have been anything—jealousy, hatred, greed, revenge—but I knew the killing itself was cold-blooded because the hole had been dug well in advance of the burial. The killer couldn't have been sure the necessary equipment would be on the scene unless he'd set it up that way. When Violet disappeared, her money had disappeared as well. Ostensibly, she'd taken possession of the fifty thousand dollars in her safe deposit box. She'd also borrowed two thousand from her brother and five hundred dollars from her mother, in addition to the jewelry she'd stolen. So where did all the money and the jewelry end up? It was always possible the stash would be found in the car, but if the killer knew she had it, why not help himself to the money before he bulldozed the dirt back into the hole?

He had to be someone she knew and probably a local, since he was sufficiently familiar with both the Tanner property and the building of New Cut Road to feel assured he'd have privacy. He must have had a cover story to account for the time he'd spent digging the hole. That meant he was either his own boss, in which case he could take all the time he needed, or if he was a nine-to-five kind of guy, he was off on vacation or he'd called in sick. With the holiday weekend, he might have had the time off.

Foley Sullivan was still at the top of my list. Granted, I'd found the man sympathetic, but he'd had years of practice declaring his innocence. I believed him when he spoke of his love for Violet, but that didn't mean he hadn't killed her.

I went back to the notes I'd taken after talking to Chet Cramer. I couldn't see what he had to gain, but I didn't rule him out. He didn't strike me as a fellow with much experience operating heavy equipment, but I'd jotted down an offhand remark he'd made. He'd said you could always hire somebody to do your dirty work.

I thought about Winston Smith, who'd been fired because of Violet. While Cramer had rehired him the following week, he hadn't known about that when she vanished. I was iffy about him. He was convinced she'd ruined his life, which in some ways she had. If he'd gotten the education he'd planned, he wouldn't be selling cars and he might not be married to the woman who now proposed booting his butt out the door.

I knew little about Tom Padgett, but he was worth checking out. Steve Ottweiler? Nah. I put a tick by his name, but only in the interest of being fair. As long as I was suspicious of the other guys, I might as well include him. He'd been sixteen at the time, and from Violet's point of view, he was probably fair game. However, if the two had engaged in a torrid affair, why kill the golden goose? I added BW's and Jake's names to the list.

I kept thinking I'd overlooked something obvious, but I couldn't think what it was.

I took a break and made myself a peanut butter and pickle sandwich for my supper. I substituted a paper napkin for a plate and thus reduced the dirty dishes to a bare minimum. I was just in the process of washing my knife when the telephone rang.

The woman on the other end of the line said, "This is Anna Ericksen. I believe you left a message on my machine."

"Are you the Ericksen who once lived at 3906 Land's End Road in Serena Station?"

There was a cautious silence. "Why do you want to know?"

"I'm sorry. I should have explained myself earlier. I'm interested in contacting the family who lived next door to Foley and Violet Sullivan in 1953."

"That was my parents' house, where I grew up."

"Really? Wow, that's great. I'm lucky you didn't get married or I'd have never tracked you down."

"Oh, honey. I'm gay. You couldn't pay me to get married. I got troubles enough."

"Do you remember Violet?"

"Not directly. I was a little kid back then, but people have been talking about her for years and years. We lived next door to the Sullivans when I was growing up. I suppose you know they found her buried in her car."

I said, "So I heard. Look, I know this is a long shot, but is there anything you can tell me about Violet?"

"No, I'm sorry to say I don't remember her, but I do remember that Fourth of July."

"You're kidding. You remember that particular Fourth of July?"

"I sure do. We'd gone to the fireworks and afterwards Daisy's friend Tannie spent the night with me. I can't tell you how thrilled I was. I was five years old and she was nine, and I just admired everything about her. She talked me into jumping on the bed in my room, which I wasn't allowed to do. So there we were bouncing away, having the time of our lives. She bumped me and I toppled off and broke my arm. The bone didn't heal right and I got a hump in it to this day. It's one of my first concrete memories."

I could feel myself blinking, wondering if the woman had made a fundamental mistake. "I was told Tannie went to the fireworks with her dad."

"Oh, she did, but we ran into them at the park, and Tannie's father asked Mother if we could keep her overnight. He said he had something to take care of and wasn't sure what time he'd be back."

"Did he say where he was going?"

"If he did, it didn't register with me. He might have told Mother, but she's long dead. Why not ask Tannie? She might know."

"I'll do that, thanks. I truly appreciate your help."

"You're entirely welcome."

27

LIZA
Saturday, July 4, 1953

Liza Mellincamp often thought about her fourteenth birthday, which fell on July 3, 1953, the day before Violet Sullivan left Serena Station. Years later, she found it hard to believe so much changed in that forty-eight-hour period. She'd spent the morning of her birthday cleaning her room. Violet was taking her out for lunch, and Liza wanted to be ready in plenty of time. She had never eaten in a real restaurant and she could hardly contain herself. She and her mother had shared sandwiches at drugstore lunch counters, but that wasn't the same.

At 9:30 she turned on her Philco clock radio and listened to *The Romance of Helen Trent* and *Our Gal Sunday* while she made her bed, emptied the wastebasket, and shoved her dirty clothes into the hamper. Monday, she'd take everything to the Laundromat as she did every week. She'd end up doing most of the household chores in any event because her mom was usually too drunk to do much except lie on the couch in the living room, smoking cigarettes and burning holes in the rim of the wood coffee table. She tidied and dusted her desktop, night table, and bookshelves. She shook out the scatter rugs off the porch rail and left them there to air. She wet-mopped the linoleum on her bedroom floor and then went over it with Johnson's Jubilee, liking the glossy wet shine, though she knew it would dull as it dried. In the bathroom, she scrubbed the tub, toilet, and sink with Bab-o cleanser. There were too many chips and stains to make a difference, but she felt better knowing it was done.

At 11:00 she ironed her best white Ship'n Shore blouse with the Peter Pan collar and baby doll sleeves. She took a shower and got dressed. Violet had called to say she had a big surprise, and when she and Daisy swung by the house at 11:45, she was driving a brand-new Chevrolet. She laughed at Liza's wide-eyed response. Liza couldn't remember ever even sitting in a new car, and here she was marveling at the white sidewall tires, the dashboard, the interior upholstery, and shiny chrome window cranks.

Violet drove into Santa Maria, where the three of them had lunch in the tea room at the Savoy Hotel. Liza and Violet both had shrimp cocktails for a first course and then this tiny cup of chicken soup and a plate of finger sandwiches—brown bread with cream cheese and chopped nuts, egg salad, ham salad, even one with watercress and thinly sliced radishes. She and Violet ate with their little fingers crooked up, pretending to be oh so lah-di-dah. Daisy had buttered noodles, which was just about the only thing she'd eat except for Welch's grape jelly on bread. They had layer cake for dessert, and Liza's arrived with a candle in it, which she blew out, blushing with pleasure as the waiters and waitresses stood around and sang to her. Just when she thought life couldn't be any more perfect, Violet handed her a small box wrapped in beautiful lavender paper. Liza opened the gift with trembling fingers. Inside there was a silver heart-shaped locket about the size of a fifty-cent piece. Inside there was a tiny photograph of Violet. "And look at this," she said.

She pulled the photo aside to reveal a second heart-shaped compartment behind the first. "That's for your true love," Violet said, pointing to the blank space. "I predict within a year, you'll know exactly who it is."

"Thank you."

"Oh, Sweetie, don't cry. It's your birthday."

"This is the best day of my life."

"You'll have others much better, but enjoy. Here, let's put it on."

Liza turned around and lifted her hair while Violet fixed the clasp. Liza put her hand against the locket that was nestled in the hollow of her throat. The silver was already warm from contact with her skin. Her lucky charm. She could hardly quit touching it.

Violet paid for lunch out of a thick wad of bills, making sure everybody noticed. She seemed pleased as Punch and more than once remarked that life was soon going to be one hundred percent improved. Liza thought if that were really true, she wouldn't have to repeat it four times during the meal, but Violet was like that.

"Oh geez Louise, I almost forgot," she said. "I need a babysitter tomorrow night. Are you free?"

Liza's smile faded. "Not really. Kathy and I are going to the fireworks."

Violet looked at her with a momentary consternation,

having assumed she'd agree. "Couldn't you skip just this once?"

"I don't know. I told her I'd go with her, and I don't want to break a date."

"Trust me, if you're going out with a girl, it's not a date. It's marking time."

"Couldn't you get someone else?"

"Oh for heaven's sake, Lies. At this late date? There's no chance. Besides, Kathy's a sourpuss. I've seen the way she bosses you around. Aren't you ever going to stand up to her?"

"Maybe I could come for a little while. Until eight forty-five. We could hold off going over to the park till then."

Violet fixed Liza in her clear green gaze. "If you sat the whole evening, you could have Ty come over. You know I wouldn't care. Missing the fireworks isn't *that* big a deal. There's always next year."

Liza was stricken. What was she supposed to say? The day had been so perfect, all because of Violet, who wanted only this one small thing.

Violet's eyes widened. "Please, please, please? You can't let Kathy take up all your time. I really need the help."

Liza didn't see how she could refuse. She sat for Violet all the time. Violet had been counting on her even if she forgot to ask. And Kathy had been such a pill of late. "All right, I guess. Maybe I can do something with her on Sunday instead."

"Thank you, Sugar Bun. You are too too sweet."

"That's okay," Liza said, flushing with pleasure. Praise of any kind always made her warm.

After lunch, for the finale, Violet took Liza and Daisy

to see a 3-D movie called *Bwana Devil*, with Robert Stack and Barbara Britton. It had been in the theaters for seven months, but it hadn't come to Santa Maria until recently. The three of them settled in front-row seats with their cardboard glasses, wearing wax lips for fun, munching popcorn and Milk Duds. Violet told her that for the early 3-D movies, one lens of the give-away glasses was green and the other was red. This was new technology, Polaroid, with both lenses clear, though Violet wasn't quite sure how either process worked. Why one green and one red lens would produce a 3-D effect was beyond her, she said. The credits began and they settled in. Unfortunately, the first time a lion jumped straight out of the screen at them, Daisy got hysterical and cried so hard Liza had to take her out to the lobby and sit for an hour. Still, it was the best birthday Liza could remember, and she hated to see the day come to an end.

After they got back to the Sullivans', Liza sat with Daisy for an hour while Violet ran an errand. Thankfully, Foley didn't get home until 6:00, so she didn't have to deal with him. True to form, Violet took longer than she said, so it was close to 5:45 by the time Liza finally got to her house. Her mother heard her come in and called her into the living room. Liza stood at the door while her mother struggled into a sitting position. Her mother had that fuzzy look that made Liza want to scream.

"What," she said. She didn't want to spoil the good mood she was in, but she knew better than to ignore her mom.

"Word of warning. Kathy Cramer came by with your birthday present, and when she found out you weren't here, she got that look on her face." Her mother's consonants were only slightly soft. In her own curious way, she was aware of what was going on.

Liza felt her heart sink. The last thing in the world she wanted was for Kathy to find out she'd had lunch with Violet and had seen *Bwana Devil* afterward. Kathy had been talking about *Bwana Devil* for weeks, trying to get her dad to drive them into town and drop them at the theater. Liza didn't feel she was under any obligation to wait and go with her, but she knew Kathy would see it differently. "What'd you tell her?"

"I forget. I made some excuse for you. She woke me from a sound sleep, standing on the porch, pounding on the front door like the house was burning down. I hollered for her to hold her horses, but by the time I got there, she was already acting like she had a stick up her butt. I told her I didn't have a clue where you were and she got all snotty and sullen. Honestly, Liza, what do you see in her? She's chained to you like a rock and she's dragging you down."

"You didn't mention Violet?"

"Why would I do that?"

"Where'd you put the present?"

"She took it to your room and said she'd leave it on your desk."

Liza made a beeline for her room, suddenly worried that Kathy had taken advantage of the opportunity to snoop. Her room was much as she'd left it, but when she went to check her diary, hidden behind the bookcase, she couldn't be sure if it had been moved or not. She sat on the bed and leafed through the pages, waves of anxiety coursing through her. She'd recorded every detail of her romance with Ty Eddings, and if Kathy had read the last few entries, she was doomed. According to Kathy,

even the use of Junior Tampax was an affront to the notion of Absolute Purity.

Liza found a new hiding place for the diary and then
sat on her bed and opened Kathy's present, which was
beautifully wrapped in pink-flowered paper with a pretty
pink bow on top. Pink was Kathy's favorite color. Liza
herself preferred shades of purple, which was also Violet's favorite.

When she saw what Kathy had given her, she could
hardly believe her eyes. The box of lily of the valley dusting powder was the same one she'd given Kathy for her
birthday in March of the year before. She checked the
bottom of the box and, sure enough, there was the same
drugstore sticker she'd torn in half when she'd tried to
peel it off. Clearly Kathy hadn't used the powder and
didn't remember who'd given it to her. Now what?

Liza didn't want to call her at all. On the other hand,
she thought she'd be smart to get it over with. If Kathy
had read her diary, she'd never pass up the opportunity
to chide and condemn her, superior as always.

Liza went to the phone in the hall and dialed Kathy's
number. Mrs. Cramer picked up.

"Hi, Mrs. Cramer? This is Liza. Is Kathy home?"

"Just a moment." She put a hand across the mouth-
piece and Liza could hear her holler up to the second
floor. "Kathy? Liza's on the phone."

There was a long pause while Kathy clumped down
the stairs. "Hope you had a good birthday," Mrs. Cramer
remarked while they waited.

"I did. Thanks."

"Here she is."

Kathy took the handset and said, "Hello," in a voice
that was dead and remote.

"Hi. I called to say thanks for the bath powder. It's really nice."

"You're welcome." Even the two words sounded snippy and clipped.

"Is something wrong?"

"Why would you say that?"

"Kathy, if something's bothering you, just tell me."

"Well, where were you? That's what's bothering me. We had a date."

"We did?"

"Yesss. This afternoon. My mother was supposed to take us to the five-and-dime . . ."

Liza could feel the cold envelop her body as Kathy went on in her martyred, accusatory tone. "We were supposed to pick out a pattern and fabric so we could sew matching skirts and weskits for our new fall wardrobe. Don't you remember?"

"I remember you mentioned it, but that was weeks ago and you never said what day."

"Because it was so *obvious*. It was for your *birthday*, Liza. I didn't think I had to spell it out. We drove over to pick you up for lunch and you were gone. Your mom didn't even know where you were."

"I'm sorry. I forgot—"

"How could you forget? We always spend our birthdays together. It's traditional."

"We've done it twice," Liza said. She knew she'd pay for the sass, but she couldn't help herself.

"Well, I guess it means more to me than to you," Kathy said.

Liza couldn't think of a response so she said nothing.

"So where did you go?" Kathy asked.

"No place in particular. Just out."

"I know you were *out*. I'm asking where."

"Why do you care?" Liza couldn't believe she was being so ornery, but she was sick of catering to Kathy's moods.

"I care, *Liza*, because I want to know what's so important you had to stand me up."

"I didn't *stand you up*. I forgot, okay?"

"I know you forgot. You already told me that a hundred times! You don't have to rub it in."

"Why are you so mad? It was an honest mistake."

"I'm not mad. Why should I be mad? I asked for an explanation. Since you were so rude as to violate our agreement, I think you owe me one."

Liza felt her temper climb, Kathy having neatly maneuvered her into a corner. If she told her where she'd been, Kathy would raise a big stink or she'd sulk for days, or she'd do both, but in no way would she ever leave the subject alone. Liza had seen it before. Once someone made Kathy mad, she never let 'em off the hook. "I was busy."

"Doing *what*?" Kathy said, exasperated.

"What difference does it make?"

"In other words, you won't tell. Thanks so much. I'd never do anything that horrible to you—"

"Oh, stop exaggerating. It's not *horrible*."

"I thought we were best friends."

"I didn't say we weren't."

"But that's not how you treat a best friend—keeping secrets and being mean."

"I'm not being mean."

"You know what? That's the difference between us, what you just said. You can't admit the truth. Moral Rearmament has made me a better person, but Absolute

Unselfishness doesn't mean a thing to you. It's whatever you want, whatever you feel like doing, and then you lie about it afterward . . ."

Liza said, "I have to go. My mom's calling me."

Kathy's voice had a quaver now. "You know what? Absolute Honesty? You hurt me. Deeply. All week long, I looked forward to seeing you. It was going to be the bright spot of my day. Put yourself in my place and think how I felt when I heard you hadn't even left a note."

"Kathy, it's not like I did it on purpose. I made a mistake."

"Then why didn't you call me when you got home?"

"That's what I'm doing. I'm on the phone. I'm calling you. What else could this be?"

"Oh sure, hours later."

"I just now walked in the door!"

"You were gone *all day*?"

"Why are you making such a fuss?"

"*I'm* making a fuss? So now it's *my* fault?"

"I didn't say it was your fault, but you don't have to make such a big deal of it. You do things without me. Why can't I do one tiny thing without you?"

"Fine. Be that way. I'm sorry I brought it up."

Liza could feel herself crumble. This would go on for the rest of her life unless she found a way out. "Look, I'm really sorry, okay? I apologize."

There was a momentary silence. Kathy didn't like giving up the power position. "Do you mean that?"

"I do. Sincerely. I didn't want to say where I was because it had to do with my mom and her . . . you know . . . her problem."

"Oh you poor thing. Why didn't you say so?"

"I was embarrassed. I hope you'll forgive me."

"Of course. I completely understand. But really, if you'd confided in me, we could have avoided this misunderstanding."

"Next time I will. I'm sorry I wasn't completely honest with you."

"That's all right. Liza, it's not your fault what she is."

"I appreciate your being so nice about it." Having capitulated, why not grovel as well?

"So what time do you want to go to the park tomorrow night? You think six is too early? I made some deviled eggs. I thought we could take a picnic."

Liza was at a loss for words.

"Liza?"

"I'm here. The problem is I can't go. That's another reason I called. My mom's kind of sick and I have to stay home because she needs me."

"But won't she be better tomorrow?"

"I'm not sure. I don't think so. She doesn't look good."

"You can't even leave her for an *hour*?"

"I better not."

"What's wrong with her?"

"I don't know. I'm calling the doctor as soon as I hang up from you. She's been sick all day so it might be serious."

"You want me to come keep you company? I don't mind skipping the fireworks. We could make popcorn."

"We better not. She could be contagious. She's calling me right now so I gotta go. I'll talk to you tomorrow, okay?"

"Sure. I hope she feels better."

"Me too."

When Liza placed the handset back in the cradle, the

small of her back was damp. She played the conversation over and over in her mind, reconstructing Kathy's tone, wishing she'd been quicker on the draw when Kathy tried to shoot her down. She shouldn't have lied about her mom, but what else could she do? She didn't see how Kathy would ever find out. She knew Kathy was full of pity for her because of her mother's drinking and often told her she prayed for her in church, citing Absolute Love. Didn't feel like love to Liza, but what did she know?

She decided to fix her mother an early supper, since she and Ty were going out that night. She couldn't wait to tell him all the stuff Kathy said. He didn't like Kathy in the first place and he'd be tickled to hear she'd finally stood up to her. For as long as she had. You couldn't handle everything at once.

She set the water on to boil for the Minute Rice and then opened a can of Libby's corn and a can of Libby's green beans. She tried to make sure her mother got a balanced meal, but half the time her mother didn't want to eat, no matter what it was. Liza had fixed Spam two nights before, so she took the chunk out of the refrigerator and cut a fresh slice, which she fried in oleo. Once the meal was fully prepared, she arranged everything on a tray, added a paper napkin and utensils, and took it into the living room. Her mother was dead to the world, cigarette still burning in the ashtray. Liza put it out and took the dinner tray back to the kitchen. She set it on the counter where her mother would see it later. Then she washed the pots and pans and put them away.

Ty picked her up at 9:00, driving his uncle's truck, which he did whenever he could cadge it. When she got in, he handed her a package with a bow clumsily affixed. "What's this," she asked, taking out a bottle of what looked like Champagne.

"Cold Duck. I got it at the minimart so we could celebrate. Happy birthday."

"You bought alcohol?"

"I look like I'm twenty-one so I do it all the time. The guy never even carded me."

"You better hope your aunt doesn't find out."

He smiled, flashing white teeth and dimples. "I got something else for you too, but that's for later."

Liza smiled, cheeks burning. She'd never received a present from a boy. Right away, she hoped for an ID bracelet, engraved with both their names, something to commemorate their love.

They drove out to the Tanner property as they had on two previous occasions. They couldn't very well ride around town. If the two were seen together, he'd be in trouble with his aunt.

The new road had been graded, but only partially paved. A trench had been dug to form a culvert, and lengths of corrugated pipe had been brought in by crane. Now as Ty swung off the frontage road, they could see that a temporary Road Closed sign had been set up, blocking access. A line of orange cones ran across the road to further discourage traffic, and a No Trespass sign had been posted. Guess they meant business. Since the Fourth fell on a Saturday, government offices were closed on Friday, the day before. No court, no mail delivery, no library, and no banks. The county road crew had apparently been given the three-day weekend as well.

Ty drove around the barrier, passing the dirt mounds and heavy equipment. A bulldozer seemed to glow in the fading light of day. He'd scoped out the house and grounds in advance of their first visit and discovered the open shed he now used to conceal his pickup. He helped her out of the passenger side, leading her by the hand as far as the expansive wooden porch that ran along the back of the house. Faintly, in the distance, they could hear the hush of passing cars out on the 101.

He said, "Hang on a sec." He went back to the truck and returned moments later with a bundle under one arm. "Sleeping bag," he said. He kept a hand on her back, guiding her as they made their way through the darkened kitchen and up the servants' stairs. The house was stuffy after being closed up for so long. Once they reached the master bedroom at the front of the house, Ty opened all the windows to let the heat out. The breeze coming in across the sill was warm, but at least it created some circulation. He laid out the bulky sleeping bag and stretched out a hand, pulling her down beside him.

He opened the bottle of Cold Duck and offered her the first swig. It tasted better than she expected, and she liked how warm and fuzzy it was making her feel. They passed the bottle back and forth until half of it was gone. She lay on one side, head propped on her hand while they talked in whispers. She started to tell him about Kathy, but he kept interrupting her with kisses and deep, meaningful looks. He said, "Your present. I almost forgot."

He took out a small jar of Vaseline, holding it out to her with a smile.

"What's that for?"

"You know. Just in case."

Liza felt her stomach knot and she sat up. "I don't think we should do this. It's not a good idea."

"Don't worry about it. You don't have to decide anything right now. It's completely up to you," he said. He
pulled her down beside him and kissed her again. By
now they'd progressed from the innocent petting of their
early dates into more treacherous territory, and Ty took
it as a given that each time they were together they'd
pick up where they left off. He was already intent on the
business of stripping her down. Liza wasn't entirely willing, but she knew she couldn't refuse. The kissing did
feel good, and she was lucky he'd chosen her when any
other girl in school would be happy to take her place.
She found herself floating in the moment, carried along
by his determination and her own inability to resist. In
the back of her mind, a tiny voice was whispering that his
insistence and Kathy's bullying weren't all that different,
but the Cold Duck had made her feel sleepy and too relaxed to care. Easier to give in than to raise any more
objections. It's not like it wasn't nice.

He was kissing her bare boob when she saw a flash of
headlights swing across the ceiling. Down below, gravel
crunched, the vehicle so close to the house they could
hear the driver pulling on his brake. Liza gasped and
broke free, scrambling to her hands and knees as the car
door slammed. "Oh my lord, someone's here!"

Ty crawled over to the window and peered out.
"Don't panic. It's fine. He isn't coming this way."

Liza eased in behind him, her eyes just above sill level.
The driver was on the far side of the vehicle, which was
ten yards away. She picked up the smell of smoke before
she saw the speck of red hot ember at the end of his cigarette. Liza said, "Who is that?"

"He must be a security guard. Looks like he's checking the equipment."

"We gotta get out of here." She crawled back to the sleeping bag and snatched up her clothing, piling her shoes on top. Ty pulled on his jeans and they scurried across the room to the walk-in linen closet, where they shut themselves in. They finished dressing in haste, Liza feeling so anxious she nearly wet her pants. Ty looked over at her, saying, "You okay?"

"What if he sees the truck? He'll know someone's here."

Ty opened the closet door and peered around the frame. The house was dark, but she could make out his profile. So beautiful. He motioned to her and the two emerged from their hiding place. Liza listened intently but picked up no sounds of activity inside the house itself. Ty reached for her hand and the two eased over to the window and peered out again. Liza could see the swinging beam of a flashlight as the fellow walked across the road, adjusting cones as he went.

Ty said, "Let's move it. I think we can make it to the truck before he turns around and comes back."

They picked their way out of the room and tiptoed along the corridor until they reached the back stairs and started down. Liza nearly fell over Ty, not realizing he'd stopped to listen again. Nothing. Liza held on to his T-shirt as they passed the butler's pantry and from there traversed the cavernous kitchen, which was bathed in soft gray light. The moon, in its last quarter, was visible through one of the kitchen windows.

Outside they race-walked across the grass to the shed. Ty felt his way down the length of the truck until he could open the driver's-side door. Liza climbed in first and crawled across the seat to make room for him. Ty climbed in after her and slid under the wheel. He pulled the door shut without slamming it, careful not to make a sound. They sat then, scarcely daring to breathe. Ty torqued himself around, staring out the rear window at the darkened yard. The width and breadth of the house blocked all view of the front, but there was an illusion of hearing more acutely when one stared at the source.

Liza said, "Do you think we should risk it?"

"Not yet."

Liza had a sudden thought and put a hand on his arm. "We forgot the sleeping bag!"

"Don't worry about it. We can pick it up next time."

"But what if he comes across it?"

Ty held a finger to his lips and they fell silent again. Ten long minutes passed and then they heard the grumbling of one of the big machines, engine grinding to life, shattering the stillness. When the racket continued, Ty took advantage of the noise to cover the starting of his truck. He backed out of the shed and crept along the service road with his headlights out.

When they cleared the house, they could see a shape as lumbering as a tank crawling in the opposite direction. Ty continued down the service road with Liza praying he wouldn't steer them into a tree. Finally, he felt safe enough to turn on his fog lights, which provided sufficient illumination for their agonizingly slow escape.

Saturday morning, the Fourth, Liza called the Cramer house. She hoped to have a conversation with Kathy in which she could casually mention her mother's illness to reinforce the fib. Telling the same lie more than once made it seem more real. Mrs. Cramer answered and said Kathy really wasn't able to come to the phone. Her voice was chilly, and Liza knew Kathy had blabbed to her about their fight. "Well, would you tell her I called?"

"Of course."

Liza didn't see how Kathy would ever find out she was babysitting for Violet instead of staying at home with her mother as she'd claimed. Ty had begged her to let him come over to the Sullivans' and keep her company and, of course, she'd agreed. Early in the afternoon she wandered over to Violet's. Foley was off somewhere, and Liza was hoping she and Violet could have a heart-to-heart talk. Unfortunately, Daisy was in the bedroom, playing with her paper dolls, and it didn't seem advisable, given the subject matter. She'd hung out for a while and then she'd gone home. She sat on the front porch in an old aluminum lawn chair, hoping Kathy would pass the house and see her there.

By 6:15 she was back at the Sullivans', minding Daisy in the bathtub while Violet and the yapping Pomeranian went out the door. She made sure Daisy dried herself and got in her pj's. They sat at the kitchen table and ate vanilla ice cream until 8:15. Daisy was easily confused about telling time, so Liza said it was 9:00 and marched her off to bed. Liza gave her the pill Violet'd left and watched as Daisy swallowed it with half a glass of milk. Twenty minutes later she was safely tucked in bed and limp with sleep.

Liza went out the back door and sat down in one of the two lawn chairs that overlooked a scruffy patch of grass. The wooden fence was less than six feet tall, but a thick tangle of honeysuckle spilled over the top, obscuring her view of the street. It was hot and her T-shirt was sticking to her back. She went inside again and sat in the living room, where she turned off the overhead light and let the table fan blow across her face.

At 9:00 she heard Ty scratching at the back screen. He stood outside the door, and the gaze he fixed on her was as hungry and as patient as a fox's. She let him in and he kissed her, pressing himself against her. For once, she had the presence of mind to slip out of his grip.

"Ty, I'm not going to neck with you in here. What if Daisy wakes up or the Sullivans come back?"

"Come on. Foley's at the park and I saw Violet barreling down the road in that fancy car of hers. Neither one of them are coming back for hours."

"I don't care. I'm not going to do it."

"How about we go out to my pickup? It's parked in the alley out back. I spread some blankets in the bed so we can lay there together and look at the stars."

"Are you crazy? I can't leave Daisy by herself."

"I didn't say we'd go anywhere. It's just someplace private where we can talk without waking her."

"I don't think it's right. I'm supposed to stay in the house."

"Did Violet say that specifically?"

"No, but that's what she pays me to do."

"Half an hour. An hour. No one's ever going to know."

He'd wheedled and coaxed, making it all sound easy and insignificant. Finally, she'd given in and followed him through the yard to his pickup. Of course, the minute they were stretched out in the truck bed he'd started in on her. The night was warm, but Liza found herself shivering. Her fingers were so icy, she had to tuck her hands in her armpits. Ty was solicitous. He'd brought two paper cups and another bottle of Cold Duck. Liza drank more than her share, hoping to quiet her nerves. While they talked, the fireworks display started in Silas.

They'd hear thumps and then sprays of green and blue sparkles would erupt, showers of red like umbrellas raining out of the sky. For thirty minutes they watched, transfixed. It was like a movie Liza had seen where this man and woman had been kissing and kissing and the curtains had blown open at the window and the sky had been alight.

After a while she lost track of time, didn't even care how long they'd been there. She was feeling so close to him. He wrapped his arms around her and murmured against her neck. "How're you doing, Lies? I gotta take good care of you so you won't catch cold." He slid his hand underneath her shirt.

"Oh, don't."

"I'm not doing anything." He unbuttoned her shorts and moved his hand down along her belly.

"Maybe we should stop."

"Stop what?"

"We can't keep doing this."

"Don't you like it?"

"I do, but I don't want to go too far, okay?"

"Just let me touch you once," he said. He'd managed to get a finger between her legs.

She grabbed his hand and held it. "Wait. I can't do this. I have to go in. What if they get home?"

"They won't. They never come in before the Moon closes. You know that about them. They're off drinking and having fun, and we're right here close by. Violet won't care. She likes me."

"I know, but we have to be careful."

"I will. I'll be careful. Here, have one more little sip of wine. I'm just so crazy about you, Liza. Don't you love me even a little bit? I know you love me." He took the empty cup from her hand and whispered against her hair, kissing her neck and her breasts until she burned. "Be sweet. Please be sweet to me just this one time."

She should have pulled away, but she felt suspended, passive, as though she had no control over what would happen next. On he went, telling her he loved her, that it was torture not having her when he loved her so much. By then he had her shorts off. "Let me put it in," he whispered. "Just one time. Please."

She'd said no at first, but he'd been so excited at the idea and so persistent, she'd relented. What was the harm when she wanted him, too. "You promise you'll pull out in time?"

"Of course. I swear. I wouldn't do anything to hurt you. I love you. You know I do. Angel, I want you so much it's driving me insane."

She felt at the same time powerful and afraid, but he was so beautiful and fearless. No one had ever said such incredible things to her. He seemed so sweet and eager. She had her eyes closed, but she could hear the rustling of his clothes. She made a sound at the shock of his naked body against hers. He was smooth and muscular. His skin was hot and he smelled of soap. She couldn't remember where the jar of Vaseline came from, but there it was. And he was pressing himself and putting her hand on him and moving against her and wanting her to open up to him and then she did. She knew he'd already gone too far, but he'd pushed in. Then he was moving and didn't seem to hear her feeble protest. He moved and he was moving and then he made a sound like he was lifting something heavy. He groaned, out of breath, and then he slumped over her, relaxed. "Oh, Lies. Oh geez. That was fantastic. That was so beautiful."

It hadn't even been a minute. She shifted her hips and he slipped out of her, leaving her goopy and wet.

"What's the matter? Are you okay?"

"No, I'm not okay. You said you'd pull out!"

"I'm sorry. I meant to, but I couldn't help myself. Baby, it just felt so good. I went crazy for a minute and the next thing I knew, it just happened."

"Shit. What time is it? I gotta go."

"Not yet. It's not hardly midnight. Don't leave me. Here, feel this." He took her hand and pressed it against him.

She'd stayed where she was, half-underneath him, warm only in the places where his body covered hers. The rest of her was cold, her limbs pinned to the blanket by the weight of him. "I have to go in. What if they come home and I'm not there?"

"You can tell 'em you came out for a breath of air."

"Let go of me. Please," she whispered, but he kissed her again, murmuring, "You're great. You're amazing. I love you."

"I love you too," she said. "Ty, I have to go in." She twisted out of his grasp and groped along the truck bed until she found her underpants. She pulled them on and then searched for her shorts and T-shirt.

"Look, I'll see you tomorrow morning, right?"

"Maybe."

"All day. We'll spend the whole day together."

"I can't."

"Yes, you can. Meet me out on Porter Road. I'll borrow my uncle's truck and we'll go for a drive. Eight o'clock."

She could tell her underpants were on wrong-side out. She lifted one hip so she could strip them off.

"Damn it! Now I got stuff running down the inside of my leg. Give me a handkerchief or something so I can clean myself off."

He handed her his T-shirt, which he'd wadded up and tossed aside. She jammed it between her legs and cleaned herself as well as she could. She eased into her underpants again and hooked herself into her bra. She pulled on her T-shirt and shorts and used her fingers to get the snarls out of her hair. Once dressed, she climbed over the tailgate.

Ty said, "Eight o'clock tomorrow morning. You're not there, I'm knocking on your door and I don't care who sees."

She kissed him in haste, told him that she loved him, and then hurried toward the house and let herself in the back door. The screen whined softly. The kitchen light was off, but she could see the luminous hands on the wall clock. 1:15. Violet and Foley usually didn't get home until after 2:00 so she was fine. Everything was okay. The same table lamp was burning in the darkened living room. The fan rotated at a steady pace, pushing hot air this way and that. Both bedrooms were dark. She paused outside Daisy's room, listening to the child's slow, deep, regular breathing. She was fine.

Liza crept into the bathroom. In the glow from the night-light, she pulled down her shorts and checked her underpants. The crotch was wet with semen, stained with blood. She had to talk to Violet. She knew she should have made him use a rubber, but he promised he'd pull out, and now what? Violet would know. Violet knew everything there was to know about sex. Liza returned to the living room, where she lay on the couch, hugging herself. What was done was done. He'd told her he loved her—he'd actually said that to her—and he was the one who brought up the subject of seeing her again, so it wasn't like she was chasing him or anything like that. Still, she wished she hadn't done it. She could feel her eyes burn as the tears spilled out. As soon as Violet came in, the two of them would talk and she'd be fine.

28

I put a call through to Sneaky Pete's. I could hear the strains of the jukebox in the background and a steady hum of voices. This was Saturday night, but it was only 6:45 and the place wasn't going to rock until well after 9:00. Tannie answered the phone.

"Hi, Tannie. This is Kinsey. You have a minute?"

"Sure, if you don't mind the interruptions. I'm tending bar and the gal who's scheduled to work called in sick an hour ago."

"I'll try to be quick. You heard about Violet?"

"I did. What happened to the poor woman? I know she was killed, but nobody's said how."

"I haven't heard a word about the cause of death. I guess we'll know more after the autopsy's done."

"Autopsy? Somebody told me she was just a bunch of bones wrapped up like a mummy so you couldn't even see her face."

"Well, that's not quite true. As I understand it, she

was wrapped in a length of fabric, but it was falling apart. That's hardly mummylike," I said.

"Did you get a look at her?"

"Not me, and Daisy didn't either. Detective Nichols gave her the news, but he didn't want anyone getting close to the car."

"How's she taking it?"

"She's okay. I don't think the reality has sunk in."

"I thought about calling, but I didn't have the nerve. Maybe tomorrow. So what's up with you?"

"I've been putting together a timeline for that Fourth of July weekend, trying to figure out where everyone was. You went over to the park with your dad?"

"Didn't we talk about this? I was supposed to go with my brother, but he went off with his friends so Pop ended up taking me himself."

"Were you there the whole time?"

"I don't remember for a fact, but I can't think why not."

"Here's why I ask. I managed to track down the woman who lived next door to the Sullivans back then. Anna Ericksen. Do you remember her? She was five at the time."

"Vaguely."

"We just had a chat, and according to her recollection, she and her mother ran into you at the park. She says your dad asked if her mother could look after you because he had something to take care of, so you ended up spending the night at her house."

"Nah, don't think so. It doesn't ring a bell. Are you sure she doesn't have me confused with somebody else?"

"Do you remember bouncing on the bed? She says you bumped into her and she fell and broke her arm."

Tannie let out a startled laugh. "That was *her*? Oh my god, I remember the little girl, but I'd forgotten her name. Was that the same Fourth of July? Shit, she had bone sticking through her skin. It was sickening."

"You have any idea where your father went that night?"

"Probably the hospital to see Mom. He was there most nights. What's this about?"

"I'm not sure. It's really just a gap I was hoping to fill in."

"I can ask the next time I talk to him and see what he says."

"Why don't you hold off and I can talk to him myself. I'm driving up again Monday, probably early afternoon."

"You're still working for Daisy? I thought you'd be done."

"This is what you call mop-up. She paid me in advance and I owe her a day."

After we hung up, I realized I should have downplayed the subject even more than I had. I didn't want Jake to know I was pursuing the point. If Tannie mentioned it and he needed to cover his tracks, he'd have time to fabricate an excuse. Maybe he *had* left Tannie in Mrs. Ericksen's care so he could visit Mary Hairl. The only time we'd talked, he hadn't said anything about that. In fact, he'd spoken in such detail about Foley's behavior at the park that I'd assumed he'd been there. Not to brag, but I myself am really quite skilled at lying and I can tell you how it's done. Like a magic trick, you distract from the sleight-of-hand by focusing attention on the irrelevant.

I took a moment to call Cheney Phillips and we chatted for a while. I asked about the conference and then filled him in on my discovery. He offered to meet me at Rosie's so he could buy me a drink, but I was feeling reclusive and thought I better level with him. "Nothing personal, but all I want to do is sleep in my own bed and not talk to a soul. The past four days I haven't had a minute to myself and it's driving me nuts."

"Got it. Sounds like you're in the thick of things, which I can understand. Call when you come up for air, and we'll have dinner."

"Perfect."

"Hey, Kinsey? You be careful with yourself. Whoever this guy is, he's gotten away with murder now for thirty-four years. He's not going to let you march in and blow it for him."

"All I'm doing is a records search and after that, my job's done. Trust me. I'm leaving any rough stuff to the sheriff's department. That's their bailiwick."

After we hung up, I sat and thought about what he'd said. I knew he was right. I'd already had my tires slashed and that was before the car was unearthed and the bodies had been found. I unlocked the cabinet where I'd been keeping my handguns. I owned three. My favorite, a little .32-caliber semiautomatic my aunt Gin had given me as a kid, had been vaporized in an explosion that was meant to kill me. The next gun I acquired was a .32-caliber Davis that I bought because I liked the looks, thus opening myself to scorn and derision from all the gun nuts who considered it inferior. In deference to them, I bought an H&K P7 and an H&K P13, both serious weapons. The P13 was really more gun than I could comfortably handle, so I put it back in the cabinet with the Davis. I took out the box of Winchester Silvertips, loaded the P7, and put it in my shoulder bag.

I was now technically prepared, but far from feeling reassured, I was just flat scared.

I spent Sunday morning typing up my notes. After lunch I drove over to the office and sorted through the mail that was piled on the floor. The mailman had stuck so many envelopes through the slot that they'd spread out across the carpet like a welcome mat. I sorted through the bills and then had no choice but to sit down and write checks. I listened to my messages, which were surprisingly few; none required my immediate attention. On the way home I went by the post office and dropped my paid bills in the box at the curb. I spent the rest of the day cleaning my apartment—good therapy for those of us who cherish solitude. Scrubbing toilet bowls, you're hardly ever troubled by others eager to pitch in.

Monday morning, I put my typewriter and all my notes in the car and drove into downtown Santa Teresa. I parked in the public lot across from the courthouse, put my handgun in the glove compartment, and locked my car. Everything I hoped to accomplish could be done in a two-block radius and none of it required me to be armed. My first stop was the title company on the corner. I was looking for information about Santa Maria property transactions in 1953. The original deeds are recorded and sent back to the new property owner, but photocopies are kept in the County Recorder's office, quite possibly forever. The easiest way to get to them is to put in a request at the customer service counter at one of the local title companies. I do most of my business with Santa Teresa Title because their library is extensive and they'll run a simple search without charge. Currently deeds are indexed according to the property address, but in the '50s, transactions were indexed by name. I asked the clerk for anything they could find for me under the names Jake Ottweiler, Chet Cramer, and/or Tom Padgett. She asked me to come back in an hour.

I crossed the street to the Hall of Records in the Santa Teresa County Courthouse. Since 1964 the estates of Santa Maria residents have been administered in the Santa Maria branch of the probate court, but in 1953 wills were filed at the courthouse here. I'd never thought of wills as hostile instruments, but I was in for a surprise. Cora Padgett's will was straightforward. On her death on March 2, 1959, she'd left everything to Tom, making him a very rich man. The attached Exhibit A indicated that the real property, including a house and four funeral parlors, was valued at close to two million dollars. Her personal assets—cash, stocks, bonds, and jewelry— bumped the number up another three quarters of a mill. I paid the fee for a certified copy of her death certificate, which listed the cause of death as bilateral bronchopneumonia. Nothing iffy about that.

I moved to the wills of Calvin and Violet's parents. Roscoe Wilcox died May 16, 1951, leaving a will that was signed and dated December 21, 1949. The will had been filed for probate on May 24, 1951, proved, the assets collected and identified, and the claims of the creditors paid. The terms were simple. Violet's brother, Calvin Wilcox, was appointed executor. There were two specific bequests: the first, the sum of ten thousand dollars, which Roscoe left to his church, and a second, which read "To my daughter, Violet, in appreciation for the love and devotion she evidenced during our lifetime, the generous sum of one dollar, which is twice what she is worth." All of his tangible personal property and the remainder of his estate he left "to my wife, Julia Faraday Wilcox, if she survives me, and if not, to my son, Calvin Edward Wilcox."

Julia Wilcox, by the terms of her will, also signed and dated December 21, 1949, left everything to her husband or, in the event that he predeceased her, to her son, Calvin. The remaining provisions of both wills spelled out the attendant clerical details: inventory valuation, the payment of funeral expenses, debts, Federal and California taxes, and any claims made against the estate. Clearly Violet had been denied any expectation of money (save that one surly dollar) by reason of her indifference, lack of compassion, or abundant bad character. Chet Cramer had implied that Calvin stood to profit by her death, but since both wills predated her disappearance, Calvin was already in line to inherit everything and therefore had nothing to gain by killing her. He might have disliked her, but I couldn't see why he'd risk his life or his freedom to get her out of his hair. Violet was a nuisance, but that was about it.

Hairl Tanner's will was the eye-popper. He'd apparently drawn up a new one on July 6, 1953, thereby revoking all previous wills and codicils. He named a trust officer at his bank to be executor and established two trusts, one for Steve Ottweiler and one for Tannie. The trusts were to accumulate all income, with no distributions whatsoever, until the two reached twenty-five years of age. He further specified that his tangible personal property was to be similarly held in trust until each was twenty-five years old. I had to go back and read that provision again. Essentially what he was saying was that Steve wouldn't have access to the money in his trust until

1962 and Tannie wouldn't be eligible for her portion until 1969. The valuation of his personal property—art, silver, and antiques—was estimated at six hundred thousand dollars, but neither grandchild could sell, borrow against, or enjoy ownership for years. What was that about? At first I thought he was being punitive toward his two grandchildren, but then it occurred to me that Jake Ottweiler was the object of his wrath. Old man Tanner apparently wanted to make sure Jake couldn't collect one red cent of his money even in support of his own two kids. Given the terms of Tanner's will, Jake would have been forced to dig into his own pockets to cover his children's expenses in addition to his own. Had Hairl made Jake the executor or a trustee, he might have at least petitioned for reasonable sums of money related to their health, welfare, and education. So how had Jake come up with his share of the purchase price of the Blue Moon?

While I was at the courthouse, I asked about DBAs, those being a record of applications for fictitious business names, hoping to pick up a tidbit or two about how they'd taken ownership. Unfortunately, an application expires five years from the date it's filed and those files are purged after ten years; 1953 had long been relegated to the shredder. I tried the tax assessor's office across the street, again hoping for information related to the Blue Moon, but the clerk told me the basement of the courthouse had flooded and any records prior to 1962 were lost. Some guys have all the luck. Here I was trying to pry into Jake's business and I was having no success.

I left the courthouse and returned to the title company, where I picked up a manila envelope full of photocopied documents. I went back to my car and sat in the parking lot, leafing through my little pile of treasures. I started with the information related to Tom Padgett. There was an Affidavit–Death of Joint Tenant, in which Cora's name was removed from the deed to the house. Over the next several years, Tom Padgett had bought numerous properties on money borrowed from a Santa Maria bank, but most had been paid off according to the Full Reconveyances on file.

I gave a cursory look at the grant deeds in the names of Calvin and Rachel Wilcox, all of which seemed unremarkable, and then moved on to Jake Ottweiler. He and BW McPhee had purchased the property on which the Blue Moon was situated on December 12, 1953, for the sum of twenty-two thousand dollars, a figure I calculated from the line of tax stamps pasted along the left margin. I remembered BW mentioning the "couple thousand dollars" he'd thrown into the pot, which meant that Jake had come up with roughly twenty thousand dollars. There had to have been a hefty additional sum to cover the liquor license, expansion, and remodeling they'd done.

I sat and thought about what I'd found, then started the car and backed out of the slot. Time to hit the road.

29

As soon as I reached Santa Maria, I pulled into a gas station and filled my tank, then parked to one side of the service bay and used the pay phone. I put a call through to the hospital where Daisy worked and asked for the Medical Records Department. Once she was on the line, I told her I was back in town. "Is there any way I can park myself at your place? I've got notes to type up and some calls I want to make."

"Sure, no problem. There's a house key hidden under the flowerpot sitting on the porch."

"That's not such a keen idea, Daisy. Everyone hides the key under a flowerpot. Burglars know that and it's the first place they look."

"Well, goody. I'm happy to hear. Frustrate a burglar and next thing you know he's busting your windows or gouging at the locks. Oh, and as long as you're there, would you mind switching the clothes out of the washer and into the dryer?"

"You just ran a load. Is that all you do?"

"Hey, it's a harmless vice," she replied.

At Daisy's, I let myself in and then did as she'd asked, after which I set my typewriter on the dining room table and assembled my notes. I picked my way through my index cards, looking for loose ends. I knew I'd missed something, but it wasn't immediately obvious going over my notes. Or possibly it was so obvious I couldn't catch sight of it. In the process of collating the bits and pieces, I came across Ty Eddings's name. He'd been at the Tanner property with Liza on Friday night, and while she remembered nothing of the car that had pulled up in front, he might make a better witness.

I put a call through to Liza. "Hey, this is Kinsey. I'm sitting here squinting at my notes and thinking it might be helpful if I could talk to Ty Eddings."

"Why?"

"To ask about the guy you spotted at the Tanner property that night. You have any idea where Ty is at this point?"

"No."

I waited and then tried a prompt. "Not even a guess?"

"I told you I never heard from him again so how would I know? Dead or in jail for all I care."

"What about his aunt? What was her name?"

"York. Dahlia. She left town when her husband died and I don't know where she went."

"What about kids? Someone told me Ty had a cousin named Kyle. Is York his last name?"

"Yes."

"Liza, why are you making this so difficult? Are you mad at me?"

There was a silence. Finally, frostily: "Not to chide

you for your lack of sensitivity, Kinsey, but did it occur to you I might be upset about Violet's death? You treat it like 'Ho-hum, oh well. One down and on to the next.'"

I could feel myself wince. "I'm sorry. I didn't think about that. You're right and I apologize. I get focused on what I'm doing and I forget about the emotional end of things."

Silence.

"You want to talk about it?" I asked. The question felt lame in the wake of her criticism. If you have to be told how to behave, it doesn't count.

"Not particularly. I'd like time to grieve in private, if it's all right with you."

"Of course. I didn't mean to intrude. Look, I'm hanging out at Daisy's. Why don't you call me later if you feel like conversation."

Silence. I could hear her breathing. Finally, she said, "Kyle York lives in San Luis Obispo. He's an allergist." She hung up abruptly, leaving me to deliver my penitent "Thank you" to dead air.

I tried Directory Assistance, asking for a listing for Kyle York, M.D. I expected an office number, but surprisingly the operator offered me a choice. "You want the office or his home?"

"I might as well take both."

She gave me the numbers, which I jotted on a card. I knew if I called the office, I'd either be left on terminal hold, listening to shitty music, or some officious receptionist would quiz me at length about my need to speak to him. I was thinking I'd wait until the end of the day and try his home phone, but on impulse I dialed. After five rings, a woman picked up. I said, "Mrs. York?"

"Well, yes, but you're probably looking for my

daughter-in-law, and she's not here right now. She's taken the dog to the grooming shop and won't be back for an hour and a half. May I tell her who called?" Her voice sounded slightly wobbly, as though from disuse.

"Are you Dr. York's mother?"

"Yes, I am. May I help you with something?" She sounded pleased that I knew of her existence. I wasn't sure that she'd be quite so pleased when I told her my purpose.

I had one split second to decide how to play the conversation. The truth didn't have a chance. "I'm actually an old friend of Kyle's from elementary school. We lost touch years ago, but someone said he had a practice in San Luis Obispo so I thought I'd give him a call."

"That's very sweet of you. What did you say your name was?"

"Tanner—Tannie—Ottweiler."

"You must be Jake Ottweiler's girl."

"Yes, ma'am, I am."

"How's your father?"

"He's fine. He sends his regards."

"Oh, he always was the sweetest man. I haven't seen him now for sixteen or seventeen years. I didn't leave Serena Station until a couple of years ago, when I moved in with Kyle and his wife," she said, warming to the subject. She went on for a bit, clearly lonely and desperate for human contact. Of course I felt like a heel, but I never set her straight. It's not nice to lie to old ladies. Even I know that much.

We exchanged reminiscences, hers real, mine invented. Then I slithered my way over to the point. "Whatever happened to that cousin of his, the one from Bakersfield?"

"You mean Ty?"

"Exactly. As I remember, he went back to Bakersfield on the spur of the moment and that's the last I heard. How's he doing these days?"

"Fine."

"Do you have a number for him?"

"Well, dear, he's in Sacramento, but I don't understand why you'd want to talk to him when you called to speak to Kyle."

"I thought I might as well round up the whole gang while I was at it," I said. I was trying to sound casual and jolly, but I couldn't pull it off.

I could feel the chill through the line. The lady might be old, but her intuitions were alive and well. "You're Liza Mellincamp, aren't you?"

"Actually, I'm not." This was the only moment in the conversation when I'd told her the truth and I was hoping to get credit.

"Well, whoever you are, I've already told you as much as I deem wise. Thank you for calling, but don't call again." She hung up with perhaps more force than I thought appropriate in a woman her age.

I hung up on my end and then took a quick break. Sometimes lying is sweaty work and leaves me feeling short of breath. I hadn't expected to be put on the carpet like that. I went and folded some of Daisy's clothes just to give my brain a rest.

I returned to the phone and called Directory Assistance in Sacramento and asked for a number for last name, Eddings; first name, initial T, Ty, or Tyler. This time my only option was his office number. As it turned out, Ty Eddings was an attorney in a law firm with a string of names that went on with all the lilt and cadence of a nursery rhyme.

The receptionist connected me with his secretary, who told me Mr. Eddings was in court. I gave her my name and Daisy's number, asking her to have him return the call. "May I ask what this is in regard to?"

"A death."

"Oh dear."

"Yeah, well, that's the way it goes," I said. "By the way, what kind of law does he practice?"

"Criminal."

"In that case, tell him it's about a murder and I need to hear from him as soon as possible."

I spent the next hour typing up my notes. This was my last day on the job and I wanted to leave Daisy with an organized account of what I'd done. I wasn't entirely satisfied with myself. There were too many loose ends and the legwork itself didn't add up to much. On the other hand, she'd now found her mother, which was what she'd wanted to begin with. Among the many unanswered questions, one issue that troubled me was the lace curtain. Foley had torn down the first panel in the course of the fight he and Violet had Thursday night, the second of July. An infuriated Violet had torn down the rest and she'd thrown them in the trash. Foley claimed great remorse, so much so that he'd gone out and bought her the Bel Air the very next day. If he'd killed her and buried her in the car, why wrap the body in the curtain? If the body were ever found—which of course it was—why leave behind an item that would link the deed to him? Foley might be cursed with a limited imagination, but he wasn't *that* dumb.

Having typed my way through to the end of my notes, I stacked the pages of my report and tucked them into a folder. I went back and read the various sections of the newspapers I'd photocopied, both before and after Violet's disappearance. When I reached the item about Livia Cramer's "home demonstration" party, I realized that the Mrs. York who'd been awarded one of the prizes was, in fact, the same Mrs. York I'd spoken to less than an hour before. This is the amusing thing about information: Facts exist within a framework. Data that might seem meaningless in one context can later serve as a little window on reality.

I was cruising through the remainder of the newspapers when I stumbled on an item I hadn't seen before. On July 6, in the second section, there was a small item about a man named Philemon Sullivan, age twenty-seven, who was arrested for "drunk and disorderly conduct." The fine was $150, and he was given a suspended sentence of 125 days in the county jail. Was that Foley? The age was right, and I knew from the names in the city directory that he and Violet were the only Sullivans in town. I checked the date again. July 6. The article didn't specify when the fellow had been picked up, but Foley swore he'd never had another drink after Violet vanished. Until the other night, of course, but who cared about that?

I pulled out the phone book and looked up the number for the Presbyterian church where Foley was employed. I picked up the handset and then found myself hesitating. I didn't want to have to drive to Cromwell, but it didn't seem smart to question him by phone. Better to be present so I could see his reaction. There's sometimes much to be learned from observing body language and facial expressions. Aside from that, I was hoping Ty Eddings would call, and if I tied up the line, he wouldn't be able to get through. I made sure the message machine was on, shoved the file in my bag, then grabbed my car keys and headed out the door.

I found Foley in the sunny church kitchen, using an oversized polisher to buff the mottled beige-and-white vinyl floor tiles. He moved with the awkwardness of a man in pain. He was a mess. His facial swelling had diminished some, but that didn't improve his looks. The adhesive tape was peeling from the splint on his nose. His eye sockets were deep lavender, as though he'd used eye shadow to intensify the blue of his eyes. The bruising had migrated down his cheeks, the pull of gravity creating a beard of subcutaneous blood that darkened the lower portion of his face. Black sutures sprung from his still-puffy lips like the whiskers on a catfish.

When he realized I was in the room, he shut down his machine and sank gratefully onto a kitchen stool.

I pulled out a second stool and perched. "Shouldn't you be in bed?"

"I don't like being idle. It's better if I work so I can earn my keep. What brings you this way?"

"I've been thinking about the lace curtain the body was wrapped in."

He dropped his gaze to his hands. "I wish I hadn't torn those curtains down. That's what drove her away. I know there's no changing what is, but if she hadn't left when she did, she might still be alive."

"That's not where I was heading, Foley. I didn't drive all the way out here to make you feel bad," I said. "When did your trash usually get picked up?"

He had to stop and think. "Fridays."

"But it couldn't have been picked up that Friday because of the holiday, right?"

He shrugged. "I'll take your word for it. It was too many years ago."

"Well, think about it. The banks were closed. No mail delivery, no government offices open, and no city services, except maybe the bus line if Serena Station had a bus back then."

"That sounds right."

"Which means the curtains were sitting in the trash for two full days—all day Friday and all day Saturday—before they landed in that car. The Bel Air wasn't buried until after nine thirty that night."

He gave me a startled look, but I headed him off. "Just bear with me here. Where did you keep the trash cans?"

"Alley behind the house."

"So somebody could have stolen the curtains without being seen."

"Stolen them? What for?"

"Because the guy already knew he was going to kill her and bury her in that hole. The curtain-ripping fight was common knowledge. Violet told the story all over town. So on the off chance someone stumbled across the car, his wrapping her in the curtain would point a finger at you."

I could sense the wheels laboring in Foley's head. I pushed on. "Who's Philemon Sullivan? Is that you?"

"My mother laid that on me, but I always hated the name so I called myself Foley."

"Weren't you picked up for drunk and disorderly conduct right around that time?"

"Who told you that?"

"I saw an item in the paper about a suspended sentence and a hundred-and-fifty-dollar fine. This was on July sixth, but there was no mention of the date the arrest was made. When did that happen?"

"I don't want to talk about it now. It was a long time ago."

"Thirty-four years to be exact. So what difference would it make if you tattled on yourself?"

He was silent for a moment and then conceded the point. "I was arrested late Friday afternoon and spent the night in jail. I got drunk at the Moon and I guess I was out of line. BW phoned the sheriff's department and they came and arrested me. Once I was booked, I called Violet, but she wouldn't come get me. Said it served me right and I could sit there and rot for all she cared. I was so hung over, I thought I'd die. They finally let me out the next morning."

"On Saturday, the Fourth?"

He nodded again.

"Did anyone see you?"

"Sergeant Schaefer left the station the same time I did and he offered me a ride home. Tom Padgett would verify that as well because we picked him up along the way. His truck battery was dead and he was on his way home to pick up some jumper cables."

"You told me you had 'a job of work' as you put it, early Saturday afternoon. Do you remember what it was?"

"Yes ma'am. Sergeant Schaefer asked if I'd help him put together a workbench he was building in his shed. I'm good at carpentry—maybe not finish work, but the kind of thing he needed. He already had the lumber and we knocked together a workbench for his power tools."

"When's your birthday?"

"August 4."

"Well, here's a belated birthday present. You're off the hook for Violet's murder. Somebody dug that hole between Thursday night and Saturday afternoon, but it couldn't have been you. Thursday night you were home with Violet, tearing up the house. Later, the two of you went over to the Moon and got drunk. Somebody saw a guy operating a bulldozer out at the Tanner property Friday night, but you were in jail by then. So between your jail time and your work for Sergeant Schaefer Saturday afternoon, your whereabouts are accounted for."

He stared at me. "Well, I'll be damned."

"I wouldn't celebrate quite yet. You'd be smart to go ahead and hire an attorney to protect your backside. In the meantime, I'll be happy to tell Daisy about this."

On the way back through Santa Maria, I stopped in at Steve Ottweiler's auto-repair shop. The whole business about Hairl Tanner's will was bugging me and I didn't want to ask Jake. Steve showed me into his office, assuming I was there on automotive business. I waited until the chitchat subsided. "Can I ask you about something?"

"Go right ahead."

"Tannie told me Hairl Tanner died a month after your mom."

"In a manner of speaking."

"Meaning what?"

"He shot himself."

"Suicide?"

"That's right. He was a bitter and disillusioned old man. My grandmother was gone. My mom had just died and he had nothing to live for, in his mind at any rate."

"He left a note?"

"Yes. I still have it, if you doubt my word."

"Did he give any explanation about the disposition of his estate?"

"What's this about?"

"I'm wondering why Hairl Tanner was so angry with your dad."

He snorted as though amused, but his eyes went dead. "What makes you think he was mad?"

"I saw the will."

"Oh? And how'd you manage that?"

"I went down to the courthouse and looked it up. I checked a couple of other wills at the same time so don't get the idea that I was picking on your dad. Your grandfather set it up so Jake couldn't touch a nickel, not even for the two of you."

"I don't see the relevance."

"This is my last day on the job. I leave it to the cops to figure out who killed Violet, but I hate to sign off without knowing why she died."

"Aren't those two questions the same thing?"

"I'm not sure."

"It's obvious you have a theory or you wouldn't be here."

"I think she was killed for the stash she'd put together so she could run away."

"What's that have to do with my father?"

"I've been wondering where he got the money to buy the Blue Moon."

"You're implying, what—that he killed her for the cash?"

"All I'm asking is how he financed the purchase of the bar."

"If you want an answer to that question, you better go over to the Moon and ask him. In the meantime, I'm not going to sit here and put up with your half-assed interrogation on a subject you know nothing about."

"Why don't you answer the question and save me the trip?"

"To make your life easy?"

"To avoid a subject he might find embarrassing. I think you know more than you've told me so far."

I knew he was angry, but I could see him wrestling with himself. "If it's any of your fucking business, my mother had a life insurance policy. Dad collected sixty thousand dollars, put half in savings accounts for Tannie and me, and used the rest to buy the Moon. The subject is now closed and I want you out of here before I call the police." He got up from his desk and with his hand on my elbow, escorted me unceremoniously from the premises.

By the time I got back to Daisy's it was 4:00 and I was ready to pack it in. Clearly I'd reached the stage in the investigation where people were not only getting pissed off, but resorting to rudeness, sarcasm, and manhandling. Steve Ottweiler had to be as aware as I was that there was no way to verify his claim about his mother's life insurance. Jake was never going to tell me which insurance company it was, and after thirty-four years, I couldn't think how to get the information independently of him. I probably should have gone straight over to Jake's and pressed him on the point, but in truth I was ever so faintly intimidated by the man. After I left Steve's office, he had plenty of time to call his dad and tell him what was going on. All Jake had to do was repeat the story Steve had told me and I'd be none the wiser.

I sat down and typed the additional three conversations into my report. Mrs. York, Foley, and Steve Ottweiler. This was strictly make-work. By now it was not so much about being conscientious as it was about giving myself time to think. While my fingers traveled across the keys, my brain was busy with something else. I simply didn't know what it was. The phone rang just as I was finishing up, and I answered with my attention still riveted to the page. "Hello?"

"Miss Millhone?"

"Yes."

"This is Ty Eddings. You left a message for me."

30

KATHY
Friday, July 3, 1953

Kathy stood behind the dining room door, forking cold Chef Boyardee ravioli from a can. The little pillows of dough were soft and the tomato sauce clung to the surfaces like cream. Dinner wasn't coming up for half an hour, and Kathy was treating herself to a little snack beforehand. Kathy's mother had decided it was important to experience food from foreign countries, so the first Friday of every month she'd try a new recipe. This she called "educating their palates." Last month she'd cooked this Chinese dish called Subgum Chicken Chow Mein that she served over English muffins with lots of soy sauce and crunchy brown noodle-things on top. In May she'd cooked Italian spaghetti, and in April she'd made a French dish called Beef Boigheenyawn, which to Kathy's way of thinking was just like beef stew. Tonight they were having a Welch dish that Kathy herself had prepared under her mother's watchful eye. First she'd opened a package of Kraft Old England American cheese slices that she melted in a double boiler with a can of evaporated milk. Then she'd stirred in Worcestershire sauce and half a teaspoon of dry mustard, and that was that. Oh, yum. She could hardly wait. The ravioli was just in case there wasn't enough to go around.

The problem was that ever since the gym teacher, Miss Carrico, made that remark about Kathy's losing thirty-five pounds, her mother had been keeping a close eye on her, serving her portions so small she left the table with a stomachache. The first time it happened Kathy thought she'd done it by mistake, but when she'd asked for a second helping, her parents had exchanged a look that made her cheeks burn. It was like they'd been discussing her behind her back and secretly agreed with the teacher, which didn't seem fair.

When Kathy first told her mother what Miss Carrico had said about how fat she was, her mother had been livid. She'd gone straight to the school principal to complain about the teacher's lack of tact and her sticking her nose into other people's business where it didn't belong. The principal must have turned around and given Miss Carrico a serious talking-to because now she made a point of ignoring Kathy, avoiding the sight of her altogether as though she didn't exist. Not that Kathy cared. If Miss Carrico tried to make trouble over her PE grade, she intended to tell her mother about the way she acted around Miss Powell, the home economics teacher. When Miss Carrico thought no one was looking, she got all weird and intense. It was almost like she had a crush on the other woman, which Kathy didn't think was right. She'd talked to her minister about it after one of the Moral Rearmament meetings, and he'd told her he'd look into it, but in the meantime to keep the information "under her hat." Kathy wasn't sure how long she was supposed to wait before she took matters into her own hands.

Actually, she thought it was possible Miss Carrico resented the Cramer family for their position in the community. On the second of June, for instance, for Queen Elizabeth's coronation, the principal had especially asked if Kathy's dad would bring in their tabletop Ardmore television set, so Kathy's class could watch the pageant all the way from England. He'd carried the TV into school and set it up right there in her seventh-grade homeroom. All the kids had gathered around to watch the ceremony and afterward, the principal made a point of personally thanking her in front of everyone. Miss Carrico had been standing in the back of the room with a smirk on her face, obviously not realizing Kathy could see straight through to that jealous heart of hers.

By the same token, Kathy hoped the principal's praise and recognition hadn't made Liza feel bad. Liza might be prettier and get better grades, but that didn't make up for the fact that Kathy came from a better family. Her father was a well-known businessman and her mother was often mentioned in the society section of the local paper. Kathy and her parents went to church together every Sunday, Kathy wearing her short white gloves and carrying the white leather Bible she'd been given at Easter. So what if she had to buy her clothes in the chubby department? Her mother said it was all baby fat and she'd turn into a swan. Poor Liza's mother was divorced and she drank all day long. Kathy didn't know how Liza could hold her head up, but Livia had explained that girls from broken homes deserved sympathy, not blame. She said Liza was doing the best she could under the circumstances. The important thing was not to lord it over her.

Kathy could see her point. Not only did Kathy have nice clothes, but her mother had a new two-door GE refrigerator with a separate freezer compartment. Also, the refrigerator came with a magic ice tray you twisted and the cubes popped right out. For Christmas, her father had given her mother a brand-new Waring blender that Kathy used to make real milkshakes after school every day until her mother stopped buying ice cream. Livia said Kathy should count her blessings, which she most certainly did. She knew how lucky she was to have a real job working at her father's dealership while Liza could only earn money babysitting and ironing Violet's clothes, which made her practically a servant.

Kathy's mother wanted her to see the value of helping those who couldn't help themselves—an important lesson in life that Kathy'd taken to heart. She was the one who'd come up with the sewing project. Her plan was that she and Liza could make their entire school wardrobes, using her mother's Singer sewing machine. Liza hadn't seemed that interested. She'd twice postponed their shopping trip to buy the pattern and fabric. She'd had a good excuse each time, but Kathy was still hurt. When she'd complained to her mother, Livia suggested Liza might be too embarrassed to admit she didn't have enough money to pay her share. Kathy understood completely. She'd even set aside ten dollars from her own weekly allowance to share with her friend. She'd appeared at Liza's door that morning, ready (finally!) to make the trip into town, thinking how excited Liza would be when she realized Kathy was going to make her dreams come true. Kathy could just picture them in their matching outfits, not the same fabric or color, of course, because each of them needed to express her individuality, like it said in *Seventeen* magazine. But at school, come fall, seeing the similar style of their skirts and weskits, everyone would know they were the very best of friends. She'd been furious when she found out Liza was gone, but she'd decided to turn the other cheek. The principle of Absolute Love had taught her she could rise above petty disappointments. She'd even left a lovely birthday gift in Liza's room as a surprise for her friend.

At the five-and-dime, she was so caught up in the notion of her own largess, she bought two patterns, one for each of them. In part, this was to show that all was forgiven and in part because she needed a much larger size. She bought three yards of pink wool for herself and a nice big remnant of gray corduroy for Liza. She was eager to share the news, but when Liza called to thank her for the bath powder, Kathy forgot her resolve. Disappointment had welled up and she'd nearly burst into tears until Liza finally explained. Poor, poor thing. She couldn't help it if her mother was weak.

When Kathy heard her father's car pulling into the drive, she quickly hid the half-empty ravioli can behind the silverware canteen, then scampered into the living room and flung herself in a chair, her legs over one arm of it. *The Howdy Doody Show* was on, and for all he knew she'd been sitting in the same casual posture for half the afternoon. "Daddy, is that you?"

"Yes."

One word and she could tell he was in a bad mood. She wasn't in such a hot mood herself after her fight with Liza on the phone. It was true what she'd said to her. She'd sooo been looking forward to their shopping trip.

They used to go shopping or see a movie every Saturday afternoon until Violet came along. Livia would drive them into Santa Maria and treat them to lunch at the soda fountain, after which she'd give them each a dollar and let them buy anything they wanted. Kathy could still picture the tuna melt and the BLT. Kathy had imagined the two of them walking arm-in-arm into adulthood, best friends, loyal and true, still thrilled to be together the same as they'd always been.

It had taken her half the school year to realize something was wrong. At first, Liza was just busy. Kathy could understand that because when they finally got together, it felt like it always had. They'd giggle and eat popcorn, pour Dr Pepper over ice and have burping contests. Gradually she realized how distant Liza had become. She seemed cool, evasive, and Kathy couldn't think why. Her mother was the one who pointed it out: first, there'd been Violet, then Ty. Liza had her hands full, so it should come as no surprise she had little left to give. And now that she babysat all the time, what was Kathy supposed to do?

After she'd delivered the birthday present to Liza's room, she'd spent a few minutes wandering around, touching Liza's things. Her hairbrush smelled exactly like her and the teddy bear Kathy'd given her was still propped up against the pillows, which she thought was a good sign. She hadn't meant to snoop, but when she spotted the diary wedged in that dark, cobwebby space behind the bookcase; she'd sat on the bed and leafed through the pages in hopes of feeling connected. She knew it was a form of make-believe, but she loved the illusion of Liza sharing secrets, even though she hadn't actually confided anything for quite some time. She was also a tiny bit worried Liza was saying unkind things about her behind her back. It was possible Liza had an objection or complaint she was too scared to tell her to her face. Kathy thought perhaps if she could see herself from Liza's point of view, she could correct whatever it was that was making Liza pull away.

On she read, somewhat discomfited to realize she wasn't mentioned at all. The entries about Ty created a sharp pang. She suddenly understood that while she, Kathy, was focused on normal teen concerns, Liza was moving into womanhood. The details of Liza's relationship with Ty created a weird sensation of heat between Kathy's legs. At times she'd felt something similar when reading *True Confessions* and she'd known it was wrong. She'd done her best to steer Liza away from tawdriness and back to the safety of movie stars and movie magazines. She assumed she'd succeeded so it was doubly shocking to realize that Liza was caught up in the same conflicts that filled trashy publications. How degrading for her. No wonder she couldn't bring herself to confide. Kathy could just imagine the stories: "Too Ashamed to Tell My Best Friend!" "His Love Is Leading Me Down the Wrong Path but I Can't Stop Myself!" "If Only I Had Someone to Turn To: One Young Woman's Struggle to Stay Pure."

Instantly, Kathy knew she could be of help. As desperate as Liza was, she'd never be able to confess her plight. And, quite naturally, Kathy couldn't admit that she'd read the diary behind Liza's back. No wonder Liza was withdrawn. Given Kathy's high standards, Liza probably thought she'd be repulsive to her. How could she aspire to Absolute Purity when she was already compromised? Tampax had been the first step. The insertion of a tampon might even have unleashed slumbering impulses of the lowest sort. She had to find a way to let Liza know there was hope, that she hadn't strayed so far that there was no turning back. She was fully prepared to offer her friend whatever help she needed. It was just a matter of eliciting the information she wasn't supposed to have.

While she'd waited for Liza's call, she rehearsed various ways of broaching the subject. It wasn't Liza's fault. Liza's father didn't even live in the same state. Liza scarcely saw him, and when she did, it was only, like, every six months, and Liza said they didn't really talk. In effect, she had no moral guidance whatever, so what could you expect? In most of these scenarios, Liza would weep with gratitude, and Kathy would comfort her at length.

Hours passed and Kathy was seriously alarmed by the time her mother finally hollered up the stairs. "Kathy? Liza's on the phone."

Kathy's stomach was knotted with dread. What if Liza had spent the whole day with Ty? What if he'd kissed her and she'd found herself melting at his touch. Kathy had meant to convey her utter trustworthiness, but she'd forgotten about the bath powder and Liza's thanking her for the gift had thrown her off. Next thing she knew, all her pain had poured out. She sensed how pathetic she was, but she longed for the familiar Liza, instead of this alien person who'd been locked in the arms of a "Boy from the Wrong Side of the Tracks!" Liza hadn't even seemed contrite. She said she was sorry, but it didn't sound that way. Kathy had been so *relieved* when she realized the problem was Liza's mother. Sick and contagious? Well, no wonder. What did the woman expect at the rate she smoked cigarettes and drank? Kathy comforted her friend as best she could, but there wasn't any way to steer the subject around to you-know-what. Even so, by the time they hung up, everything seemed fine. She'd still have to find a way to worm the truth out of Liza, but at least things were back to normal. The problem was, she didn't feel happy and she couldn't figure out why.

That's what had driven her to the can of Chef Boyardee, not hunger so much as confusion and despair. Her mother called her for supper and she was finally able to sit down at the table. She ignored her parents' little spat and focused on her plate. She'd been looking forward to the Welch Rabbit, which was every bit as good as she'd hoped. Soft, warm cheese oozing across the golden brown raft of Wonder Bread. She'd put oleo on the toast and the taste of melted margarine under the puddle of rich cheese was enough to make her weep. Her pain was receding and she was almost feeling safe when her father made an offhand remark about Liza. Kathy could hardly pay attention. She was starving. She hadn't finished the can of ravioli and she knew if her parents noticed how eagerly she was plowing through her food, they'd snatch it away from her and leave her desolate. She'd suffered losses enough.

At first, the notion of Liza having lunch with Violet was absurd. Where'd he get that? She knew he said it to be mean, but he didn't usually make things up. Then she caught his mistake. "Very funny. Ha ha. And where's Daisy all this time? Did you forget about her?"

"She was sitting right there with a big bowl of buttered noodles she was slurping through her lips."

That was the line that clinched it. Her father had never even been around Daisy. How could he know about her slurping her noodles unless he'd actually seen her do it? She'd protested, arguing the point, but only because she didn't want him to see he'd gotten the best of her. Her mother's feeble attempt to intervene only made it worse.

By the time her father left the house, Kathy was taking the steps two at a time, on her way to her room. She slammed the door and locked it. Weeping, she threw herself across her bed. This was the worst day of her life! She'd never felt so betrayed. Liza had lied about everything. On her very own birthday, she'd chosen to be with Violet Sullivan. They'd spent the whole entire day in a fancy restaurant, eating shrimp. All Kathy had ever wanted was to be with her friend and now look what she'd done.

She wasn't sure how long she'd been crying when she heard a little tap at her door and her mother calling her name. She knew her eyes were swollen to the size of Ping-Pong balls and her nose was so snotty she wondered if she was coming down with a cold. "Go away!"

"Kathy, I brought you something. Do you mind if I come in?"

"Just leave me alone."

"I have a little treat for you."

"What."

"Open the door and you'll see."

Reluctantly Kathy blew her nose on a hankie and wiped her eyes with the hem of her T-shirt. She got up and unlocked the door.

Her mother stood holding a glass of milk and a plate of brownies. "I made these for my canasta club, but I have plenty. They're your favorite—double chocolate with walnuts and pecans."

"I don't feel like eating."

"Not even one? You hardly ate your supper so you must be a little hungry. Can I come in? Just for a minute?"

"I guess."

Kathy went back to her bed and sat down. Her mother put the glass of milk and the plate of brownies on the bed table. She could tell the brownies were still warm because she could smell the chocolate, as heady as perfume. She couldn't remember when her mother last offered her something to eat. Usually it was the other way around. Yet here they were, Kathy with her heart broken, her mother sitting on the other twin bed, her expression filled with concern. "Are you feeling better?"

"No." Without looking at the plate, Kathy reached out and took a brownie and held it in her hand.

Her mother said, "I can see how upset you are."

"So."

"I can understand why you're mad at Liza for lying, but is there anything else?"

"Like what?" She broke off a corner and put it on her tongue. She could feel tears sting her eyes.

"I don't know, Sweetie. That's why I asked. I get the impression there's more here than meets the eye. Is there anything you want to talk about?"

Kathy couldn't figure out what her mother was getting at. "Not really."

"Kathykins, I don't want us keeping secrets. That's not what a mother and daughter do when they want to feel close."

Her mother hadn't called her "Kathykins" since she started her menstrual periods a year and a half ago. Her mother had already bought supplies—a box of sanitary napkins and this strappy elastic-belt thing you had to wear around your waist to hold the pad in place. Demonstrating how to stick the long, gauzy part of the pad in the fastener, she'd had the same worrisome look on her face, like maybe Kathy was suddenly vulnerable in ways she couldn't bear to explain. Her mother went on in that same loving tone. "I know you're withholding something. Can you tell me what it is?"

"I'm not withholding anything." She broke the remainder of the brownie in two and put half in her mouth.

"You know I'll always love you, no matter what you've done."

Kathy looked up with astonishment. "Muuther, I didn't do anything! How can you think such a thing when I don't even know what you're talking about."

"Then what? I want you to be absolutely honest. Whatever you tell me will never leave this room."

Kathy was silent, staring at the floor. She didn't exactly have a secret but she did have something that seriously concerned her. She knew her mother would have good advice, but she wasn't really sure she could trust her with this. "You'll tell Dad."

"No, I won't. As long as it doesn't have anything to do with your health or safety. Short of that, this is just between us."

"It's not about me."

"Then who? Liza? Did she say something ugly about your weight?"

"No-oo." Two syllables. Something ugly about her weight? What ugly thing could her mother possibly have in mind? She was the one who talked about inner beauty.

"But it has to do with her?"

"Sort of."

"Has her mother's drinking gotten worse?"

Kathy shook her head, avoiding her mother's gaze. "I'm just worried, that's all."

"Oh? And why would that be?"

Kathy had vowed to herself she'd never utter a word of it. Once she figured out how to get Liza to confess, she pictured the two of them in long, heartfelt conversations, sitting up half the night the way they'd done in the past. They'd roll their hair in bobby pins and smear Noxzema on their faces so they wouldn't get zits. Gently, she'd help Liza see the error of her ways and guide her to safer ground.

Her mother studied her. "I don't understand what could possibly be going on with Liza that you're too ashamed to say."

Kathy felt she was under a certain amount of pressure here, torn between her loyalty to her best friend and her longing to throw herself into her mother's arms. "I promised I wouldn't tell."

"Does this have anything to do with Liza touching herself?"

"Touching herself with what?"

She saw something shift in her mother's face. "Oh my lord. Is she letting Ty Eddings have his way with her?"

Kathy could feel a little mustache of perspiration forming on her lip.

"Answer me."

Kathy murmured a reply, keeping it as vague as possible to keep from lying to her mom.

"Speak up."

"She let him touch her boobs and put his hand . . ." She managed to mumble that last.

"Where?"

"Down there."

Livia looked at her, aghast. "She told you that?"

Kathy shrugged one shoulder.

"Are you absolutely sure?"

Kathy said nothing, but she moved her mouth in a way that suggested she was sure. After all, she'd read about it with her very own eyes.

Her mother's gaze was searching. "You wouldn't lie about a thing like this to get back at her?"

"No."

"How far have they gone?"

"Not very. Just petting."

"Petting? Is that what you call 'petting'—when he puts his hand on her privates? That's disgusting. Outside of her clothing or inside?"

She hadn't expected her mother to probe for this kind of detail. The diary hadn't been specific and Kathy didn't like having to commit herself. Outside, inside. Pick one. "Out."

"How do you know?"

"Because she would have told me if he put his hand inside."

"Well, thank heaven for small favors. You wait right here. I'm going to take care of this."

"What are you doing?" Kathy wailed. "You can't tell anyone. You promised."

"Don't be ridiculous. Ty Eddings was sent here to shape up after the unfortunate situation he created in Bakersfield. If Dahlia York ever found out I knew about this and didn't go straight to her, she'd never speak to me again, and rightly so. I've entertained her in my own home and I owe her that much."

"But what if Liza finds out?"

"She's not going to find out. Trust me. Your name won't come into it."

Kathy listened with something close to horror as her mother went downstairs to the phone in the lower hall. Kathy hadn't meant to tell on Liza, but her mother just seemed to jump to the right conclusion before Kathy even said a word. She heard Livia give the operator Dahlia York's number and then there was a silence while she waited to be connected.

Kathy's stomach felt queasy, like she might have to go to the bathroom and do number two. The situation had gotten out of hand, but it wasn't her fault. She couldn't lie to her very own mother, could she? What kind of person would that make her? Besides which, if Liza'd been honest to begin with, she never would have breathed a word of it because that's what best friends do. Petting was wrong. The pastor said it created temptation, that kids might lose their self-control and go all the way. So maybe it was just as well she'd spoken up when she did. She couldn't stand by and let something that horrible happen to her friend. It was like her mother said to Dahlia, her voice drifting up the stairwell: "That boy is sure to take advantage if the situation isn't nipped in the butt." Her mother's voice went on and on until Kathy tuned her out.

Anyway, how would Liza ever know where Ty's aunt got the information?

31

My conversation with Ty Eddings was polite and to the point. I gave him a brief synopsis of the situation—the discovery of Violet's body buried in the Bel Air, the speculation about the hole and how long it would have taken to dig. I also repeated what Liza'd told me about the man she and Ty had seen at the Tanner property on Friday night. "Do you remember anything about the make or model of the car? Liza thought it was dark-colored, but that's the extent of it. She says she was so scared she didn't really look."

"It wasn't a car. It was a late-model black Chevrolet pickup truck."

"It was? I'm amazed. How do you remember things like that?"

"Because my dad had one like it, only his was a '48. This one was newer."

"What about the guy? What did he look like?"

"I don't remember him. Old."

"Like what? You were seventeen."

"Thirties, forties, something like that. In other words, he wasn't a kid."

"No one you recognized?"

"I'd been in town for all of three months. I didn't know anyone to speak of except my high school class-mates."

"Good point." I asked a couple of other questions, but he wasn't any help.

I was moving into my wrap-up tone of voice, not wanting to waste his valuable lawyerly time, when he said, "How's Liza doing?"

"Great. I'm so glad you asked. She's divorced. She bakes cakes for a living. She's just become a grandmother for the first time, but you'd never guess by looking at her because she's gorgeous. Too bad you didn't keep in touch."

"Don't blame me. That was her decision. I wrote six or seven times, but I never heard back. I assumed she wasn't interested."

"That's not what she says. You disappeared the same weekend as Violet. She was devastated. Even now she says you were the love of her life. 'A bad boy, but so adorable.' Her words."

"Are you *matchmaking*?"

I laughed. "I don't know. Are you available?"

"Actually, I am. My wife ran off with my secretary eighteen months ago. Talk about a loss. The wife, I don't miss. My secretary was the most efficient woman I ever met in my life."

"Liza's married name is Clements. She's in the phone book. If you remember anything else, I'd appreciate your giving me a call."

"Will do," he said, and clicked off.

I tried Liza's number. She was either out or screening her calls, so I left a message on her machine, asking her to get back to me. My purpose had nothing to do with her erstwhile boyfriend. She'd lied to me about Foley and I wanted to know why. I glanced at my watch. It was 4:35, and at best I owed Daisy another hour and a half. It's not that I was punching a time clock, but I felt honor-bound. The problem was there was almost no point in confronting anyone else because who'd be dumb enough to volunteer the truth? You'd have to be a fool to admit anything when most claims couldn't be proved or refuted after thirty-four years. The best I could hope for was to encourage folks to rat each other out. Even then, the answers wouldn't be definitive. A clever killer would make it his business to implicate someone else. In any event, the problem wasn't mine to solve. The sheriff's department was handling the homicide, mustering all the authority, expertise, and technical advances at their disposal. All I needed to do, with Daisy's permission, was to pass along my report, which might or might not help.

However.

Ty Eddings had given me one small lead to pursue. If anyone was going to know who once owned a black Chevrolet pickup it would be the man who sold them. I'd talked to Chet Cramer twice and he'd struck me as a nice enough man. He knew his inventory and his customers, and he was passionate about both. What harm would it do to run the question by him? For the second time that afternoon, I picked up my jacket and shoulder bag and went out to my car.

*   *   *

As I'd anticipated, Cramer was on the premises. In the interest of snagging business, the dealership stayed open until 9:00 every night. Chet told me that at the end of a hard day's work (and a couple of stiff drinks), many a man found himself in the mood to look at new cars. What better reward for a job well done than to sit in a red-hot Corvette, with a salesman fawning over you, demonstrating all the bells and whistles, offering to cut you a deal. You might pretend you were window-shopping until you realized you could actually drive a new car home.

Cramer was schmoozing with a married couple when I walked in. He was such an old hand at selling that I doubted they even realized what was happening. He had Winston fetch the keys and he watched with something close to parental pride when Winston went off with them on a test drive. He caught sight of me and greeted me warmly, perhaps thinking I was finally in the mood to buy.

I said, "I'm here to test your memory. I'm trying to find out who owned a black late-model Chevy pickup truck back in 1953."

He smiled. "Half the men in town," he said. "Let's go up to my office and I can check."

"Glory be. You still have records from that era?"

"I have records dating back to 1925, the year I got into the business."

I climbed the stairs behind him and followed him to his office. He opened a door and led me into a storage area easily as large as his office. File cabinets lined the walls on three sides, each drawer neatly labeled with dates and vehicle types.

I said, "I don't believe this."

"Well, I'll tell you why I keep these. Every vehicle I sell represents a future sale. Customer comes in, I can talk about the cars he's owned and every servicing he's had. I can compare last year's model to this year's, compare this year's model to the one he was driving six years ago. Good points and bad. He knows he can trust me because I have the facts at my fingertips, and I've taken the time to look them up before he walked in the door. Guy dies, I talk to his son, reminisce about the old man, and maybe sell him a car as well."

Without mentioning Ty by name or detailing the circumstances, I told him what I knew.

Cramer regarded me with interest. "So you're saying this fellow would have recognized the truck because his father had the 1948 model."

"Right. And it couldn't have been later than 1953 because the '54 models wouldn't have come out as early as July."

"You're correct on that point. So a span of five years. That shouldn't be too hard. Have a seat and I'll pull what I have. There's a tin of chocolate chip cookies on my desk if you want to help yourself. My wife made them. Caroleena. She's a fabulous cook."

The cookies were incredible, so I treated myself to another while I waited for him. Five minutes later he emerged from the room with an armload of files, saying, "I keep these cross-referenced. Customer's name with the type of vehicle he's bought from me before. I don't go so far as to color code, but I can lay hands on the contract for every vehicle I've sold. What I have here is the Advance Design Series, 1949 through 1953."

He handed me a scratch pad, pen, and two of the files while he took the other three. We sat and went through them contract by contract, checking the color of the pickup, noting down the names of anyone who'd bought a black one. Twenty-five minutes later, we each had a list, though mine wasn't at all enlightening. He got up and made copies of both lists and gave them to me.

I ran my eye down the names on his list. "No one I recognize."

He shrugged. "The truck might have been repainted."

"In that case, we'd have no way to find the owner."

"Another possibility, the fella might have borrowed the truck. In those days, nobody locked their doors, and half the time people left their keys in the ignition."

"I've heard that before and it actually makes sense. You go out to dig a grave, you don't want use your own truck complete with California plates. Well. I'm sorry I wasted your time."

"I guess every lead you get isn't going to pay off."

"That's for sure. Mind if I pick your brain about something else?"

"I'll help if I can. It's not like I have total recall of anything much beyond this dealership."

"Understood. I've been digging and I've come up with something quirky."

"That being?"

"Hairl Tanner's will." I went on to tell him what I'd discovered about the terms.

"I hadn't heard about that. Sounds like the old man had a mad-on about something. Wonder what it was?"

"I think Jake and Violet had a fling and he found out."

Some of the complacency faded from his eyes. "I don't believe it."

"What, that they had a fling or that Tanner found out?"

"Violet and Jake. I can't imagine such a thing."

"Why not? Jake must have been handsome. I mean, he's not bad-looking now, and I can just imagine how he must have looked back then. His wife was dying of uterine cancer so his sex life couldn't have amounted to much. If he ran into Violet at the Moon, what with all the drinking that went down, it wouldn't be surprising if the two of them stumbled into a relationship. From what I've heard, she went after just about every man she saw." I was so intent on persuading him that I hadn't paid attention to his reaction. Now I caught a glimpse of his face and I flashed on the fact that he was married to a bloated Violet Sullivan clone. He had access to any number of pickup trucks and I had no idea what he'd been doing with his time in the days before she died. How dumb could I get? Here I sat, about to lay out the evidence I'd gathered, when for all I knew, he was as capable of killing her as anyone else.

"Go on," he said.

I backpedaled. "That's about it. I don't have any proof. I was hoping you might've heard a rumor to that effect."

"I did not and it would grieve me to learn it was true. Mary Hairl was a lovely woman, and if Jake fooled around on her he should be ashamed."

"Well. I trust you'll keep the notion to yourself. It's pure speculation on my part and I wouldn't want him to suffer your ill-opinion if he's innocent."

He straightened up abruptly, dismissing me with a wave. "I best get back to work. I've got things to do."

"Sure. Sorry to keep you. I appreciate your help." We shook hands across the desk. As I was leaving his office, I glanced back and noticed he hadn't moved.

I went down the big staircase to the ground-floor showroom. I wanted to have a conversation with Winston to see if he had any reason to believe there was a link between Violet and Jake. He was in his office but so deeply engrossed in a telephone conversation he didn't look up. I went out to the parking lot, where I unlocked my car and slid under the wheel. I was reaching for the ignition when the penny finally dropped. For days I'd been convinced I was missing something obvious, but the more I tried to pin it down, the more elusive it became. Now, without warning, I finally *got* what it was.

The dog.

Daisy's car was in the drive when I arrived at the house. I'd returned the key to its hiding place beneath the flowerpot. Rather than walk in unannounced, I rang the bell politely and waited on the porch until she opened the door. I took one look at her and knew something was wrong. She was still wearing her work clothes. The pallor in her complexion had shifted to the gray end of the spectrum and her eyes were pinched with tension. I didn't think she'd been weeping, but she'd suffered a shock.

"What is it?"

She put a hand against her mouth and shook her head. Like a sleepwalker, she crossed to an upholstered chair and sank down on the edge. I closed the front door behind me. I moved to the sofa and sat down with my knees nearly touching hers. "Can you tell me what it is?"

She nodded, but said nothing. I had to wait her out. Whatever it was, she'd been hit hard. A minute passed and she sighed. Was her father dead?

Another minute passed.

When she finally spoke, her voice was so low I had to lean close to hear. "Detective Nichols was here. He left a few minutes ago, and when you rang the bell, I thought he'd come back."

"Bad news?"

She nodded and fell silent again. "They found two brown paper bags filled with my mother's clothes in the trunk. It's clear she was leaving us or at least she believed she was."

"You must have guessed as much," I said.

"That's not it."

I put a hand on her arm. "Take your time. It's fine. I'm not going anywhere."

"He said if there was any way to avoid telling me he would, but he was worried word would leak out and he didn't want me to hear it from anyone else."

I waited.

"The techs went over the car."

I waited.

She took a deep breath and exhaled with an audible sound. "When the pathologist peeled the curtain away from her body, they realized my mother's hands were bound behind her back. They think she was alive for some time. It looks like the dog was killed with a shovel they found in the bottom of the hole once they got the car out. It's possible the guy knocked her out and he put her in the car, thinking she was dead. At some point she must have come to and realized what was going on."

She stopped, fumbling in her pocket for a tissue. She blew her nose. "Even tied up, she'd tried to claw her way free. Her fingernails were broken off and some were caught in the upholstery fabric. There were tiny shards of glass embedded in the bones of her heels. She managed to kick out the window, but by then he must have started filling in the hole."

She paused, struggling. All I could do was look on, allowing her to take whatever time she needed. The air felt heavy, and I could sense the weight of the darkness Violet must have known. Why scream for help when the silence would have been profound, thick yards of soil muffling any sound? The blackness would have been absolute.

Daisy went on, addressing her remarks to the crumbled tissue. "I asked him. I asked . . . what it would have been like for her. How she died. He said carbon dioxide poisoning. I forget some of it . . . the technical stuff. He said basically, how deeply you breathe is regulated by your arterial oxygen pressure and carbon dioxide tension, some kind of pH that controls the reflexes in your lungs and chest wall. If there's not enough oxygen in the mix your breathing picks up. Your body has to have oxygen so it's compelling . . . this instinctive drive to take in air. Her heart would have started racing and her body heat would have spiked. She'd sweat. She'd be having chest pains that would only get worse. She'd breathe faster and faster, but every breath she took would use up more oxygen and produce more CO_2. She'd start hallucinating. He said her systems would shut down, but eventually there might have been a kind of peace . . . once she resigned herself to her fate.

"Can you imagine dying like that? All I can think is how scared she must have been, how cold and dark it was, and how hopeless she felt."

I found myself veering away from the images, searching for safety. I could understand the bind Nichols had been in. Once he laid out the facts, that's the picture she'd carry for the rest of her life. But if word ever reached Daisy from an unofficial source, she'd be reeling anyway. Adding his betrayal to the horror would only confound any healing she might hope for in time.

Daisy blew her nose again and moved on to something else. I could see the shift. There was only so much she could process. Little by little she'd assimilate the information, but it was going to take a very long time. She picked up six round black circles that were lying on the table. She said, "He gave me these."

"What are they?"

"My mother's bracelets. Sterling silver. I'll polish them and wear them, the last thing I'll ever have from her." She set them back on the table. "I thought you'd be gone by now."

"Me too."

"Are you finished?"

"Not quite. Let's go sit in the yard. We need space." I'd nearly said "air" but I'd caught myself in time. Daisy must have heard the unspoken word because she winced.

We sat together on the back patio in the waning light of day while I laid out my reasons for concluding that Foley was in no way connected to her mother's death.

"That's some comfort," she said.

"Not much, but it's the best I can do. The rest of it— what happened to your mother—makes my blood run cold."

"Please let's change the subject. Every time I think about it I feel like I'm suffocating myself. What's left to do? You said you weren't quite finished."

"I'm wondering where your mother got the dog?"

The question wasn't anything she expected. "It was a gift."

"From whom?"

"I never heard. What difference does it make?"

"Did the dog have papers?"

"You mean, was she pedigreed? I think so. Why?"

"Because a purebred Pomeranian must have cost a fair penny, even in those days. I think the guy—the mystery lover—bought her the pup. That's why she doted on the little bugger, because the dog came from him."

She thought about it. "Yes, I can see that. You have anyone in mind?"

"I've got a feeling about Jake sitting in the middle of my gut. We know she took him to small-claims court because a dog of his killed hers."

"I remember that. A toy poodle named Poppy. Mom had taken her outside. Jake's pit bull attacked her and killed her on the spot. Mom was beside herself."

"So maybe he thought giving her the new pup was a way of making it up to her."

"Are you going to ask him?"

"I think not. There's no way I can force him to tell the truth. I'd like to track down the breeder and find out who paid for the dog. I may not have any luck, but I think it's worth a few calls. There are still lots of people around who were part of the picture back then."

"I'll make supper. We have to eat."

While Daisy puttered in the kitchen, I sorted through my file and pulled the photocopies of the Serena Station and Cromwell business listings for 1952. There were no breeders. Damn. Nothing's easy in this world. I did count two pet hospitals, five veterinarians, and three pet-grooming shops. I hauled out the local phone book and did a second search, coming up this time with still no dog breeders, six pet hospitals, fifteen grooming shops, and twenty-seven veterinarians. By comparing addresses, I could see that none of the earlier pet-related enterprises had survived to the present day. I didn't picture a grooming shop being passed down tenderly from father to son, but I did think a profitable business might be bought and sold over the years and still retain the original name. Not so here.

I decided to fold pet stores into the mix, and I started making calls, telling my story until I had it down pat. I couldn't think of a reason why anyone would want information about the sale of a pedigreed Pomeranian in the spring of '53, so I was forced to tell the truth. Geez, I hate that. "The dog was killed some years ago and for reasons too complicated to go into, I'm looking for the breeder. This would have been the spring of 1953. Do you know if someone was breeding Pomeranians in the area back then?"

The responses varied from curt to conversational, long stories of much-loved dogs and how they perished, tales of cats crossing state lines to reconnect with owners after long-distance moves. There were more succinct replies:

"No clue."

"Can't help."

"Sorry, the boss is gone for the day and I've only worked here three weeks."

"You might try Dr. Water's Pet Hospital out on Donovan Road."

"I already talked to him, but thanks."

"What makes you think it was someone around here. Pomeranians are bred and sold all over the country. The dog could have come from another state."

"I'm aware of that. I was thinking along the lines of

an impulse buy. You know, you pass a pet store, you
glance in the window, and there's the cutest little pup
you've ever seen."

I chatted with veterinarians and vet's assistants, pet-
store owners, clerks, and dog groomers. I felt as though
my tongue were starting to swell. I was on call number
twenty-one when the receptionist at a twenty-four-hour
emergency facility dropped the first helpful suggestion
I'd heard: *If I were you, I'd try Animal Control. They
might keep records going back that far, especially if you're
talking about a puppy mill and there was ever a complaint.*

"Thanks. I'll do that."

As it turned out, Animal Control kept no such files.
The man who answered the phone was apologetic, and I
thought for a moment that would be the end of it, but
he said, "What's this about?"

I went through my truncated account at the end of
which there was a moment of quiet. "You know who I
think you're looking for? There was a woman who operated a boarding facility about six miles out Highway
166, right where it intersects Robinson Road. I believe
she got into breeding Pomeranians in the early fifties,
though it didn't come to much. Rin Tin Tin was the
popular dog in that day."

"Is she still in business?"

"No, the kennel shut down, but I know she still lives
there because I pass her house two and three times a
month when I go to visit my grandkids in Cromwell.
House hasn't changed—same bright blue wood frame
and the yard's a mess. If the place sold, I should think the
new owner would have the good taste to clean up and
repaint."

"You have her name?"

"Daggone it, I sure don't and I knew you'd ask. I was just trying to think. I can't say for sure, but I'd say Wyatt . . . Wyman . . . something along those lines."

"You're my new best friend," I said, and blew him a kiss.

I went back through the phone book and within thirty seconds I was talking to Millicent Wyrick, who sounded old and cranky and not all that happy to be hearing from me. "Hon, you have to speak up. You want *what?*"

I raised my voice a notch and repeated my spiel, hoping I sounded winsome and sincere while I was yelling at her. "Is there any chance you might have the information?"

I listened to a silence that seemed to bristle with aggravation. "Mrs. Wyrick?"

"Hold your horses. I haven't gone anywhere. I'm setting here trying to think. I know I have it. Whether I can find it is another matter."

"Is there any way I can help?"

"Not unless you want to dig through my shed. I'm fairly certain I can lay hands on the litter record, but not right this minute. I'm setting down to supper and then I have my shows to watch. Call back at nine and I can tell you if I've had any luck."

"I'll do better than that. I'll drive out to pick it up."

32

Daisy and I finished supper a little after 7:00—salad and pasta with a sauce that came out of a can. Neither of us had much appetite, but the normality of eating seemed to lift her spirits. I left her to read the paper while I rinsed our few dishes and put them in the machine. I heard the phone ring. Daisy picked up and then called into the kitchen. "Hey, Kinsey? It's Liza."

"Tell her to hang on. I'll be right there."

I closed the dishwasher and dried my hands on a kitchen towel before I went into the living room. Daisy and Liza were chatting away so I waited my turn. I wanted to ask Liza why she'd lied about Foley, but I didn't think I should raise the subject with Daisy in the room. She might have had a good reason, and there was no point in jeopardizing their relationship if what she had to say made sense. Daisy finally surrendered the phone.

"Hey, Liza. Thanks for returning my call."

"I didn't mean to be short with you earlier. Violet's death has been hard. I know I should have seen it coming it, but I guess I was holding out that one small hope."

"Understood," I said, knowing she didn't know the half of it. "Listen, can you spare me half an hour? There's something we need to talk about."

"That sounds serious. Like what?"

"Let's don't go into it now. I think it's better in person."

"When?"

"Now, if possible. It shouldn't take long. I have an appointment at nine, but I could swing by in the next half hour."

"That sounds okay. Kathy's coming over in a bit, but I suppose that would work. Can you give me a hint?"

"I will when I get there. It's really no big deal. See you shortly."

I signed off before she had a chance to change her mind.

I leaned against the counter in Liza's kitchen, watching her decorate a cake. She wore an oversize white apron over her jeans and white T-shirt. A scarf was tied around her head to keep her hair out of her eyes and off the cake. I could see one curve of the silver locket visible under the apron bib.

"How's your granddaughter?"

"She's great. I know everybody says this, but she really is gorgeous. Big eyes, little pink bow mouth, and this fine brown hair. I can't wait to get my hands on her. Marcy let me hold her for a half a minute, but she was hovering the whole time so it was no fun at all."

She'd smoothed on the first two coats of frosting before I arrived and she was now piping an elaborate design on the top. "This is for a kid's birthday party. Actually, a thirteen-year-old who's into Dungeons and Dragons, in case you're wondering."

She'd set up a series of parchment-paper cones, each filled with a different vividly tinted icing, each capped with a metal tip cut to produce a specific effect—leaves, shells, scrolls, flower petals, and rope bordering. With a practiced hand and steady pressure, she created a dragon with a strange dog-shaped face. Switching cones, she defined its arched body in vibrant lime green and orange frostings, and then added strong red frosting to detail the flames that twisted from the dragon's mouth.

"I've seen that dragon. It was on a kimono hanging on the back of Daisy's bathroom door."

"That was her mother's. I've got the image burned indelibly on my brain."

I felt myself tripping backward to the notion of Violet buried alive, as though I were in the car instead. Given the size of the Bel Air, there would have been sufficient oxygen to last for a while. The suffocation would have been slow, shutting her down by degrees. Anyone with asthma or emphysema would identify with her panic and suffering. I could only guess. Still, I found myself breathing deeply for the pure pleasure and relief.

When Liza finished decorating the cake, she opened the refrigerator door and tucked it on a shelf. She untied her apron and tossed it over the back of a kitchen chair. "What's this about?"

I'd hoped to be subtle, working my way around to the subject by some delicate route, but I'd been sidetracked by the image of the dragon and came right out with it. "I think you lied about Foley."

"*I* did?" She seemed taken aback, her tone tinged with surprise, as though falsely accused. Thousands might have lied about Foley, but surely not her. "About what?"

"The time he came in."

She picked up and then put down the tube of bright blue icing she'd used to form the ground on which the dragon writhed. Apparently my approach wasn't that persuasive because she didn't 'fess right up.

I tried again. "Look, Liza. His story's been consistent for the past thirty-four years. He may have omitted an item or two, but most claims he's made have been verified."

"How do you know that?"

"Because I did the work myself and I'm here to testify."

"I don't understand what you're getting at."

"Liza, please don't play games. It's too late for that. My guess is he got home when he said he did and your account was just bullshit."

"What do you want me to say, that I'm sorry?"

"No point apologizing to me. He's the one you wronged."

"I didn't *wrong* him. Everything that's happened to him he brought on himself."

"With a little help from you."

"Excuse me. Did you come over here to lay shit on me? Because *that*, I can do without. I've got a lot going on."

I raised my hands. "You're right. I take it back. Life is tough enough as it is."

"Thank you."

"Just tell me what happened. Look, I'm sorry about

Violet, but I don't understand what went on that night. Were you in the house or not?"

"Kind of."

"Meaning what? Somewhere in the neighborhood?"

"Don't be a shit or I won't say another word."

"Sorry. I forgot myself. Please go on."

There was a pause and then, reluctantly, she said, "Ty came to the house. He parked his truck in the alley and we necked. I was less than twenty feet away so if anything had happened, I'd have been right there. Violet knew he was coming over because we talked about it and she said it was fine."

"Good. That helps. How long was he there?"

"A while. When I finally came in, the bedrooms were dark. I looked in Daisy's room and knew she was okay. I never thought to check their bedroom. He was probably there if he said he was. Afterwards, I couldn't admit I was irresponsible so I made up a story about the time. Next thing I knew, this deputy was pressing me for answers so what was I supposed to do? By then, I'd painted myself into a corner and I had to stick to my guns."

"Got it."

"Good. So now you know."

There was a moment wherein she was thinking that the subject was closed and I was thinking we were finally going to get some place. I had a theory and I was gingerly feeling my way. "You went to live with your dad in Colorado, didn't you?"

"Yes."

"I hear that arrangement didn't work out so hot."

"It was short-lived. A failed experiment, but such is life." She crossed to the kitchen faucet where she dampened a sponge so she could wipe down the counter. Preoccupied, she scooped a few crumbs into her palm and tossed them into the sink.

"Is this painful to talk about?"

She smiled briefly. "I don't know. I've never had occasion to talk about it."

"The first time we met, do you remember what you said?"

"About what?" She moved her decorating tips aside, wiping under them as well.

"Losing Violet and Ty. You said, 'You play the hand you're dealt. There's no point in dwelling on it afterwards.'"

"I must have been waxing philosophical. It doesn't sound like me."

"Did you get pregnant?"

Her eyes sought mine. "Yes."

"From that night?"

"First and last time with the guy and boom."

"What happened to the baby?"

"I put her up for adoption. Would you like to see a picture?"

"Please."

She set the sponge aside and reached for the heart-shaped locket, pulling it out from under the bib of her apron. She opened it and leaned forward, holding it so I could see. There was a black-and-white photograph of Violet. She flipped the inner rim, revealing a second frame hidden behind the first. In it there was a photo of a newborn. The baby looked frail and wizened, not one of the worst I'd ever seen but certainly not the best. Liza looked down, her expression wistful and proud. "She was so tiny. I couldn't believe it when I saw her, how delicate she was. Know what Violet said when she gave me this? She said, 'That's for your true love. I predict within a year you'll know exactly who it is.' And so I did."

"Did you get to hold her?"

"For a while. The nurse advised against it, but I knew it was the only time I'd ever get to spend with her. I was fourteen years old and my father wouldn't consider my doing anything else. I should have stayed with my mom. Despite her problems, she was a good egg and would have found a way to make it work."

"You have no idea where the baby is?"

"Probably in Colorado. A few years ago, I wrote her a letter and left it with the agency so if she ever wants to reach me, she'll have my name and address."

"Ty never knew?"

"I'd have told him, I think, if I'd ever heard from him."

"I talked to him."

"I know. He called me right afterward and said you'd given him my name and number."

"Only your married name. He looked up your phone number on his own, which I think should count in his favor. He said he wrote to you. Did he tell you that as well?"

She nodded. "His mom probably intercepted his mail. Or maybe the letters reached my mom and she never sent them on."

"Or maybe she sent them to your father's house and he decided not to let you know."

"That would fit. What a shit-heel he was. I've scarcely spoken to him since. I'm sure he thought he was doing what was best. God save us from the people who want to do what's best for us."

"What happens now?"

"I guess we'll wait and see. Ty said he'd call again and we'd find a way to get together. Wouldn't that be strange after all these years?"

"Will you tell him about his daughter?"

"Depends on how it goes. In the meantime, are the two of us square?"

"Totally."

She flicked a look at the clock. "Your appointment's at nine?"

"It is. I'll hang out at Daisy's until I have to hit the road."

"Why don't you stick around? Kathy should be here any minute. You could wait and say hello."

"To tell you the truth, I'm not all that fond of her, but thanks anyway."

Liza laughed. "What about Winston?"

"Him, I like."

"Well, he's apparently on the warpath and she's furious. That's what she's coming over to discuss."

"Wow. I'm surprised. I'd love to hear about that."

As though on cue, the doorbell rang and then Kathy opened the door and banged in with a bottle of white wine in hand. She tossed her purse on a chair, saying, "That guy is such an *ass*hole!"

She was wearing heels and hose, a T-shirt, and a floral cotton skirt that was slightly too short for the shape of her legs. She stopped when she saw me. "Sorry. I didn't realize you had company. I can come back later if you're tied up."

"No, no. Not a problem. Kinsey's met Winston, but I'm sure her lips are sealed."

I raised my right hand, as though being sworn in.

Kathy was in motion again, coming into the kitchen,

where she placed the bottle on the counter. "Well, shit. I don't care who knows about the prick. It serves him right." She went about the business of opening the wine—cutting the foil, augering out the cork. She crossed to one of the kitchen cabinets and removed three wine-glasses, which she lined up on the counter. I declined, so she filled the other two and handed one to Liza.

It was odd to see the contrast between the two blondes. Liza's features were delicate—straight nose; fine, flaxen hair; and a wide mouth. She was slender, with small hands and long, narrow fingers. Kathy's hair was thick, with a slightly frizzy wave that probably got worse when the humidity went up. She was built along sterner lines, with the look of someone who has managed to lose weight but will surely gain it back.

Liza said, "So what's he gone and done?"

"He hired a divorce attorney. That guy, what's-his-butt, Miller, the one whose brother got killed."

Liza wrinkled her nose. "*Colin* Miller? Kathy, that's bad news. He's horrible when it comes to women. I don't know how he gets away with it. He must have an in with the judges because his clients do great and all the ex-wives end up screwed. Joanie Kinsman wasn't awarded enough support to cover the mortgage. She was forced to live in her car until Bart came along."

"Perfect. That's just what I need. I don't know what got into him. He must have been burning up the phone lines because the jerk got me served. Can you believe it? I get home from my tennis lesson and there's a process server on my doorstep, shoving all this shit in my face. I felt like a criminal. And get this. He's refusing to leave. Last week I talked him into finding his own apartment and everything was set. Now he won't budge. He says he's paying for the house and he intends to live there and if that doesn't suit me, I can move out myself. Where does he get off? You know what else he said? He says if I give him any guff, he'll default on the loan, quit his job, and take off."

"Geez, *that's* extreme. Have you talked to your dad?"

"Of course! I called and told him everything."

"What'd he say?"

"He said I should keep my mouth shut and get a good attorney of my own. He says Winston's a great manager and as much as it would grieve him, he'd have to hang with him."

"Ouch."

"Yeah, ouch. Anyway, I'm sorry to bust in. I know I sound like a raving lunatic, but I'll be feeling better in a minute. Cheers." She lifted her wineglass in a toast and then drank it half down. I could hear her epiglottis working with every gulp she took.

Liza took a sip of wine and set it down. She was fiddling with the sponge again, but she wasn't cleaning much. "Guess who called?"

For an instant Kathy seemed surprised that someone other than herself would be the topic of conversation. "Who?"

"Ty."

"Eddings? You're putting me on. Talk about a voice from the past. What the hell did he want?"

"Nothing. He was calling to touch base. He lives in Sacramento."

"Doing what?"

"He's a criminal lawyer."

"Oh, please. Given his history, I'm surprised he didn't wind up in jail."

"I guess he saw the error of his ways."

"Fat chance of that," Kathy said. "Anyway, I called Winston the minute the process server left. I was so damn mad, I could hardly keep a civil tongue. I mean, I managed, but just barely—"

"He told me your mother was the one who blew the whistle on us."

That stopped her cold. "Are you serious? Well, that's weird."

"According to Ty, Livia called his aunt Dahlia, who turned around and called his mom. And that's why she drove in and hauled him off."

"Huh, that's funny. I had no idea."

"Me neither. I was shocked."

"Maybe she did you a favor."

"A favor?"

"Come on. The guy was a *loser.* You were so ga-ga over him, you couldn't even see straight."

"Why was that any of Livia's concern?"

"Liza, you know how judgmental she was. She thought she was right. You were barely fourteen years old and had no business taking up with the likes of him. If Ty's mother hadn't showed up, no telling what kind of trouble you'd have gotten yourself into. All that petting? Get real. Can't you see that he was setting you up?"

"But how'd she find out?"

"What?"

"We know Livia told Dahlia, but who told her?"

"Don't look at me. All the kids at school knew. That's all they ever talked about—the fact that the two of you were fooling around. I can't tell you how many times I had to come to your defense."

Liza looked at the counter. "Really."

"Trust me. I was on your team. Remember Lucy Speiler and that guy she was hanging out with? What a mess he was—"

"Kathy, don't go on and on. You're the one who told."

"Me? I can't believe you'd say that."

"Well, I did. You were jealous of Violet and you were jealous of Ty. Remember the day you brought over my birthday gift and I wasn't home? You went to my room and read my diary and that's what you told your mom. God knows why. Maybe you thought you'd been anointed to save my immortal soul."

"Maybe I was. Did it ever occur to you how gullible you were? You were so pathetic. Violet could make you do anything. Whatever she wanted—didn't matter how outrageous it was—you'd lie down, roll over like a pup, and start licking her hand."

"We were friends."

"What kind of woman makes friends with a thirteen-year-old? You know why she did that? Because no one her age would have anything to do with her. She was cheap. She was sleazy and she slept all over town. She'd have liked nothing better than to have you in the same boat with her. You know what they say, misery loves company."

"You didn't know her the way I did."

"I knew her well enough. Same thing with Ty. He might have been cute, but he had no class at all. Anyway, enough of this. It's over and done. There's no sense going over the same ground twice."

"I agree. We can't change the past. No matter what went down, we're accountable."

"Exactly." Kathy reached for the bottle and topped off her wine, wiping her mouth against the back of her hand.

"Lola says I should talk to that divorce attorney from San Luis Obispo. Stanley Blum. He's a real shark according to her. He charges a fortune, but he's good. She says I gotta fight back, and I better be quick."

"You remember Moral Rearmament?"

"Ha. You're talking to the all-time champ here. Moral Rearmament was my middle name."

"You still think it's right? Absolute Honesty?"

"Are you kidding? Of course."

"And that's what friends do, help one another when we stray from the path?"

Kathy rolled her eyes in exasperation. "Look, Lies, don't think I'm unaware of your snotty tone. You can be as mad as you want, but I did it for you. I agonized—honestly—but I had to follow my conscience. I make no apology for that so I hope you're not waiting for one. You want to blame me? Well, fine, you go right ahead, but you should be thanking me instead. What if you'd ended up married to the guy? Have you ever thought about that?"

"Aren't you even sorry?"

"Haven't you heard a word I said? I'm not going to apologize for doing what I thought was right. I didn't want you making a mistake you'd regret for the rest of your life."

"Never mind. All right. I get that."

"At long last."

"I guess, if it came down to it, I'd do the same for you."

"I know you would and I appreciate your saying that. You're a good friend." Kathy leaned forward as though to hug her, but Liza remained upright and Kathy was forced to convert the gesture into something else. She brushed a speck from her skirt and then took another sip of wine with a hand that trembled slightly.

"As a matter of fact, I did."

"Pardon?"

"I did the same thing for you. You meddled in my life so I decided I should meddle in yours."

Kathy lowered her glass.

Liza's tone was mild but her gaze was unwavering. "I called Winston this afternoon. I told him about Phillip."

"You *told* him?"

Liza laughed. "I did. Every last detail."

I hadn't meant to stay at Liza's as long as I did, but once Kathy left, we had to sit and do a postmortem. Liza seemed lighter and freer than I'd ever seen her. We laughed and chatted until I happened to glance at my watch. 8:39. "Wow, I gotta get out of here. I didn't realize it was so late. Where's the sheriff's substation?"

"It's on Foster Road over by the airport. Here, I'll draw you a map. It's not hard," she said. "The quickest route is to cut down from Highway 166 to Winslet Road on Dinsmore."

"Oh yeah, I've seen that," I said.

Liza drew a crude map on a paper napkin. The scale was off, but I got the general idea.

I tucked the napkin in my pocket. "Thanks. As soon as I get this last piece of information, I'm heading over there. I trust they have a copier. The originals are Daisy's, but I want one set for my files and one set for theirs."

"You'll be driving home after that?"

"I have to. I've got a stack of files on my desk, plus

mail, plus calls to return. If I don't get back to work, I won't eat this month."

We hugged quickly. When I left, she was standing in the doorway, silhouetted in the light from the living room. She watched until I was safely in my car and then she waved. I started the engine and pulled away from the curb, taking another quick peek at my watch. Mrs. Wyrick struck me as a stickler for punctuality, someone who'd lock the door and turn the lights out if you were one minute late. She'd love nothing better than to shut me down.

The temperature had dropped and the night was considerably colder than it had been when I left Daisy's. I sped over to Main Street, which turned into Highway 166. Traffic was light and once I had Santa Maria at my back, the darkness stretched out in all directions—broad fields of black rimmed in lights where a house or two backed up to the empty land. The air smelled damp. My headlights cut a path in front of me into which I rushed. I had only a rough idea how far away she was. This section of the county was uncomplicated, five or six roads that ran in straight lines, cattywumpus to one another so that they occasionally intersected. I was currently heading toward the ocean, which was somewhere ahead, fenced off by a low rim of hills marked in darker black against the gray-black of the sky.

Now and then I passed an oil rig and farther on a huge storage tank, lighted from below as though to emphasize its mass. Barbed-wire fences ran on both sides of the road. I could see the ghosts of irrigation pipes zigzagging across a field where the available moonlight picked out the lines of PVC in white. A stand of frail pines was the only feathery interruption to the skyline. I caught a flash of bright blue—Mrs. Wyrick's house, a hundred feet off the highway and planted in the middle of a junkyard.

I slowed and turned onto the rutted dirt driveway. She lived in a landscape of rusted farm equipment, disabled vehicles, piles of lumber, wood pallets, and scrolls of chicken-wire fencing. This was apparently where old bathroom fixtures came to die once the renovations were done. I could see sinks, toilets, and upended bathtubs. In another area, sections of wrought-iron fencing had been laid against a wooden shed. There were sufficient discarded iron gates to enclose a pasture if you soldered them together side by side.

There was a doghouse, of course, and chained to it, a heavy-chested brindled pit bull. The dog's choke collar made its bark sound like whooping cough was on the rise. I thought about Jake's pit bull killing Violet's toy poodle and hoped this dog was properly secured.

There was no place to park, but a hard-packed dirt lane encircled the house, where I could see lights still burning. I pulled in beside a vintage truck up on blocks, wheels gone, its black tailgate down. I killed the engine and got out. I kept my attention half-turned on the pit bull while I picked my way to the front porch. The wooden steps creaked emphatically, which threw the pit bull into a frenzy. The dog lunged repeatedly with such force that the shuddering doghouse humped closer by a foot. Looking out across the yard, I could see a number of old cars dotting the landscape. Maybe Mrs. Wyrick sold salvaged auto parts along with all the other junk.

The top half of the front door was glass, with a panel of cloth that might have once been a dish towel concealing the rooms from view. The sound from a television set suggested a sitcom in progress. When I knocked, the glass windowpane rattled under my knuckles. After a moment, Mrs. Wyrick peered out and then she opened the door. The overhead light was on in the living room and a brightly lighted kitchen was visible beyond it.

She was softer than I'd imagined her. When I'd spoken to her on the phone, I'd pictured a harridan, stooped, not quite clean, with flyaway white hair, rheumy eyes, and bristles on her chin. She'd mentioned her shed, and I had images of a crone who'd been saving *Life* magazines since 1946. I envisioned a house filled with newspapers, head-high, with narrow walkways between, stray cats, and filth. The woman who greeted me had a round, doughy face. Her body looked spongy, rising and swelling as she moved until the flesh filled all the little nooks and crannies in her dress. She may have had some fermentation action under way as well because the snappishness I'd encountered on the phone had now mellowed. She seemed vague and irresolute, and she smelled like those bourbon balls people give you at Christmastime. She was eighty-five if a day.

The minute she saw me, she turned and lumbered back to her easy chair, leaving me to close the door. The rise and fall of a laugh track churned the air, not quite camouflaging the fact that nothing being said was funny in the least. "Did you take out the garbage?" Screams of laughter. "No, did you?" The more witless the line, the more hilarious was the outbreak of merriment. Mrs. Wyrick picked up the remote and lowered the sound. I spotted the half-empty pint of Old Forrester sitting on the end table near her chair.

We skipped right past all the social niceties, which was just as well. She was too looped to do much more than navigate from the chair to the door and back. I said, "Did you have any luck?"

Something flickered in the depths of her blue eyes—cunning or guilt. She picked up a folded piece of paper that fluttered lightly from the palsy in her hands. "Why do you want this?"

"Do you remember Violet Sullivan?"

"Yes. I knew Violet many years ago."

"You must have heard that her body was found."

"I saw that on the television."

"Then you know about the Pomeranian in the car with her."

"I believe the fella said a dog. I don't remember any mention of a Pomeranian."

"Well, that's what it was, and I think the dog was one you sold. Is that the litter record?"

"Yes it is, hon, but I can only tell you who bought the puppy. I wouldn't know anything about where the dog went from here."

"I understand. The point is I suspect the man who bought the dog gave her to Violet and he's the one who killed both."

She began to shake her head. "No, now you see, that doesn't sound right. I can't believe that. It doesn't set well with me."

"Why not?" I caught a flash of light and glanced over my shoulder, thinking a car was pulling into the drive. The dog barked with renewed vigor.

Mrs. Wyrick touched my arm and I turned back to her. "Because I've known the man for years. My late husband and I were longtime customers of his and he treated us well."

"You're talking about the Blue Moon?"

"Oh, no. The Moon is a bar. My husband didn't hold with alcoholic beverages. He never had a drink in his life."

"Sorry. I didn't mean to jump to conclusions. Do you sell automobile parts?"

"Not for the kind of car you have. I heard you when you drove up. It sounded foreign to me. I may be deaf in the one ear, but the other one hears good."

"What about Chevrolet parts?"

"Them and Fords and whatever, but I don't see how that applies to this question of the dog."

"May I see the paper?"

"That's what I'm still talking over in my head, whether I should pass this on. I don't want to cause any harm."

"The harm's already been done. I'd be happy to pay for the information if that would help you decide."

"A hundred dollars?"

"I can do that," I said. When I reached for my wallet, I noticed my hand was shaking. I had to get out of there.

She laughed. "I was just saying that to see what you'd do. I won't charge you anything."

"Then you'll give it to me?"

"I suppose so since you drove all the way out."

"I'd appreciate it."

She held the paper out.

It was like the Academy Awards. *And the nominees are . . .* I opened the fold and looked down at the name, thinking about the presenter who pulls the card from the envelope and knows for one split second something the audience is still waiting to hear. *And the winner is . . .*

"Tom Padgett?"

"You know Little Tommy? We always called him Little Tommy to distinguish from his daddy, who was Big Tom."

"I don't know him well, but I've met the man," I said. I thought about how rich he was now that his wife was dead, how desperate he must have been while she was still alive.

"Well, then I don't see how you can think he'd ever do a thing like that."

"Maybe I'm mistaken." I could feel the fear welling up. I tucked the paper in my bag and put one hand on the doorknob, prepared to ease out.

She seemed to be rooted in place but fidgety at the same time. "He always said if anybody ever asked about the dog I should let him know. So I called and told him you were coming out."

My mouth had gone dry and there was a sensation in my chest like a faraway electrical storm. "What did he say?"

"It didn't seem to worry him. He said he'd drive over to have a chat with you and get it all straightened out, but he must have been delayed."

"I thought someone pulled in just a moment ago."

"Well, it must not have been him. He'd have knocked on the door."

"If he shows up after I'm gone, would you tell him I was thinking of someone else and I'm sorry for the in-convenience?"

"I can tell him that."

"Mind if I use your phone?"

"It's right there on the wall." She nodded toward the kitchen.

"Thanks." I crossed the living room to the kitchen and picked up the handset from the wall-mounted phone. The line was dead. I set it back with care. "It seems to be out of order so I'll just be on my way. I can probably find a phone somewhere else."

"Whatever you say, Hon. I enjoyed the visit."

I left by the front door, and the porch bulb went out as soon as my foot hit the step. For a minute I was blinded by the sudden shift from bright lights to darkness. The dog had taken up its barking, but he didn't seem any closer to the house. I could hear the rattle of its chain as he paced back and forth. I stood there, waiting for my eyes to adjust. I scanned the area around the house. I spotted my VW, parked where I'd left it. There were no other cars in sight. The highway extended in both directions with no passing cars. I found my car keys and listened to them jingle as I went down the stairs. My hands were shaking so badly I could barely unlock the car door.

Automatically I checked the backseat before I got in. I made sure both doors were locked and then started the car, shoving the gear into reverse. I took my gun out of the glove compartment and laid it on the passenger seat, putting my shoulder bag over it to weigh it in place. I threw my right arm over the top of the passenger seat, my eyes on the path behind me as I backed out of the yard. I swung out onto the highway and shifted into first. All I had to do was reach the sheriff's substation, less than ten miles away. I'd have to cut south from Highway 166 to West Winslet Road, then cut south again on Blosser, which Liza had penned in parallel to the triangle of land where the airport sat. Foster Road was close to the southernmost boundary.

The alternative was to take 166 straight into Santa Maria and pick up Blosser on the outskirts. The problem was Padgett Construction and A-Okay Heavy Equipment sat on Highway 166 between me and the town. My car was conspicuous. If Padgett were looking for me, all he had to do was wait for me to pass. I shifted from second to third, engine whining in a high-pitched protest. I tried to picture the roads that connected the 166 and West Winslet. There were three that I remembered. The Old Cromwell and New Cut were now behind me so scratch that idea. The one choice remaining was a road called Dinsmore.

I leaned on the gas until I spotted the sign and took a hard right-hand turn. It was black as pitch out there. I kept scanning for headlights, my eyes flicking back and forth from the darkened road ahead of me to the darkened road behind me, spinning away in my rearview mirror. On my right, lengths of thirty-six-inch pipe were lined up along the road, in preparation for who knows what. An excavator and a bulldozer were parked across the road. I was guessing they were laying gas lines, collection mains, something of the sort.

I was on the verge of making a U-turn when a set of headlights popped into view behind me, filling the oblong of mirror with a glare that made me squint. The vehicle was closing rapidly, coming up behind me at a speed far greater than I could coax out of my thirteen-year-old tin can. I pressed down on the accelerator, but my VW was no match for the car behind. I picked up a blend of silhouettes as the car swung wide and passed me with a crew of teenage boys inside. One of them tossed an empty beer can out the window, and I watched the aluminum cylinder bounce and tumble before it disappeared.

The red of taillights diminished and winked out.

A minute later, I saw a fork in the road ahead where Dinsmore split. One arm continued straight ahead and a second road shot off to the left. There was a row of four barriers across that arm. The devices were hinged like sawhorses with a two-by-four-foot panel across the top, painted in series of diagonal orange and white stripes. Each had a reflecting light on top that seemed to blink an additional caution. I slowed to a stop, remembering Winston's description of the barriers he'd seen the night he'd spotted Violet's car.

I had two choices: I could take the barrier as gospel, warning of repairs or obstructions on the road ahead, or I could assume it was a ruse, drive around one barrier and straight onto Winslet Road. I flicked on my brights. I could see the front end of a truck parked about a hundred yards away. I understood the game. At that point the angle of the two roads was probably no more than forty-five degrees, the distance between them widening over the course of four hundred yards. Padgett could be waiting in between, biding his time until I chose one or the other. It really made no difference which I picked. I backed up and yanked the steering wheel hard to my right. I completed the turn, shifted from reverse into first, and headed back the way I'd come.

I checked my rearview mirror, expecting to see some sign of a vehicle. Nothing. I thought I might be okay until I heard the *whap-whap-whap*ping of my tires. I struggled with the steering, which was suddenly clumsy and stiff, trying to control the car as the pressure in my tires diminished. I slowed to a stop. I was right. Padgett had stopped off at Mrs. Wyrick's earlier that night. An ice pick would have been the perfect instrument to create four slow leaks. Not as dramatic as his tire-slashing methodology at the Sun Bonnet Motel, but he wanted to make sure I could drive on the tires for a while. At least long enough to find myself out here.

That's when I saw the headlights behind me.

Padgett took his time. My engine was idling, but I knew I couldn't outrun him. I wanted to open the door and flee, but I didn't think I'd get far. Even if I ran as swiftly as I could across one of the wide dark fields, I wouldn't be hard to catch as long as he was driving his truck. I reached for my handgun and pulled the slide back.

He pulled up behind me and slowed to a stop, his engine idling as mine was. He waited for a minute and then got out of his truck. He left his headlights on, flooding my car with an unearthly glow. He strolled along the road, coming up next to my car on the passenger side. He knocked on the window despite the fact that I was looking right at him.

"Flat tire?" His tone was conversational, his voice faintly muffled. I hated his smile.

"I'm fine. Get away from me."

He leaned back and in an exaggerated display of skepticism as he checked the tires on that side. "Don't look fine to me." He rested his arm on the roof of my car, watching me with interest. "Are you afraid of me or what?"

I pulled the gun up and pointed at him. "I said get the fuck away from me."

He said, "Whoa!" and put his hands up. "I believe you have the wrong idea, Missie. I'm here to offer help . . ."

I should have shot him right then, but I thought there had to be another way out, something short of killing the man where he stood. I simply couldn't sit there and blast him in the face.

I stepped on the accelerator and the car jolted forward. This threw him off balance, but far from becoming angry, he seemed amused. Maybe because he recognized my fleeting moment of cowardice. I put the gun in my lap and pressed on at a much-reduced speed. I knew I was ruining my rims, risking a broken front axle, and god knows what else, but I had to reach civilization. As I shuddered my way forward, I could see Padgett shake his head, bemused. He ambled toward his truck.

He got in, shifted into gear, and followed me, taking his sweet time, knowing his vehicle was always going to be the faster of the two. The rims were now cutting through my tires, trimming off streamers of rubber. The rims ripped along the pavement, throwing up a rooster tail of sparks. The steering was almost impossible to control, but I hung on for dear life. We continued this slow-speed pursuit, Padgett riding up against my rear bumper, giving me the occasional quick bump just to remind me he was there.

I could see Highway 166 in the distance. It was 10:00 at night and there wasn't any traffic to speak of, but there had to be a business open, a gas station at the very least. Cromwell was closer than Santa Maria and if I could make it as far as the highway, I'd head in that direction. Padgett had slipped his gear into neutral. I heard him revving his engine and then he popped it into first again and lurched into the back of my car with a thunderous bang. I clung to the steering wheel, my knuckles white with the tension of my grip. I spotted the construction site ahead, the bright yellow bulldozer and an excavator parked on the left. Padgett slammed into me twice, doing as much damage as he could, which turned out to be plenty. I smelled burning oil and scorched rubber, and something made a scraping sound every time my tires flopped around. Black smoke roiled across the rear window. My car limped along, like some sad, crippled beast while I listened to the screech of metal like the howling of the dead.

He tried another one of his gear-popping tricks, but he outsmarted himself and his engine stalled. He turned the key and I could hear the starter grind. Once the engine coughed to life, he backed up, veered around me and eased on down the road. I thought he'd given up, but that was just my inner optimist rearing her sunny little head. He pulled onto the gravel berm, cut the lights, and got out of his truck. I watched him as he proceeded at a casual pace, crossing to the bulldozer. He grabbed a handhold on the side and pulled himself up, using the track as a foothold as he climbed into the cab. He settled in the seat and leaned forward. He turned the key and the bulldozer grumbled to life. He flipped on the headlights and I watched him reach for the levers that controlled the big machine. I couldn't figure out what his intention was—beyond the obvious, of course— until I spotted the mound of dirt in the middle of the field to my right. He'd dug a hole for me.

He was heading right at me. I braked and reached for the door handle. The engine died and by the time I turned back, he was on me. He laid the lip of the bucket up against the driver's side of my car, making it impossible to open. He downshifted and began to push my car sideways toward the mound of dirt. I couldn't see the hole, but I knew it was there. The VW was rocking, sliding sideways, raw dirt piling up against the passenger's-side door. I stuck the gun down in the waistband of my jeans and slid over into the passenger seat. I pulled back on the door handle and then shoved, trying to push the door open against the rapidly increasing buildup of soil and rock on the other side. This was never going to work. I abandoned the effort and cranked down the window, working as fast as I could. By then the dirt accumulating against the side of the car was almost to the window. I hoisted myself onto the sill, making a low sound in my throat when I saw how fast we were moving. Five miles an hour doesn't sound like much, but the pace was steady and relentless, leaving me very little room to negotiate. I rolled out, kicking to free myself, barely managing to clear the car as it scraped past me and tumbled into the hole. The 'dozer came to an abrupt halt while the VW hit bottom with a bang and a shudder that left the rear wheels spinning.

I staggered to my feet and headed out across the raw dirt field, hoping to make a wide circle back to the road. The ground had recently been plowed and the soil was broken into chunks that forced me to lift my feet high like a member of a marching band. Running across the rows was like running in a dream, agonizingly slow with no progress to speak of. Behind me, Padgett, in his 'dozer, trundled along at a same nifty five miles an hour, easily cutting the distance between us. I tried veering left, but he had no problem correcting the direction of the 'dozer, which proved to be remarkably agile for a machine weighing in at forty thousand pounds.

I pulled the gun from my waistband, for all the good it would do. In the time it would take me to stop, turn, and aim the gun, he'd mow me down. My only hope was to reach his truck, which I could see ahead and to my left. My breathing was ragged and my chest was on fire, my thigh muscles burning while the weight of my jogging shoes seemed to suck me deeper into the earth with every step. I headed left, stumbling toward the road at an angle while the 'dozer behind me clanked and banged, metal treads leveling the very ground that cost me everything to traverse. The size of the yellow excavator was diminished by distance, but I knew when I reached it, I'd be on the road. I felt like I was wading, my own weariness slowing me as I slogged on, trying to gain sufficient ground to make a stand. The yard-high lengths of pipe on the far side of the road grew marginally larger and the yellow excavator began to assume its proper dimensions. I was just about out of steam when I felt a change in the terrain. I was on the hard-packed berm. I reached the asphalt and ran. Once I gained the protection of the pickup, I turned and rested my arms on the side of the truck bed to steady my aim. I could see Padgett work to raise the bucket. In that split second, I squeezed the grip safety and then I fired off four rounds. I had to be dead-on or die, because there wasn't going to be time to check for accuracy and then correct my aim.

The 'dozer rumbled on, continuing at full throttle. Its path was unwavering, its bulk aimed directly at the excavator. I backed up rapidly and moved to my left until I had Padgett in my sights again. He'd slumped sideways and I could see the blood pouring out of the hole that I'd nicked in his neck. The 'dozer slammed into the excavator and Padgett tumbled forward. I stood and waited, holding the gun until my arms trembled from the weight. Did I consider approaching him with an eye to rendering first aid? Never crossed my mind. I lowered the gun, went around the truck, and got in on the driver's side. I put the gun on the seat and reached for the keys he'd left in the ignition. The truck started without complaint. I dropped it into first and headed toward the lights along the 166.

EPILOGUE

It was almost a year before I saw Daisy again. Technically, there wasn't any reason to be in touch. I'd been paid in advance, and when my final written report was met with silence, I didn't think much of it. As the weeks went by, however, I found myself feeling ever so faintly miffed. It's not that I expected effusive gratitude or praise, but I would have appreciated *some* response. I had, after all, put my life at risk and killed a man in the process. In the wake of his death, I was subjected to the scrutiny of the Santa Teresa County Sheriff's Department, which (as it turns out) looks unkindly on fatal shootings, whether justified or not.

I suppose I could have initiated contact with Daisy, but I really thought the move should be hers. This was one of those rare instances where our professional relationship had veered closer to friendship . . . or so I'd thought. On the few occasions when I stopped in at Sneaky Pete's, Tannie didn't know anything more than I did, which generated a certain sulkiness on both our parts.

I went about my business, taken up with other matters in the intervening months. Then, late morning on the last day in August, I returned to the office to find her sitting in her car, which was parked out front. I unlocked the door, letting it stand open while I picked up the mail. Moments later, Daisy followed me in.

I tossed the stack of envelopes on the desk and said, "Hey, how are you?" in that breezy offhand manner that conceals emotional injury. I sat down in my swivel chair.

She took the seat on the other side of the desk. She seemed uncomfortable, but I wasn't going to make it any easier on her. Finally, she said, "Look, I know I should have called you, and I'm sorry. I stopped by Sneaky Pete's, and Tannie's so mad she's hardly speaking to me. I owe you both an apology."

"You did leave us hanging."

"I'm aware of that," she said. Her gaze traveled over the surface of my desk. She was probably desperate for a cigarette, but the absence of an ashtray must have made her think better of it. "I know this sounds feeble, but I didn't know what to say. It's taken me this long to figure it out. I knew I was depressed, and it didn't seem right to inflict myself on anyone until I felt better about life."

"I can understand the depression," I said.

"I'm glad *you* can. It surprised the hell out of me. I don't know what I expected. I guess I thought if I ever found out what happened to my mother, everything would be different, so I was sitting around waiting for the big magical change. One day I realized my life was the same old shit heap it's always been. I was still drinking too much and taking up with all the wrong men. I was also bored out of my mind."

"With what?"

"You name it. My job, my house, my hair, my clothes. I had one session with a new shrink, and the whole time I was pissed off about the money I was having to spend."

"What'd you do?"

"I quit therapy for starters and then I just waited it out. Yesterday I got it. I was sitting at my desk transcribing some doctor's notes and doing a damn fine job of it as usual, when it occurred to me that I'd spent the first seven years of my life trying to be good so my mother would love me and take care of me. Well, that clearly didn't work. Then, after she left, I kept on being good, thinking maybe I could make her come back."

"And when she didn't?"

Daisy shrugged, smiling. "I decided I might as well be bad and enjoy myself. Turns out she was dead the whole time, so my behavior didn't matter one way or the other. Good, bad? What difference did it make?"

"And *that* made you feel better?"

She laughed. "No, but here's what did. It dawned on me that if she'd lived . . . if she'd been alive . . . she might have come home of her own accord. She might have missed me a lot, and maybe she'd have realized how much she cared. She might have decided to swing back, pick me up, and take me with her this time. I'll really never know, but I have just as much reason to believe in that possibility as the opposite. What made me feel better was realizing I don't have to live like someone who's been rejected and abandoned. I can choose any view I want. Death took away her options, but I still have mine."

I studied her. "That's nice. I like that. So now what?"

"I'll look for a new job, maybe in Santa Maria, maybe somewhere else. I doubt I'll quit drinking, but at least I'm not biting my nails. When it comes to men, I don't know, but I decided it's better to be by myself until I get my head on straight. That's a big one for me."

"That's huge."

"Thanks. I thought so." She let out a big breath. "So now I'm wondering if you're in the mood for a spicy cheese-and-salami sandwich. My treat," she said.

"Sure, if I can have it with a fried egg on top."

"You can have it any way you want. Tannie said she'd be heating up the grill."

And that didn't seem like a bad way to have the matter end.

T IS FOR TRESPASS begins slowly with the day-to-day life of a private eye, but Grafton suddenly shifts from the voice of Kinsey Millhone to that of Solana Rojas, introducing readers to a chilling sociopath. Excruciating tension builds as the reader foresees the awfulness that lies ahead. Will Millhone will realize what is happening in time to intervene?

PUTNAM | Penguin Random House

1

SOLANA

She had a real name, of course—the one she'd been given at birth and had used for much of her life—but now she had a new name. She was Solana Rojas, whose personhood she'd usurped. Gone was her former self, eradicated in the wake of her new identity. This was as easy as breathing for her. She was the youngest of nine children. Her mother, Marie Terese, had borne her first child, a son, when she was seventeen and a second son when she was nineteen. Both were the product of a relationship never sanctified by marriage, and while the two boys had taken their father's name, they'd never known him. He'd been sent to prison on a drug charge and he'd died there, killed by another inmate in a dispute over a pack of cigarettes.

At the age of twenty-one, Marie Terese had married a man named Panos Agillar. She'd borne him six children in a period of eight years before he left her and ran off with someone else. At the age of thirty, she found herself alone and broke, with eight children ranging in age from thirteen years to three months. She'd married again, this time to a hardworking, responsible man in his fifties. He fathered Solana—his first child, her mother's last, and their only offspring.

During the years when Solana was growing up, her siblings had laid claim to all the obvious family roles: the athlete, the soldier, the cut-up, the achiever, the drama queen, the hustler, the saint, and the jack-of-all-trades. What fell to her lot was to play the ne'er-do-well. Like her mother, she'd gotten pregnant out of wedlock and had given birth to a son when she was barely eighteen. From that time forward, her progress through life had been hapless. Nothing had ever gone right for her. She lived paycheck to paycheck with nothing set aside and no way to get ahead. Or so her siblings assumed. Her sisters counseled and advised her, lectured and cajoled, and finally threw up their hands, knowing she was never going to change. Her brothers expressed exasperation, but usually came up with money to bail her out of a jam. None of them understood how wily she was.

She was a chameleon. Playing the loser was her disguise. She was not like them, not like anyone else, but it had taken her years to fully appreciate her differences. At first she thought her oddity was a function of the family dynamic, but early in elementary school, the truth dawned on her. The emotional connections that bound others to one another were absent in her. She operated as a creature apart, without empathy. She pretended to be like the little girls and boys in her grade, with their bickering and tears, their tattling, their giggles, and their efforts to excel. She observed their behavior and imitated them, blending into their world until she seemed much the same. She chimed in on conversations, but only to feign amusement at a joke, or to echo what had already been said. She didn't disagree. She didn't offer an opinion because she had none. She expressed no wishes or wants of her own. She was largely unseen—a mirage or a ghost—watching for little ways to take advantage of them. While her classmates were self-absorbed and oblivious, she was hyperaware. She saw everything and cared for nothing. By the age of ten, she knew it was only a matter of time before she found a use for her talent for camouflage.

By the age of twenty, her disappearing act was so quick and so automatic that she was often unaware she'd absented herself from the room. One second she was there, the next she was gone. She was a perfect companion because she mirrored the person she was with, becoming whatever they were. She was a mime and a mimic. Naturally, people liked and trusted her. She was also the ideal employee—responsible, uncomplaining, tireless, willing to do whatever was asked of her. She came to work early. She stayed late. This made her appear selfless when, in fact, she was utterly indifferent, except when it was a matter of furthering her own aims.

In some ways, the subterfuge had been forced on her. Most of her siblings had managed to put themselves through school, and at this stage in their lives they appeared more successful than she. It made them feel good to help their baby sister, whose prospects were pathetic compared with their own. While she was happy to accept their largesse, she didn't like being subordinate to them. She'd found a way to make herself their equal, having acquired quite a bit of money that she kept in a secret bank account. It was better they didn't know how much her lot in life had improved. Her next older brother, the one with the law degree, was the only sibling she had any use for. He didn't want to work any harder than she did and he didn't mind bending the rules if the payoff was worthwhile.

She'd borrowed an identity, becoming someone else on two previous occasions. She thought fondly of her other personas, as one would of old friends who'd moved to another state. Like a Method actor, she had a new part to play. She was now Solana Rojas and that's where her focus lay. She kept her new identity wrapped around her like a cloak, feeling safe and protected in the person she'd become.

The original Solana—the one whose life she'd borrowed—was a woman she'd worked with for months in the convalescent wing of a home for seniors. The real Solana, whom she now thought of as "the Other," was an LVN. She, too, had studied to become a licensed vocational nurse. The only difference between them was that the Other was certified, while she'd had to drop out of school before she'd finished the course work. That was her father's fault. He'd died and no one had stepped forward to pay for her education. After the funeral, her mother asked her to quit school and get a job, so that was what she'd done. She found work first cleaning houses, and later as a nurse's aide, pretending to herself that she was a real LVN, which she would have been if she'd finished the program at City College. She knew how to do everything the Other did, but she wasn't as well paid because she lacked the proper credentials. Why was that fair?

She'd chosen the real Solana Rojas the same way she'd chosen the others. There was a twelve-year difference in their ages, the Other being sixty-four years old to her fifty-two. Their features weren't really similar, but they were close enough for the average observer. She and the Other were roughly the same height and weight, though she knew weight was of little consequence. Women gained and lost pounds all the time, so if someone noticed the discrepancy, it was easily explained. Hair color was another insignificant trait. Hair could be any hue or shade found in a drugstore box. She'd gone from a brunette to a blonde to a redhead on previous occasions, all of which were in stark contrast to the natural gray hair she'd had since she was thirty.

Over the past year, she'd darkened her hair little by little until the match with the Other was approximate. Once, a new hire at the convalescent home had mistaken the two for sisters, which had thrilled her to no end. The Other was Hispanic, which she herself was not. She could pass if she chose. Her ethnic forebears were Mediterranean; Italians and Greeks with a few Turks thrown in—olive-skinned and dark-haired, with large dark eyes. When she was in the company of Anglos, if she was quiet and went about her business, the assumption was that she didn't speak much English. This meant many conversations were conducted in her presence as though she couldn't understand a word. In truth, it was Spanish she couldn't speak.

Her preparations for lifting the Other's identity had taken an abrupt turn on Tuesday of the week before. On Monday, the Other told the nursing staff she'd given two weeks' notice. Soon her classes were starting and she wanted a break before she devoted herself to school full-time. This was the signal that it was time to put her plan into operation. She needed to lift the Other's wallet because a driver's license was crucial to her scheme. Almost as soon as she thought of it, the opportunity arose. That's what life was like for her, one possibility after another presenting itself for her personal edification and advancement. She hadn't been given many advantages in life and those she had, she'd been forced to create for herself.

She was in the staff lounge when the Other returned from a doctor's appointment. She'd been ill some time before, and while her disease was in remission, she'd had frequent checkups. She told everyone her cancer was a blessing. She was more appreciative of life. Her illness had motivated her to reorder her priorities. She'd been accepted to graduate school, where she would study for an MBA in health care management.

The Other hung her handbag in her locker and draped her sweater over it. There was only the one hook, as a second hook had a screw missing and dangled uselessly. The Other closed her locker and snapped shut the combination lock without turning the dial. She did this so it would be quicker and easier to pop the lock open at the end of the day.

She'd waited, and when the Other had gone out to the nurse's station, she'd pulled on a pair of disposable latex gloves and given the lock a tug. It hadn't taken any time at all to open the locker, reach into the Other's bag, and remove her wallet. She'd slipped the Other's driver's license from its windowed compartment and put the wallet back, reversing herself as neatly as a strip of film. She peeled off the gloves and tucked them into the pocket of her uniform. The license she placed under the Dr. Scholl's pad in the sole of her right shoe. Not that anyone would suspect. When the Other noticed her license was gone, she'd assume she'd left it somewhere. It was always this way. People blamed themselves for being careless and absentminded. It seldom occurred to them to accuse anyone else. In this case, no one would think to point a finger at her, because she made such a point of being scrupulous in the company of others.

To execute the remaining aspect of the plan, she'd waited until the Other's shift was over and the administrative staff were gone for the day. All the front offices were empty. As was usual on Tuesday nights, the office doors were left unlocked so a cleaning crew could come in. While they were hard at work, it was easy to enter and find the keys to the locked file cabinets. The keys were kept in the secretary's desk and needed only to be plucked up and put to use. No one questioned her presence, and she doubted anyone would remember later that she'd come and gone. The cleaning crew was supplied by an outside agency. Their job was to vacuum, dust, and empty the trash. What did they know about the inner workings of the convalescent wing in a senior citizens' home? As far as they were concerned—given her uniform—she was a bona fide RN, a person of status and respect, entitled to do as she pleased.

She removed the application the Other had filled out when she applied for the job. This two-page form contained all the data she would need to assume her new life: date of birth, place of birth, which was Santa Teresa, Social Security number, education, the number of her nursing license, and her prior employment. She made a photocopy of the document along with the two letters of recommendation attached to the Other's file. She made copies of the Other's job evaluations and her salary reviews, feeling a flash of fury when she saw the humiliat-

ing gap between what the two of them were paid. No
sense fuming about that now. She returned the paperwork to the folder and replaced the file in the drawer,
which she then locked. She put the keys in the secretary's
desk drawer again and left the office.

2

DECEMBER 1987

My name is Kinsey Millhone. I'm a private investigator in the small Southern California town of Santa Teresa, ninety-five miles north of Los Angeles. We were nearing the end of 1987, a year in which the Santa Teresa Police Department crime analyst logged 5 homicides, 10 bank robberies, 98 residential burglaries, 309 arrests for motor vehicle theft and 514 for shoplifting, all of this in a population of approximately 85,102, excluding Colgate on the north side of town and Montebello to the south.

It was winter in California, which meant the dark began its descent at five o'clock in the afternoon. By then, house lights were popping on all over town. Gas fireplaces had been switched on and jet blue flames were curling up around the stacks of fake logs. Somewhere in town, you might've caught the faint scent of real wood burning. Santa Teresa doesn't have many deciduous trees, so we aren't subjected to the sorry sight of bare branches against the gray December skies. Lawns, leaves, and shrubberies were still green. Days were gloomy, but there were splashes of color in the landscape—the salmon and magenta bougainvillea that flourished through December and into February. The Pacific Ocean was frigid—a dark, restless gray—and the beaches fronting it were deserted. The daytime temperatures had dropped into the fifties. We all wore heavy sweaters and complained about the cold.

For me, business had been slow despite the number of felonies in play. Something about the season seemed to discourage white-collar criminals. Embezzlers were probably busy Christmas shopping with the money they'd liberated from their respective company tills. Bank and mortgage frauds were down, and the telemarketing scamsters were listless and uninterested. Even divorcing spouses didn't seem to be in a battling mood, sensing perhaps that hostilities could just as easily carry over into spring. I continued to do the usual paper searches at the hall of records, but I wasn't being called upon to do much else. However, since lawsuits are always a popular form of indoor sport, I was kept busy working as a process server, for which I was registered and bonded in Santa Teresa County. The job put a lot of miles on my car, but the work wasn't taxing and netted me sufficient money to pay my bills. The lull wouldn't last long, but there was no way I could have seen what was coming.

At 8:30 that Monday morning, December 7, I picked up my shoulder bag, my blazer, and my car keys, and headed out the door on my way to work. I'd been skipping my habitual three-mile jog, unwilling to stir myself to exercise in the predawn dark. Given the coziness of my bed, I didn't even feel guilty. As I passed through the gate, the comforting squeak of the hinges was undercut by a brief wail. At first I thought *cat, dog, baby, TV.* None of the possibilities quite captured the cry. I paused, listening, but all I heard were ordinary traffic noises. I moved on and I'd just reached my car when I heard the wailing again. I reversed my steps, pushed through the gate, and headed for the backyard. I'd just rounded the corner when my landlord appeared. Henry's eighty-seven years old and owns the house to which my studio apartment is attached. His consternation was clear. "What was *that*?"

"Beats me. I heard it just now as I was going out the gate."

We stood there, our ears attuned to the usual sounds of morning in the neighborhood. For one full minute, there was nothing, and then it started up again. I tilted my head like a pup, pricking my ears as I tried to pinpoint the origin, which I knew was close by.

"Gus?" I asked.

"Possibly. Hang on a sec. I have a key to his place."

While Henry returned to the kitchen in search of the key, I covered the few steps between his property and the house next door, where Gus Vronsky lived. Like Henry, Gus was in his late eighties, but where Henry was sharp, Gus was abrasive. He enjoyed a well-earned reputation as the neighborhood crank, the kind of guy who called the police if he thought your TV was too loud or your grass was too long. He called Animal Control to report barking dogs, stray dogs, and dogs that went doo-doo in his yard. He called the City to make sure permits had been issued for minor construction projects: fences, patios, replacement windows, roof repairs. He suspected most things you did were illegal and he was there to set you straight. I'm not sure he cared about the rules and regulations as much as he liked kicking up a fuss. And if, in the process, he could set you against your neighbor, all the better for him. His enthusiasm for causing trouble was probably what had kept him alive for so long. I'd never had a run-in with him myself, but I'd heard plenty. Henry tolerated the man even though he'd been subjected to annoying phone calls on more than one occasion.

In the seven years I'd lived next door to Gus, I'd watched age bend him almost to the breaking point. He'd been tall once upon a time, but now he was round-shouldered and sunken-chested, his back forming a C as though an unseen chain bound his neck to a ball that he dragged between his legs. All this flashed through my mind in the time it took Henry to return with a set of house keys in hand.

Together we crossed Gus's lawn and climbed the steps to his porch. Henry rapped on the glass pane in the front door. "Gus? Are you okay?"

This time the moaning was distinct. Henry unlocked the door and we went into the house. The last time I'd seen Gus, probably three weeks before, he was standing in his yard, berating two nine-year-old boys for practicing their ollies in the street outside his house. True, the skateboards were noisy, but I thought their patience and dexterity were remarkable. I also thought their energies were better spent mastering kick-flips than soaping windows or knocking over trash cans, which is how boys had entertained themselves in my day.

I caught sight of Gus a half second after Henry did. The old man had fallen. He lay on his right side, his face a pasty white. He'd dislocated his shoulder, and the ball of his humerus bulged from the socket. Beneath his sleeveless undershirt, his clavicle protruded like a budding wing. Gus's arms were spindly and his skin was so close to translucent I could see the veins branching up along his shoulder blades. Dark blue bruises suggested ligament or tendon damage that would doubtless take a long time to mend.

I felt a hot rush of pain as though the injury were mine. On three occasions, I've shot someone dead, but that was purely self-defense and had nothing to do with my squeamishness about the stub ends of bones and other visible forms of suffering. Henry knelt beside Gus and tried to help him to his feet, but his cry was so sharp, he abandoned the idea. I noticed that one of Gus's hearing aids had come loose and was lying on the floor just out of his reach.

I spotted an old-fashioned black rotary phone on a table at one end of the couch. I dialed 9-1-1 and sat down, hoping the sudden white ringing in my head would subside. When the dispatcher picked up, I detailed the problem and asked for an ambulance. I gave her the address and as soon as I hung up, I crossed the room to Henry's side. "She's saying seven to ten minutes. Is there anything we can do for him in the meantime?"

"See if you can find a blanket so we can keep him warm." Henry studied my face. "How are you doing? You don't look so good yourself."

"I'm fine. Don't worry about it. I'll be right back."

The layout of Gus's house was a duplicate of Henry's, so it didn't take me long to find the bedroom. The place was a mess—bed unmade, clothes strewn everywhere. An antique chest of drawers and a tallboy were cluttered with junk. The room smelled of mildew and bulging trash bags. I loosened the bedspread from a knot of sheets and returned to the living room.

Henry covered Gus with care, trying not to disturb his injuries. "When did you fall?"

Gus flicked a pain-filled look at Henry. His eyes were blue, the lower lids as droopy as a bloodhound's. "Last night. I fell asleep on the couch. Midnight, I got up to turn off the television and took a tumble. I don't remember what caused me to fall. One second I was up, the next I was down." His voice was raspy and weak. While Henry talked to him, I went into the kitchen and filled a glass with water from the tap. I made a point of blanking out my view of the room, which was worse than the other rooms I'd seen. How could someone live in such filth? I did a quick search through the kitchen drawers, but there wasn't a clean towel or dishrag to be found. Before I returned to the living room, I opened the back door and left it ajar, hoping the fresh air would dispel the sour smell that hung over everything. I handed the water glass to Henry and watched while he pulled a fresh handkerchief from his pocket. He saturated the linen with water and dabbed it on Gus's dry lips.

Three minutes later, I heard the high-wailing siren of the ambulance turning onto our street. I went to the door and watched as the driver double-parked and got out with the two additional paramedics who had ridden in the back. A bright red Fire Rescue vehicle pulled up behind, spilling EMT personnel as well. The flashing red lights were oddly syncopated, a stuttering of red. I held the door open, admitting three young men and two women in blue shirts with patches on their sleeves. The first guy carried their gear, probably ten to fifteen pounds' worth, including an EKG monitor, defibrillator, and pulse oximeter. One of the women toted an ALS jump bag, which I knew contained drugs and an intubation set.

I took a moment to close and lock the back door, and then waited on the front porch while the paramedics went about their business. This was a job where they spent much of their time on their knees. Through the open door I could hear the comforting murmur of questions and Gus's tremulous replies. I didn't want to be present when the time came to move him. One more of his yelps and they'd be tending to me.

Henry joined me a moment later and the two of us retreated to the street. Neighbors were scattered along the sidewalk, attentive in the wake of this undefined emergency. Henry chatted with Moza Lowenstein, who lived two houses down. Since Gus's injuries weren't life-threatening, we could talk among ourselves without any sense of disrespect. It took an additional fifteen minutes before Gus was loaded into the back of the ambulance. By then, he was on an IV line.

Henry consulted with the driver, a hefty dark-haired man in his thirties, who told us they were taking Gus to the emergency room at Santa Teresa Hospital, referred to fondly by most of us as "St. Terry's."

Henry said he'd follow in his car. "Are you coming?"

"I can't. I have to go on to work. Will you call me later?"

"Of course. I'll give you a buzz as soon as I know what's going on."

I waited until the ambulance departed and Henry had backed out of his drive before I got in my car.

On the way into town, I stopped off at an attorney's office and picked up an Order to Show Cause notifying a noncustodial spouse that a modification of child support was being sought. The ex-husband was a Robert Vest, whom I was already fondly thinking of as "Bob." Our Bob was a freelance tax consultant working from his home in Colgate. I checked my watch, and since it was only a few minutes after ten, I headed to his place in hopes of catching him at his desk.

I found his house and passed at a slightly slower speed than normal, then circled back and parked on the opposite side of the street. Both the driveway and the carport were empty. I put the papers in my bag, crossed, and climbed his front steps to the porch. The morning newspaper lay on the mat, suggesting that Bobby wasn't yet up. Might have had a late night. I knocked and waited. Two minutes passed. I knocked again, more emphatically. Still no response. I edged to my right and took a quick peep in the window. I could see past his dining room table and into the darkened kitchen beyond. The place had that glum air of emptiness. I returned to my car, made a note of the date and time of the attempt, and went on to the office.

SUE GRAFTON

"No private eye comes close to Sue Grafton's endearing California sleuth, Kinsey Millhone."
—*New York Times Book Review*

For a complete list of titles and to sign up for our newsletter, please visit prh.com/SueGrafton